SHADOW IN THE DEEP

THE BINDING OF THE BLADE

BY L. B. GRAHAM

Beyond the Summerland
Bringer of Storms
Shadow in the Deep

Shadow in the Deep

L. B. Graham

Page design by Tobias Design
Typesetting by Lakeside Design Plus

Printed in the United States of America

Library of Congress Cataloging-in-Publication Data

Graham, L. B. (Lowell B.), 1971–
Shadow in the Deep / L. B. Graham.
p. cm.—(The binding of the blade ; bk. 3)
Summary: The people of Kirthanin continue their fight against their ancient enemy, Malek.
ISBN-13: 978-0-87552-722-2 (pbk.)
ISBN-10: 0-87552-722-1 (pbk.)
[1. Fantasy.] I. Title.

PZ7.G75267Sha 2006
[Fic]—dc22

2006041689

For James, Nathanael, and Noah, once students, now friends,
with thanks for all your help

And

For Tom and Shane, best of friends, for dreaming the dream with me

CONTENTS

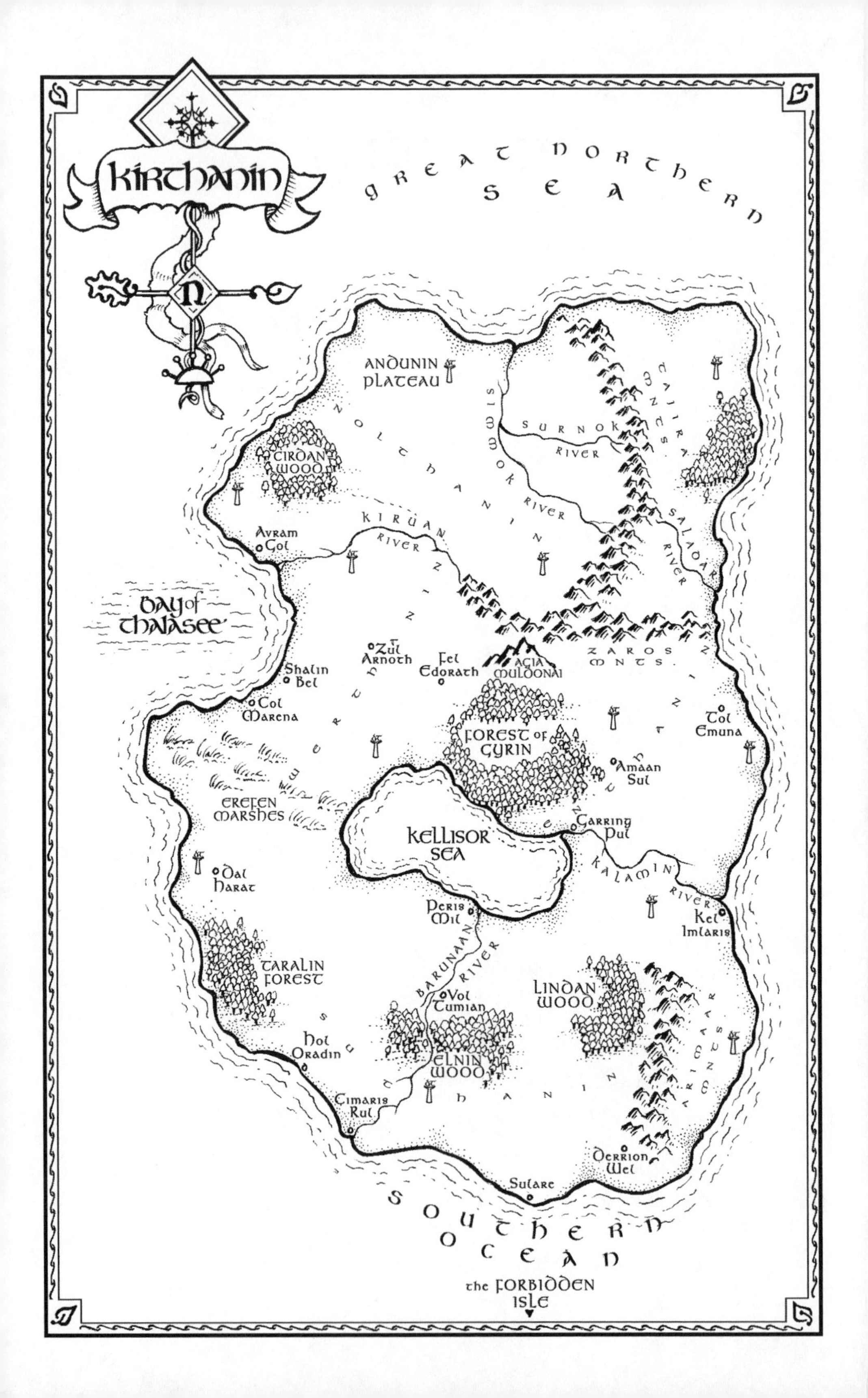
KIRTHANIN
N
GREAT NORTHERN SEA
ANDUNIN PLATEAU
CIRDAN WOOD
SURNOK RIVER
SALADAR RIVER
KIRUAN RIVER
Avram Col
BAY of THALASEE
Zul Arnoth
Fel Edorath
AGIA MULDONAI
ZAROS MNTS.
Shalin Bel
Col Marena
FOREST of GYRIN
Col Emuna
Amaan Sul
EREFEN MARSHES
KELLISOR SEA
Garring Pul
KALAMIN RIVER
Dal Harat
Peris Mil
Kel Imlaris
TARALIN FOREST
BARUNAAN RIVER
Vol Tumian
LINDAN WOOD
Hol Oradin
ELNIN WOOD
Cimaris Rul
Derrion Wel
Sulare
SOUTHERN OCEAN
the FORBIDDEN ISLE

PROLOGUE: FARIMAAL'S REWARD

FARIMAAL COUGHED AS HE walked through the rough-hewn, dimly lit tunnel. The sound of hammers striking rock echoed up and down the corridors all around him. Despite the fact they had been working more than ten years already, there seemed to be no end in sight to the ongoing excavations. Malek was digging into the very roots of the Mountain, and it had been a long time since the Nolthanim had dared to hope that their sojourn beneath the earth, cut off from the sun and stars, would be brief.

Arriving at a dark junction where two of the smaller corridors intersected, he paused. He had only recently started coming down this way, and he was still getting his bearings. As sure as he was ever going to be that the correct way was to the left, he kept moving with his torch held firmly before him. The tunnel was made for men and was much too small for Malekim, let alone Vulsutyrim, but from time to time Black Wolves came down this way. It wasn't that the children of Rucaran scared him, but he didn't like surprises, especially when they brushed past his legs in the dark.

A few turns and several minutes later he found the mid-sized, reasonably well-lit room that he had been looking for. His friend Ronan had shown him the room a few weeks earlier, and ever since, Farimaal and the other captains of the Nolthanim had used it as a sort of common room far from the populous and sometimes-crowded rooms and caverns on the upper levels of Malek's new home. The modicum of distance the Nolthanim managed to keep from the rest of Malek's hosts was hard to maintain inside the Mountain, but as the labyrinth of tunnels and rooms continued to grow, the opportunity to reestablish that distance increased.

Three men sat at a table along the near wall, but only Bralis looked up as Farimaal entered. He nodded in acknowledgment and Farimaal reciprocated, moving silently past them toward the table much farther inside the room where Ronan sat, waiting.

"Do you have it?" Ronan said as Farimaal sat down at the table.

"Yes," Farimaal answered, pulling a small, carefully wrapped package from the pouch that hung at his waist and putting it on the table. Ronan picked up the package and unwrapped it carefully.

"Freshly cooked rabbit," Ronan said under his breath as he pulled a strip of meat away from the bone and dropped it into his open mouth. His face broke into a wide smile as he chewed silently, looking at Farimaal and shaking his head. "You are going to get yourself killed if you keep going down to the edge of Gyrin on your own. I don't care how good of a hunter you are, one of these days a patrol of Great Bear is going to catch you, and you aren't going to come back."

"Maybe," Farimaal answered, watching his friend enjoy the gift. "But I don't think you really want me to stop going."

"True." Ronan nodded, having taken another bite. "There are benefits to your foolhardy ideas."

"Indeed," Farimaal answered. "I would not go if there were no benefits."

Ronan continued to eat the rabbit, and Farimaal watched in silence. He had eaten his own fill, for he had caught three and brought them back the previous night. What he didn't eat he stored in his room, but he always brought Ronan a portion, even though his friend had gone with him to Gyrin only once, many years ago when they first retreated into the Mountain.

Seeing motion out of the corner of his eye, Farimaal turned back toward the door. Another man entered and took a seat with the other three Nothlanim officers. Farimaal turned back to Ronan, who was still eating the rabbit, watching Farimaal closely. "What is it?" Ronan asked.

"What is what?"

"What's on your mind?"

Farimaal shrugged and shook his head.

"Don't say *nothing*," Ronan said, pausing for the first time before taking another bite. "You're pondering something."

Farimaal looked back over his shoulder at the four men, who were far enough away that they surely couldn't hear. "I'm thinking about going to Malek about his most recent offer."

Ronan choked, a small chunk of rabbit meat falling out of his mouth and onto the floor. "You're wasting my meat," Farimaal said evenly.

"Yes, and I'd better not, because if you just said what I think you said, you won't be getting me any more. Are you mad? I mean, I know you're a little out there, but I didn't think you were really mad."

Farimaal shrugged again.

"By the Mountain, Farimaal, you're serious! I can't believe you. I know you don't want to live the rest of your life in here, but if you want to die so badly, one of us could run you through and get it over with. Why travel all the way to that dragon tower just to be a meal for a Grendolai?"

"Malek says he'll give the one who subdues the Grendolai the power to rule at his right hand when we get out of here. Not only could I secure all the things we've dreamed of for our people, Ronan, but Malek would give me life, long life."

"Farimaal." Ronan looked and sounded completely incredulous. "You would have to survive the journey and compel the Grendolai to reforge their bonds with Malek before he gave you anything. What makes you think you could succeed at what even Malekim and Vulsutyrim couldn't do?"

"I have to."

Ronan's expression changed from shock to bewilderment. "What do you mean, you have to? You don't have to do this. No one really believes what Malek is asking can be done, unless Malek goes himself, and even then there are doubts. You saw what the Grendolai did to the dragon near that dragon tower in Suthanin. He ripped a gaping hole right through the dragon's scales and tore him up inside. You think you're going to walk into that dragon tower and tell the Grendolai what he has to do?"

"I have to."

Ronan shook his head. "Why do you keep saying that?"

"I have the disease."

Ronan's face changed again. The shock was back, but this time there was more. He was sobered, and Farimaal knew Ronan now understood just how serious he was. "Are you sure?"

"Yes. I have all the signs: the bruises, the cough, everything."

"It can't be," Ronan muttered. "Not you. Of all people, not you."

"Why not me?" Farimaal said, returning Ronan's gaze levelly.

For several moments, neither of them said anything. The sound of laughter drifted across the room from the other table, but neither of them turned to look. "Even if it is true," Ronan said at last, "some have lived a couple of years with the disease. There is no point throwing away what time you have left."

"I don't want a couple of years. I don't even want ten or twenty years. I want all the time it will take to leave this place, to walk out under the sun and sky and lead my men back into the field. I want to live to see the Nolthanim returned to their rightful home and enjoying the life on the land that they should never have lost. Doing this is the only way I can have these things."

"Are you sure Malek can give them?"

"I will make sure the terms of the offer are clarified before I go."

Ronan's eyebrows rose. "Oh you will? And what is to prevent Malek from telling you whatever he likes just to get you to try? You are Nolthanim. You know the history of Malek's promises."

"I know."

"So what certainty could he give you?"

"None. But I have no choice. Nothing else can save me."

"Farimaal—"

"Besides," Farimaal continued, "if I do this, if I'm successful, is it not possible that Malek will fear me? Will not all the men and all the creatures in this place fear me? If I do what no one believes can be done, don't you think Malek will keep his promise to me?"

"You will become legend, that is sure," Ronan said, "but how can it be done?"

"That is for me to worry about."

Ronan had pulled all the meat there was to eat from the bone, so he tossed it away from the table and licked his fingers. "Thanks again for the rabbit."

"You're welcome."

"You're still crazy," Ronan added.

"Maybe."

"You know, even if you somehow did succeed in subduing the Grendolai, and even if Malek did heal you from the disease and grant you long life, you won't be leading your men out onto the battlefield again one day. If Malek doesn't move again in the lifetime of this generation, you will lead out our children or grandchildren. Who knows how many generations removed they will be? We will all be dead."

"Unless you come with me. Maybe Malek will give you long life too."

Slowly Ronan shook his head. "I'm sorry, friend. I want to walk beneath the sun and sky again too, but I'd rather spend the remainder of my days here than die in this foolishness. That's what it is, you know. I'm sorry you have the disease, but I wish you wouldn't throw away the months and years you have left in the vain hope of a miracle."

"I understand, but I am decided."

"When are you going to Malek?"

"After I have seen the keeper."

"Nalson? Why are you going to him?"

"Because he is the keeper. He knows what the rest of us have forgotten. He is the memory of the Nolthanim, and if anyone knows anything about the towers or the Grendolai that I can turn to my advantage, it is Nalson."

Ronan nodded. "Can I come with you?"

"Sure. I'm meeting with him tomorrow."

"And if you don't learn anything that will help you? Will you give up this idea then?"

"No."

Ronan sighed. "I didn't think so."

"Then why did you ask?"

"Habit."

Farimaal smiled. "Come, Ronan," he said, standing. "Let's not spend the remainder of the day debating the issue. Tomorrow we will see what the keeper has to say."

Nalson Kirisuul clasped his hands tightly together and peered at Farimaal over them. On the wall behind his bed was the tapestry of Harak Andunin, the symbol of Nolthanin that each keeper passed on to the next, along with the stories of the Nolthanim. He was ten years older than Farimaal and had only been keeper about that long. "The dragon towers?"

"Yes."

"Everything?"

"Yes."

"All the Kirthanim, with the aid of the Great Bear and under the direction of some of the Twelve, built them early in the First Age. The rock was quarried—"

"Perhaps not everything," Farimaal interjected, and he didn't turn to look at Ronan, who he knew would be smirking. "I was thinking more in terms of their design than their history."

Nalson nodded. "The towers themselves exist purely as a stand for the gyres on top. There is nothing inside them except a narrow spiral stair. The walls are extra thick to support the gyres' weight, leaving little room for anything else. The gyres on top are like great bowls of smooth stone. They are open except for a small roof that stands over the center of the gyre."

"The roof was to shelter the dragons?"

"No, the roof was meant to protect signal fires. The Novaana used beacons to summon dragons, and if the weather was bad, they needed to be covered. Each gyre has a great door in the floor. Dragons would descend from the gyre into the large supply room below if they desired shelter from bad weather or if they wished to partake of any of the supplies the men and Great Bear would sometimes leave for them there."

"The narrow stairs you spoke of, they were big enough for Great Bear carrying supplies, then?"

"Big enough for Great Bear, yes, but only just. Great Bear could ascend the stairs if they went on all fours and squeezed through the narrow doorway at the top. If they brought supplies, they probably dragged them up behind or pushed them up ahead."

"So how did the Grendolai get up into the supply rooms? Could they also fit up the stairs if they climbed on all fours?"

"Oh no, the Grendolai are too tall and far too broad to ascend inside the towers, but they didn't need to. Their arms are so powerful that they can ascend the outside of the towers. Their claws were made to be stronger than even the strongest stone, and up they went, sinking their claws into the exterior walls. Once up on top, they most likely slipped down into the great rooms beneath the gyre and waited for dragons to come. There they could attack the dragons where they were most vulnerable, in the underbelly. Before warning could spread among the dragons of the Grendolai's existence and danger, many of Sulmandir's children died at their hands, and before long the dragons forsook the towers altogether for the safer climes of the mountains. So the towers have been dark and abandoned by all but the Grendolai these past fifteen years, and so they shall be as long as the Grendolai live."

"And how long will that be?" Farimaal asked, but only half seriously, for he knew it was a question that neither Nalson nor anyone else could answer, perhaps not even Malek, their maker.

Nalson shrugged. "I cannot say, but there they are and there they will remain."

"The Grendolai," Farimaal started, bringing Nalson's attention to the other subject of his inquiry, "they are less than three spans tall, are they not?"

"Yes, two and half, maybe a hand or two more."

"Still, you are sure they cannot use the stairs in the towers?"

"No. You have seen them. Their shoulders are massive, two or three times as wide as any Great Bear's. The passage is too narrow to allow it."

"So their only way in and out of the towers is from above. They must go out through the gyre and down the outer wall."

"Yes, though I don't think they are frequently outside."

"But surely they eat."

"Yes, they do, but I think their need of food is far different from our own. They can go long periods of time without eating; indeed their metabolism is not unlike that of a hibernating animal. This is no doubt why they are reluctant to leave the towers. They have great rooms that are completely dark and isolated."

"And their weakness?"

Nalson shook his head. "I don't know of any."

"But if even a dragon is vulnerable like you said, underneath, than surely the Grendolai are weak too."

"Perhaps, but I don't know where."

"If a swordsman could get close enough, could he not be successful at the joints? The eyes? Somewhere?"

"I don't see how anyone could get close enough. Not only are their hands strong, but their arms are unusually long, nearly as long as their bodies. And the Grendolai are as fast as any living thing. A swordsman would be ripped into pieces long before he was able to bring a single stroke home."

"What about arrows?"

"Arrows? Their hides are virtually impossible to penetrate, except perhaps by another Grendolai's claw, or a dragon's. You would need an arrow the size of a battering ram to penetrate that hide."

"A spear then?"

"A spear might work in theory, but I can't see how it could be used in reality. A man couldn't lift a spear large enough to deal a mortal wound to the Grendolai, let alone strike with it, and one stroke is all he'd get, if that. A spear of regular size just wouldn't work. If it pierced the armor at all, which would be unlikely unless the head was exceptional, it would inflict but a pinprick. More likely the Grendolai would catch and smash the spear on its way, then he would catch and smash the spearman."

"There must be some point of weakness," Farimaal muttered.

"Perhaps a Grendolai could be crushed under the gyre if it could be dropped on him, but I don't know of a force in all Kirthanin that could dislodge the stones of the tower, for they were made with extraordinary skill and blessed by the Twelve. They have weathered two thousand winters and show no diminished structural resilience at all, save only where the claws of the Grendolai have chipped their exterior.

"I will add this much to what I have already said: In the right place, with the right equipment and enough men, a Grendolai could be killed. Especially if it was daylight, for they hate the light of the sun. But in a dragon tower, where they live in darkness in a confined space, the Grendolai are essentially unassailable."

Farimaal nodded, and when Nalson said no more, he stood to go. Ronan stood as well. "Keeper, I thank you for sharing the knowledge of our people. May you live long and keep safe the memory of the Nolthanim."

Nalson nodded. "You are welcome," he answered, again peering carefully at Farimaal. "You will need the knowledge of our people and more if you intend to do more than ask questions."

Farimaal nodded, not wishing to discuss the matter, though Nalson had clearly guessed at his purpose for coming. Nalson added, "Please send Derrod in as you go out. His lessons for the day have only just begun."

"I will." Farimaal left the room, followed by Ronan.

Farimaal ignored the voice that seemed to drone endlessly behind him in the corridor. He grew weary of Ronan's chatter, but Ronan didn't appear to grow weary of chattering. "Are you listening to me?" Ronan said, his volume escalating.

"No," Farimaal said without turning around.

Ronan grabbed his arm, and Farimaal spun, stopping to meet Ronan's gaze with fire in his own eyes. "You heard what Nalson told you last week. You can't go into the dragon tower to fight the Grendolai and hope to come out. This mission is impossible."

Farimaal scoffed. "The boundaries of the possible change all the time. If no one ever tried the so-called impossible, most of the world's greatest accomplishments would never have come to pass."

"Maybe so, but this is beyond you. Let it go."

"I will not."

Ronan's frustration turned to sadness. "Then you will go to your death alone." He let go of Farimaal's arm and stepped back.

"Very well then. I will go to my death, but at least I will go to it. It will not come to me as I sit skulking in this hole. I at least will die a man's death."

"No, Farimaal, you will die a fool's death."

Ronan left, and Farimaal turned back in the direction he was going. A quarter of an hour later he approached Malek's chamber, and a small contingent of soldiers stood before the entrance, talking quietly among themselves. They were Nolthanim as well, but because they served on Malek's private guard, they held themselves aloof from regular officers of the Nolthanim.

"What business brings you here, soldier?"

"I'm here to see Malek."

"Are you indeed?" The man laughed and looked at his companions as though Farimaal was out of his mind. "Go away, fool, you don't come to this door unbidden. Malek will call you if he has need of you."

"He has and he does. Malek has these last three months repeated his invitation for any who would subdue the Grendolai to come forward."

The man laughed again, as did his friends, but when he looked back at Farimaal, the laughter died in his mouth. His eyes narrowed, and he stepped toward Farimaal, sniffing. "I smell no ale on your breath, but even so, you must be drunk. Make your purpose here plain and have done with you."

"I have, but if you are too slow to follow me, repeating myself will do no good."

Anger flashed across the man's face, and he made to draw his sword, but one of the other guards stayed his hand. "Let it be. If he is serious, he will die soon enough. If he isn't, well, he will learn firsthand that no man makes a mockery of Malek."

Farimaal stood still, his hand resting casually on the hilt of his sword. The guard who intervened took Farimaal in soberly, then spoke with measured tones. "I know you. You are the one they call Farimaal, aren't you?"

"I am."

The guard nodded. "You are fearless in battle, that I remember. I believe you are here in earnest, but I cannot see how even your success on the battlefield gives you cause to believe you can do this. We will announce your name and reason for coming, if you are decided."

"I am."

"Very well." The guard motioned to another guard, who went inside and closed the door. The guards and Farimaal stood silently, no one moving, until the man returned. "The Master will see you. Go in and have a seat."

Farimaal nodded and stepped through the door. The room inside was scarcely lit by a low, flickering candle near a single chair. Farimaal crossed to it. He could hear from the echo of his own footsteps on the stone floor that the room was much larger than the small candle revealed.

"So, you have come in answer to my call," a voice said from the shadows, and the hair on Farimaal's arms tingled at the sound.

"I have."

"You are willing to go to the dragon tower and confront the Grendolai?"

"I am, if you can give me what I desire in exchange."

"If I can give you what you desire?" Malek sounded mildly amused.

"Yes."

"What do you desire, man of Nolthanin?"

"Time."

"Time?"

"Yes, I want more time. I have the sickness."

"Ahh, I see," Malek answered in smooth and even tones. "You are dying anyway, so you thought you'd go out and see the world one more time. You thought you'd cross over into the ancient homeland of your fathers for one last journey. You thought that this would be a more interesting way to make an end than dying a slow and painful death here in the Mountain with the rest of my servants. Is this so?"

"It is so, but I have not reconciled myself to death as you suppose. I mean not simply to subdue the Grendolai but to kill it and so deliver the allegiance of the remainder to you again. That is why I am here."

A sound of scraping on the stone floor drew Farimaal's eyes, and a stooped figure in dark blue robes stepped forward to the edge of the candlelit area. Malek's hand took Farimaal's chin in a strong grip. Piercing blue eyes peered out from under Malek's hood, which was drawn up over his dark hair, and for a long moment, Farimaal returned Malek's stare. At last Malek began to nod. "Yes, I see. You are determined to try your hand at this thing."

"I am."

"Then you have my promise," Malek answered, his voice almost a whisper. "If you give me back the Grendolai, I will give you all the time you want. Is that the answer you were looking for?"

"It is."

"What hope have you for success?"

"Little, but hope I do have. I have a plan, but I won't really know whether it can succeed until I am there."

"When will you head out?"

"I need to make a trip to the Kellisor Sea—"

"The Kellisor Sea? Why?"

"There are two things I need. One I could possibly get here, but the other almost certainly I could find no place closer than there."

"These things are necessary?"

"I can think of no way around it."

"Very well then. I have waited this long for someone to come forward; I can wait a little longer. How long will you need?"

"To go around Gyrin and reach the coast and get back I will need perhaps two months."

"So be it. Come to me upon your return. I will have an escort ready."

The escort Malek promised consisted of half a dozen Nolthanim and about as many Malekim, but the number of Nolthanim had swollen to more than thirty by the time they were out of the Mountain and headed north to the dragon tower.

Apparently, word of Farimaal's venture had spread throughout the Mountain rapidly, and there was talk of little else during his absence. Speculation about his sanity, the terms of his agreement with Malek, and the purpose for his mysterious trip to the Kellisor Sea swirled through the tunnels and corridors of the Mountain like great gusts of wind. The general consensus on each of the questions appeared to be that too much time underground had indeed deprived Farimaal of at least part of his senses, that Malek promised Farimaal a throne in Avalione, and that the trip to the Kellisor Sea involved some sort of quest for a magic weapon, perhaps hidden by Malek during the Invasion. Farimaal's return from the sea caused such a stir that it reminded him of the days before they departed from Nal Gildoroth to board the ships for Suthanin more than fifteen years ago.

On his departure from the Mountain, just six short days later, word again quickly spread, and several, especially among the younger Nolthanim, hastily joined the party. At first the additional Nolthanim rode at some distance behind Farimaal and his escort, watching the quiet, lean, and grizzled man make his way steadily toward one of the most feared places in Kirthanin. After a few days, however, they joined the other Nolthanim in the escort and all traveled together, though Farimaal consistently rebuffed their attempts to engage him in dialogue of any kind. He did not speak rudely or dismissively; he simply did not speak to them at all.

Farimaal knew why they had come. They were there to see him fail, but he would not fail. At first they kept their murmurs and mockery to themselves, but by the end of the first week, the uninvited Nolthanim began to mock and ridicule Farimaal and his quest openly. They rode beside, before, and behind him, laughing at his folly and speculating as to the specifics of the hideous and certain death that awaited him. And so, in this way, the remainder of their journey passed until they were camped perhaps half a league away from the dragon tower, now visible above the tops of the trees that surrounded it in the distance.

The following day, the men and Malekim of the escort, as well as the hangers on, made no motions to accompany him.

He packed his saddlebag and prepared to ride on alone as the others sat around a fledgling fire.

"What did it feel like, waking up for the last time?" one of the more contemptuous of the uninvited Nolthanim asked as Farimaal mounted. "All this time you've spent traveling, first to the Kellisor Sea and now here to the dragon tower, and the Grendolai will probably kill you in less time than it takes me to drink a cup of water on a hot day."

"Even so," another added, "we thank you for the excuse to leave our digging and our duties behind us. It has been pleasant to ride abroad again, even through this wilderness. What's more, though you will likely be dead before we lie down to sleep this evening, we'll remain here for a week or so on the pretense of waiting for your return. Then we'll take to the road again, enjoying every moment of our journey, before having to feign sadness at your failure. We are greatly in your debt."

"Greatly," a third chimed in, "but we regret we will have no chance to repay what we owe."

"When I return," Farimaal said, looking down at them serenely from his horse and enjoying the shock on their faces at hearing his voice for the first time in reply, "I will exact payment from each of you in my own time and way."

He turned his horse away and spurred it forward.

Farimaal stooped beside the bones of the Vulsutyrim scattered beside the door to the dragon tower. As he had suspected, the giants died outside the tower. It was comforting to have been right, and alarming at the same time. He would have to limit his excursions outside the tower to times when the sun was fully up and shining, and even then he'd be quick about his business. The Grendolai who inhabited this place still used the exterior of the tower as a ladder, and however odd it seemed, the only safe place for Farimaal was inside the tower and on the spiral stairs.

He pulled the heavy saddlebag off his horse but left the saddle on. He stroked the horse gently for a few moments, then picked up a stick from the ground and struck the beast hard upon the hindquarters. The startled animal started off and ran several spans through the trees before slowing to a trot. He disliked having to be cruel to the poor creature, but he feared it would be supper for the Grendolai otherwise. With any luck it would make its way back to the camp and the others and so return again safely to the Mountain.

Farimaal shouldered his saddlebag and walked to the great iron door that stood slightly ajar at the base of the dragon tower. He hesitated, gazing up the exterior wall to the gyre high above him. He wondered just what exactly he would find up there, but he did not allow the question to delay him for too long. He pulled a torch from his saddlebag, lit it, and wrenched the door open just enough to slip inside.

The stairs were much like he had imagined them. They were narrow and steep, very steep. He ran his hands along the smooth stone of the interior walls and marveled at the quality of the work. The joints were still solid, and whatever had been used for mortar was not crumbling. The stones did not seem to have groaned under the weight of all they upheld for so many years. He was glad, for his plan, at least in part, depended upon their stability.

He pulled the door almost entirely closed behind him, but not quite. He couldn't bring himself to close it completely. The torch flickered, burning brightly enough to illuminate the small space. Farimaal set his foot cautiously upon the first stair and started up. Though he knew he could not hide his presence from the Grendolai for long—indeed, it was essential to his plan that the Grendolai know of him and be aware of him—he felt the urge to be quiet and so stepped up gingerly and delicately, so that each footstep made almost no sound.

Around and around, upward and upward he went, the torch flickering. Occasionally his pack, so heavy it pulled him constantly toward the outer wall, would hit the stone, and a slight echo would reverberate up and down the spiral staircase. Then he would pause, frozen on the steps, listening. But every time he stopped to listen, he heard nothing except his own breathing. He didn't know if the Grendolai heard him or smelled him or detected him in any way, and though he'd spent much time in dark corridors and tunnels of late, he felt a bit unnerved.

He stopped again, but this time he was smiling. He was unnerved by the mystery, by the unknown, by the uncertainty of what he would find above, and it was precisely the power of these things to unnerve and disconcert that his plan was based upon. But, he wondered, and not for the first time, would these things affect a Grendolai like they affected a man? Could a Grendolai be unnerved and disconcerted? Or were they so secure in their dark homes that Farimaal's hopes were based on impossibilities? Were they so sure of their invincibility that they could not be baited?

Farimaal started upward again. He needed the Grendolai to be so confident, but he also needed him to be capable of doubt and capable of being provoked. For Farimaal this would require patience, almost inhuman patience. He would have to endure long hours and days and perhaps weeks in this unsettling darkness as he worked bit by bit to prepare the Grendolai for that one brief moment when everything would hinge on the strength of the tower's stone, the speed of Farimaal's reflexes, and the Grendolai's desire to rip him to pieces.

Eventually, Farimaal reached the top of the stairs. The uppermost steps moved up and out, extending toward a small open space of perhaps half a span framed by an open doorway. The fact that the stairs were just as steep here, and that there was a slightly greater number of stairs within view of his torchlight, was encouraging. He had worried about whether the tower would be both wide and long enough for the pole he had in mind, but he could see now that it was.

He didn't waste much time thinking about that, though, for there would be plenty of time later to set the trap. What would take more time, and what he needed to turn his attention to first, was presenting the bait and convincing the Grendolai to care enough to go for it.

Farimaal stood a couple of steps down from the top. With less than a span between the top step and the doorway, he wasn't about to go all the way up, where the Grendolai's arms, infamous for both their length and their strength, would be able to reach him. Instead he gazed through the open door into the darkness of the storeroom beyond. He couldn't see much, but he could see that the space beyond was large, much larger than the narrow landing.

For a long time he stood there, waiting and listening. He felt a growing curiosity to explore the room, but he knew that would be foolish. *Patience,* he reminded himself, *I can only do this with patience.*

And then, almost as if on cue, a soft and even soothing voice spoke from the darkness. "Greetings, stranger. Welcome to my home. Why wait outside my door? Having come so far so boldly, why not see what you have come to see?"

The Grendolai's voice was so inviting that for a moment he forgot the danger. Farimaal felt his foot rising to ascend, but he forced it back down. "No thank you," Farimaal called when he had gathered himself. "I am not yet worthy to stand in your presence. I will come in when I have earned the right."

There was a pause, and then the Grendolai spoke again. "There is no need to prove yourself here. All are welcome. Come in."

"I am afraid not," Farimaal said, almost laughing. "I have seen how you welcomed your more recent guests, and I have no wish to remain in your company in that state. I have not come to stay forever, unfortunately. I'm only here until I have done my master's bidding."

"And who is your master?"

"You know my master, for he is your master too."

"I am my own master. No one rules over me."

"You are wrong, for you have both a maker and a master, and they are one and the same. I am sent here by him to secure the return of your allegiance."

Low laughter echoed in the darkness beyond the doorway. "You are a jester, sent here for my amusement. What crime did you commit that Malek sent you here to atone for it? Is there an army hidden behind you, crouching on the stairs? Surely you haven't come alone. Even if you haven't, you have come here in vain. You will not leave this place with my submission. Indeed, unless you flee, you will not leave at all."

"I will not flee."

"Good," the soothing voice said with genuine enthusiasm. "I have gotten used to regular meals again. I don't suppose you will make more than a snack, but I will eat and give thanks to my maker for his provision all the same."

"Do as you please with me if you catch me," Farimaal answered. "I expect no mercy from you, nor will I grant any."

For a second time laughter came floating through the darkness. "Good, little messenger, I consider myself duly warned. Even so, my submission you will not have."

"I am not here for your surrender. I have come for your head."

The laughter ceased, and Farimaal wondered what was happening now in the quiet darkness. When no words or laughter or sound of any kind came after several minutes, he threw his torch as far into the room as he could. It landed many spans inside, and the small flame still burning on the stone floor made precious little difference in the dark expanse. Farimaal waited, and still nothing happened. He held his breath, but soon doubt began to creep in, doubt that the Grendolai's hatred of light was as strong as rumor claimed. Then a dark form moved across the small circle of light the torch had created, and for a brief instant Farimaal saw a towering form as a great foot came down upon the torch, thrusting the tower into darkness.

As soon as the light was extinguished, Farimaal retreated instinctively and reached around for his pack and another torch. As he did, though, his foot slipped and he lost his balance, falling several steep steps before he could stop his momentum. He clenched his teeth to keep from howling and held his shin where it had crashed against the stone. As he did, a voice, seeming to come from just above, floated down the stairs. "Watch yourself, little messenger. You'll find my head hard to come by. How secure is yours?"

Farimaal sat as still as he could until the throbbing in his leg had diminished enough for him to descend again. He went down about ten steps, then emptied his pack entirely, distributing on the stairs the things he had brought with him. He took out what food he had left and his supply of torches. Then he removed the coil of rope he had obtained from the shipping yard on the Kellisor Sea. Lastly, he set out a hammer, three iron rings, and the great iron piece fashioned by the blacksmith there, which weighed the better part of half a dozen stone. This he set cautiously on a stair against the wall. He didn't want to step on that by accident, so he lit a torch and surveyed his items. Moving gingerly, he descended the great stair to the bottom.

Pushing the iron door open, he stepped back out into the sunshine. He breathed deeply, as though coming up for air. For a moment he drank in the sunshine on the leaves of the trees, the slight breeze, and the feel of space around him. Then, with his empty pack, he set about the task at hand. Moving slowly around the tower and out under the nearest trees, he started filling his pack with rocks.

That night, Farimaal slept on the stairs of the dragon tower. It was every bit as uncomfortable as he had imagined it would be, but he didn't dare sleep outside. Nor did he dare sleep within reach of the iron door at the bottom or the storeroom door at the top.

Eventually he did sleep, and when he awoke, he had no concept of whether it was day or night. He picked up one of the iron rings and the hammer and silently ascended to the top. He stepped onto the small landing outside the open door for the first time, and sweat began to bead on his forehead. This was one of the stages in his plan that made him nervous, even more than most of it did, but there was nothing for it. If he couldn't get the rings in, there was no plan. Reaching overhead, he could not feel the ceiling. It had looked the previous day, in the torchlight, to be just over a span and a half, so he knew it would be close. Setting the hammer and ring on the top stair, he went back down. As he filled his pack with rocks the previous day, he found two broad, flat stones, which he now lugged up the stairs one at a time. He set each gently on the edge of the top stair, then slid them into the middle of the landing. There he set the one on top of the other, and with hammer and ring in hand, stood on them.

With the added height, he could place his hand flat against the ceiling. He felt around with his fingertips for one of the joints, and having found it, raised the iron ring. The ring was about half a hand in diameter, with a long iron piece coming out of one side, tapering to a sharp point. This point he lined up on the joint. Then, looking nervously at the door that opened onto the darkness beside him, he raised his hammer.

Ching! Ching! Ching! The hammer flew up and down, and the sound of metal on metal split the silence and echoed in the darkness. It took several strokes before he felt the ring move at all, and he kept pounding. He needed to drive the ring all the way in and get out of this vulnerable spot. He kept hitting, over and over, aware that every stroke exposed him further. Suddenly the sound of scraping against stone came to him between strokes, and without hesitation he let go of the ring and with hammer in hand leapt off of the stones in the direction of the stairs. This time, miraculously, he kept his balance when he landed.

He scrambled down several steps, then squatted, listening. After a moment, he heard the Grendolai's voice. "Piling stones at my door, little messenger? Do I not have enough stone about me that you need to bring more? Do you hope to shut me in by walling off my door? Pile away. If these are the biggest stones you can carry, know I can squeeze them into dust."

When no further words were forthcoming, Farimaal slipped back down and grabbed a second ring. He didn't dare continue the actual work of driving them in today, but as he had nothing else to do, he could always begin his siege on the Grendolai's patience. Settling onto one of the stairs as close to the top as he dared, he set down the iron ring and started tapping it firmly, over and over. Sitting there in the dark, listening to the echo of the hammer, he thought of life inside the Mountain. He could only hope the Grendolai found this disruption of his quiet life as irritating as Farimaal did.

All he did the rest of the day was tap the iron ring, over and over, but if he was provoking the Grendolai, there was no sign of it. Eventually he went to sleep again, passing a second uncomfortable night on the stairs. When he awoke, he slipped up to the top again. He felt for the stones that he'd left on the landing, and sure enough, they were still there. Slowly, quietly, he stepped back up onto them. He reached up and felt around on the ceiling until he found the iron ring again. He was pleased to find that he had driven the iron shaft above the ring solidly into the mortar of the joint. In fact, it was more than halfway in, and a few solid blows would be sufficient to drive it the rest of the way. It might have been secure enough as it was, but Farimaal didn't want his plan to fail because he hadn't completely secured the ring. He lifted the hammer to finish the job, but paused, turning to stare at the open doorway. Suddenly he felt quite sure it would be a mistake to strike the ring, so he stepped off and hastily scrambled down the stair and found the iron ring he'd spent the previous day tapping. Picking it up and returning to a place only six or seven stairs from the top, he struck the ring as hard as he could so that the sound rang up and down the stairs.

No sooner had he struck the ring than something sailed over his head and smashed into the wall. That something smashed into pieces, some of which fell on Farimaal's head. He scrambled back down and, lighting one of his torches, examined what had broken. It only took a moment to recognize the fractured pieces of a large skull, probably that of a Malekim, for it was too small to be a giant's and too big to be a man's.

Farimaal smiled as he grabbed his pack and moved as close as he dared to the top of the stairs. "I appreciate your cooperative spirit," Farimaal called out, "but that was not the head I was after."

There was no response from within, and after several moments, Farimaal drew open the pack and stacked several stones on the stair beside him. Then, standing, he took a few in his left hand and again threw his torch as far into the open room as he could. This time the massive form quickly crossed the small circle of light and stomped it out. Just as quickly, Farimaal began throwing the stones in the direction of the great form. Half a dozen stones he threw, and though he tried to hear what they struck, he could not tell if any had hit anything but the stone floor.

The Grendolai's soft, low laugh sounded right above him. Panicked, Farimaal moved clumsily down several stairs. If the Grendolai wasn't standing in the doorway, he was right beside it. "This is your plan, little messenger? Draw me out into the open with your torches, then throw these pebbles at me? What do you think they will accomplish? Tell me you haven't come all this way and pinned all your hopes on that. Tell me there is more to your dread plan than stones and persistent sounds. Come now, servant of Malek, show me something to fear, for my only fear right now is that I will grow bored with you."

Farimaal didn't speak but listened for the Grendolai's next move. The sound of another object smashing against the wall, followed by a second, both dropping heavily onto the stairs, told him he had been right to be cautious. He groped around in the darkness and found one of the broad stones that had been sitting on the landing. Part of it had been broken off by the impact, but it was basically intact, which was good news. It would have been inconvenient had the Grendolai taken the stones away, but the only inconvenience now was that Farimaal would have to put them back.

He found the other and stacked them both together before heading to the bottom. He would leave the ring alone for today. He would leave the Grendolai in silence, leave the creature to wonder if he'd been scared away. Farimaal had other things that needed taking care of, and now was as good a time as any.

Outside in the sunshine, he walked among the trees that surrounded the dragon tower. Most of the trees were old, very old, but he spotted new growth here and there, and these trees he examined carefully. None of them was exactly the right size. Though he looked all day, he did not find what he wanted. He marked the tree that came closest, but he was not yet ready to give up on finding the perfect one. The one luxury he had now was time, for the longer he dwelt upon the tower stairs, the longer the Grendolai lived with the mystery of his presence, the better his chances that when the right moment came, the creature would respond as he desired.

The better part of the next day Farimaal searched again, and not long before sundown he found what seemed the perfect tree. The diameter was ideal, he was sure of it, and the trunk was straight and solid. The tree was taller than he could lift or carry, he knew that, but better too big than too small. He could cut it down to a manageable size, but now was not the time. As the sun sank, he marked this tree as well and quickly made his way back inside.

His fourth night on the stairs was just as miserable as the first three, and after drifting in and out of sleep several times, he decided that it was time to finish with the first ring. If the Grendolai was camped out close to the doorway, this could be the end of everything, but sooner or later, he was going to have to try. He had not ascended to the top in almost two days, and when he reached the two stones, he found himself strangely calm. One at a time, he lifted them back up to the landing and stacked them there again. With no hesitation he stepped up onto the stones, found the ring with his left hand, and sent the hammer flying. *Ching! Ching! Ching!*

Six strokes. That was all it took. The ring was flush with the ceiling, driven in as far as he could drive it. A great arm swept past him in the darkness. A great arm was what it had to be, for something sharp as nails ripped through his shirt and cut his side as he leapt down several steps. He felt the wounds, two shallow, bleeding cuts.

"Your flesh is soft, Nolthanim, for that is what you are, isn't it? The land around my tower was once your home, or at least, it was the home of your fathers before you became Malek's slaves. Malek is not your maker, and yet you serve him. He is my creator, but I defy him. I am my own master. Why do you care if I serve Malek or not? Why come here and give your life away in service to him? What has he done for you, except conquer your homeland and subjugate your brothers and sisters? Go back to the Mountain, or go make your way north. If you stay here, you will die. One way or another, you will die."

"Malek is my master," Farimaal called, "but I'm not here for him. I'm here for me. If killing you will get me what I want, so be it. I will kill you and not think twice about it. I will not die here."

"So be it, little messenger. You have sealed your fate."

That was all Farimaal had from the Grendolai, so he tended his wound and settled in for sleep once more.

The next day, the fifth since his arrival, Farimaal returned to his tree. With only his hammer and a slender wedge, he set about cutting the tree down. It was slow going, for he had to drive the wedge in as far as he dared without getting it completely stuck, and then work it out so he could drive it in elsewhere on the trunk. A few times he stopped a hair's breadth shy of too far, and the wedge was almost pinched beyond recall. Still, each time, he patiently and successfully removed it. Eventually, after making perhaps a dozen cuts into the tree, he heard a cracking and knew that the tree was ready to be toppled. He leaned against it and pushed, and with all the force he could bring to bear, he forced the tree to the ground. He sat down next to it and rested. He would come back in a day or two and measure out how long he wanted it to be, but he couldn't bring himself to start that laborious process now. He retreated into the tower.

The following day, though, he did not go back to work on the tree. Rather he spent the first half of the day finding three more large, smooth stones that he could stand upon when inserting the second and third rings. Each of these he carried up the tower and stacked on the landing several hands away from where the first stack had been. The original stones he also moved so that he had a wider base on which to stand.

Feeling the ceiling for a joint, he lined up the sharp end of the next ring and started to drive it in. He worked until it was in far enough to stay without him holding it, and then he quickly ducked down and stooped nearby on the stairs. He waited, but nothing happened. Nothing came flying through the door; no voice called or laughed from within. He lit a torch, stood, and hurled it into the room. The Grendolai did not go to it immediately, but he did go, and Farimaal marked that he approached the torch from the far side. He had not been waiting by the door, nor had he come to it when Farimaal started to hammer. Even so, he thought he wouldn't press his good fortune any further today.

He went downstairs and outside, but not back to the tree. His food supply was running low. He didn't know what kind of creature might live in close proximity to the tower and the Grendolai, but he thought he'd have a look. He was making good progress, but even so, he was several days, perhaps even weeks away from being ready to move forward with his plan. Sooner or later he was going to have to try his hand at hunting.

Hunting proved futile. He had imagined that the selection of living creatures near the dragon tower would be slim, but it seemed as though everything that walked or slithered or crawled upon the earth had fled. Only the birds remained, but even these seemed always to be flying overhead, not resting where they could be caught. Any hope Farimaal harbored for substantial sustenance slipped away. His only consolation was the plentiful occurrence of locusts, especially on the trees of the north. He might not eat well when his food ran out, but he would eat.

The next three days he spent doing three things in uneven shifts. In sporadic and brief bursts, he worked on driving home the second iron ring just above the edge of the small landing. That complete, he set about pounding in a third, this one into the slightly sloping ceiling just above the first stair. All told, this took up perhaps only a quarter of an hour of his time, though it was far and away the activity that dominated his mind the most as he lay down to sleep each night.

When he wasn't about the nerve-racking business of securing the iron rings, he was dividing his time between cutting the tree to his desired specifications and sitting near the top of the stairs, tapping the heavy iron piece with his hammer. Long years beneath the Mountain had all but made him deaf to the clanging of hammers, but he hoped that the Grendolai's long years in silence had made him especially sensitive to the piercing notes. Still, the creature gave no sign of irritation. If his plan was working, he had no proof of it. Farimaal could only hope that despite the apparent calm, the Grendolai would eventually grow angry enough to become careless.

On the tenth day, as Farimaal climbed to his place near the top of the steps to continue his psychological assault, a voice greeted him from inside the room.

"Nolthanim, the pole you are shaping down below fascinates me."

Farimaal felt his heartbeat falter. In his mind's eye he imagined the tree broken into pieces or gone altogether. All that work, and now he would have to start over. Worse, perhaps the Grendolai had figured it out: the hammering, the tree, the plan. He was unmasked. How could he have been so careless as to leave his work lying on the grass overnight? He knew the Grendolai was not confined to the tower. Why had it not occurred to him that the creature might find his handiwork?

"Still," the creature continued, "if you have aspirations to be a carpenter, I can't see that you have any future here. Like the stones you have piled outside my door, what good will that pole do you? It may be a mighty tree to you, but I assure you it is but a twig to me. I would snap it in my hand, as you would break dead branches from a tree. Go home, little messenger, and leave your scheming and your irritations behind. You have worn out your welcome here, and when you eventually find the courage to come out from your hiding spot, I will sharpen one end of that stick of yours and spit you upon it."

Farimaal did not dare speak for fear he would give away his panic. If he was undone, he would find out for himself down below. He would not, though, as his enemy had done, give anymore of himself or his plan away involuntarily. He had at last confirmation that he was succeeding in irritating the Grendolai. The voice was the same, but the message and words were different. He wanted Farimaal gone or dead, whatever would silence him. But Farimaal would not be silenced. He took up his hammer and started tapping.

When his hand was exhausted from the motion of the hammer, he made his way quickly down the stairs and outside. Hurrying through the trees to the place where he had left his pole on the ground, he saw it still lying there. If it had been touched, he could not tell. He set to work, for he did not want to leave it out even one more night. He cut and shaped and peeled what remained of the bark. He needed it smooth, completely smooth, and by the early evening, the surface was like the slick stone of the tower wall. Returning to the tower at a run, he grabbed the great iron piece and his hammer and the four solid nails he had left with his rope.

Back in the dying light of day, he carefully slid the top of the wooden pole into the open end of the large iron piece, which was thick and solid and more than two hands in diameter. Yet at the top, the piece formed a point so sharp that it could have slid between Farimaal's finger and his fingernail. The tree slid snugly almost a hand into the sharp point, and with the hammer, Farimaal drove the four nails through the holes prepared for them and into the hard wood. He clasped the thick edge of the iron piece and tried to tug it off, but it would not move at all.

The sun had nearly set, and he dared not risk being found by the Grendolai, so he expended the last of his energy on dragging the tree into the tower. It was almost completely dark when he set the tree down some twenty stairs up, securing the edge of the great iron head on the stair to keep it from sliding down. He considered retrieving his hammer, but he would have to leave it out tonight. Better to lose his hammer than his life.

The next day, he returned to the place where he had shaped and smoothed the tree, but his hammer wasn't there. He looked all over the small clearing, but he couldn't find it. It was useless to conjecture whether the Grendolai had destroyed or taken it; in the end it didn't really matter. The groove on the tree he could make with the wedge, which the Grendolai had not taken with the hammer. Perhaps he had overlooked it, for it was still lying in the grass. He took up the wedge and returned to the tower.

Ascending to the top of the stairs, he stepped quietly onto the stones and threaded the end of his rope through the three rings so that the end almost touched the landing. He couldn't light a torch to see what he was doing, because it was imperative that the Grendolai never see the rope. He was going to have to use his hands and arms to measure distances in the dark, which meant he was going to have to brave his way across the landing to the door. It wasn't the only time his plan called for this, but it would be the most vulnerable time. If the Grendolai was lurking there, all Farimaal's efforts were in vain.

Holding the rope he had fed through the loops, he started to crawl, groping through the darkness. He made his measurements. If the iron head was to be free to swing through the doorway, Farimaal must give the rope enough slack to prevent the point from going straight into the ceiling.

The pole was just over two spans long, and with the iron head attached, it was almost all Farimaal could do to lift it. Even after he had made the groove and attached the rope, it took him two full days of yanking and tugging and pulling to move the contraption up the stairs. He had to go quietly, for great screechings and scrapings would have alerted the Grendolai to the nature of the danger that Farimaal was preparing. All Farimaal could do was lift the pole, step by step, setting it down on each successive stair and keeping firm hold on the rope should the pole start to slide. In this way he brought it all the way up to the place where he had been sleeping the previous twelve nights. He was ready to put the plan in motion. All that remained was to spend one final day baiting the hook.

The next morning, Farimaal took all but three of his remaining torches and climbed to the top of the stairs. He removed the stones that he had used on the landing, as they would only get in the way now. A sizeable stack of smaller stones remained. Lighting one of the torches and throwing it into the room, he again took aim at the form of the Grendolai stomping out the offending light. This Farimaal did at random intervals throughout the day, until his supply of both torches and rocks was exhausted. The Grendolai said nothing as this pattern was repeated, and neither did Farimaal. He felt as though they had established a connection, a clear and almost tangible bond. There was no more use for words. Neither would speak again until the other was dead.

The morning of the fifteenth day came at last, and Farimaal stretched on the stairs. Today was the day. He would go down and look on the outer world once more. If he failed and these were his final hours, he would spend them in the sunlight, under the trees.

In the early afternoon he ascended the stair once more. The way was now familiar, and his feet moved quickly and quietly up the long spiral stairwell. When he reached the pole, he went right to work moving it up, step by step. With every step, he became increasingly sensitive to the slightest sound. He spent ages lowering the pole at an almost imperceptible rate, all with the hope that no sound at all would be made. In this way, he moved slowly toward the landing. When at last he was there, he took off his shirt and wiped the sweat from his face. Crouching beside the pole, he made sure it was centered on the stairs and that nothing might impede it.

He stooped at the bottom of the pole and gave it a slight push. It didn't move. He frowned in the dark. Had he made it too heavy? It was lighter than he was, but was it light enough? He would have momentum and he would pull as hard as he could, but would that be sufficient? With both hands he grabbed the pole, and straddling it, he pushed it up. It slid a little bit. He eased it back down gently until it rested on the stair again. He felt relieved. If he could move it like that from the bottom, then surely he would be able to propel it forward when the time came.

Back up top, he took hold of the rope end that wasn't fastened to the pole and fed it through the loop closest to the door. It was a delicate process, as even on his tiptoes he could barely reach the ring. He then pulled the rope back toward the stair, and through the second and third rings. When he had pulled the rope all the way through, he stepped back up onto the landing. Standing on the edge, he could hold both lengths of rope in either hand, the taut one securely tied to the pole and the loose one dangling slack down the stairs. He closed his eyes and imagined the whole process again. As he did, he started to feed some of the rope back through the rings. He didn't want there to be tension in the rope when he first grabbed it. He wanted some slack to play out before the rope jerked taut and pulled the pole. He felt both bits of rope again. The amount of tension felt right now. All that remained was to take the excess that was sitting in a jumbled heap beside the pole and move it over until it sat against the wall. He needed that part of the rope to hang to the side. It would be catastrophic if he grabbed the wrong piece.

Satisfied that everything was ready, he faced the open room. There was no time like the present, and the longer he waited, the more nervous he would become. He'd imagined this moment a thousand times, and he didn't need any more time.

Pulling out his last three torches, he lit them all. He held two in his left hand and, stepping right up to the doorway, threw the third as far into the room as he could. As the torch fell to the floor, some ten spans inside the room, he moved a second torch into his right hand. As he did, he passed through the doorway, at last entering the domain of the Grendolai.

He had not gone far when the Grendolai's large figure glided into the circle of light and stomped out the torch. The second torch was already in the air on its way toward the Grendolai, and heavy footsteps echoed through the room, telling Farimaal the creature was now moving his way, and quickly. He turned and ran. As he was turning, he caught a glimpse of the torch gliding past the ducking form of his pursuer. He expected that at any moment the long arm of the creature would reach out and seize him, but it didn't. He flung the last torch along the wall as he shot out of the room and onto the landing. Grabbing the dangling rope, he leapt as high and as hard off of the top stair as he could.

For the briefest of moments he soared out into the air, but he barely had time to feel the power of his leap before the slack in the rope was played out and the weight of the pole on the other end altered his trajectory, swinging him in a downward arc. He had known that this would hurt, and he tried to brace himself for the impact of his body against the stone stairs, even as he tried midflight to pull the rope with all his might.

His body swung at full speed into the stairs, and pain erupted all across his body. His leg and ankle hit the hardest, but as he struck he twisted, and the side of his head whacked the corner of one of the stairs. He lay there for a second groaning. He was still holding as tightly as he could to the rope, and as he pulled against it, he was momentarily encouraged by the fact that there was not give at all. That was a good sign.

Even so, his encouragement was only momentary. As his mind raced back over the leap, he realized that in no part of his memory could he locate a cry or shriek or scream from the Grendolai. If the plan had worked, surely some outcry of shock, of pain, of indignation would have been forthcoming.

Slowly, and with much pain, Farimaal started back up the stairs, using the taut rope as a handle to pull himself up and along. As he neared the top, he saw the bottom of the pole lodged firmly against the top step. Farimaal's heart sank. The angle seemed much too sharp. The pole rose too high, too quickly. He had feared this, that after all his work he might succeed in doing nothing more than lodging his makeshift spear in the stone arch above the doorway.

But even as his heart was sinking, he stopped in his tracks. The torch that he had cast aside was still glowing, and silhouetted in the doorway by its light was the thick and imposing form of the Grendolai. He stood where he was, still holding the rope, and stared.

It took a moment for his eyes to adjust to the faint light, but as they did, he noticed two things. The first was that the Grendolai did not move, not at all. The silhouette was completely still.

The second was that the pole had not struck the stone arch, for the long, thick shaft passed through the doorway beneath it.

Hope and excitement began to rise in Farimaal. He stepped onto the landing and moved closer. He stopped again. Even if the iron point had struck the Grendolai, it might not have killed or even seriously wounded the creature. He waited.

Eventually, he sat down. He had waited this long to spring the trap, he could wait a while longer to make sure the trap had worked. Still, the Grendolai did not move or speak. Several hours passed. The second torch that Farimaal had thrown into the room went out. The third, which he could not see from where he was, burned very low. He would wait no longer; it was time to go in.

He rose and went forward, then realized that there was not enough room on either side of the Grendolai to pass through. He dropped onto his hands and knees and crawled under the creature's legs. He walked over and grabbed the dim torch. Moving back to the Grendolai, he stood beside it and took a closer look. Even from the side, the sight was dramatic. The Grendolai's head was braced against the stone above the doorway, as though leaning there for a rest. In the gap between the body and the wall, Farimaal could see the pole firmly embedded in the creature's chest not far below his neck.

He touched the Grendolai's arm. There was no response. He held the torch up as close to the shoulders as he could. No reaction. Farimaal breathed deeply. The plan had worked. The Grendolai was dead.

He tugged on the body, but he couldn't tilt it away from the wall. He studied the situation for a few moments, but as he stood there, his torch went out. He had one more in reserve for this very moment, but it was down the stairs. As he retrieved it, he had an idea. Returning to the top of the stairs, he cut the rope from the pole and took it with him as he passed between the Grendolai's legs for the third time. Fastening the rope to one of the Grendolai's ankles, he stepped back from the great body and pulled as hard as he could. Three times he pulled, and three times nothing happened. The fourth time, though, the legs began to slide out from the wall and the whole body began to shift, and after a few more tugs, the Grendolai's head slid into empty space and the great body tumbled down.

Fortunately for Farimaal, the pole kept the Grendolai from falling flat on the floor, and it now propped him up at an odd angle. It took some maneuvering, but Farimaal managed to use the pole to push the Grendolai onto his side and lower him to the ground. With much wrestling and wrangling, Farimaal managed to remove the great iron head and pole from the Grendolai's chest. Stepping close with his torch, he took a closer look at the wound.

The Grendolai's hide, even where penetrated, was most impressive. Farimaal ran his finger around the circumference of the wound. Nalson had said it would take an arrow the size of a battering ram, and he'd been right. The hide was wondrously tough, and Farimaal knew he had been fortunate to strike it so hard, straight on.

As he stooped over the Grendolai, he had an idea. A smile crept across his face as he ran his fingers over the unbroken hide. When he returned to the Mountain, he would claim and receive his gift of time from Malek, but before he left this tower, he would carve from the body of his vanquished foe a very different kind of reward, a very different kind indeed.

FLIGHT

A FOOL'S HOPE

RULALIN LOOKED BACK over his shoulder at Col Marena. Flames from some of the buildings in the small port city rose in the distance, sending plumes of smoke into the dark sky. It was early Third Watch, ushering in the second day of Winter Rise. The wind was cool and the rain steady, so Rulalin wished himself a bit closer to the fire in the distance, if only to be near the heat.

"Rulalin," Soran whispered sharply. Rulalin turned. Soran said nothing but motioned with his head toward Farimaal's tent not more than ten spans away. Rulalin peered through the dark night, seeing only two cloaked figures standing before the tent, partially lit by the torches. As Rulalin watched, the men started across the grass in their direction.

As they neared, the man nearest them looked up at Rulalin and Soran and nodded with a smile as he passed. Rulalin clenched his teeth and returned the faint nod with an even fainter one of his own. He still didn't know what role Synoki played in Malek's service, or how highly Malek might prize him, but Rulalin figured just about everyone was higher in rank than he, so he'd better be polite to them all, regardless of how he felt about it.

The two men disappeared into the darkness, and Rulalin turned back toward Farimaal's tent. Tashmiren stood before it now, and he motioned to Rulalin and Soran to come over. Even though it was too dark to make out any details of Tashmiren's face from this distance, Rulalin envisioned the look of smug, arrogant disdain that Tashmiren wore so frequently. He felt rising inside him a different kind of loathing for Tashmiren than the loathing he felt for Synoki. He trusted neither man, but he sensed with Synoki a need to be wary, for mystery surrounded this man he had first met so long ago and so far away. Even Synoki's revelation inside the Mountain had not fully explained the mystery. Though he didn't like to admit it, at some level, Rulalin feared him.

He did not fear Tashmiren. To be sure, he feared what might happen to him if he did to Tashmiren any of the things he'd like to do, but to Rulalin that was an important distinction. As he crossed the damp grass swiftly, he fantasized about how good it would be to bury his sword up to the hilt in Tashmiren's chest. Pushing that thought from his mind, he nodded in acknowledgment, and Soran remained outside as Rulalin stepped through the open flap.

Farimaal was in his usual position for receiving company, slumped sideways in the wide wooden chair that had been hauled from inside the Mountain. The grey stubble on his face was thicker and scragglier than usual, and Farimaal was scratching it with all four fingers of his right hand as Rulalin came in.

"Sit," Farimaal said without looking at him.

Rulalin settled onto an uncomfortable bench, the only other piece of furniture in the large tent. Rulalin didn't enjoy sitting on that bench for any reason, especially not tonight, when their enemy had eluded them and slipped out to sea. He waited for Farimaal to speak.

"We have a quandary," Farimaal said at last, and still he didn't look in Rulalin's direction. Rulalin waited, and another long pause followed. Farimaal turned from whatever he had been gazing at and fixed his stare on Rulalin. "This Aljeron Balinor, your friend, has taken all the ships in Col Marena."

"Yes, sir, I know," Rulalin said, coughing and clearing his throat.

"Most of them are still visible out in the Bay of Thalasee, but we think he'll head south soon. Do you?"

"Yes. The only explanation I can think of for his refusal to defend Shalin Bel or Col Marena is that he wanted to slip away to try to find aid among the Suthanim. I'd guess he's headed for Cimaris Rul."

"As are we," Farimaal answered, turning his head back to the side of the tent, scraping at his stubble again.

After a few moments, Rulalin asked, "You mean to go through the marshes?"

"Yes."

"The wagons won't make it."

"We won't take them. At least, we won't take most of them. We'll have to rely on the land to feed us along the way."

"It is a long way, and there are long open stretches with little but grass. It will be muddy and slow going in all this rain."

Farimaal gazed at Rulalin. Rulalin saw in those bright eyes the flash he had seen there before. Was it laughter somewhere buried deep below the impassive face? He couldn't tell, and as quickly as it came it went. "We will move quickly, for we don't want to give him time to fortify Cimaris Rul. When we reach the city, if it still stands, your services will be again required, both as a soldier and as an ambassador, though I suspect they won't surrender as long as Balinor leads them. Between now and then, I may need you as a guide. You are the only one among us who has passed through Suthanin anywhere west of Lindan Wood. At least, you are the only one who has passed that way in the last thousand years."

Again the sparkle rippled through Farimaal's eyes, and once more he turned his head away. "Go and prepare your men for the crossing of the marshes. We leave at dawn."

"Yes, sir." Rulalin rose and exited into the wet, cold night.

"Well?" Soran asked as they walked away together through the darkness.

"We are leaving at dawn."

"Where to?"

"South. We are headed to Cimaris Rul."

"As you guessed. And the route?"

"We are making for the marshes."

"As you feared."

"Yes, as I feared," Rulalin said, keeping his head down to shield his face from the cool rain. "I imagine it will not be the last time that following Malek will take us somewhere I don't want to go."

Aljeron stood at the port side of the *Summer Sun,* gazing across the dark waters of the Bay of Thalasee at the fires that still burned in Col Marena. They began early that morning, in the half-light of dawn, and continued all day. Even so, Aljeron hoped that the steady rainfall had tempered their spread and that much of Col Marena might survive to be rebuilt one day. *There is much that will need rebuilding, but who will be around to do it?*

It was not a cheery thought, for it took Aljeron's thoughts many leagues east to Shalin Bel. The enemy had pressed hard after them, so it was possible Malek's armies had not stopped to burn the city, pull down the walls, or pillage its buildings. It did not take long to start fires, however, and the destruction of Col Marena did not give Aljeron much hope for Shalin Bel, now empty and exposed.

It is the people, not the stones that matter, he reminded himself as the fires burned in the distance. If Allfather had been merciful, the people of Shalin Bel were many leagues north or south by now. He hoped Malek's pursuit of his army had diverted the enemy forces long enough. While he could offer no protection now to the Werthanim on the run, he had bought them precious time that might keep them alive, at least a while longer.

He scanned what little he could see of the port city. He hated sitting out here on the water in safety when he didn't know who might still be alive and desperate to get out of the city. Men of his, perhaps, separated during the flight down the coast, might even now be trapped between their pursuers and the sea. For the first time in the last month, Aljeron prayed for the ever-present, all-pervading rain to fall harder, faster, and stronger. He prayed for the rain to put out the fires and preserve what few shelters and hiding places might remain in Col Marena.

A step behind him on the deck drew his attention, and he looked back over his shoulder to see Aelwyn approaching. She was wrapped in the heavy dark-grey cloak that she'd worn all the way from Shalin Bel. An image of her setting out, sitting astride her sleek black horse in the cold grey morning came back to him. He had looked back over his shoulder as they rode out from the city, and he saw almost instantly in the vast crowd her face, beautiful and determined and turned toward him, her long black hair pulled loosely behind her.

As she approached now, her hair was pulled much more tightly and secured in a simple knot at the back of her head, but she was no less beautiful; indeed, she was even more so as she smiled at him. She reached up and took his arm gently. "Why stand here alone, Aljeron? Your closest friends and advisors are gathered here. Why do you avoid their company?"

"It is not their company that I'm avoiding, but their questions. I would happily go to them to be advised; it is the advising I wish to avoid. I cannot give them the guidance that they seek." Aljeron gazed once more across the water. "I was comfortable as commander of the army of Shalin Bel. I was confident besieging the city of Fel Edorath to bring Rulalin Tarasir to justice, but that's no longer my role. I've suddenly become Aljeron Balinor, commander of the Werthanim in flight before the might and power of Malek, and I have no idea how to do that. It is beyond me. It is beyond any man."

Aelwyn didn't answer but held onto Aljeron's arm. He looked down at her and saw not only compassion but affection. Thoughts of fire and rain and war slipped away from him for the first time in days. He smiled.

"It is so good to see you smile," Aelwyn whispered, reaching up to stroke the smooth skin of his unscarred cheek. "You carry so much weight, so many burdens. If I bring no other good to you and to this army but an occasional smile, I will consider my service to you and to Shalin Bel meaningful."

Aljeron turned toward Aelwyn, placing his big hand on her cheek, touching the smooth skin of her face for the first time. Aelwyn blushed, but she did not pull back. "I don't understand, Aelwyn, why me?"

"Because you are beautiful," she answered, without hesitation.

"But my face—"

"Yes," Aelwyn said. She lifted her other hand and ran her fingers along the ridges of the large scars that dominated the other side of Aljeron's face. "I know you don't think anyone could think you are beautiful because of these, but that's rubbish. Anyone who can't see beyond the scars can't see at all."

Aljeron looked intently into Aelwyn's eyes. He saw complete sincerity and earnestness there. "Aljeron, I want you to do me a favor."

"What?"

"You're free to love me or not love me, but I'm asking you to accept that I love you the way any woman would love a man. Time, our time, may be short. Let's not go over this ground again."

Aljeron nodded. "All right. I'll take you at your word."

"Thank you."

"As for loving you," Aljeron said, "I hardly know where to begin. I've been consumed by war for so long. I'd given up on the possibility of love, but when you touch me, when I feel your hand on my arm or your fingers on my face, I feel like a boy again. Laughter is never far from my heart when I dream of a face like yours to look into my own. Do I love you? I don't honestly know, but I know that I'm glad you're here. I know that when I think there's nothing beautiful left in this world, seeing you reminds me that I'm wrong. I know that if our lives weren't unraveling with each passing day, I'd gladly devote my days to spending time with you. These things I know, Aelwyn. It may not be an answer to your question, but it's a start, isn't it?"

"It's a start," Aelwyn said, smiling. "And a start is all we need right now. I've adored you since I was a little girl. I don't expect you to be on my timetable."

"Ahem." They turned, and Aljeron could feel his face blushing as he looked up into Aelwyn's sister's face.

"Good evening, Mindarin."

"I trust I wasn't interrupting anything too important," Mindarin said, smirking as she looked back and forth between them, "but I've been sent to find you, Aljeron. Gilion just arrived by longboat. Everyone is here now."

"Have the others gathered?"

"Yes. All we need now is you."

"Thank you. Please take word to them that we're coming."

"I will," Mindarin said, turning and heading back across the deck.

Aljeron turned back to Aelwyn, "I'm sorry, Aelwyn."

"Don't be. Every moment we are able to steal together is a gift. Let's treasure each in hope for a day when we'll have all the time we want."

"Wouldn't that be nice?"

"Yes, it would."

The large, open stateroom that belonged to the wealthy merchant who owned the *Summer Sun* was opulent, bright with gilded wood furniture, including a long oval table engraved with swirling patterns. Tall, bronze lamps firmly bolted to the walls to prevent them from tumbling over in rough seas and setting the ship ablaze lit the room. Even the timber pillars that supported the deck above were dressed up with painted landscapes that must have been hung there to remind the merchant of home during his long sojourns at sea.

Spread out on the large table was a great map of the western coastline of Kirthanin, stretching all the way from the Bay of Thalasee to the mouth of the Barunaan River in the south and the great city of Cimaris Rul. Which of the ships the map had come from, Aljeron didn't know. Certainly no one in the fleet had objected. The sailors and crews who worked these ships were only too willing to set sail once they understood from what they were fleeing. Not all the captains and owners were as happy to relinquish control to Aljeron's officers, but as the flames rose from Col Marena early that morning, a change of heart overcame even the most stubborn. For most of these men, the only thing worse than losing control of one's vessel was losing the vessel itself.

As Aljeron and Aelwyn joined the meeting, he took in the weariness that characterized the faces around the table. It was a weariness mixed with sorrow, for Valzaan's passing was still fresh with them all. Even now, images of the prophet's demise flashed before him. He could see the swirling sands whipping around the heads of the Vulsutyrim, and the sinking sands beneath the Black Wolves. He could hear the children of Rucaran howling on the beach, and the terrified neighing of the horses as they reared in fear, many of them throwing their riders.

He could also see the dark and horrible form of the Bringer of Storms walking through the maelstrom, his arm raised, holding that mighty hammer. He could see the whole scene unfold as the giant stood opposite Valzaan, dwarfing the prophet. Valzaan's mouth moved, calling down Allfather's pronouncement of doom upon the arrogant creature, and then the sound of deep laughter and the flash of incredibly bright light flew out from the Vulsutyrim's hands and struck Valzaan, casting him backward into the sea. Aljeron had stared for a moment, stunned as he watched the body of the white-haired old man soar above the waves. Then Valzaan struck the water and disappeared beneath the whitecaps, and the spell was broken. Aljeron wheeled his horse around and charged after his men, who were flying ahead of him down the beach. Fear and rage drove him, and somehow they reached Col Marena ahead of their enemy. They managed to drive through the town to the docks, calling out for the people to flee at once. As they loaded every ship in the harbor with both man and beast, he expected to see their enemy charge into the city, but the Bringer of Storms never arrived. They loaded until darkness fell, then the ships in the harbor, seventy-three in all, sailed out from Col Marena to wait in the dark waters far from shore.

Aljeron's only explanation for the delay of their enemy was that Valzaan's final effort to throw the enemy into confusion with the shifting and sinking sand must have persisted even after his death. Perhaps they could not recover from their disarray. Whatever had happened, whatever had held them up, he thanked Allfather with all his might. Without Valzaan, they could not have held the enemy at bay while the ships were loaded. They would have been cut down on the quays, and all would have been for naught.

"Aljeron?" He flinched in surprise. Evrim, lean and weary, rose from his seat and stepped closer to Aljeron. "Is everything all right?" he asked quietly.

"Well, no," Aljeron said just as quietly. "I wouldn't say that. But I'm all right, if that's what you're asking."

"I was," Evrim said, smiling. "Good. Everyone's ready, come take your seat."

Evrim motioned to an open chair at the head of the oval table, then took the seat at Aljeron's left hand. Before sitting, Aljeron stooped by Koshti, who was curled in the near corner of the room. Aljeron had been on a ship with Koshti before, on that ill-fated journey to the Forbidden Isle so many years ago, and Koshti's feelings about travel by sea had not changed much. He had not left this room since before the ship left port. "It's all right, Koshti," Aljeron murmured as he rubbed his battle brother's head and scratched his ears playfully. "We will return to land before long, don't worry."

The tiger looked up at Aljeron, not appearing to be much consoled, and Aljeron stood reluctantly to take his place at the table. Aljeron sat, looking down the table at the place beside Mindarin where Aelwyn had settled herself. She looked up at him, and he smiled again. He couldn't help it. She blushed, but she didn't look away.

Aljeron forced himself to survey the room. Gilion sat to his right, the captain's beard and clothes as fastidious as ever. No situation could ruffle him, or at least no situation could make him look ruffled. Next to Gilion was Caan, his long grey hair braided and resting on his shoulders. The sparkle that normally shone in Caan's eyes was gone, and Aljeron tried to gauge the warrior's intensity. He knew the man grieved, for Valzaan's loss was heavy news to Caan, but there was more. Aljeron sensed anger, deep anger, and Caan did not grow angry lightly.

Beside these elder statesmen sat Corlas Valon, the young officer from Fel Edorath, and beside him were the three Great Bear, who filled the rest of that side of the table. Even had there been enough chairs, the bears would not have needed them. As it was, their heads towered above the table and almost touched the ceiling's support beams. Sarneth sat closest to Valon, and next to Sarneth was his son, Erigan, and then the patrol bear from Lindan, Arintol.

Brenim sat at the opposite end, leaning back in his chair with a dejected look. Aljeron knew that on top of the despair they all felt was the disappointment that Rulalin lived. They had come so close to bringing him to justice for the murder of Brenim's brother, Joraiem, but now he was roaming free and, worse, aiding the enemy. The discovery was hard on everyone, but perhaps hardest of all on Brenim. Mindarin and Aelwyn sat next to him, huddled close together where two chairs had been forced into the group to accommodate them.

Next to the women was Saegan, who perhaps showed the least wear of the past several weeks. He looked to Aljeron little different than when the anticipation of their impending victory over Fel Edorath had buoyed their spirits. Beside Saegan was Bryar, her hair cut short and her clothes rough, a stark contrast to the sisters. Pedraal and Pedraan occupied the middle of that side of the table, and beside them was Benjiah. The young man sat upright and still, the staff Valzaan had entrusted to him leaning against the table, the carved windhover atop it hooked on the edge to keep it from slipping. Next to Benjiah was Evrim, completing their number.

Ten men, three women, and three Great Bear, Aljeron thought as he studied them. The fate of the Werthanim, and perhaps the fate of Kirthanin, was entrusted to them. How had it come to this? What had brought each of them to this moment, where so much would depend upon their decisions, so much would depend upon their actions? They would have to choose well and act decisively, and even then their choices and actions might avail little. The strength against which they were matched was too great. If Valzaan could not stand against it, who could?

"Thanks for coming," Aljeron started. He knew that the meeting would not begin until he spoke, and yet he didn't know where to lead them. He had made Valzaan a binding promise on the beach, and he had not yet spoken of that promise to anyone. He decided to discern the spirits and thoughts of his men first. "What report from you, and what report from the men who serve under you?"

His question was not followed by silence as he had expected, for Gilion jumped on the question. "We have escaped the net of our enemy and are safely put out to sea. Whatever clouds still hang over us, even these unnatural rains that have followed us from the Mountain, we have gone farther than most believed we would. See where Allfather has brought us; He will take us on from here, though it might now seem impossible."

"It is true," Evrim said. "We have achieved no small feat in outrunning our enemy. I don't know what kept them from falling upon us in Col Marena, but I can think of nothing other than divine deliverance to account for this providential escape."

"You speak of providence and divine deliverance," Brenim said, scowling. "Tell me how we have but delayed our doom? Will we think ourselves fortunate that we did not fall in Col Marena or Shalin Bel or Zul Arnoth when our enemy throws his full might upon us in Cimaris Rul? And now Valzaan has fallen. Who will hurl sand and stone against our enemy next time? There is no hope for us. Wherever we go, Malek will find us, and we will be destroyed."

"No!" Benjiah said, leaning over the table, his right hand gripping Valzaan's staff so tightly that Aljeron could see his knuckles turn white. "There is always hope, always. As long as Allfather rules the heavens and the earth, there is a power greater than Malek. If Valzaan taught us anything, that is it. Did we not despair at Zul Arnoth when the Bringer of Storms came against us? And yet Valzaan threw him back. And again we despaired upon the beach, and again Valzaan delivered us. And though Valzaan has fallen, Allfather has not. It was not his own power that Valzaan wielded, but Allfather's, and that power remains with us. I cannot say where we should go, for I cannot see it, but I know that we are not hopeless. I will carry Valzaan's staff, but we must all carry his hope."

"Carry what you like, Nephew," Brenim replied, "but Valzaan is at the bottom of the sea. All the hope in the world couldn't save him."

"You dare not—"

Caan rose from his seat and motioned to Benjiah to sit back.

"Enough, both of you. We will not argue, not tonight. Though a soldier never has a guarantee that he will survive his mission, a good soldier always undertakes the task set before him. We will do what must be done, or we will die doing it. That is all. I don't want to hear another word about whether it can be done. That is irrelevant."

"So," Aljeron said as Caan sat back down, knowing that the real questions of the evening could not be delayed. "What do we do?"

Several looked up at this question, and Saegan, who didn't usually say much at these meetings unless he was called upon, leaned forward and looked down the table at Aljeron. Their eyes met, and Saegan held his gaze for a long, probing moment before speaking. "I'm not sure I understand the question, Aljeron. Our objective is clear: We must head south to Cimaris Rul and rally support among the Suthanim for a stronger defense of Kirthanin, right? What's changed?"

The eyes and attention of all those gathered turned in unison from Saegan to Aljeron. The moment could be avoided no longer. "Valzaan spoke to me before he opposed the Bringer of Storms. He said, in effect, that Sulmandir might be alive."

Whispers and exclamations spread around the table. Everyone turned to see if the shock of the statement had registered on their neighbors' faces, and each of them found that it had. As quickly as the chatter flared, it died, and they turned once more to Aljeron for answers.

"What is this?" the normally calm and dignified Gilion said for them all. "Could it be?"

"I know only what Valzaan told me. He said that when Sulmandir flew from Agia Muldonai and was never seen again, he did not die, at least not right away. Valzaan went north some nine hundred years ago, and at least at that point, Sulmandir was alive. Why Valzaan never spoke of this, I don't know. I had no time to ask questions. Perhaps Sulmandir wished him not to, or perhaps Allfather bid him keep it silent. Even so, Valzaan could not guarantee that Sulmandir was still alive. He said he had not seen Sulmandir since."

"Not seen in nine hundred years!" Brenim said. "Then there is indeed little hope that he is alive. Why speak of it now?"

Aljeron looked down. "Valzaan said that finding Sulmandir might be our only hope against our enemy. He made me promise to go and look for him."

"What?" Pedraan said, his face betraying his shock. Aljeron looked at him, but only for a moment, as he wanted to see the reaction in Aelwyn's more restrained expression. She met his eyes, but only for a moment, quickly looking down into her lap. It was evident, even in that brief moment, that she might not be far from tears. "Why did you promise to go north?" Pedraan said again. "We need you. Your place is here with us."

"I promised because a prophet of Allfather bid me promise!" Aljeron replied hotly. "What's more, it now constitutes Valzaan's dying wish, and I will not betray my word to him."

"How can you question Aljeron, Pedraan?" Mindarin asked. "You knew Valzaan. He would not lead us astray."

After a pause, Corlas Valon leaned forward, gazing up and down the table at the others. "Far be if from me to contradict a prophet of Allfather, but surely this is a fool's hope. Nine hundred years since Sulmandir was last seen alive, and even with all his knowledge, Valzaan could not give you more surety than that. What's more, what if the Father of Dragons is alive? What hope do you have that you will survive the long trek through the wilderness that is Nolthanin? And where exactly are you to look for him? Are you to comb all the land above the Holy Mountain and below the Great Northern Sea?"

"Valzaan said his lair was in Harak Andunin."

"Harak Andunin!" Gilion said, wonder in his voice.

"What is Harak Andunin?" Benjiah asked when no one else said anything.

"It is said," Caan began, looking at Benjiah, "that when the Nolthanim fled their home, the men in the army named the tallest mountain in the Tajira Mountain Range 'Harak Andunin,' or, 'the Spear of Andunin.' The name was a testament not to Andunin's might, but to his shame. They loved him dearly, as they proved by following him even when they knew Malek's plan would not succeed, but they felt the burden of his betrayal of Allfather and the sorrow of their impending exile."

"Where is the mountain?" Aelwyn asked quietly, and Aljeron saw she had composed herself, looking as calm as any of them.

"I'm not sure," Aljeron said, "but if the old maps of Nolthanin are right, it is a long journey north and east from here. The Tajira Mountains run south from a place where the range almost touches the Great Northern Sea. Once we find it, we'll look for the biggest of them all."

They sat quietly until Corlas spoke up again. "I don't know who else I speak for here, but your answer is neither comforting nor encouraging. Harak Andunin may indeed be the biggest mountain in Nolthanin, but it may not be any easier to find than the tallest tree in a great forest. I say it again, this is a fool's hope."

"A fool's hope it may be, but I will keep my promise. The rest of you will go south, as planned. I will go north, alone."

"No," Evrim said. "You will not!"

"If Sulmandir is dead or the wilderness is impassable, I will not need your help to discover these things. What's more, if Sulmandir is alive, then I will find him just as quickly alone as I could with a whole company at my command."

"I don't care," Evrim replied. "Some dangers can be overcome only with the help and strength of many men. Don't be foolish. At least a handful of men should go with you. So few will not greatly diminish the strength of the army, but so many will greatly multiply your readiness to meet the unknown trials of that road."

"I will go with you," Benjiah said, looking intently into Aljeron's eyes. "Perhaps Allfather will reveal through me the location of the mountain or the road to take there."

Aljeron shook his head, "You will not come, Benjiah. With Valzaan gone, your responsibility is to the people of Kirthanin, not to me alone. In all likelihood, Malek is already planning his move south. He surely knows that is where our army is headed, and he will move with his full strength to sweep over the land. Peril lies in every direction, but as Allfather's prophet, you must go with the leaders of the army to aid and advise them as Allfather enables you. I am sorry. You cannot come."

"I agree," Evrim said, looking at Benjiah before turning back to Aljeron. "My responsibility, however, is to you personally."

"As is mine," Gilion echoed.

Aljeron raised his hand to quiet all those who looked ready to speak and perhaps to volunteer as well. "You cannot both come, for I must entrust the guidance of the soldiers to someone. I am afraid it must be you, Gilion, for you are the officer they know best and have known longest. Evrim, if you are insistent, you may come, but I am resolved that most of the rest of you will go south. Caan, having lived in Sulare for so long, your aid in this southern campaign could be invaluable, and your leadership is essential. Brenim, you are a Suthanim, so you, too, must go south and help where you can. Pedraal and Pedraan, your commitment to Wylla Someris to see Benjiah safely home also takes you south. Sarneth, your draal lies that way, and it may be that your influence with the Great Bear will be needed before long. You also, Corlas, as the commanding officer of the men of Fel Edorath, you must head south. Mindarin and Aelwyn, the women you have led here will look to you for leadership, as Saegan and Bryar will continue to be needed by the scouts."

"Command of the scouts can be left ably in Bryar's hands," Saegan said. "Leave the scouts in Bryar's care while I go with you."

After a moment, Aljeron nodded, feeling relief. Though he had come determined to go only with Koshti, he was bolstered to think that Saegan and Evrim would accompany him. "So be it. You will come too."

"As will Erigan and Arintol," Sarneth said. "I will go south, and I will rouse the support of the Great Bear as Allfather grants me opportunity, but Arintol and Erigan will go with you. Their wisdom and strength may be of use to you in that desolate land, and they are not easily lost, even in a great wilderness."

Aljeron looked from Sarneth to the other two, but he found their faces as serene and inscrutable as ever. In the end he simply nodded. "I will gladly accept your offer of aid, Arintol and Erigan. I am honored."

Gilion addressed Aljeron, his voice betraying a hint of dissatisfied resignation. "If this is your will, what directions do you have for me and for us?"

"Only that you, Gilion, and you, Corlas, submit yourselves and your men to Caan, for it is Caan who must lead you all now. We are no longer men of any one city. We are Kirthanim, and men of Shalin Bel and Fel Edorath must unite. None of us knows what you will find when you reach Cimaris Rul, but I trust you to make the best of it. Go there as quickly as you can and summon what strength they have. Secure the city if you think it defensible. If not, you will need to decide whether to retreat by land north to Amaan Sul or to sail around the coast up to Kel Imlaris. I cannot give you any further guidance; all I can do is promise that I will seek Allfather's blessing upon you every day that I am gone."

"And you?" Caan said when Aljeron finished. "What will you do and where will you go from here?"

"I will stay behind with the others on the smallest of the ships. If the flames die down and there is no sign of the enemy ashore, tomorrow night I will try to see if any of our missing men have survived and are in Col Marena."

"Why?" Aelwyn said. "Your promise to Valzaan does not mandate this."

"No, it doesn't," Aljeron said, "but my responsibility to my men does. I will not take any needless risks, and if I see evidence that the city is still held against me, I will be on my way. Either way, my course will take me across the Bay of Thalasee to Avram Gol."

"Avram Gol." Evrim whispered the name.

"Yes," Aljeron said. "We will each of us go where we must go, and for me, my journey will begin there."

2 SURVIVORS

THE OTHERS HAD GONE, most to prepare to sail south with the morning light. Koshti still lay snugly curled in the corner of the stateroom, and though his eyes were closed, Aljeron could tell by watching his breathing that he was not asleep. Were they headed south, Aljeron would have had little hope to offer Koshti, but they would soon leave the rolling waves behind and take to the land again, for better or for worse.

Aljeron noticed movement at the door and looked up to see Aelwyn leaning against the doorframe, watching him. "I thought you were going with Mindarin to meet with the women," he said.

"She said I should stay and say goodbye."

"That was nice of her."

"Yes," Aelwyn said, smiling just a bit. "From time to time my sister can be very kind. Many are surprised by that."

"I'm not surprised," Aljeron said, motioning for Aelwyn to come over and sit down. As she took the seat that Evrim had vacated, he continued. "You know, when Mindarin and I were in Sulare, she had a reputation at first for being pretty harsh. There was an edge to her looks and her laughter, not to mention her words. But when she and the other women were taken captive, she showed her softer side as she helped the younger ones pull through that experience. At least, that's what the other women said after they were set free. I'd say your sister is probably a pretty good person to have around in a crisis."

"Yes, she is," Aelwyn nodded. "You don't have to tell me. I've seen her at work." Aelwyn set her folded hands on the table and shivered as she leaned forward. "This really is a crisis, isn't it?"

"Yes." Aljeron stretched out his hand to cover Aelwyn's and hold them both. "Perhaps *the* crisis."

"I wonder if we'll come through it," Aelwyn said, looking down.

"I don't know. The odds seem to be against it."

"I know you have to go to Avram Gol, and I know you have to go across Nolthanin to find Harak Andunin, but why go ashore tonight? Why not start across the Bay at first light when we head south?"

"I was on the last ship out of Col Marena," Aljeron said, a distant look in his eyes. "As I peered back across the water, it seemed to me I could see someone on the quay, though I can't be sure. What if it was one or more of my men?"

"Send someone else to look. You don't have to go yourself."

"I know, but you must all leave as soon as possible to go south. Malek will pursue you wherever you go. He will chase you the length and breadth of the land. If I am delayed a day, so be it, it will not greatly affect what I have to do. The fleet headed south must not be delayed, not even for a day."

"It is a needless risk."

"I won't go ashore if there is any sign of trouble."

"So you say."

"I will check the waterfront quickly, just to reassure myself no one was waiting, hiding, hoping, and then I'll go."

"And if someone is there?" Aelwyn asked. "The ships will have headed south by then. What will you do? Will you take them with you to the wilderness? What if they're injured? How will they keep up? Won't they be better off fending for themselves in the Werthanin countryside?"

"Maybe." He had considered these possibilities at some level, dismissing most of them without careful consideration. He kept telling himself that he could do only one thing at a time, that he would first see if anyone lived, and then he would decide what to do. He hoped against the odds that he would find many men, and that they would be strong enough to cross the Bay of Thalasee with him and then, after depositing him at Avram Gol, take the ship south after the others. He knew this was unlikely, and that it was possible he would find himself with a difficult decision to make regarding whomever he found. "I don't know what I'll find, Aelwyn. I only know that I need to go."

Aelwyn nodded but didn't speak. Pulling her left hand out from under Aljeron's, she clasped his big, calloused fingers in her tiny, smooth ones. They sat together in silence for a few moments, with no sound except the creaking of the boards above and below. Aljeron stood after a moment and scooted his chair around the side of the table until it was right beside Aelwyn's. Sliding as close to her as he could, he put his arm around her shoulder and leaned her back to rest against him. As she did so, she laid her head flat against his chest and took his other arm tightly in her hands.

They sat this way until the sound of footsteps in the hall reached their ears. Aljeron wondered if Aelwyn would sit up before whoever it was came to the door. She didn't, and he didn't push her away. He looked up to see Evrim step into the room. If his friend was surprised by what he saw, he didn't give it away.

"The longboats are ready to take us to the *Sea Horse.* We can go whenever you and Koshti are ready."

"All right," Aljeron said. Evrim left. Glancing over, Aljeron saw Koshti's eyes open. The tiger lifted his head slightly and looked in the direction of the door. Aljeron stroked Aelwyn's hair. "I don't really want to go," he whispered in her ear.

"Me neither."

"I have to, though."

"I know." Aelwyn looked up into Aljeron's face. She lifted her own hand and traced the ridge of the scar that ran down his cheek. "I want to store the memory of your face in my fingertips, in case the darkness and the rain wash all my other good memories away."

Aljeron leaned down and kissed her. He wanted to linger there, his lips upon hers, but he didn't. If he lived to hold her again, he would perhaps be bolder. "I want to promise you that we'll meet again, but I can't. Like you, I fear the rain and the dark that seem more and more like they'll never go away. All I can say is that no storm yet has lasted forever. This one may not either."

"It won't last forever," Aelwyn said with conviction. "I know it won't. Still, I know we may not both survive to see one another again."

"We may not, but like you said on deck, let's part in hope. Hope is pretty much all we have left."

"We will part in hope," Aelwyn said, smiling again as she looked up at him, "but it isn't all we have left."

"No?"

"No," she said, shaking her head. "We have love too. I love you, Aljeron Balinor, and dare I say it, despite your uncertainty, I begin to suspect that you are beginning to love me."

"You may be right," he said, smiling as they rose.

"I will bid you farewell here," Aelwyn said, "for it is time, and I hate long goodbyes."

Standing on her toes, she stretched up to kiss him on the cheek. "Goodbye, Aljeron, and may Allfather grant you protection on your journey and success on your mission."

"Goodbye, Aelwyn," Aljeron replied as she walked to the door. "Allfather's blessing be upon you."

She was gone. Aljeron stepped over to Koshti and stooped to rub the tiger's fur. Koshti stood as Aljeron patted him twice on his hindquarters. They stepped toward the door. "Love her? I just might," Aljeron said half to himself and half to the tiger beside him. "I miss her already."

Aljeron, with Koshti at his feet and Evrim beside him, stood in the stern of the *Sea Horse* as the last of the small fleet disappeared from view. It was Third Hour already, and the day, though gloomy and uninspiring under a thick canopy of grey clouds, was probably as bright as it was going to get.

Turning, they joined Saegan and the two Great Bear, Erigan and Arintol, in the middle of the deck. The Great Bear sat comfortably while Saegan leaned against the mast, gazing north over the Bay of Thalasee in the direction of Avram Gol.

Aljeron came up beside Saegan. "All these years living so close to the bay, but I've never wanted to cross it and go there. Still, we've sailed together to the Forbidden Isle and walked the streets of Nal Gildoroth. We can pass through Avram Gol and traverse the wastes of Nolthanin and hope to return, can't we?"

"Of course," Saegan answered. "Avram Gol has been abandoned for two thousand years."

"Nal Gildoroth was supposed to have been abandoned for almost a thousand."

"True." Saegan shrugged. "Still, I don't fear this ruin any more than I feared Zul Arnoth when I first rode there. The land beyond Avram Gol, though, is another matter. It is not the legends that I fear, but the long trek north through difficult land in winter. It will be cold there, Aljeron, very cold."

"I know."

"If this rain is as steady there as here, and if it changes into something other than rain, this may be a hopeless quest."

"We shall have to wait and see."

"Yes," Saegan said, turning and putting his hand gently on Aljeron's shoulder. "We shall see."

"I'm glad you're coming along, Saegan. I don't know why my mind goes back to Sulare and our adventures there so much these days, but it does. I'm glad there are two of us here."

"Yes," Saegan said, smiling. "Despite what was lost, those were good days, weren't they?"

"The best."

The rest of the day passed uneventfully as they settled into life on the *Sea Horse.* The area below deck was divided into three rooms. One occupied half of the space and had been employed as a stable for several horses when the Werthanim fled Col Marena. The horses were still on board, for with no real way to transfer them from the *Sea Horse* to one of the other ships, Aljeron was stuck with the three he needed and a half a dozen extra. The other two rooms were cabins, and the two Great Bear settled into one and the three men and Koshti into the other. The small captain's cabin above deck was left empty. For Aljeron, it symbolized his hope that he would find many men ashore who would need this extra space. The room could hold half a dozen men, more than enough to serve as a crew on the *Sea Horse* after Aljeron and the others were delivered to Avram Gol.

As darkness fell over the Bay of Thalasee and Col Marena, Aljeron and Evrim boarded the longboat. Though neither had a lot of nautical experience, Aljeron and Saegan, by virtue of their training under Ulmindos in Sulare, were the two most experienced sailors on the *Sea Horse,* and it didn't seem wise for both to leave the ship at the same time. So it was that Evrim accompanied Aljeron ashore.

Quietly they paddled across the cold water toward the docks. The fires had burned down or out, and Aljeron had nothing but the image of the port, fixed solidly in his mind, to guide them. The rain fell cold and light, but the clouds were thick and dark, and the thin sliver of Winter Rise's new moon was virtually invisible. Onward they paddled, somewhat consoled that the darkness would cloak their approach, should unfriendly eyes be watching. Aljeron, though, was increasingly doubtful that danger lay ahead, for he reasoned that while men afraid for their lives might hide in the ruins, it seemed more likely that the enemy, if he still held the city, would have his fires blazing to make his presence known.

One of the pylons supporting the docks suddenly appeared, and Aljeron leaned forward to catch the column and steer the boat aside before they struck it. He let the motion of the boat carry them forward until they sat half under the wharf. For several moments he and Evrim listened to the quiet creaking of the wooden docks. Aljeron looked at Evrim. His friend had uncanny hearing, part of his giftedness at hunting and tracking, but Evrim showed no sign that he could hear anything Aljeron couldn't. Eventually, Evrim shrugged, and Aljeron backed them out from under the dock with his oars and directed them to a place where they could tie up next to a ladder.

Aljeron stepped lightly onto the dock, and he and Evrim moved silently to the firm ground of the quay beyond. There they squatted below the burned remains of a wagon that was tilted forward so that the charred back end pointed almost straight up into the dark sky. They positioned themselves there and waited. Aljeron sat on the smooth stones and periodically surveyed as much of the quay as he could, which wasn't a whole lot.

"Well," Aljeron whispered after several minutes. "Do we risk a torch?"

"No," Evrim said. "Let's head out without one. I'd like to see more of the city before I take that step."

"All right." Aljeron moved around the cart and started toward some of the burnt buildings at the edge of town. The closest building had probably been a warehouse; its facade was enormous and the doorway unusually wide. The doors, though, were gone, and through the opening they could see the sky above the roofless space. They paused in the doorway, peering into the shadows.

"I guess if someone's hiding in a place like this, they'll need to come out when they see us," Aljeron said.

"Yes," Evrim whispered, "I guess so. We certainly won't find them in the dark, not if they've hidden well."

They moved from building to building along the waterfront, poking their heads into as many open doors as they found, and forcing their way into obstructed entries. As time passed, they became less cautious about making noise and spoke more freely as they moved in and out of the buildings of Col Marena.

It was approaching Second Watch when they entered a small building that might have been an inn before the fire. A slender post dangling a length of chain hung above the door, which was broken off at its hinges and leaning against the front of the building. They stepped inside, and immediately the smell of burned flesh assaulted their noses. Aljeron reeled from the horrific odor. Evrim coughed and raised part of his soggy cloak to cover his nose.

At that moment a creak in the floorboards above them echoed in their ears, and without saying a word, both drew their swords. Aljeron forced himself to step into the dark entry hall, Daaltaran held up before him. They moved forward slowly, shuffling as quietly along the sooty floor as they could. Again, the sound of creaking came from above, this time from farther back in the house. They stopped to listen, and the sound of feet on stairs sounded lightly just ahead.

Aljeron stepped out of the hall into a larger room, perhaps a common room of sorts, and Evrim joined him. There they waited, shoulder to shoulder, facing a pair of doors in the direction of the noise. More creaking sounded, and Aljeron felt his pulse quicken. He hadn't thought the footsteps heavy enough to be a Malekim's, but what if he'd been wrong? What was moving through the dark?

As though in silent answer to his question, a soft voice called out, "Hello?"

Aljeron and Evrim exchanged a quick glance. There wasn't any guarantee the voice belonged to an ally, but they'd come to find survivors. "Who's there?" Aljeron called.

"I'm Karras, a soldier of Shalin Bel, is this your inn?"

"No, Karras," Aljeron said, smiling in the dark at Evrim, "I am Aljeron Balinor, commander of the army of Shalin Bel."

"Master Balinor!" Karras replied, stepping into the room. "Can it really be you? The ships set sail today. I saw them from the upper window."

"All the ships set sail but one. I have come ashore to see if any like you have survived the enemy's work here. Are you alone?"

"No, a fellow soldier, Tornan, is here with me." Karras crossed the room. "He was injured in the battle on the beach two days ago, and though we rode here together, our horse came up lame and we fell behind. We arrived shortly after the last ship had departed for the safety of the bay." Aljeron could see he was only a youth, perhaps nineteen or twenty years old. Excitement etched his face.

"We will hear your whole story soon enough, but take us to your injured friend now," Aljeron said. Karras led them back through the hall to the back stair and up to the second floor. The rooms just at the top of the stair were roofless, as the rafters had given way and the roof had collapsed. Ducking under a beam that stood diagonally in the small hallway, they made their way to the intact front rooms.

The smell of burned flesh was especially pungent here. Aljeron coughed and almost gagged. “What is up here, Karras?”

Karras paused at the end of the hall. One of the doors was cracked open, and he pointed to it. “There are several bodies in that room. They’re huddled together and look like maybe a family trapped by the fire. We hid here because we thought the smell might throw any Black Wolves or other creatures tracking us off our scent. I think Malek’s forces left last night, but we haven’t dared go out and check yet.”

“No, I suppose not,” Aljeron said as Karras pushed the door opposite the death room open.

“Tornan,” Karras said as he led them to a mattress on the floor, “Master Balinor and Evrim Minluan are here!”

The figure lying on the mattress slowly raised his head, and Aljeron stooped beside the mattress and looked into the wide eyes of the astonished face. “It is true, Tornan, we are come to rescue you. We will take you from this place.”

Aljeron could see the man’s shocked face begin to quiver, and tears flowed almost immediately. Aljeron knelt and took the man’s head in his arms and cradled it gently. Tornan sobbed, trying to say something Aljeron couldn’t understand, so he whispered, “Shh, don’t talk now. Later, we’ll talk about it later.” The man stopped trying to speak, but the tears continued. Aljeron leaned sideways off his knees so that he could sit on the floor, and he held Tornan until the crying finally ceased.

Below, Aljeron lowered Tornan to the ground after carrying him down the narrow stairs and out in front of the building. The soldier had a wicked looking gash in his leg made by the paw of a Black Wolf. The cut looked like it might be infected, and the skin around it was swollen and discolored.

"We'll take you to our longboat, but it is a fair walk from here, and we'll have to carry Tornan. I'll take him as far as I can, but I may need a rest along the way," Aljeron said.

"Are we headed back to the *Sea Horse*?" Evrim asked.

Aljeron turned to Karras. "Have you seen any other survivors?"

Karras shook his head. "No, sir, I haven't. There may be others, but I doubt it. We spent quite a bit of time searching up and down the quay for even the smallest of rowboats to try and make it out to one of the ships, but there weren't any."

"We swept the waterfront clear of anything that would float, or just about," Aljeron said.

"That you did, and by the time we realized that we'd made the wrong decision—to stay in the city and look for a boat I mean—we heard the thunder of horses clamoring down the stone streets behind us."

"What did you do? How could you have eluded the enemy?"

"We were out on one of the docks, and we had nowhere to go but into the water. We jumped in and moved as far back under them as we could. We spent all of that night and the next day in the water. It was brutally cold, and there were a few times when I thought our chattering teeth would give us away, but I guess there was enough noise above us that no one thought to look down through the slats of the dock.

"By last night, though, we had to get out of the water. We both knew we wouldn't survive another night. Our fingers were ripped and bleeding from holding onto the pylon, and we were numb from the cold. I honestly thought that being caught and tortured would be better than staying in the water. So we waited until we couldn't hear any movement above us, and we crawled onto the dock.

"We couldn't see anyone, so we made our way to the edge of the waterfront buildings. The first one we came to was open but empty and without a roof. We made our way down, building by building, until we found this one, and this is where we've been."

"And you saw no one and nothing as you moved from building to building?" Evrim asked.

"No, nothing," Karras answered.

"Curious," Aljeron said. "They must have already pulled back."

"It makes sense," Evrim added. "There was nothing more they could do here. They had come after us, but we were safely out to sea. Why stay and keep watch? What did we have to gain by coming back? Why should they have waited? Their interest in this place disappeared with the ships this morning."

"Yes, but it sounds like they were gone before the ships set sail," Aljeron said.

"Anticipating our next move," Evrim said. "It's what I would do."

"Me too," Aljeron said. "Well, Evrim, let's light a torch. If I'm going to carry Tornan, I don't want to trip over any debris along the way. Let's get back to the boat as quick as we can and be on our way."

Evrim drew a torch out of his pack, and in a moment it was flickering in the cold night air. "Let's go," Aljeron said, hoisting Tornan onto his shoulder.

They were almost back to the pier where they'd tied up their longboat when a shadow appeared in a doorway right in front of them. In a flash, Evrim drew his sword and Aljeron stepped behind Evrim, moving toward the nearest wall, where he lowered Tornan to the ground.

"Who goes there?" Evrim called out, raising the torch in his left hand and extending the sword in his right.

"Just a sailor, left behind," came the soft reply. The figure stepped into the light. It illuminated his face, and he held his hands at chest level so Evrim could see he was unarmed. As he moved forward, he shuffled with a marked limp.

Aljeron, seeing his face in the light, stood. "I, I know you," he said, hesitating. "It's been seventeen years, but I'd know your face anywhere. Synoki?"

The man peered at Aljeron, and after a moment, a broad smile broke on his face. "Aljeron Balinor, what are you doing here?"

"I should ask you the same question," Aljeron said. "How did you come to be lurking in a building that we not long ago found empty? If you were in the city when the army of Malek came through, how did you survive? Explain?"

"I wasn't in the city when either army came. I was visiting a friend who lives south of here, along the coastline. So when the army of Shalin Bel, which I assume is what brought you here to Col Marena, passed through the city and took the ships, word of events came south with some of the refugees. I, like many of my friends, watched the city burn from a distance. I came back tonight because the fires were gone and the city was dark, and I wanted to see how my warehouse had fared."

"Your warehouse?"

"Indeed, for in the years since we parted, I have prospered enough to become part owner of a small merchant vessel based here in Col Marena. I am a minor partner, to be sure, but it is better than being a hired hand. Unfortunately, my ascendancy to the ranks of the owners and financers of vessels and voyages has been short-lived, for my ship is gone and my property destroyed."

Aljeron stared at the impassive face. His mind soared back over time and space to the distant, hot afternoon when he had first seen Synoki trudging through the sand along the beach of the Forbidden Isle. As he listened to Synoki, whose face and voice were unaffected by the gravity of his losses, Aljeron thought of that first tale Synoki had told them of his shipwreck and suffering. How odd, Aljeron thought, to stumble across him again in a forsaken place just after fortune had robbed him once more of everything. "I'm sorry to hear about your loss, Synoki. I hope Allfather will grant you better fortune soon. I hope He grants us all better fortune."

"It seems unlikely."

"Yes, I guess it does," Aljeron replied awkwardly.

Synoki looked from Aljeron to the wounded Tornan to Evrim and Karras. "I have told you my story, though in brief, will you now not tell me yours?"

Aljeron soon found himself narrating the retreat to Col Marena and the desperate flight to sea. He did not speak in detail, and he did not give specifics of his own role in any of the events. He found himself, perhaps struck by the curiosity of the coincidental meeting, reluctant to say more than he needed to, though he could see no real harm in letting Synoki know any of those things. The man had been a companion on the perilous journey into Nal Gildoroth and risked his life in the pursuit of the Vulsutyrim who had abducted the women on the Forbidden Isle. Aljeron dismissed his reluctance as he finished his brief account.

"It appears you've found the survivors you sought."

"Yes, we were fortunate to find these two alive and well, for the most part."

"Yes, I would say you were fortunate," Synoki added, looking at Karras and Tornan again. "I should doubt that many remained behind, and that few of those escaped the fires alive."

"Indeed, which is why we were just headed back to our longboat to head back out to our ship and be on our way."

"I thought all the ships left this morning," Synoki said, looking intently at Aljeron.

"The rest of them did. We stayed behind on the last one."

"Which ship is it?"

"The *Sea Horse.*"

"Oh." Synoki sounded disappointed.

"Not yours?"

"No. I don't know that one." Synoki paused but then pressed forward. "Why stay behind, Aljeron? Surely you didn't stay just to look for survivors?"

"No," Aljeron answered, and he noticed Evrim turn from Synoki, whom he had been watching closely. He looked at Evrim's face and thought he read there a warning to be careful.

"Then why?" Synoki pressed unabashedly.

"It is nothing, really," Aljeron tried to dismiss the subject. "Someone was needed to take care of an errand, that is all."

"Surely not," Synoki replied. "Even in Col Marena your name is known. You are the commander of the army of Shalin Bel, are you not?"

"I am."

"Then I don't believe you would be left behind on an errand of little importance. You don't have to tell me what it is, but perhaps I can be of help. It seems that once again I am at your disposal, if I could be of service."

"Well, we do have a short voyage to undergo, and an experienced seaman could be of help—"

"Excellent," Synoki exclaimed, a hint of excitement showing now in his face. "Then perhaps this time I may be able to repay the debt I owe you for my rescue."

"Synoki, it may be a very dangerous journey."

"Danger seems to find me even when I hide from it. There's nothing here for me but flight and possible death at the hands of the hosts of Malek. Why not spend my final days at sea and in the company of noble men such as yourselves?"

After a moment Aljeron said, "Well, before you decide to join us, you should know where we're headed. You all should." He looked from Synoki to Karras and then down at Tornan. "We're going north, across the Bay of Thalasee."

"Across the Bay?" Karras said quietly.

"Yes."

"Where are you going?" Synoki asked, his face again impassive.

"We are headed to Avram Gol."

Synoki nodded. "Where is your longboat?"

"Nearby."

"Go ahead of me. I will join you there before long."

"What are you doing, Synoki?" Aljeron said as Synoki started off through the darkness.

"Don't worry, Aljeron. There are some things not far from here that might be of use in the voyage and beyond. I will retrieve them. Surely an hour's wait will not slow you down overmuch?"

"No, but don't be any longer."

Synoki nodded and disappeared into the dark.

Aljeron held the torch up and peered across the dark quay. There was still no sign of Synoki, though well more than an hour had passed. Aljeron looked back over his shoulder at Karras, who was sitting on the dock with his back to Col Marena, gazing out over the water. Tornan lay beside him. The young soldier had listened intently when Aljeron explained the necessity of heading north into Nolthanin. Admirably, he did not object to what he might have seen as a fate worse than being left behind in Col Marena. Instead, he said only, "We are yours to command, Master Balinor, in this as in all things."

"The lad is trying hard to be brave," Evrim said, and Aljeron turned to see his friend looking not at Karras but him.

"I like him," Aljeron said. "I almost wish I could leave him here."

"You could, you know," Evrim replied. "The enemy is likely gone, and Col Marena, at least for a time, will be safer than most other places in Kirthanin. The war will roam far from here, perhaps never to return."

"Perhaps. But I cannot leave him here."

"Then what will you do? I know you hoped there would be enough survivors to take the *Sea Horse* south, but even if Karras were a genius on the sea, he alone with a wounded Tornan is not enough. Even if Synoki went with him, it would be hard, two men to work the ship. It is a risk to think you and I and Saegan can handle it. What do you intend?"

"I intend for Karras to come with us."

"And Tornan? You will take a wounded man with a badly infected leg with us into Avram Gol and beyond?"

"Yes."

"Why?"

"Because my duties have collided. My duty to my men, as sworn before Allfather to watch over and care for them, has led me ashore tonight and to these men. My duty to Valzaan, Allfather's prophet, who made me swear that I would seek Harak Andunin and Sulmandir, will take me north. These recent weeks have taught me that I am not in control of my own destiny, and that powers much larger than I are at war in this world. I can only be faithful to the tasks set before me. The rest is out of my hands."

Evrim did not reply, and they both returned to watching the darkness through the rain. After a moment, the sound of footsteps echoed through the night, and Evrim reached out and took Aljeron's arm. "There are two people coming across the stones."

Both men drew their swords, and Aljeron wondered what this could mean. Had two more of his soldiers survived? Had two townsmen? Had the torch drawn the attention of enemy soldiers left behind to keep watch over the deserted city?

"Who goes there?" Aljeron called.

"It's me," Synoki answered in the dark, and at that moment the limping Synoki appeared within the beams of Aljeron's torchlight, accompanied by a second man. He was tall and well built, though not as tall as Aljeron. He had the mustache and bearded chin with clean-shaven cheeks sometimes found among those who made their living at sea. A dark rag tied his hair back, but long braided locks fell past his shoulders.

"Who is this?" Aljeron asked, relaxing his grip on his sword a little bit.

"This is Cinjan, a friend."

"Why did you not tell me you were going for a friend?"

"Would it have mattered? I told you there were things nearby that could help, with them was Cinjan, one of my most loyal and trusted friends. He will be of more use to us on this expedition than any of our supplies."

"How is that, exactly?" Aljeron asked, looking at the man carefully.

"I'll tell you." Synoki smiled. "Cinjan is one of the few men living, perhaps the only one, who has traveled extensively in Nolthanin. He has been to Avram Gol and beyond, and where we go blindly, he has walked before."

Cheimontyr stood in the rain, water streaming down his face and running over his bare chest. Farimaal stood close by in the dark, his cloak hanging loosely about him and his stubbly grey beard matted to his face.

"You are sure about this?" Cheimontyr said. Even his whisper echoed like thunder.

"Word came to me just minutes ago."

Cheimontyr turned to the Vulsutyrim beside him. "Go, bring Varatyr to me at once. Tell him I have need of him. He will know what I mean."

The giant disappeared into the night, and Cheimontyr turned back to Farimaal. "Can you feel it, Farimaal? The power of my storm grows. Even now the boundaries of my reach stretch farther south. Long before we arrive, the waters of Suthanin will begin to rise. By the time we reach Cimaris Rul, all will be more than ready, and the Kumatin will be unleashed."

Farimaal nodded. "Yes, I feel the power growing. You have done well."

Cheimontyr looked at Farimaal, then turned his face up to the dark sky. He closed his eyes and laughed. "It won't be long now, Farimaal. We've both waited so long, but not much longer. No, not much longer at all."

A moment later, the Vulsutyrim who had been dispatched returned with a second, taller and broader. Varatyr walked straight up to Cheimontyr, and Farimaal watched as he bowed ever so slightly. All the Vulsutyrim were impressive, but this Varatyr was almost as fearful in countenance as Cheimontyr himself. They stood eye to eye, two immensely powerful creatures, their arms thickly muscled like their chests, and their legs as thick as trees.

"You are needed in the north," Cheimontyr said, but Varatyr said nothing. "A small party of men, Werthanim from the army we have just driven into the sea, are heading that way. They are headed across the bay, and from there they will head inland. To where exactly, we don't know. Track them down and kill them."

Varatyr nodded, adjusted the large pack on his back and the long cruel sword that hung from it, and moved out into the darkness, running swiftly north.

3

THE CITY OF THE SETTING SUN

SAEGAN, KOSHTI, AND BOTH the Great Bear were on the deck of the *Sea Horse* when the longboat came up alongside not long before dawn. The longboat was quickly drawn up even with the deck, and as Aljeron and Evrim prepared to help Tornan out, Synoki and Cinjan scrambled onto the deck. The sight of Koshti standing not more than a span away, alert and watching them, brought both to a standstill.

"Still have your tiger friend, I see," Synoki said. Cinjan only stared.

"Yes," Aljeron said. He and Evrim handed Tornan out to Saegan, who carried the wounded soldier to the captain's cabin and set him against the wall. "You remember Koshti."

"I do indeed," Synoki said, keeping his eyes on the tiger.

Aljeron placed himself between them and Koshti. Koshti was tense, perhaps reacting to the sudden appearance of four unknown men. He placed his hand on his battle brother's head and stroked the fur gently. "Koshti has been my constant friend and companion these many years, a quarter of a century now. He is the very picture of fidelity in a world where even dear and trusted friends can prove faithless and untrue."

Synoki looked from the tiger to Aljeron. "You are speaking of Rulalin."

"I am."

Synoki nodded. "I heard, of course, of the murder. All of Werthanin did. Probably all of Kirthanin. One of the Suthanim Novaana, married to the Enthanin heir, murdered in the Summerland by a Werthanim Novaana; when news reached Col Marena it was all anyone could talk about."

"I'm sure," Aljeron answered, still stroking Koshti's head. "It was all I could think about for years."

"I am sorry about Joraiem. He was a pleasant companion."

"He was a true friend." Synoki did not reply, and Aljeron patted Koshti's head and turned from the tiger. "You know, Synoki, since that showdown with the Malekim and Vulsutyrim just north of Lindan Wood I have often wondered what would have happened if you hadn't saved Rulalin's life. If that Malekim had killed him, what would my life look like now? To be sure, my life might well have been no different over these last few weeks, but before Malek's coming? If Joraiem had never been killed, what then?"

Synoki shrugged. "I am sorry for your loss, but I couldn't leave Rulalin to die. For all I knew, he had a great and promising future ahead of him."

"I know. I don't blame you for doing what any one of us would have done. None of us could have foreseen what Rulalin would do, even those of us who knew him well. You could not have been expected to see the trouble he would cause."

"Indeed," Synoki said. "After all, I was but a castaway you discovered on the Forbidden Isle, barely in my right mind and long isolated from human contact."

Saegan, finished making Tornan comfortable, now approached Aljeron, Synoki, and Cinjan. "I see that it is you, Synoki, but it is very strange. After all these years, I can't believe we have met again, and in circumstances like this."

"Yes, it is strange, is it not?" Synoki said, smiling in the misty morning light.

"Do you remember me?" Saegan asked.

"Of course I remember you, Saegan. You were one of my rescuers. I owe you my life."

"You owe me nothing. We were all rescued by Eliandir. You, though, helped us pursue and defeat our enemy. We owe you our gratitude."

"Please," Synoki said, raising his hands in a gesture of dismissal, "I did nothing. I had long since given up hope of ever leaving that island. All I did was ride north with you, which was on my way home anyway. Truth be told, I grew somewhat attached to you all. In getting to know you on the Forbidden Isle, I saw great value in remaining in your number. I was almost sorry to say goodbye."

"Well, welcome aboard the *Sea Horse,*" Saegan said. "I'm sure you've already told your story to Aljeron. I'll hear it later, I suppose. For now, just make yourself at home."

"Thank you," Synoki said, "I will."

"And who is this?" Saegan asked facing Cinjan.

"This is my friend Cinjan. Like me, Cinjan lost everything in the fires of Col Marena. He will be of great use to us, because he has traveled extensively in Nolthanin, including Avram Gol, and few indeed can say that truthfully."

"Oh?" Saegan asked, his eyes widening.

"Yes," Cinjan said, though he stole a nervous glance at Koshti. "I have always been fascinated with the stories and legends of the Nolthanim and of their land, and like Synoki I came from humble beginnings. I have journeyed to Avram Gol and beyond on more than one occasion, in search of both knowledge and profit."

"And what have you learned from your travels?" Aljeron asked.

"I have learned that the land is hard but not impassable. But that you must already know, or else you would not be going there."

"I am going there because I have to and for no other reason. When my job there is done, I will gladly leave and not look back."

Aljeron went to Karras, who was stooping beside Tornan. Tornan had not been away from Col Marena long, but already the distance between them and the burned-out buildings had made a world of difference. He held his head up as he sat against the wall, and he smiled as Aljeron approached. "Well, men, your little holiday excursion is over, I'm afraid. Duty calls you again to service."

"Never has the voice of duty sounded so sweet," Tornan said, a broad smile on his face. "You can take me to Avram Gol or anywhere you like, so long as we leave this place. Keep me far from there and keep me out of the water, and I will be happy."

"I will do my best."

Evrim caught Aljeron's eye, motioning away from the cabin. Aljeron excused himself and stepped to the starboard side with Evrim. There they could see both Karras and Tornan and the others, who had moved down the deck to where the Great Bear sat. Saegan was introducing Arintol and Erigan to Synoki and Cinjan, or in the case of Arintol and Synoki, reintroducing them. Cinjan appeared as wary of the Great Bear as he had been of Koshti, who had padded his way across the deck and seated himself at Aljeron's feet.

"We need to talk about this Synoki and Cinjan," Evrim said quietly.

"What about?"

"If this is really the man you found on the Forbidden Isle, don't you think it odd that he was also in Col Marena, with no one else but two dazed survivors?"

"Yes, it is a remarkable coincidence."

"Too remarkable."

"What do you mean?"

"I don't trust him."

Aljeron smiled. "We aren't either one the trusting type, not anymore at least."

"No, but that's not what I mean. I don't like him, or his friend."

Aljeron looked at them down the length of the ship. "I understand. I always assumed his eccentricities were a consequence of where we found him."

"Maybe they were, and maybe they weren't."

Aljeron turned back to Evrim. "If you are suggesting we be cautious around him, I agree. But you don't really mean to suggest that Synoki, after seventeen years, has conspired some evil plot against us, do you? He's just a lame sailor from Col Marena! Such a thing would be ludicrous."

"It's all ludicrous. It doesn't fit or make sense, and I don't like things that don't make sense."

"So what do you think we should do?"

"I think we should have Synoki and Cinjan help Karras take Tornan and the *Sea Horse* south after we reach Avram Gol. It makes sense at least, since taking a wounded man with us into Nolthanin is less than ideal."

"But if Synoki and Cinjan are to be taken at their word, we could use them both, especially Cinjan. They could be timely aid sent by Allfather. On the other hand, if you are right, and if they are somehow dangerous and up to no good, how could

I send them south on the *Sea Horse* with Karras and Tornan? They could easily dispatch of Karras, and Tornan would be helpless to defend himself. No, Evrim, even if I knew beyond question that they were up to something terrible, entrusting two of my men to them, one wounded and the other but a boy, would be out of the question."

"So instead you mean to take a wounded man with us into the Nolthanin wild, along with two strangers—because really, that's what they both are—one of whom happens to have appeared out of nowhere at two of the most desperate times of your life?"

"Tornan's leg will heal. As for Synoki and Cinjan, we will be careful. There are five soldiers here, even if Tornan is wounded, and we have two Great Bear and Koshti. The two of them don't pose much of a threat to us. You are being paranoid."

Evrim shrugged. "Maybe I am, but I don't like him."

"You don't have to."

"All right. As with things we've disagreed on in the past, I'll submit to your decision. You're in charge. I just wanted you to know I'm not happy about this."

"I appreciate that, and I am glad you are willing to disagree with me. That's one of the reasons I need you. Now let's get underway. The sun is rising, and it is time we were off."

Avram Gol appeared on the horizon shortly after dawn on the seventh day of Winter Rise. The passage across the Bay of Thalasee was uneventful, though the steady rain churned the sea into rough waves. Koshti had remained below deck, and every time Aljeron visited him, the tiger's great bright eyes seemed to plead with him to end the misery and take him ashore. "Soon," was Aljeron's constant refrain, and now at last that *soon* had arrived.

Word quickly spread through the *Sea Horse* that Avram Gol was within view, and before long, the men and the Great Bear lined the bow as they faced their goal. As they neared what had once been the city quay, several Merrion soared overhead, the bright blue stripes on their wings clearly visible.

"It looks as though Avram Gol is not completely given over to the dark beasts of nightmare and legend," Aljeron said almost cheerily. "The Merrion give me hope."

"Don't get carried away," Cinjan said a few steps away, and Aljeron turned to see the man staring straight ahead. "I have seen many living things in Avram Gol, not all of them pretty, nor omens of hope and good fortune."

Aljeron turned toward the stern. "Synoki, come help me guide the ship in."

The process of bringing the ship into port required some small amount of nautical skill, and Aljeron realized that without Synoki's help, it might have been a very different story. The waters around the docks were hazardous, for large parts of the stone quay had long since crumbled off the main and fallen into the harbor and did not necessarily protrude above the water. Synoki stationed the others in strategic places to keep lookout. With everyone's help, Aljeron managed to bring the ship all the way in to one of the few docks that looked relatively sturdy.

Even with Synoki's guidance, Aljeron did not gauge his speed well, and the bow of the ship struck the stone quay none too gently, throwing Karras across the deck. The dock was discolored from centuries of weathering, but it was in better shape than most. In many places, docks disappeared mere spans away from the stone quay, no doubt the victim of the unrelenting sea swell and surge. In other places, great wooden or stone pylons rose out of the water, no longer supporting anything, but remaining as an enduring monument to what had once been.

"Avram Gol," Saegan said as Aljeron came alongside him in the bow again. "Once the greatest city of Kirthanin, or so they say."

"Yes, the City of the Setting Sun," Aljeron replied.

"The City of the Setting Sun?" Tornan asked as he held firmly to the rail. His leg had improved enough over the past few days that he had taken to standing for as long as he could, though it was a struggle for him to last more than a quarter of an hour upright.

"Yes," Aljeron said. "My father told me that Avram Gol was called the City of the Setting Sun because there was a saying in the First Age that the sun rose over Kel Imlaris, peaked above the Holy Mountain, and set over Avram Gol."

"The City of the Setting Sun," Saegan muttered. "The sun set on this place two thousand years ago. It has lain in darkness ever since."

Aljeron turned to Arintol and Erigan, who stood on all fours nearby, also fascinated by this city of ancient legend. "We will need your help, Arintol and Erigan, with the ramp for the horses."

Arintol answered, "We are yours to command."

The work was trickier than Aljeron had expected. The ramp for loading and unloading live cargo doubled as part of the deck that ran lengthways along the starboard side. It could be unhooked from below and lowered on its massive hinges, but to do so without dropping the heavy ramp with a thud to the floor below required fine dexterity to work the multiple hooks and latches and also great strength. It was likely a job performed by the whole crew under normal circumstances, but Aljeron had only six healthy men and two Great Bear, so while Karras sat on Aljeron's shoulders to reach and work the hooks, the two Great Bear stood ready to hold and lower the ramp once it was unlatched.

Eventually the job was completed, and the ramp was successfully in place. The nine horses, no doubt relieved by the prospect of emerging from their dark stables, followed Evrim's and Saegan's leads gladly and ascended the ramp one at a time until all stood patiently above deck.

"Now comes the tricky part," Aljeron said, grimacing as the wind-blown rain fell on a slant. "Getting these horses onto that dock."

"Right," Evrim said, looking down to the dock. "I was wondering how we were going to do that."

"No dock crane, no unloading ramps. No one has unloaded live cargo here in two thousand years," Saegan said.

"I thought about using the winch that lowers the longboat—" Aljeron began.

"You must be joking," Evrim said. "The winch on the horses? How would you distribute their weight evenly? You'd end up hanging them before you got them down."

"Not necessarily. There could be a way, but you didn't let me finish. I had thought about that, but now I have another idea. Let's break the deck ramp off of the *Sea Horse* and use it where the quay loading ramp would go, right here on the side of the ship."

"Are you serious?" Saegan asked.

"Completely."

"But how? The ramp doesn't fit the space, and there is nothing on it to attach it to the side of the ship. It is too long for this job and would likely fall beyond the edge of the dock. Further, once broken off, it will never go back on the *Sea Horse.*"

"As for going back on the *Sea Horse,* that hardly matters. The *Sea Horse* will likely never leave this dock. And, yes, it might be too long and it will certainly be too steep, but we will find a way to attach the top part and shorten the bottom. I don't have any other ideas, do you?"

"No, I don't."

"Then this is our plan."

For the better part of an hour, they worked on the great iron hinges until they broke the top part of the ramp loose. Though heavy and awkward, they eventually detached the ramp and secured it in place. The horses were not easily coaxed into mounting the steep ramp, and it took both Evrim and Saegan, both well-schooled and adept at handling horses, to get them up onto and then down the short steep drop. Soon, all nine horses stood on the stone quay, and the seven men, two Great Bear, and Koshti joined them.

Two of the horses they loaded with as many supplies as the men thought might be handy on the journey, but truth be told they didn't have a whole lot. The horses themselves might prove the most valuable, Aljeron remarked to Evrim, for if the wild proved too unforgiving, they might eat several meals from the meat two extra horses could provide.

Aljeron scanned the port city's ruins. They were nothing like Col Marena's, where fire brought sudden, dramatic destruction; nor were they like Zul Arnoth's, whose destruction was wrought by human hands. Nor was Avram Gol like Nal Gildoroth, empty but intact. The buildings bore no signs of human violence, but in a number of places roofs and upper stories had toppled inward where support beams gave out after many hundred years of untiring work and thankless labor. Strong storm winds had caved in weak walls, and collapsing buildings had crushed their neighbors like tall trees falling in a wood.

"So," Aljeron said, looking from the ruins to Saegan, who sat mounted on his horse, "what do you think now of Avram Gol?"

"I think nothing of it I did not think before."

"So, you don't worry that we walk now in a city cursed by Allfather, as the superstitions hold?"

Saegan shrugged. "Perhaps the city was cursed by Allfather, but so long as the curse doesn't forbid the men of Kirthanin to set foot in the city, as He has forbidden us to set foot on Agia Muldonai until the Mountain should be cleansed, then I do not fear. For why would the curse of Allfather on this place frighten me when it is Allfather's purpose that brings me here?"

"And you, Evrim?" Aljeron said. "What do you think?"

"I think I'll be happy when we're through the city and out the other side. I have no desire to cross Nolthanin, but I have even less to pass through this empty mockery of a city. Let us proceed, for the sooner we begin, the sooner we may finish."

"Cinjan?" Aljeron called, and the man looked over from his horse beside Synoki.

"Yes?"

"You have been in Avram Gol before?"

"Yes."

"Well, we need to pass through and come out on the northeast corner, or at whatever point would be advantageous for our trek across Nolthanin. Where should we go from here?"

"I have not found any one way better than another. All may be empty and easily passed, or if danger lies ahead, it could lie anywhere."

"Then take us the most direct way you remember."

Cinjan answered by spurring his horse forward, and the others fell into line with the Great Bear and tiger moving alongside them.

As they passed from street to street, Aljeron kept thinking of riding into Nal Gildoroth, though the only similarity was the feeling of being in a once great city, now dead and empty. Otherwise, the two places could not have been more different. The day they rode into Nal Gildoroth had been hot and bright and clear as any summer day could be, and this day was cold and grey and thick with steady, penetrating rain. Nal Gildoroth's large buildings of dark, almost black stone were built on a scale to accommodate Vulsutyrim. Avram Gol was full of graceful white buildings, almost fragile in their slender designs and high rounded roofs. While Nal Gildoroth, abandoned a thousand years, still looked sturdy enough to withstand any assailant, even without living defenders, it seemed to Aljeron that most of the buildings in Avram Gol would fall down if he but rested his hand upon them.

And yet he kept going back to that day. He looked at Saegan nearby and Synoki not far ahead. They had been with him then, and Koshti too. He glanced at his battle brother trotting along gracefully over the wet city streets. Almost as if Koshti knew Aljeron was thinking of him, the tiger glanced up and made contact with his eyes. *All these years you have walked the earth beside me, battle brother. I am so very grateful. May Allfather grant you a life longer than my own. I don't want to walk any streets without your softly padding feet alongside.*

The rain stung his face, it was so cold. Though several days due north of Col Marena, Aljeron had not expected the temperature to drop so far so quickly. He pulled his cloak tight and held onto the reins of his horse with one hand, tucking the other inside his cloak to keep it warm.

As they rode on into the afternoon, the sound of several high calls like wolves or wild dogs rang out from somewhere nearby. Aljeron's horse reared, and his single-handed grip proved insufficient. He was thrown down upon the smooth stone street.

"Aljeron, are you all right?" Evrim called as he steadied his own horse and dropped down onto the street to see what had happened.

"Yes, I'm all right," Aljeron answered, standing and taking hold of his horse to calm him. "The only thing hurt is my pride. I haven't tumbled off my horse like that since I was ten years old and racing my cousins across unfamiliar terrain. I don't think I've ever fallen off a horse that was barely walking faster than I do."

"It was those howls," Saegan said, scanning the streets. "I wish we could see what was calling, and to how many of its kind."

"Do you think it could be wolves, Black Wolves?" Evrim asked Aljeron as they remounted.

"I don't know. It didn't sound like that to me, though I couldn't be sure."

"Whatever made those sounds—" Cinjan didn't finish, for several distinct howls echoed down the empty streets, this time closer than the last. "I would suggest we kept moving," Cinjan said.

"Stay close together," Aljeron said. The men pulled their horses in tighter as Arintol and Erigan walked together near the front by Cinjan's horse, or at least as close as the poor frightened beast would allow. Koshti looked to Aljeron positively delighted at this turn of events. He was jogging around them, sometimes darting out in front and then dropping behind, stopping to smell and listen every few seconds.

"He has no idea what is out there or how many there are," Aljeron said proudly to Saegan, "but he's hunting. Can you believe it? He's hunting. Even when fleeing before a superior enemy, I've never seen Koshti really in retreat. He is always on the prowl, always looking for the attack and the advantage. He is remarkable."

They moved forward, each of them quiet, ears straining to hear anything above the splashing raindrops that would warn of an attack. Aljeron kept a hand on the hilt of Daaltaran and looked forward, for Saegan turned regularly to watch behind them.

Another group of howls pierced the cold afternoon, this time from not far ahead on their right. Without any command to do so, the four who had served with Aljeron in his campaign against Fel Edorath, wheeled almost as one in that direction, and Synoki and Cinjan followed suit. The Great Bear stood, drawing their long wooden poles off their backs.

They didn't have to wait long. A dozen or more scrawny wild dogs came down a small street, trotting briskly. Koshti was upon them in an instant. They had obviously not taken note of his scent from a distance, for when he ran into their midst, ripping dog flesh and fur and crushing their emaciated frames with ease, howls of pain and surprise mingled. One succeeding in slipping past Koshti only to be struck by a smooth stroke of Erigan's great staff, which flung the poor creature a solid ten spans up the road and through a shuttered window.

What remained of the pack disappeared far more quickly than they had come, and Aljeron found himself laughing in the cold rain at the thought of what he had just witnessed. "Are these the wild beasts of Avram Gol, Cinjan? Are they the creatures of legend that walk these abandoned streets and inhabit these deserted buildings?"

"You laugh, but were you here alone and on foot, it wouldn't be so funny."

"Were I here alone and on foot, if I had Daaltaran with me, I would have had all the fun, but today it was Koshti who was the benefactor of this good fortune."

"It would be foolish to assume every danger here will be so easily overcome," Cinjan went on. "These are not all that dwell here, nor are they the worst of the inhabitants of this land. Many things live here and in the Nolthanin wild that are more fearful than those feral dogs, sharing only their ravenous appetite."

"Yes, and you have seen these things with your own eyes and lived to tell?" Saegan asked, his voice betraying no emotion.

"I have seen some of them, indeed I have," Cinjan answered, but he would say no more. In the end, they spent little time at the place where Koshti slaughtered the dogs, and they pushed forward, on through the city.

The rest of their journey to the northeastern corner passed without event, though the great square of Avram Gol sparked some interest in Aljeron and Evrim. "Do you notice what is missing, Evrim?" Aljeron had asked.

"A mound."

"Yes."

"Of course there would be no mound in a city abandoned before the end of the First Age."

"No, but it is weird all the same. I've never been in any town, no matter how small, that did not have a mound, much less a great city such as this."

They reached the outskirts of the city by nightfall. They stopped near a passage through a short wall. Aljeron supposed a tree had fallen many years before and knocked a hole the width of a man in the wall and then rotted away. Aljeron dismounted and examined the loose stone on either side of the small gap. "We will easily be able to widen this hole enough for our horses to pass through, but we will wait until the morning. Let's spend the night here where this small building can serve as shelter. Out there"—he pointed with his thumb behind him at the hole in the wall—"we will probably wish we had shelter of any kind, even that of Avram Gol."

The men dismounted and led their horses back toward the building. Evrim joined Aljeron as he stared out through the gap in the wall. "Can you imagine building a city so great and so wondrous with so short a wall to protect it? This is less than a span high and only a single layer of stone thick."

"I doubt the wall was meant for protection. In the First Age, what would it have protected the people from? It was probably ornamentation of some kind, or a symbol, a picture of where the city met the wild, perhaps."

Evrim was silent. "It was a different world then."

"Yes, a very different world."

Inside the men made themselves as comfortable as they could on the cold stone floor. They had been successful in scavenging enough wood to build a reasonable fire.

"We've been so long on ships, on the run, and in rain that I'd almost forgotten the beauty of a fire," Saegan said as he gazed into the flames.

"Not me," Tornan said, shaking his head. "I like being warm as much as anyone, but I've seen and felt and smelled enough of fire to last me a lifetime."

"I understand," Synoki said. "The fires in Col Marena were fearful to behold, even in the rain. It was like watching the waters of a flood overwhelming everything in its path. Even now, after all these years that living creatures have walked the earth, the mightiest forces in the world are still fire and water."

"I wonder about the First Age," Aljeron said, his mind still churning over his exchange with Evrim about the wall.

"What about it?" Synoki asked.

"About fire and water. Were they so destructive then, back when the world knew peace? Back when the world was peace?"

Arintol sat forward. "The memory of the Great Bear is long, and our homes are among the great trees of Kirthanin. We have no stories of fire run wild that I know."

"You think of the beginning," Saegan said. "When I sit here, in this place, I think of the end. Once this city was alive. Now it is dead, like the men who built it. In Tol Emuna, as long as our children still walk the streets we pave and repave, the city lives. But when no one repairs the holes in the roofs or lights fires in the hearths, a city dies. Avram Gol is dead. Whatever may scavenge here, the city is dead. Will it always be so? When Allfather restores all things, will He restore Nolthanin? Will the streets of Avram Gol teem with life again?"

Synoki laughed, and Aljeron turned to him. "Is the question so funny, Synoki?"

The man shrugged. "Not so much funny as pointless."

"How so?"

"All I know," Synoki said, speaking clearly and slowly, "is that this place has been disintegrating for two thousand years. Kirthanin has been hoping for restoration two thousand years. Maybe I'm a pessimist, but at some point I think we have to consider the possibility that this is all there is, and there isn't anything more coming, now or ever."

"But Allfather Himself promised restoration." Karras's irritation showed in his voice.

"He didn't promise me."

"He didn't promise you what?" Saegan asked coldly, his voice almost a growl.

"Look, I don't want to start a fight. All I'm saying is that all these prophecies and things everybody is counting on happened a really long time ago. As for me, I've pretty much seen it all. I tend not to believe something until I see it or can hold it in my hand."

"Sounds like a hopeless way to live," Evrim answered.

"Maybe so, but I haven't found that hope gets you a whole lot in this world. All you can do is work and plan, and even then, things will get in your way. That's just how it is."

Not long before dawn, a cold hand shook Synoki awake. He sat up and looked at Cinjan, who sat beside him. The man motioned to him to be quiet. Synoki looked at the others, all fast asleep beside the now small fire. Aljeron, who volunteered to keep the first watch, had fallen asleep where he was sitting, and now sat slumped over on the far side of the fire.

Following Cinjan's lead, Synoki slipped out quietly. The horses were tied up outside, but they didn't seem to be startled by or even interested in the sudden emergence of the two men from the building. Synoki wiped the sleep from his eyes with one hand and took hold of Cinjan's collar with the other, pulling him close. "What are you doing? You know we are likely to be suspected. Calling me off like this will only heighten their suspicion."

"I want to do it now," Cinjan said, and Synoki saw the eagerness in his face, in his bright, gleaming eyes, and in his hand clutching the dagger concealed under his cloak.

"No."

"But he's asleep. We can do it and be on our way."

"I said no," Synoki responded, no louder but with an added edge. Cinjan sheathed the dagger, relenting. "We will wait until we know why Aljeron has come, why he has left his army to come here of all places. Cheimontyr will have sent Varatyr after us. He will pick up our trail soon enough. When he catches up, he will kill the others, and we can take Aljeron and force him to tell us what he's doing here."

"I will make him tell."

Synoki smiled and patted Cinjan on the shoulder. "That's why I love having you along, Cinjan. You're so eager. Just remember we have time, plenty of time—time that I want, moreover. I don't just want to know what Aljeron is doing here, I want to know if he is the one I seek, the one I've been seeking for so long. I know Joraiem Andira wasn't. I know it might be Aljeron Balinor, but I don't know for sure. It would be good to know one way or the other by the time Varatyr comes."

"Yes, but even if it isn't him, you'll still let me kill him, right?"

"Cinjan, I have not forgotten my promise. Make no mistake, whether he is the child of prophecy or not, Aljeron will die."

Varatyr gripped the leg of the cow by the thin bony part just above the hoof and turned the meaty shank over the fire. The broken shambles of the small house burned brightly and made an excellent cooking fire. He had devoured most of the cow already, but he was very hungry. He had been on the move for three days and knew he wasn't many days away from the Nolthanin border. He also knew that he couldn't expect to find much food there, not so easily, anyway.

He pulled the leg back from the fire and took a big bite. The meat was not as well done as he would like, but he was impatient to be on his way. He would go a little farther before dawn and then find an out-of-the-way place to sleep.

He looked at the bodies of the man and woman who had lived in this house. Varatyr probably had no real threats to hide from, most of the soldiers of Werthanin having fled south on the ships. Still, he was alone, without his brothers, and though he was not afraid, neither was he stupid. He was more than a match for any of the villages and small towns he had so far passed, but he wasn't invincible. He was covering a lot of ground by night and knew that even if the party he pursued left their ship on horses, he would overtake them. He could afford to be careful.

His teeth struck solid bone as he gnawed down the leg. Having stripped it of meat, Varatyr flung the leg away. He picked over the cow's remains, finding nothing of much appeal. He gathered up his things and started off into the night, headed north.

4
TIMES LIKE THESE

WYLLA PAUSED BEFORE a narrow shop with an open door and, looking in, surveyed a table covered with candles of myriad colors, shapes, and sizes. The shopkeeper looked up from the other side of the table, and a look of recognition and surprise crossed her face. Wylla smiled, that reassuring smile meant to put Enthanim at ease around their queen. She lifted her hand in a gesture of acknowledgement as she moved on.

Yorek walked beside and slightly behind her, not because she required it, but because he seemed more comfortable there. Today was not quite as cold as it had been in recent days, though the light rain continued to fall and the drab grey skies that had greeted them every morning for weeks remained unchanged.

"With the coming of winter and all this rain, the color seems to have gone out of the world, Yorek," Wylla said, looking heavenward as small raindrops fell upon her upturned face. "I find myself dreaming of summer things, of a hot Full

Summer sun in a blue summer sky. I dream of thick green grass fringed with golden brown, and wispy white clouds drifting lazily across the horizon. Then I wake, and everything is wet and grey and just as it was the day before. It feels interminable, and there are days I simply don't want to get out of bed."

"The rain and overcast skies are oppressive, my queen," Yorek said.

Wylla glared at him. He saw her look and glanced away, across the street. After a moment, he continued, but he dropped the formality. "We were made to be creatures of light. Like plants we thrive upon it. So much dark and dreary weather is unnatural. Probably many feel as you do, Wylla."

"Do you?"

Yorek smiled. "On many days I struggle to get out of bed, but I cannot blame that on the weather. Sadness can itself be like a persistent cloud between us and the light. Sometimes it parts, and the rays of delight shine upon me, but I've never known a time devoid of those clouds. Coming to work in your house, however, has done much to brighten my days."

"Even with everything else going on in the world?"

"Yes. I am old enough to know that some of the very best things in life come at unexpected moments. I don't question them anymore. It is enough to accept them and be grateful."

Wylla nodded and adjusted her hair, which she'd wound tightly in a knot for her excursion into the market. "You are right, Yorek. Into the midst of my deepest sorrow, Benjiah was born. He was a light in dark times, and I was very grateful. I am decided; today I will not let the rain get me down. I am here to get a present for Elnah. Her time is near and I want to celebrate with her."

She turned and continued down the street with Yorek following closely. They passed several more shops and stalls, and Wylla stopped to browse some of them. Wherever she did stop, she offered a smile and a kind word to the shopkeeper and other Enthanim. She could see her newfound cheerfulness rippling through the faces and laughter of the people around her. She wondered if she could spread merriment to all of Amaan Sul in this way. It was encouraging to think that her smile could have this much power.

She stopped after a small group of women had passed them, their faces reflecting Wylla's warm smile. Turning once more to Yorek, she asked, "Do you think all smiles are so contagious, or do they smile because I am their queen and have smiled at them?"

"I don't know. Perhaps both are true. Smiles and kindness may be contagious, but to see their queen moving about their streets without fear probably calms them. They look to you to read their own peril, and it is no doubt comforting to see light and hope in your eyes. It even comforts me."

"You, Yorek? But surely you see through me and past my throne. You knew me as a little girl. I didn't awe you then; why should you look to me for anything?"

"You underestimate yourself and your throne, for you have long since ceased to be a little girl. You are as regal a queen as any could be. Beyond that, you underestimate the need for the heart to find comfort from above. I am older than you and have known you for a long time, but you are my queen, and it comforts me to see happiness in your face."

"Even when it was you who encouraged me to have it there?"

"Yes, even so."

Wylla turned her focus once more to the shops, and she continued browsing. Soon she entered a dressmaker's shop, where some dresses hung around the room, and a folio of patterns lay open on a small counter.

"Good morning," said the greying woman behind the counter. She looked up with a smile. Her smile did not disappear when she realized who it was, but Wylla saw both the startled flash of wonder and the comfort her own smile brought to the dressmaker. "Your Majesty, welcome."

"Thank you," Wylla said, looking around the room.

"Can I show you something specific, a pattern perhaps? I have some samples to show you the quality of my work."

"I see them, they are very good."

"I will be happy to make for you whatever you wish."

"I am grateful, but my need is more immediate." Wylla turned from surveying the shop and looked once more at the dressmaker. "A steward of my house is going to have a baby soon. I was hoping to get something for the child. A beautiful, warm nightshirt for these wintry days would be perfect."

Excitement crossed the dressmaker's face. "Just a moment, Your Majesty, I have just the thing."

She disappeared through an open door, and Wylla could hear her footsteps ascending stairs at the back of the shop. She turned to Yorek, who stood by the open door, his attention directed toward the street. She would not disturb him, so she stepped to one of the hanging dresses. The embroidery was excellent—the stitching elegant and strong. She ran her fingers over the texture and smiled. Even in winter and on a rainy day, there were reminders all around her of beautiful and happy things. She just needed to be more deliberate in finding them.

The reappearance of the dressmaker brought her back to the counter, where a lovely, white baby's nightgown now lay. The bottom was long and ideal for wrapping around a child to keep him snug and warm and safe in a cradle, and the woman had stitched small, bright stars at random intervals.

"It is beautiful," Wylla said as she took it up in her hands.

"Yes," the woman said modestly, "it was for my own grandchild."

Wylla looked from the garment to the woman. "Then you must keep it."

"Oh no," the dressmaker said, blushing. "My daughter is only newly married and isn't expecting a baby, not yet. This was just a silly old woman's whim. I have plenty of time to make another. I would be honored if you wanted this one."

"I do want this one, very much. May I take it now?"

"Of course," the dressmaker said, starting immediately to wrap it.

"It is finished?"

"Yes, Your Majesty."

"You will come by the palace for payment this afternoon or tomorrow?"

"Tomorrow would be fine."

"Very well, then, come by when you have time tomorrow." Wylla smiled and took the small bundle from the dressmaker's hands.

"Thank you, Your Majesty," the dressmaker said as Wylla and Yorek stepped out into the street.

"You are welcome. Thank you."

As they walked up the street, in the direction of the palace, Wylla said to Yorek. "You know, Yorek, I am proud of my people."

"Yes?"

"Yes. They know the prophecy. They have heard the news. They know Malek may come, and yet they press ahead. Making a nightshirt for an unborn baby—it is a sign of hope, is it not?"

"It is."

"An affirmation that life goes on."

"Even so."

"Life does go on, Yorek, doesn't it?"

"It always has so far."

"That wasn't a resounding yes."

"No, it wasn't."

"You think life might cease to go on entirely?"

"No."

"Then it will go on as it has before."

Yorek hesitated. "It will go on, but whether it goes on as it has remains to be seen."

Wylla had slowed her step as she listened to Yorek, but now she resumed her brisk pace. "This may be, but even so, I am proud of my people."

It was late morning by the time Wylla and Yorek returned to the palace. Strolling in from the front gate, which opened south onto the city of Amaan Sul, Wylla passed the large fountain in the front courtyard. She noticed the water level was so high that in some places water poured over the walls and onto the paving stones around the base. Wylla made a note to have the fountain shut off so the water level could recede. Maybe she would need to leave the fountain off until this unnatural rain was over and the storm had passed, whenever that would be.

When Wylla spoke of going to see Elnah, Yorek politely excused himself to go and take care of several reports that had been languishing on his desk. Wylla dismissed him with a smile and hurried through the long corridors of the eastern wing and up the narrow stairs to the stewards' quarters.

She rapped gently on the door to Elnah's room. The door swung partway open, and another steward appeared in the doorway.

"Oh," Wylla said, a little startled, "Jolianne, I'm sorry, I didn't know you were visiting Elnah."

"That's all right, Mistress Someris." Jolianne was almost seventy years old and ran the household, though she shunned any talk of her being the head stewardess. She preferred the younger stewards simply to refer to her as "Mother," and usually dispensed of other formalities, except with Wylla, whom she insisted on calling Mistress or Your Majesty even though she had bounced the baby Wylla on her knee. "I was just about to leave, come on in."

Jolianne returned to the chair by Elnah's bed and gathered up a shawl that she had draped over its back. She took Elnah's hand. "Now don't you worry anymore about this. We've seen more than a few babies into the world around here, and yours won't be any different, all right?"

"Yes, Mother," Elnah replied. "Would you tell Caylin? He's been pacing at the foot of my bed every night for a week."

Jolianne rolled her eyes. "Husbands! I tell you, Elnah, the older I get, the less use I see for them. All the really important things that happen in this world are done by women anyway."

"Jolianne!" Wylla said, walking to the foot of the bed. "I'm scandalized."

"It's true, Mistress," Jolianne said, shaking her head. "Almost fifty years I've been married, and I love Gradin, I do, but sometimes I just marvel at a man's lack of common sense. It's a wonder anything gets done at all without a woman to make decisions."

"And did you feel this way when my father was king?"

"No, Mistress, I didn't, but your dad had your mom, didn't he?"

Wylla laughed. "Oh, go on now." Jolianne bustled out the door, pulling it closed behind her. Wylla turned to Elnah, whose head was propped up on a couple of pillows. "Don't mind Jolianne, Elnah, Caylin is a good man. It's tough for the men, you know, they feel shut out of this part. He'll be all right when he holds the baby in his hands. They all are."

"I know," Elnah said, smiling as Wylla sat down in the chair.

Wylla pulled the small bundle from under her cloak where she had stowed it to keep it dry on the walk home. "I picked something up for you, and I was going to wait until the baby was born, but I can't. It's too gorgeous."

Elnah's eyes lit up as she took the bundle from Wylla's hands, but she paused short of opening it. "Your Majesty, you are too kind. You didn't need to get me anything."

"I didn't really, this is for the baby."

Elnah opened the bundle and held up the beautiful nightshirt. "It's for the cold winter nights ahead. We're going to keep this little girl or boy, whichever it is, as warm as we can. It may be cold and wet outside, but it will always be warm and cozy in his world, at least for a while."

"I wonder if it will be a boy," Elnah said as she rubbed the soft fabric in her fingers.

Wylla smiled. A memory of Benjiah as a curly-headed three-year-old running through the palace like a little madman flashed through her mind. Her smile broadened. "Whether a girl or boy, it will be good to have another baby in the palace. It's been too long. There's nothing better than holding a warm, soft baby in your arms, especially when it's your own."

"I'll take your word on that," Elnah answered, rubbing her round, protruding stomach.

"What is it?" Wylla asked, picking up on something in Elnah's voice.

"I've seen the pain in your eyes when you speak or think of Benjiah. I know it must be hard not to know where he is or what he's doing. I can't imagine how hard it is to let them go. I don't want to ever have to do what you've done. I know I can't keep my baby inside me, and I don't want to, but you know, there's a part of me that feels like my baby is safe in here." She patted herself softly as she talked.

Wylla took Elnah's hand as Jolianne had done. Stroking the back of Elnah's hand with her thumb, she spoke kindly. "Don't worry about things so far down the road. As a mother, I think we are granted strength to bear what we face at the moment, but the worries of tomorrow are not for us to carry yet.

You will have plenty of time to brace yourself for the letting go, but right now you are free to hold tight, as tight as you wish. Enjoy it. It's a precious time."

"I will." Elnah smiled. "I'm sorry to bring it up."

"Don't be. I do miss Benjiah, very much. How couldn't I? I'm his mother."

"I'm sure he's all right."

"I hope so. I really do."

For a moment Wylla just sat, holding Elnah's hand. Then, letting go, she stood and said, "Well, Elnah, I'll go and let you rest. Do you want me to put the nightshirt away for now?"

"Sure, but leave it handy. I want it to be the first thing my baby wears."

"All right." Wylla smiled, and she took the nightshirt, folded it gently, and laid it on the table on the side of the room.

"Rest well," Wylla said.

"I will," Elnah replied.

The queen pulled the door closed behind her, and for a long moment, she stood in the hall, her back against the wall beside the door. She ran her hand across her own stomach. It seemed like just yesterday Benjiah grew inside her. Where was he now? She had no idea, and it was almost too much to bear.

Wylla stood at her large, open window, feeling the fresh, cold air upon her face. A warm fire burned in her fireplace, and she would return to sit before it momentarily. For the moment, she wanted to feel the wind on her cheeks and the frost in the air.

Benjiah loved wintertime. Snow was one of his favorite things in this world. From an early age he would not stay indoors when snow covered the ground. Using all available machinations to elude her attentive care and head for the largest snowdrifts, he'd been a constant source of anxiety for a grieving widow trying to keep her infant warm and dry.

Wylla smiled as she remembered the day when Benjiah, perhaps three, found himself briefly unattended while she addressed a matter of some urgency. He slipped downstairs and roamed freely and discreetly through the palace. The young rascal managed to climb up onto the back of a large chair in the great hall, and from this vantage point succeeded in unlatching and opening a tall window. He leapt from the top of the high chair back through the window and out into a snowdrift a third of a span deep, at least.

Wylla found him just in time to witness the jump. Her heart nearly stopped as she raced across the room to find a small, Benjiah-sized hole in the snowdrift outside. Stepping out through the window, she dug in the snow until she retrieved the laughing boy from where he was lying on the ground. Despite her best intentions to severely scold him, the sight of the little smiling face contorted with giggling and chattering prevented her from mustering the requisite seriousness. She had, at a later point, impressed upon her young son the danger of such a stunt and disciplined him for his secretive disappearance, but as she held him in the chair that had been his launching pad, she was content to wipe the snow from his face and hands and hold him close.

As Wylla shut the window and turned back toward the fire, a firm knock came from her door. Resuming her seat, she called out, "Come in."

"Your Majesty?"

Wylla turned to see Yorek paused in the doorway. "Yes?"

"It is time for lunch, Your Majesty."

"That's all right, Yorek," Wylla replied. "I'm fine. I'm very tired, but not hungry."

"Yes, Your Majesty, but Captain Merias is here, remember? We were to dine with him today?"

Wylla stood quickly, adjusting her hair as she strode across the room for her bright, warm shawl. "I'm sorry, Yorek. I don't know what's come over me today. I feel so fatigued."

"That's all right." Yorek held the door open for Wylla as she passed swiftly through. He followed quietly, closing the door securely. "Even queens forget, especially when they have as much on their minds as you do these days."

"I'm so embarrassed. Has he been here long?"

"No, he's only just arrived. He need never know that you forgot."

"Thank you." Wylla paused to squeeze Yorek's arm before turning with renewed vigor to descend to the small dining room where she usually held such mealtime meetings.

Inside, Captain Merias stood, straight and still, his hands resting lightly on the back of a chair. When Wylla entered, he bowed over the chair and then resumed his posture of patient attentiveness. Wylla took her seat at the head of the table and Yorek sat at her right hand opposite Merias.

"Please, Captain, take your seat and rest with us for a while."

"Thank you, Your Majesty."

Within moments of Wylla's arrival, stewards appeared with plates teeming with cooked fowl, bread, and fruit preserves prepared and stored during the summer harvest season. Wylla took some bread thinly layered with the preserves and waited as the two men dug eagerly into the fowl.

"So, Captain Merias, how has the recruiting in the countryside and villages been going?"

"Well, Your Majesty," the Captain replied, setting down a wing and wiping his mouth carefully. "The number of those now training with the army here in Amaan Sul has grown to twelve thousand. That, of course, does not include the twenty-five hundred men encamped a day's hard ride from the Forest of Gyrin that we dispatched there two weeks ago."

"Does it include men from Tol Emuna?"

"No, Your Majesty. We have not heard yet from Tol Emuna, though such word might come any day now. Nor have we heard from the towns and villages around Jul Avedra, though I do not expect news from there for perhaps another week."

Wylla nodded, sitting back. "At least the news we have is all good."

"Well, I'm not sure about that."

Wylla straightened and Yorek set down the bone in his hand in exchange for a long drink of water. "What is it?" Wylla asked.

"News of Fel Edorath has come from Garring Pul."

"Yes?"

"It is overrun, Your Majesty," Captain Merias said softly. "People of the city who fled some weeks ago have crossed the northern waters of the Kellisor Sea by boat, seeking refuge in Garring Pul and other smaller villages along the shore. They say that Malek and his forces came to Fel Edorath and pushed quickly westward."

"What of Aljeron Balinor and the army of Shalin Bel that surrounded the city?"

"They were gone already, Your Majesty. These accounts claim that Aljeron took possession of the city, but when reports came to him of Malek's imminent arrival he withdrew, heading west with some of the soldiers of Fel Edorath."

"Some?"

"Some, the rest stayed to defend the city, against his advice."

"They were destroyed by Malek, then."

"No, they were invited to join Malek and march west with him."

"What? Surely they did not?"

"They did, for the invitation was delivered in person by Rulalin Tarasir, or so the account from Garring Pul goes."

Wylla stared hard at Merias. "You are sure of this?"

"I am as sure as I can be, not having been there. My messengers had the same story from three different families. All the accounts were consistent in everything except specific dates and times, which are easily confused."

"Rulalin," Wylla said, looking from Merias to Yorek, who folded his hands as he rested his elbows upon the table. "What do you make of this, Yorek?"

Yorek shrugged. "I am not surprised. You said the prophet Valzaan believed Malek would move first in the west, and he has. What's more, Rulalin's alliance with Malek is a smart move, since his own defeat and death was imminent."

"Smart?"

"In the sense that it has helped him to evade capture for the moment. For a desperate man, it must have held a certain appeal. He is the cat now, the mouse no longer. He has handed one of Kirthanin's great cities to Malek without a fight, so his service has already paid dividends to his new master. We may find Malek's hosts encamped outside our own walls one day, and Rulalin might be there right alongside them."

A strange and terrifying thought took shape in Wylla's mind. She gasped at the mere presence of it, and quickly she pushed it away. *Surely not,* she thought. *That couldn't be his plan.*

"Are you all right?" Yorek asked, seeing the dismay on Wylla's face.

She gathered herself and pushed this disconcerting possibility as far from her mind as she could. "Yes. As all right as I can be, I suppose. Malek has come from the Mountain and taken Fel Edorath without a fight. Fel Edorath, where Valzaan, my brothers, and my son were headed."

"There was no news of them. These who crossed the Kellisor Sea despite the strange winds and rains had no news of the prophet or any who might have been with him. I am encouraged, given the situation, that apparently no battle took place at the city. Whatever has happened to them, it doesn't look like any lives were lost trying to hold Fel Edorath in vain."

"No, but if Malek and his army headed west after Aljeron, we don't really know what has happened, do we? What of the rest of Werthanin, of Shalin Bel?"

"We don't know."

What happiness Wylla had managed to muster that morning dispersed like songbirds before a storm. The clouds descended upon her again. "What are we to do?" she asked of no one in particular.

Captain Merias jumped at this, almost literally, springing to his feet with enthusiasm and addressing her as though her rhetorical question was the opportunity he had been waiting for. "We should march out to aid them. We have more than fourteen thousand men at our disposal. Give me the order, and I will lead our men to their aid."

"Where would you go, Captain Merias?" Wylla replied, looking up in the face of her young and excitable captain, who looked for all the world like he was asking to play with a new toy, not lead men to war. "Would you head west in the wake of both armies? What do you think you'll find? Will they wait for you to arrive to engage in battle? What if you come upon a defeated Werthanin with its strong places held against you? What then?"

"I don't know," Captain Merias responded, "but I know that Malek could well destroy every city of Kirthanin, one at a time, until all things lie at his feet. We have to unite or we will all die. Our fathers of the Second Age fought side by side despite the civil war that preceded Malek's Invasion. Why shouldn't we?"

"I'm not saying we shouldn't, but how are we to do it? Have you seen a dragon in the sky lately, Merias? Its wings shimmering like hammered gold? Who will bring us news of the enemy's movements? Who can see Malek's army today and tell us tomorrow where to position our soldiers? We are blind. We have no dragons and no prophet, not here anyway. What if I send you out to the wrong place and Malek comes here in the meantime? Who will defend our walls and protect your wives while you are gone? I will not send you anywhere and leave Amaan Sul undefended, especially when our latest news is several weeks old."

"We could send out messengers, spies. We could send them west into Werthanin and south into Suthanin. We could send them to Shalin Bel, to Cimaris Rul, to Peris Mil, and to Kel Imlaris. We could send men all the way to Sulare until someone sees or hears enough to know where the enemy is and where he will be. Then we could march."

Wylla met the determined eyes of the Captain, holding them with her own. After a moment, she turned to Yorek. "And you? What do you think?"

Yorek sat back with a sigh, stroking his face. "I think the hour has passed for you to think of yourself as Enthanin's queen. We must all think of ourselves as Kirthanin's stewards, entrusted with Kirthanin's care. Saving Amaan Sul is no longer our primary goal. I believe the city cannot be saved unless Malek is utterly defeated, and Merias is right: His defeat is unlikely as things stand, with every city fending for itself.

"And yet, you are also correct. We cannot send our men to battle when we don't know where the battle is. We don't know what Aljeron intended when he withdrew from Fel Edorath. Did he fall all the way back to Shalin Bel? Did he try to hold Zul Arnoth? Would he head south through the Erefen Marshes to draw Malek away from his beloved city? Would he head south to Suthanin or try to outflank Malek's forces and come here to join with another army, to relieve his own war-weary men? Who can say? We cannot march, but we cannot be content to sit and wait."

Yorek leaned forward. "Merias is right. We must send out the spies. We must send them out now."

Wylla closed her eyes and exhaled as though she had been holding her breath for ages. "All right. This is what I want you to do. I want three hundred young men divided into groups of three. Send them everywhere you can imagine with these simple instructions: Find the enemy or definitive news of him, and then return. That is all they are to do."

"Yes, Your Majesty."

"Also, send three thousand men to Garring Pul to keep an eye on the Kellisor Sea and the Kalamin River."

"Yes, Your Majesty."

"Is there anything else, Captain Merias?"

"No, Your Majesty. Thank you." The Captain bowed and was just turning to leave when a strong knock came from the stewards' service door.

"Yes," Wylla called out, her face betraying the annoyance her voice concealed.

A steward entered. "Your Majesty, a messenger for Captain Merias has just arrived. I told him the Captain would be out momentarily, but he will not wait."

"Send him in."

The steward had barely stepped out of the room when a ragged youth, perhaps twenty years of age, entered wearing a broad smile.

"Captain, Your Majesty." He bowed, then grew serious when he saw Wylla frowning. "I bring news from Tol Emuna."

"What news, Hardin?"

"A force of five thousand men is on its way to Amaan Sul to augment our defenses."

"Five thousand!" Captain Merias said, the delight showing on his face. He turned to Yorek and the queen. "That's twice the number dispatched from anywhere else. The soldiers of Tol Emuna are the toughest in all Kirthanin."

"It is good news, indeed." Wylla said, feeling the clouds begin to lift again. In her wildest dreams, she had not dared to hope for so many from Tol Emuna, a notoriously independent city.

"Thank you, Hardin," Captain Merias said. "Go, clean yourself up and get something to eat. You will dine with me tonight and tell me of your journey."

"Thank you, Captain." The young man bowed once more to Wylla and exited.

"Now, all we need is news of the enemy, and we will bring the war to him," Captain Merias said, looking from Yorek to Wylla.

"The news from Tol Emuna is good," Yorek said, "but our fears lie in another direction, and all the good news in the world cannot allay or dismiss them. I will wait to rejoice until Malek's head has been separated from his shoulders and Kirthanin is free of him at last."

Wylla's bed was soft and inviting, and she succumbed to the temptation to take an afternoon nap for the first time in ages. Closing the shutters to block out the pale afternoon light, the queen settled into her bed and drew the large, warm quilt up over her head.

The afternoon sun above Wylla struck her as decidedly odd. It had been a long time since she'd felt its heat on her face. She didn't focus on the warmth for long, because she noticed across from her in the fine gardens a young man with shoulder-length blond hair and a wide smile.

"Joraiem?" she said, her heart quickening.

"How are you, my beloved?"

"Delighted!" She ran to him and threw her arms around him. "I thought I'd lost you forever."

"You haven't lost me," Joraiem said. "I'm always with you."

"I'm so glad." Wylla stepped back and looked up into Joraiem's smiling face. Reaching up, she felt the curve of his jaw with her finger, feeling the smoothness of his closely shaved skin. He laughed at her touch, and she smiled.

They sat down on a bench in the garden, and Wylla looked around them for the first time. The Great Hall of Sulare rose not more than twenty spans away, its towering white walls still covered with bright yellow vines. "It's so good to be back," Wylla said, leaning against her husband.

"Yes. It's like coming home."

A sudden thunder in the sky made Wylla snap upright. The garden around the Great Hall and Joraiem were gone, and darkness surrounded her. She saw the flickering firelight of the fireplace across the room, when suddenly her door was flung open and light poured in.

"Your Majesty!" shouted the silhouette in the doorway. "You need to come now! The palace is on fire!"

Disoriented, Wylla made her way down the stairs behind the steward. She discerned from fragmented statements that it was in fact the kitchen that was on fire, and not by any means the whole palace, not yet at least. The chaos and commotion increased as they approached the kitchen. Stewards were running every which way, and overhead, thick billows of smoke rolled out of the open kitchen door and into the hall and nearby rooms.

Yorek saw Wylla and cut her off. "Your Majesty, we must get you out of the palace immediately. The fire is not yet large but we can take no chances. Come quickly."

"No," Wylla said simply. She started past him.

Yorek took her by the arm. "Your Majesty, I am sorry to do this, but I must insist."

Wylla glared up at him. "We need water and lots of it and every pair of hands matters. Now let go of me."

Yorek hesitated but conceded, letting the queen go. Wylla stepped to the doorway and called above the commotion. "The open troughs in the courtyard outside the stables are overflowing with water from all this rain. Go immediately and fill as many buckets from the stables as you can carry. Bring them to me here. Go, now."

A flood of stewards, perhaps a dozen or more, ran down the hall and out into the courtyard. Wylla, waiting outside the kitchen, which was thick with dark smoke, spied Karalin coming down the hall with Kyril and Kyril's two daughters. Wylla grabbed Yorek's arm. "Yorek, take Kyril and the girls out front to the fountain. They can help with the buckets if we have to start a water line from there. Karalin, go with them and help Kyril with the girls."

"They'll be all right," Karalin said as Yorek led Kyril and the stunned girls into the cool evening. "I'll stay here and lend a hand as I'm able, same as you."

Soon the stewards started coming back with buckets in each hand, some losing water in great splashes as they ran. A pair of men positioned themselves at the kitchen door and took it upon themselves to direct the water as the others passed their buckets. Wave after wave of water was flung onto the fire inside the kitchen, and with every empty bucket, Wylla directed the steward who had carried it out to the fountain for more. With perhaps half a dozen buckets left, she called a halt to the dousing of the kitchen and stepped to the door herself. Much of kitchen was smoldering now, but she could see the fire very much alive on the ceiling.

"Up the stairs. Follow me."

Through the thickening smoke they charged up the nearby narrow stair that led to the kitchen stewards' small rooms. Dashing down the hall, they threw doors open, looking for evidence of the fire. In the second room, smoke rose from between the floorboards. Stooping, Wylla could feel even at the entrance to the room that the floor was very hot.

"Here," she called and took a bucket from the nearest steward. She slung the water across the floor and steam rose, glistening. "More!" Five more buckets were dumped into the room.

"Back down! Keep the buckets coming into the kitchen, but divert half of them up here, quickly!"

Wylla waited at the top of the stairs with Karalin. "We could use my brothers right about now, couldn't we?" Wylla said, gently squeezing Karalin's arm as they waited.

"We sure could," Karalin answered, and Wylla heard her voice catch. She said no more.

Soon feet came pounding up the stairs, and Wylla directed the young men to the correct door as gallons of water washed over and over across the floor until water seeped back into the hall. "Keep the water coming and hit both rooms on either side as well," Wylla said as she headed back down the stairs.

At the kitchen, another round of buckets was being tossed all over the kitchen by men venturing further and further into the dense smoke to douse the room. Looking up at the ceiling, she could see water running along the support beams where it was seeping through from above.

A few more rounds of water in the kitchen and above, and Wylla called a halt to the efforts. The smoke was still dense but clearing. "All right," Wylla said, "let's spread out in pairs and check all the neighboring rooms. Make a note of any place that seems to be smoldering, and keep an eye on it."

More than an hour later, there was reluctant but grateful consensus that the fire was indeed out. Lamps were lit, and the examination of the damage began. The main kitchen was almost completely destroyed. The beams above were charred black, as were the walls and tables and counters. Utensils littered the charred furniture and floors, melted into bent and twisted relics. With little or no talking, those who had fought the fire now started the work of sorting through the mess, trying to figure out what needed to be done immediately and what could wait.

A weary, sooty, and coughing Wylla stood in the middle of her once-beautiful kitchen, a bustling hub of activity at all times of the day and sometimes night. Just that afternoon she had seen it full of glistening copper pots and pans. Yorek reappeared beside her and renewed his plea. "Your Majesty, I really must insist this time. We have no idea how extensive the damage to the ceiling is. You just can't stand here."

Wylla looked up. "Was there anything above not destroyed by the smoke and water?"

"Not really. We'll have a closer look later. Don't worry about it. Everyone's all right, and there's nothing here that can't be repaired."

"Yes, that's the important thing, isn't it?" Wylla said, looking forlornly at Yorek. The crisis having passed, Wylla felt as though her strength and power to command had left her. "Everyone's all right."

"They are indeed. Come."

Wylla followed Yorek from the kitchen, and made her way to Karalin, who sat in a chair in the large open hall. "I'm sure, wherever he is, he's missing you just as much."

"I know," Karalin answered. "Just to be able to see him, to touch his skin—it would mean so much."

"I know," Wylla answered slowly.

Karalin sighed. "Waiting. I hate it."

Wylla smiled. "Yes, it is hard."

She took Karalin's hand in hers. "We'll wait together, you and I, and may your beloved bring my son home, safe and sound. Then we'll rejoice together, will we not?"

"We will."

They sat, and Wylla felt the last fragments of the energy she had mustered to fight the fire slip away. As the weariness of the evening washed over her, a steward came running up the hall. She let go of Karalin's hand and sat forward, newly attentive.

"Your Majesty," the young girl panted, "you won't believe it, but Elnah's baby, it's coming!"

Wylla moved swiftly through the halls, more swiftly than she would have thought she could just moments earlier. Karalin limped along behind her, her weariness no doubt aggravating the pain of her disfigured foot. Wylla paused to allow Karalin to catch up. "Karalin, I'll be all right. There's no telling how long this will be. Why don't you go get some rest?"

"Not if you aren't," Karalin replied.

"Don't be silly. All I'll probably end up doing is wait. Why should you have to wait too? Besides, I don't see this as a burden. I could use a little good news and simple joy today. I'll be fine."

"Are you sure?"

"Yes. Go on and get some sleep."

"All right." Karalin gave Wylla a hug and turned to go back to her room.

Jolianne and several stewards were already bustling about Elnah's room when Wylla arrived. She could tell from the doorway that Elnah's labor pains had begun. The calm, even sleepy face of the young woman had been replaced by a flushed and contorted grimace. She clung to the hand of a friend on the one side and the bedclothes on the other.

"Now, Your Majesty," Jolianne said as she stopped in front of the queen, "I've been serving as a midwife in this house for nearly thirty years, and I've never put a queen to work in the process yet. I know you'd like to wait, but maybe you'll need to wait outside. I've already had to send the husband away twice."

"Yes, Jolianne." Wylla smiled. "I'll step out in a moment. I'll just have a quick word to Elnah."

"Quick then." Jolianne said, frowning a little as Wylla moved to the bedside.

Wylla slid along the side where Elnah's free hand had a firm hold on the sheet. Wylla reached down and placed her own hand lightly on Elnah's. "Not long now," she whispered gently as she bent over the young woman.

Elnah turned to look at Wylla. A hint of a smile crossed her face, but it soon disappeared as a contraction shook her body and her grip on the bedclothes tightened.

"I'm not going far, but I'm going to wait out of the way. I'll be close by if you need me." Wylla stroked Elnah's hair, gave her another smile, and left the room.

Hours passed, and the commotion died down. Caylin appeared twice, but the male stewards who were helping him pass the time in a nearby room by regaling him with stories of their own children's births kept retrieving him. Wylla couldn't tell if the man was more eager to see how Elnah was doing or to escape his fellows.

Wylla sat outside the door in the hall, and as the night slowly moved on, she closed her eyes. Her breathing started to come more rhythmically, and though she could hear a voice in her head telling her to stay awake for Elnah, it didn't seem to her so bad to sleep for a few minutes before the baby came.

Renewed commotion awoke her. Stewards were moving up and down the hall, fairly running to and from the room. Looking more closely at the face of one, Wylla saw panic in her eyes. Wylla stood, alarmed.

Walking quickly to the door, she looked inside. A steward sat crying next to the bed, where Elnah lay still. Jolianne stood with a small crowd around the table on the far side of the room. Wylla walked to the bed. Reaching down, she felt Elnah's hand. It was cold and lifeless. She was not sleeping. She was dead.

Wylla stepped back involuntarily. "What happened?" she said quietly but firmly to the crying steward.

"I don't know. It all seemed to be going all right, but she just stopped breathing. They couldn't help her." The girl broke down into sobs again.

"They got the baby out?"

The girl nodded.

Wylla felt a moment of relief, but just a moment. It dawned on her that the room was quiet. She could hear the hushed voices of the women by the table, but no cries or screams from a newborn. She turned toward the table and slowly drew nearer.

She could see through the crowd glimpses of the child, bluish and bloody. Wylla closed her eyes tightly and mumbled under her breath, "Not the baby too, not the baby."

When she opened her eyes again, she saw Jolianne shaking her head. A few minutes later, the other stewards drifted away. Jolianne gently cleaned the dead child and then started to wrap it in the large towel it had been lying upon.

"Don't," Wylla said, and Jolianne turned, surprised. "Use this." Wylla retrieved the beautiful nightshirt she had purchased for Elnah's baby from the small stack of neatly folded clothes that had been waiting for the baby's arrival.

Jolianne did not argue but slowly unwrapped the towel and started to dress the baby in the shirt. Wylla watched her. "A boy," she said softly.

Jolianne nodded, finishing her task by taking the long train of the nightshirt and wrapping it securely around the baby. "I need to find Caylin," Jolianne said as she carried the child from the room.

Except for Elnah's friend, still crying at the bedside, the room was empty now. Wylla felt the urge to cry too, but it seemed distant and far away. She felt as empty as the room, as though life itself had fled from within her. And then, a terrible thought rolled through the back of her mind. She walked woodenly from the room, past the few stewards in the hall, and up the stairs. She slipped into her room and closed the door behind her, standing for a long moment with her back against it in the darkness.

The thought and the words were still in her head, and terrible though she knew them to be, she realized they wouldn't go away as long as they remained unspoken. She breathed deeply and then whispered them to the darkness.

"Perhaps it is better never to see the light than to be born into the world in times like these."

5 OUT OF THE DEEP

BENJIAH RAN HIS FINGERS along Valzaan's staff. The wood was solid and dense, but it felt light and smooth to the touch. He hadn't noticed until after they set sail for Cimaris Rul, but there seemed to be no nicks or gashes anywhere on it. From the long, smooth handle to the intricately carved windhover at the top, there were no marks of any kind. *Valzaan carried this staff for centuries,* he thought as he felt the damp wood in the rain, *but age seems hardly to have touched it.*

He heard laughter from across the deck, and looking over he saw his uncles doubled over at the starboard rail, which was facing seaward on this trek south. He was suddenly tired of standing alone and moved toward them. They had straightened by the time he reached them and grown almost serious again.

"Nephew," Pedraal said, wiping tears from his eyes as Benjiah leaned on the rail, "isn't it a fine day for sailing?" He motioned with his hand for Benjiah to consider the grey sky, the seemingly inexhaustible rains, and the choppy and tempestuous waves. Hardly was the question out when both of the twins doubled over again, laughing merrily as though Pedraal had said something immensely clever.

"Forgive us, Benjiah," Pedraal continued when they had achieved a modicum of control once more. "We're going stir-crazy, I think. There's no other excuse for us, is there, Pedraan?"

"No, and there never has been."

"No," Pedraal agreed, snickering, "there never was."

"Our poor mother."

"Our poor father."

"Our poor sister."

"And now," Pedraal finished, "our poor nephew. Alas, Benjiah, you are but one in a long line of people, forced to bear with us. We are truly sorry."

"Most sincerely," Pedraan added.

"You two have been at the cider," Benjiah said dryly.

"Surely not," Pedraal answered, indignant. "We don't need cider to behave as fools; we were born this way." At this, both of his uncles broke out into riotous laughter again, and it took several moments before they regained their composure.

Benjiah waited patiently, gazing out over the dark waves into the gloomy distance. Beneath his feet the *Silver Swan* bobbed, taking the waves in stride. Benjiah, who had not spent much time on a ship before, save only a few encounters with much smaller vessels on the Kellisor Sea, was glad to be on one of the bigger ships of this makeshift fleet. A few others were sailing in the front with the *Silver Swan,* but most of them were larger too. Benjiah looked out over the stern at the water behind them. Out there, the smaller ships followed. Benjiah wondered what these waves must feel like on ships like those.

"Seriously, though," Pedraan said, drawing Benjiah's attention to his uncles again. "It is great to be out at sea once more."

"Yes," Pedraal agreed. "Bad weather, wind, rain, and waves—all that aside, this is better than Gyrin, is it not?"

He asked Benjiah, who looked back out at the water, trying not to think of the seasickness that seemed always to hover nearby, even when the water was calm. "I suppose so."

"You suppose so?" Pedraan asked, his voice betraying a rare note of surprise. "How on earth could there be any doubt?"

Benjiah shrugged. "Gyrin may be a fearful place now, but it wasn't always. You know me, Uncle. I love the woods—the peace and the tranquility, not to mention the hunt. Gyrin was doubtless very beautiful once."

"But this is the ocean, boy! Gyrin may very well have been beautiful once, but you should see the ocean on a warm, sunny day. There's nothing better."

"I've never seen the ocean on a warm, sunny day."

"Then use your imagination! Look around you. Envision the blue sky, the bright sun, the birds wheeling above the ship, the smooth blue water tranquil and lovely all around us. Can you see it?"

Benjiah could imagine it. Indeed he had many times. "I think so."

Pedraan smacked Pedraal on the arm. "Brother, when all this is over, when we've buried Malek and his captains in the cold earth, let's go back to Sulare. Let's go back in summer, and let's find Ulmindos or whoever might be in charge of teaching the youngsters how to sail these days, and let's go back to the Forbidden Isle. I want to see it again. I want to sail the Forgotten Waters once more."

Pedraal nodded. A sudden, hushed seriousness descended upon him. "Yes, let's do that. We'll all go south again. As many of us as we can find. As many as are left."

"Yes, of course. We'll take Wylla and Karalin and even Mindarin, though perhaps we ought to meet her there." Pedraan's eyes twinkled.

"Perhaps we should, unless we want to be talked to death on the way." Pedraal laughed softly while looking over his shoulder to make sure Mindarin, who was standing with Aelwyn in the bow, couldn't hear.

"And you, Benjiah," Pedraal continued, looking to his nephew, "you can come too. You can see Sulare at last."

"I'd like that," Benjiah answered. "I'd like that very much."

Benjiah looked back over the rail and out to sea. How often had he dreamed of visiting Sulare and seeing for himself the place where his mother and father met, wed, and spent the entirety of their brief married life together? His mother had told him their story over and over when he was little, so much that he felt he knew the Great Hall, the majestic fountain, the long grassy avenue that led to the sea, and the carefully tended gardens. He would walk there some day in the summer sun, and he would honor the memory of the person he most wanted to know but had never met.

"You're thinking of your father," Pedraal said softly.

Benjiah looked back at his uncle and saw that the twins were completely sober now. They were watching him watch the ocean with sadness in their eyes. "Yes," Benjiah said. "I was."

Pedraal put his arm around his nephew's shoulders. "We'll take you there, Benjiah, when this is over. We will show you everything and tell you every story we remember. We will bring the place to life for you, and by the time we leave, you will feel as though you had been there with us and with him."

Benjiah smiled at his uncle's earnestness. "Thank you, Uncle Pedraal. I appreciate that. I would like to see Sulare through your eyes."

"You will," Pedraal answered.

"You know," Benjiah said, "I think I miss my dad more, now that Valzaan is gone."

"You do?" Pedraan said, not sounding all that surprised.

"I do. When he was with us, guiding us through Gyrin and beyond, I felt for the first time in my life like I had a father. No offense to either of you." Benjiah turned red as he looked at his uncles.

They smiled. "None taken," Pedraal answered for them both. "We know we aren't especially paternal. We're more like brother figures than father figures. We know ourselves well enough to know that."

"Yeah," Pedraan added, laughing, "younger brother figures."

"I'm glad you understand," Benjiah said at last. "Valzaan was teaching me about me, like I always imagined my father would have. Now that he's gone, I feel even more alone than I did before."

Pedraal squeezed Benjiah's shoulders, pulling him closer. "It was very hard for us all to lose Valzaan, for a lot of reasons, but for you, it has been harder still. We're sorry, Nephew."

Benjiah nodded and noticed that Aelwyn and Mindarin were approaching. He turned to face them, pulling away from his uncle and leaning back against the starboard rail.

"Good evening," Mindarin said. She wore a wry smile, and though he'd only recently met her, Benjiah braced himself as she opened her mouth to continue. "After all those weeks riding and camping in the rain, it is good to see you gentlemen taking advantage of the shelter this ship affords. Well done."

"Sleeping in a dry room below deck is welcome," Pedraal answered, ignoring her sarcasm, "but spending the duration of our voyage there isn't my idea of a good time, even if it is dry."

Aelwyn smiled benevolently at Benjiah. "And how are you, Benjiah?"

"All right," he answered sheepishly.

"I know the weather isn't ideal, but some of the coastline we'll pass on our way south is very beautiful. I think you'll enjoy it."

"If he can see it through all the rain and mist," Mindarin said. "Besides, you haven't been down this way since you were a little girl. Things may have changed."

"I'm not that old," Aelwyn retorted. "I think we can safely assume the coastline hasn't changed dramatically in the last fifteen years."

"I don't assume anything anymore. Anyway, it's time for dinner and I'm starving. Let's not linger up here in the rain any longer."

Benjiah and the twins stepped away from the rails and followed Mindarin and Aelwyn below deck.

Dinner was a modest affair. The hasty retreat from Shalin Bel and rapid departure from Col Marena rendered the ships unevenly provisioned. In the time they spent anchored off the coast, supplies had been ferried from ships with greater stores to those with less, but even so, it was generally acknowledged as prudent that they try to preserve as much food as possible.

With little formality in their dining these days and not much food to eat, dinner took barely more than a quarter of an hour to consume. During that brief time it was evident to all below that the weather had turned nasty, for the ship began to pitch and roll with increasing severity. Though several soldiers with nautical experience manned the decks, both the twins and Benjiah hastily excused themselves to see if they could lend a hand.

Benjiah was not prepared for what greeted him as he followed his uncles through the hatch onto the deck. The wind swept across the deck in swirling gusts, tossing everything that wasn't tied down across the soggy planks. For a moment Benjiah thought that might include him; he thought he felt the wind begin to lift him off his feet. Instead he slid sideways half a span before his uncle grabbed him by the wrist and steadied him with a smile. "If you've been missing Gyrin," Pedraal yelled above the wind, "this storm should remind you of that night near the Mountain, eh, Benjiah?"

Benjiah merely nodded as he tried to focus on pressing his feet down on the deck as hard as he could, willing them to stay put as the wind swept past with renewed vigor. Benjiah looked at the tall waves, now twice the normal height, and watched them come crashing against the side of the *Silver Swan*. He wondered how much force each wave brought to bear on the side of the beleaguered ship and how long the wood could take such a pounding before being smashed to bits.

Perhaps even more alarming than the waves and the wind was the darkness. Though dusk before dinner, now, less than half an hour later, it was as dark as midnight. The grey, misty clouds were gone, replaced by a deep, dark bank of dense cloud that seemed to stretch endlessly before and behind them. Where had such a monstrous storm come from? How could it have swept over and around them so quickly and with so little warning?

It occurred to him that perhaps the Bringer of Storms had hurled this storm at them from wherever he was at that moment. Benjiah wondered if perhaps he was sitting on some bluff or hilltop near Col Marena, waving that hammer of his in the sky, summoning the power of the heavens. A jagged flash of brilliant lightning ripped horizontally across the sky. The light was so bright, Benjiah had to shield his eyes to keep them from being seared. Following hard upon the heels of the lightning flash was a deep roll of thunder that echoed across the face of the waters and rumbled all around them for two or three times as long as the lightning had been visible.

A second burst of lightning exploded all around them, and as it did, Benjiah tightened his grip on Valzaan's staff. Instantly he felt the pull of *torrim redara,* and he found himself in slow time. The roar of the crashing waves against the ship, the howling of the remarkable winds, and the last echoes of the fading thunder all disappeared from his ears. A striking and eerie silence replaced them all, and he stood beside his motionless uncles and gazed above the *Silver Swan* at the frozen glory of the immobile lightning.

He walked across the no longer rolling deck to the side of the ship, marveling at drops of rain suspended in the air like tiny jewels, and gazed out at the great sea swells about to strike the vessel. He stretched out his hand and felt the cold, still water off the side of the ship as it hung there waiting for the chance to execute this act of aggression. As he withdrew his hand, he looked once more to the heavens and wondered at the power of their enemy to wield such might from so far away.

He is indeed mighty, a voice spoke from within him. Benjiah stood still, gripped by wonder, his hand reaching for the rail beside him to lean upon. *But he is not yet strong enough to cast a storm such as this against you from so great a distance. Do not fear, for this storm is mine. This wind, these clouds, these waves—they do my bidding. He does not yet control them.*

But hear, and know, that the range and realm of his power is growing. The master of the Bringer of Storms has poured much of his remaining power into him to grant him the strength to do these things, power received from my hand at the creation of the world. His grip on this world will grow stronger, and the shadow he is casting over the world will grow darker. So it is and so it must be. Even so, be strong and stand firm, for you are mine, and I am with you.

The voice ceased, and Benjiah felt the pull of real time tugging at him. He looked in vain to the place where he had been standing, remembering Valzaan's warning about getting back to where he had been before the stream of time pulled him back into its flow. There was nothing he could do. He was yanked across the deck of the ship at an incredible speed and flung violently into his original position.

In an instant, the crashing of the waves and the flickering of the lightning resumed. The brilliant light that had illuminated the sky throughout his experience in slow time blinked out and disappeared. The echoing thunder came rolling even more quickly behind it, and the sound seemed to swallow them as it boomed across the waves. Pedraal grabbed Benjiah by his cloak. "Come back below," he shouted. "I want you where it's safe."

Benjiah looked up at his uncle. He had heard the words, but their meaning had hardly registered. The impact of the voice still hung about him, a strange combination of awe and comfort filling him even then. "Are you all right, Benjiah?"

Suddenly Benjiah nodded vigorously, as though released at last to respond. "I'm fine," he yelled over the din. "Everything is going to be fine. This storm won't hurt us."

Pedraal looked quizzically at him through the driving rain. "Maybe not, but I still want you down below."

"All right," Benjiah conceded. Turning from his uncles, he disappeared down below deck.

When Benjiah woke up the following morning, he was relieved to find the ship sailing smoothly. The storm had pounded the ship for hours, keeping Benjiah from falling asleep until well into Second Watch. He lay awake, gripping the mattress on both sides of him as he tilted first one direction then the other. The echoing report of the monstrous peals of thunder made him tremble and shudder, and at one point he loosened his grip on the bed to try to shield his ears.

The dream. He sat up in his bed, suddenly forgetting the storm in the light of this fresh memory. How could he have forgotten, even momentarily? He threw back the covers and leapt out of the bed. The bedding that his uncles used was vacant, so he quickly dressed and exited the small cabin to search for them. They might not know any better than he what to make of his dream, but he had to tell someone.

He found them above, helping to repair a section of the rail on the port side. They explained to Benjiah that a piece of one of the crossbars on the mast had been sheered off by lightning and fell through the rail, taking about a span's worth with it. The men were using some rough-shaped posts and rope to put up a makeshift rail. It was clear to Benjiah that these men might know a lot about war and a little about sailing, but they didn't know much about carpentry.

Benjiah waited patiently, eventually sitting down on the deck at the foot of the broken mast. He ached to discuss the dream, and with every clumsy effort to patch the rail, his frustration grew. At one point he realized he had been running his fingers through his hair repeatedly, and that it was probably standing more or less straight up. Looking around to make sure no one was watching him, he discreetly licked his hands and tried to pat it down.

His uncles eventually finished their project, and he rose quickly to take them aside. They crossed the deck to the starboard rail, far from any other ears on board. Benjiah sat back down, leaned against the rail, and motioned for his uncles to join him on the deck.

"What is it?" Pedraan asked, looking intently at his nephew.

"I had a dream."

Pedraan laughed and leaned forward to pat Benjiah's knee. "It's all right, little Benji. The big nasty storm is gone. See?" He motioned to the relatively calm sky and slight drizzle.

"Good one, Uncle Pedraan," Benjiah said, annoyed.

Pedraal elbowed his brother, probably thinking he was being discreet, but Benjiah saw the quick, sharp blow and saw Pedraan wince as he was struck. "Ignore him, Benjiah. He didn't sleep much last night. He's in a weird mood."

Benjiah continued. "The dream, I don't think it was a normal dream. I think it was, well, a vision of some kind."

“A vision?” Pedraal asked.

“Yeah, or some kind of prophetic dream,” Benjiah added.

Neither of the twins spoke at first, but eventually Pedraal said, “You have our attention, go on.”

“Well, the dream, it was so clear. I’ve had dreams before that felt real, you know, where you wake up and think at first the things in the dream really happened. But this, this was even more real, down to the smallest details, and when I woke up this morning, after a few minutes, it all came back to me, everything.

“I found myself standing in a muddy field. It was raining, just like it has been for weeks, and the ground was soft and squishy under my feet. Ahead of me was a broad river, swollen with floodwaters I think. It had to be. No river in Kirthanin that I’ve ever heard of is that wide. I could hardly make out the far shore, it was so broad. I could, though, see a dragon tower reaching up into the grey sky on the other side, the dark stone towering above the great river and the empty plain.

“As I stood there watching, a solitary windhover came circling down out of the sky. I watched him descend, gracefully swooping in wide arcs, his wings outstretched. He landed in the muddy field and stood in the grass looking at me. Then it started hopping toward the river. I followed it, and it leapt into the sky and flew, then landed a distance away. In that way, in short bursts, it led me to the near side of the river.

“A small boat was caught behind the top of a scraggly tree that had probably at one point been many spans from the bank but now lay mostly underwater. I waded to the boat and climbed in. There was a broken oar in the water beside the boat and one oar intact on the bottom. I took it up and started paddling across the river.

“When I reached the far side, I dragged the small boat up onto dry ground. Turning from the river and boat, I walked through the mud to the foot of the tower. The door was on the opposite side, so I circled around the base until I stood before it. Gazing slowly up to the gyre far above, I heard a voice talking to me. It didn't come from above me or below, or from anywhere outside of me; it came from within. It said, *Light the beacon. Summon the dragons.*

"I stood there before the tower, and the windhover, which had flown ahead of me across the river, landed on my shoulder. I think the voice was Allfather's, and I think he wants me to find a dragon tower and light a beacon to summon the dragons."

Neither Pedraal nor Pedraan spoke or moved. They stared at their nephew. For several moments silence reigned. After a while, Benjiah finally said, "Well, what do you think?"

"I don't know what to think," Pedraan said.

"Yeah, that's a pretty wild dream," Pedraal added. "So, you think the dream was a vision because of the windhover?"

"Yes, in part. The King Falcon made me think of Valzaan. It's more than that, though. It was the voice too."

"You think the voice was Allfather's?"

"Yes."

"Have you heard this voice before, with Valzaan or something?"

"No," Benjiah said, squirming a little.

"Then how do you know it was Allfather's?"

"I don't, I guess, but I have heard it before. Just not with Valzaan."

"What do you mean?"

"I heard it last night in the storm."

"What?" both twins said at the same time. "What do you mean?"

"When we came out on the deck last night, when the second big lightning strike hit, I slipped into *torrim redara.*"

"*Torrim redara,* this slow time that Valzaan taught you about?"

"Yes."

"But," Pedraan said, "we were with you the whole time, and you were only above deck for a moment."

"I know, it happened really fast."

"And this voice spoke to you then?"

"It did." Benjiah told them everything that had happened and everything the voice had spoken.

The twins listened, amazement on their faces. "And this was the voice that spoke to you at the tower."

"This was the voice."

"But I don't understand," Pedraal said. "If Allfather spoke to you, why tell you to light a beacon and summon the dragons? That doesn't make sense. Isn't this what Valzaan told Aljeron to do? To find the Father of Dragons that he might summon his children to our aid?"

"Yes," Benjiah agreed. "I don't know why he would tell me to go to a dragon tower. Maybe we'll need the help of dragons sooner than later. Maybe Aljeron isn't going to find Sulmandir. After all, Valzaan couldn't say for sure that the Golden Dragon is still alive."

"Well," Pedraan chimed in, "even if Allfather is calling you to light a beacon, how will you do that? Are we supposed to abandon Cimaris Rul and take the army of Shalin Bel with us on a quest for a dragon tower?"

"And what about the Grendolai? What if they're still around?" Pedraal said at almost the same time.

"I don't know about any of that," Benjiah answered, shrugging his shoulders. "That's why I told you guys. I don't know what to do. All I know is that this wasn't an ordinary dream."

"No, we believe you about that."

"Maybe—maybe I'm supposed to go alone. I didn't see anyone else with me in the vision."

"You're not going anywhere alone," Pedraan said quickly. "Whatever this means, that won't happen."

"Perhaps," Pedraal said, "we should keep this among the three of us for now. Let's see if some sort of confirmation comes along. Allfather knows that your understanding of your gifts is incomplete. He'll give more guidance when it's time. Until then, we'll wait, but with a willingness to change our plans if He makes that clear. Agreed?"

"Agreed," Benjiah said.

"All right then," Pedraal said, taking a breath. "Looks like keeping an eye on you for your mother may prove more interesting than we thought."

"Sorry about that," Benjiah answered.

"Oh, don't be sorry, Nephew. We like interesting, don't we, Brother?"

"Oh yes, we like interesting. We do indeed. It's dull and dreary that we can't stand."

After a moment Pedraal said, "You know, we don't really have any idea if there are beacons on the dragon towers anymore."

"No, no we don't," Pedraan echoed.

"I guess we'll have to wait and see about that, like the rest of it," Benjiah said.

"Well then," Pedraal said as the three of them stood. "Let's go about our day as usual, but no more keeping things to yourself when you hear strange voices or have prophetic experiences, all right, Nephew?"

"All right," Benjiah conceded, but even as he did, he wondered what he would be able to say if Allfather did confirm that he must seek out a dragon tower alone.

Despite the storm and strange dream, dinner that night was a more relaxed and merry affair than any Benjiah had enjoyed in some time. The twins were jovial as usual, but without the teasing that often characterized their interactions. Benjiah wondered if they hadn't made a conscious decision to be more careful around him. Whatever it was, they seemed to be on their best behavior.

Whether she had decided to honor the twins' attempts at positive social interaction or simply come to dinner in a good mood, Mindarin likewise held herself to a higher standard that evening. She was playful, but without the edge in her jokes that generally cut someone else. All told, the twins' restraint, along with Mindarin's civility, set an entirely different tone, and everyone happily lingered over it far longer than usual.

When they finished, the twins coaxed the friends up on deck. Though the drizzle continued to fall, they had by now gotten more or less used to its constancy and were rather relieved that it was light and there was no sign of storm in any direction.

The twins gathered a pair of stools for the sisters and a handful of barrels for them and Benjiah, and they sat together near the starboard rail, laughing and telling stories. Before long, the twins and Mindarin started sharing tales from their trip to Sulare, and Benjiah and Aelwyn listened.

"Do you remember that night on the *Evening Star?*" Mindarin asked.

"Which night?"

"The night we were all out on deck and Elyas sang his silly song."

"Oh, that night," Pedraan groaned.

"What?" Mindarin asked. "He was hilarious. His songs always were."

"He pranced around like a little peacock," Pedraan said. "He was always doing things like that for the attention of you ladies."

"Well," Mindarin said, mischief in her smile, "he might have. But then again, he didn't go parading around barechested all the time trying to impress us with his manly girth, did he?"

Pedraan blushed as Mindarin went on. "Anyway, whatever his motivation, he amused us all, didn't he?"

"Yes," Pedraal answered. "He provided some light moments in some dark times."

"Poor Bryar," Mindarin said after a moment.

Benjiah knew who Bryar was, but he didn't really know her. He'd heard, of course, in the many stories told of the adventures surrounding his parents' time in Sulare, of the death in Nal Gildoroth of Kelvan, Bryar's love. Elyas, Bryar's brother, played a less prominent role in those stories, but Benjiah knew that he had died early in the war between Shalin Bel and Fel Edorath.

The twins fell quiet, as did Mindarin and Aelwyn, and he turned to survey the ships. Out there, on one of those, Bryar was sailing even now with members of the Shalin Bel scouting corps who were under her command. As his gaze swept over the many sails, he was again struck by the size of this makeshift fleet. Almost three hundred men were on the *Silver Swan,* crowded into three very large rooms below. He and his uncles were in the smaller of the two private cabins, and Mindarin and Aelwyn and a handful of women were in the other. In those ships that stretched into the distance, farther than he could see, thousands more sailed in groups as big as their own and as small as twenty or thirty. They fled certain death in Werthanin, looking for hope in a city most of them had never seen. They followed the commands of a man who wasn't even with them any longer, and held onto the hope that the combined strength of all the cities of Kirthanin might just be enough to stand against the hosts of Malek.

The large ship sailing almost parallel with them on their port side, though some distance away, was the *Sea King,* the largest of their ships, which carried Caan and Gilion. Another ship had come up over the course of the day on their starboard side, but Benjiah didn't know it by name or know what contingent crewed it.

"I've heard Bryar is fearless on the battlefield," Aelwyn said.

"Fearless and reckless," Pedraan said.

"Yes, though she doesn't unnecessarily endanger the lives of her men," Pedraal added. "Only her own."

"Does she want to die?" Aelwyn asked.

Pedraal shrugged. "I don't know. I don't think she cares. Having lost those she loved most, perhaps she doesn't cling to this world as much as the rest of us. At the same time, living to fight another day against Fel Edorath meant having another shot at avenging her brother. Living to fight another day against Malek means having another shot at avenging Kelvan."

Something struck the ship, rocking it toward the port side. The barrels and stools started to slide as the deck listed dramatically. "What is that?" Mindarin cried out as they all struggled to maintain their balance.

They stood and scrambled up the deck, fighting the slant to gain the starboard rail, rising higher and higher before them. Several other men milling around on deck likewise struggled to reach the rail. Suddenly the tilting stopped, and the ship righted itself quickly, throwing many of them down against the deck. Benjiah took hold of the rail and managed to keep his feet.

"By the Mountain!" his uncle whispered. "What is that?"

Benjiah didn't need to ask what "that" was, for a massive dark shape was moving just beneath the surface of the water. It appeared to emerge from underneath the *Silver Swan* and move toward the ship off their starboard side. The figure was almost as wide as the *Silver Swan,* and it extended farther and farther beyond their ship. Then, it started to descend and disappeared beneath the dark waves, which seemed themselves to be almost black in the fading twilight.

"That thing," Benjiah said, "that's what hit us and lifted us out of the water?"

"Looks like it."

"What could do that? What could lift a ship of this size out of the water like that?"

"There are stories," Mindarin said as she stood beside them at the rail, her eyes also locked on the churning waters, "told by the merchants of Suthanin, of something awful in the waters of the Southern Ocean near Cimaris Rul. But I've not heard of anything up here, just two weeks from the Bay of Thalasee and Col Marena."

"Well," Pedraan said, "the stories may not have mentioned anything awful this far north, but that looked like something awful all right."

"Where did it go?" Benjiah asked, growing uneasy.

"I don't know," Pedraal answered quietly, and for a long moment, they stood at the rail, searching the waters for any sign of movement.

Benjiah lifted his eyes and saw two great black hands shoot out of the water and take hold of the ship sailing alongside them. "There!" He pointed at the staggering sight.

The hand visible to them on the near side of the ship was enormous, and Benjiah thought each finger must have been almost the size of a man. They grasped the rail of the ship and ripped downward, tearing not just the rail but a large chunk out of the side of the ship. Aelwyn screamed, and the sound of her cry echoed in Benjiah's ears as he watched water begin to pour into the gaping hole.

Men were scurrying around on the deck but without any clear purpose. Benjiah felt their helplessness and desperation. Turning to Pedraal, he said, "Suruna. I'll get Suruna and take a shot at him if he surfaces again."

Pedraal grabbed him by his sleeve. "Suruna can't do them or us any good. Grab Valzaan's staff instead."

Benjiah ran across the deck and dropped hard into the hold. Valzaan's staff was resting beside his bed in the little cabin. He grabbed it and quickly returned above deck. He looked in dismay at what was left of the ship. It had been broken in half while he was below deck, and both bow and stern were sinking rapidly. Men clung to the flotsam and thrashed wildly in the sea.

Benjiah ran to the side of the *Silver Swan* and raised the staff. He held it aloft, praying to Allfather for something, for anything that might protect those men or hamper the creature. He waited—hoping, praying—but nothing happened. Nothing happened inside of him. Nothing happened with the staff. Nothing happened at all. Slowly, he lowered it.

"I'm sorry," he whispered.

"Don't be, it isn't your fault," Pedraal answered.

Pedraan was at his brother's side. "We have to get this ship turned toward shore. Who knows where that thing is or what it intends."

Pedraal was already moving across the deck. "For shore! For shore! We make for shore!"

Men were running in every direction. They worked the sail and rigging as the great ship slowly began to arc to the left, heading toward Kirthanin. Fortunately, someone on the *Sea King* had seen enough to know something happened, and that ship was also turning slowly. Benjiah looked astern at the ships trailing them and wondered how long it would take and how hard it would be to get every ship moving ashore.

He turned back to the starboard rail as the wreck of the ship whose name he did not know continued to spread across the water. Boards and barrels floated on the rising waves, but the men were disappearing. Where perhaps a hundred men had been thrashing about in the water, he could now see only fifty at most. As he stared in horror, they continued to dwindle in number. Man after man disappeared from sight, not slowly as a result of fatigue, but suddenly and entirely, swallowed whole by the sea.

"Allfather have mercy," he whispered as they disappeared. "What could this thing be?"

"Another nightmare unleashed upon us from the depths of Malek's dark mind," Mindarin replied evenly.

"A nightmare from out of the deep," Benjiah muttered. "A nightmare that controls the seas."

6 A CHANGE OF PLANS

BENJIAH SAT ON THE WET SAND of the beach in the darkness, gazing out at the dim outline of the ships, anchored or grounded, as far as he could see. It had been dark for hours, but still the smaller boats ferried to and from the larger ships, which had come in as far as they could, depending upon the size of the ship and weight of its load.

Not far away from him, Mindarin and Aelwyn gathered with the women they had brought from Shalin Bel. There were at least a hundred in the assembly, and that was enough. Benjiah did not turn to look at them. He was annoyed at his uncles for telling him to stay ashore when they took charge of a midsize landing boat and set out to help unload men and supplies. He was also annoyed at Mindarin for offering to "watch" him, as though he were a child in need of babysitting. He would be seventeen years old come Summer Rise. He had seen the face of battle twice now. He was a prince as well as a prophet. He was as skilled with the bow as any man in the army. He did not need to be entrusted to anyone for safekeeping, least of all this son- and husband- and brother-deprived horde of women looking for a man to take care of.

Begrudgingly, he had to admit his uncles' reasoning was sound. While Benjiah's help lifting and loading would have been welcome, more people in the boat only meant more trips, and there were enough of those already. He was still a little dazed by how quickly it had been decided to abandon the ships, but when it became clear that no fewer than four ships and several hundred men were unaccounted for, few were willing to return to the sea, though no one particularly wanted to make the rest of the journey on foot or on horseback, either.

And so the unloading had begun. No one could guess at how long it would take. Unloading at a harbor with the proper equipment would have been one thing, but unloading in water of varied depths at varying distances from shore from decks of unequal height was something no one could quite wrap their minds around. As soon as one problem was realized, discussed, and addressed, three more had arisen. It seemed likely that the unloading would proceed through the night and into the next day, and perhaps on into the following night.

Benjiah looked down at the things lying in the sand beside him. Suruna was there with his quiver, packed with arrows, most of them cyranic. Next to Suruna was Valzaan's staff. He looked at the staff, the carved windhover on top facing him. Again he wondered, as he had a half a dozen times since he'd raised it aboard the *Silver Swan,* if there was no power in the staff, why had it been entrusted to him? What was he doing, lugging this thing around with the rest of his gear, if it was little more than an ornamental stick? He missed Valzaan, that was true, but he did not need the staff to remember the prophet.

He ran his fingers along the smooth, pristine staff. Deep down, he knew he was being unfair. Whatever Valzaan had not yet had time to teach him, Benjiah had learned enough to know that Allfather controlled the prophet, not the prophet Allfather. If *torrim redara* and some of the other prophetic endowments were not fully in his control, especially at so early a stage in his development, how could he expect to wield Allfather's power with Valzaan's staff at will? He didn't even know how Valzaan had done it. Could Valzaan somehow summon a portion of Allfather's power in moments of great need? Had Allfather somehow directed Valzaan in the manner and method of the staff's usage each time, so that even he had been dependent on Allfather to wield the staff with power? Benjiah had no idea. All he knew for sure was that he could not cast great balls of light or waves of power from the staff. He had been unable to harm the enemy or save the men in the water. Whatever service he might one day be able to offer these soldiers, he could do nothing this time. They stood watching just as helplessly as he had, but he felt more responsible and more of a failure. It was just the kind of moment that called for Valzaan, and with Valzaan gone, it called for him. It called for him, and he was found wanting.

Benjiah stood, shaking the clumpy, wet sand from his cloak. He walked down the beach to the water. Even though the night air was cold, he slipped his boots off and stepped barefoot into the receding waves. The feel of the water and sand slipping away beneath his feet relaxed him, even as a new wave splashed his ankles. He tried to envision the water warm and the sun bright overhead, but it was difficult. It had been so long since he'd seen the sun shining in the sky, it almost seemed like the sun itself was a dream. All he knew anymore was cloud and rain and dreariness, day after day.

He looked out at the dark water and wondered if the creature was gone. As far as anyone could tell, in the space of a single hour or so, it had taken down four of their ships. And yet there were no further reports of it or of damage being done to any of their vessels. Perhaps it had gone away, or perhaps it had accomplished its goal: to steer the ships ashore.

The thought that the creature might be purposeful unnerved Benjiah. He didn't like to think that the beast was anything more than a monster of the deep, an unthinking machine of destruction. The possibility that it was guided by intelligence, its own or someone else's, was most unpleasant. And yet it all seemed to make sense. The Bringer of Storms was manipulating the weather, calling rain from the heavens all day long and all through the night. Was it coincidence that this new beast of Malek's had surfaced, literally, within the past year or so, depending on which of the countless stories he believed? Benjiah thought not. He couldn't fit all of the pieces together, but any doubt he held began to fade. The ceaseless rain and the creature from the deep were connected. Malek planned a new assault on Kirthanin, and he would assert his control over the waters of both sea and sky.

"Are you coming to the council?" Pedraal asked.

"Of course," Pedraan answered, looking up from his seat.

"You all right?"

"I'm tired, brother," Pedraan replied, his normal good humor wholly absent from his manner.

"Is that it?"

Pedraan looked at his brother and smiled. "No hiding it from you, I guess."

"No," Pedraal said, "guess not."

"I miss her, Pedraal. All these years I've wasted, waiting for who knows what, and here I am, far from home and far from her and quite possibly never to see her again. I'm so stupid."

"Don't beat yourself up. You were doing what you thought was right at the time."

"That's little consolation now."

"I know, I'm just saying you're not stupid. No man is stupid for doing what he believes is right. I admire you."

Pedraan looked at Pedraal closely. "You admire me?"

"Sure. I know how much you love her, and yet you showed restraint. That couldn't have been easy."

"It wasn't."

"See, and even more admirable, you came clean with her, told her how you felt, and even admitted that maybe you didn't get it right."

Pedraan didn't say anything, so Pedraal continued. "Just don't give up on seeing home again. Don't give up on seeing her."

"I haven't. Not really. It's just always so grey, so dark. It brings me down."

"I know, but hang in there. We'll get through this. We've got to. I've got to see Benjiah home, and you have to make it back for Karalin. We'll just go one day at a time, one battle at a time, one problem at a time. We'll make it."

Pedraan nodded.

"Ready to go?" Pedraal asked.

"All right." Pedraan stood up wearily, his body aching. "Let's go."

The council of the captains was quiet, and no one moved to speak first. Their options were few. Guessing that they were somewhere near the Taralin Forest, they could not head inland. They would have to go south along the coast, heading that way to Col Marena. It would be a long trek.

"Caan, if I may," Sarneth said in his deep and resonant voice that Benjiah still found unnerving. Though his words were soft and soothing, there was something like a growl woven into the fabric of his speech.

"Yes, of course, Sarneth," Caan answered. "Your counsel would be most welcome."

"We did not seek this change of plans, and yet it has come. We do not desire to head south over land, and yet we must. Perhaps this creature's attack in this place is not coincidental."

"You think this a trap of Malek's?" Gilion asked.

"No, though that is possible," Sarneth answered. "My thoughts were actually tending more the other direction."

"What?" Brenim exclaimed, incredulous. "You think the destruction of four of our ships and the gruesome death of hundreds of our men is really some bizarre form of divine guidance? You think that creature is an agent of Allfather's instead of Malek's?"

"I am suggesting that Allfather was not caught by surprise by this creature's attack. I am suggesting that Allfather can overrule the machinations of the Master of the Forge if he so desires. I am suggesting that Malek's evil intent can play a part in bringing to pass what Allfather has ordained and desires."

"Allfather desires this?"

"Allfather did not kill these men, but Allfather could use the destructive rampage of this thing to provide us with an opportunity."

"I follow the theory in what you are saying," Caan said, "but I don't see the opportunity you are speaking of. What do you mean?"

"I mean the Taralin Forest."

"What about it?"

"I told you all when I agreed to come south that I would seek an opportunity to raise the aid and succor of the Great Bear. This seems to me to be just such a time. The army will take some time to organize and head south along the beach, and as has already been pointed out, the going will not be fast. I will head into the wood and seek out the draal of Taralin. I have not traveled here in many, many years, but I am not unknown in the Taralindraal. I will lay our plight before them and see if they will send us any aid. When I have an answer, I will meet you at the southern tip of Taralin, just far enough inland for your army to encamp in relative shelter and security."

The men and women gazed at one another after Sarneth finished, and Benjiah could see the excitement he felt reflected in their faces. For the first time since Valzaan's death, Benjiah felt real hope. If the Great Bear sent aid, maybe even an army, then that would be help indeed.

Caan smiled and then laughed. Smiles broke out on faces all around. "Sarneth, if the elders of Taralindraal decide to aid us, then I am quite willing to consider our landing here a most fortuitous event. How soon will you go?"

"I will go immediately, but I do not think I will go alone."

The smile on Caan's face slipped momentarily, replaced by puzzlement. "But are not men forbidden in the draal?"

"They are, but if the elders of Taralindraal send aid, many things will need to change. I will bring a man with me, so that those who have hidden deep within the forest for the better part of the Third Age will be reminded that we are not alone in this world. I want them to see who is already fighting this war."

"Who do you want to go?" Caan asked.

"Benjiah."

"If Benjiah goes, we're going," Pedraan said quickly.

"Only Benjiah may come," Sarneth answered. "I don't know if they will allow me into the draal with one man, but I am sure they will forbid me with more than one."

"Why Benjiah?" Caan asked.

"Because he is young and carries Valzaan's staff. His story and his youth may soften the elders, and the staff and the emblem on it is known in all the draals. His connection to Valzaan can only help."

"Benjiah?" Caan asked, and now all eyes turned upon him.

"I will go," Benjiah said, trying to conceal his eagerness. To travel with Sarneth into the forest and possibly find admittance to one of the draals seemed almost too good to be true.

"Very well then," Caan answered. "It is settled. Benjiah will gather his things and accompany you. When the army is ready, it will head along the beach to the southern edge of Taralin Forest, and there we will camp far enough inland to be out of sight of prying eyes from the sea. We will wait there for you; do not be long."

"We will be only as long as we need to be," Sarneth said. "But I do not think you need to worry about us. Traveling the secret ways through Taralin will help, and whatever the elders of the draal decide, we will know their answer soon enough."

Benjiah tightened his pack on the horse. He checked to make sure Suruna and Valzaan's staff were secure, then turned to his uncles.

"Well," he said, "I didn't see this coming when I got up today."

"No," Pedraan answered. "Indeed not."

"I wouldn't let you out of my sight for anything but this," Pedraal added. "We're here to keep you safe, and goodness knows there probably isn't anywhere in this world safer than traveling through Taralin Forest under the care of a Great Bear like Sarneth. You'll be safer in there than we'll be out here, so I can't really object."

"I'm not worried about my safety," Benjiah responded.

"What do you mean?"

"I mean, Sarneth is taking me as the representative of the men of Kirthanin, what do I do? He's taking me as the one who now bears Valzaan's staff, so again, what do I do? You see? I don't know how to be mankind's envoy or Valzaan's successor."

"Ah, I see," Pedraal said, nodding.

"Look, Nephew," Pedraan said, exchanging a serious look with Pedraal. "Don't worry. Allfather's hand is on you; we can see it. The others can too. Just go. He'll show you what to do or say when the time is right."

"I'm not sure if that really comforts me a whole lot right now."

"Well, it's the best we can do, so you'll just have to take it for what it is worth. We can't go with you, but we'll see you when you come out."

Benjiah hugged his uncles, each in turn, and he mounted the horse. Turning from them, he rode to the place where Sarneth waited on the edge of the beach, where the grass gave way to the coarse, reedlike grass. He carried nothing but the enormous staff, which he carried everywhere on his back.

"Are you ready?" Sarneth asked.

"Yes."

"You know I traveled many years ago with your father when he went to the Forbidden Isle and beyond, don't you?"

"I do."

"We traveled in Lindan Wood then."

"I know."

"I could sense the hand of Allfather on your father, Benjiah. I can sense it on you too. You are like him, very much so."

Benjiah did not answer at first, but slowly he nodded. "Thanks, Sarneth. I hope I am."

"You are. You'll be fine."

"I hope so."

"Just follow me," Sarneth said as he turned and started ambling on all fours through the grass.

Benjiah spurred his horse on and set out after him toward the trees in the distance. He looked back over his shoulder at the men gathered on the beach. As far as he could see, men moved about, gathering and packing supplies for the trip south. He would miss his uncles, but he would see them again soon enough. He turned back around and set his eyes on the Great Bear moving into the forest.

Gazing out over the grasslands of northern Suthanin, rain-drenched and soggy under an interminably grey sky, Rulalin thought the expanse might be the most beautiful thing he had ever seen. Mud, gloom, and the endless march were not as appealing as a warm bed in a cozy house, but they were better than struggling through the stinking marshes. He looked over his shoulder northward at the southern rim of the Erefen Marshes, which looked like a vast tidal pool with a shallow layer of water everywhere, covering even the thin stretches of semisolid ground that wove erratically through the mire and bog. Four days they had struggled through the marshland, and without a doubt it was the most dismal place in all Kirthanin.

For five days after withdrawing from Col Marena, they waited while the Malekim left behind in Shalin Bel were sent for. Those five days, sleeping on the slightly less damp ground beneath a small grove of trees, seemed now like a haven of rest and relief unparalleled in Rulalin's memory. There had been no riding, no fighting, no stumbling or wading through putrid swamp water, only time to sit under the trees and think.

Time to sit and think held its own kind of danger, and normally Rulalin would have been vigilant to keep himself from obsessing over some risk or mistake he was just about to make or had just made. Strangely enough, he found himself free of self-doubt and inner turmoil this time. He didn't know why, but he felt sure it was somehow related to the trees. Though Winter Rise had come and the weather was cold, these trees had not yet lost their brown and wrinkled leaves. They hung tenaciously to their branches like mothers clinging to their newborn children. Above the leaves, the cloud-filled sky was nevertheless infused with the light of the long-hidden sun, and that sunlight, though scant and filtered through layers of cloud and droplets of rain, carried the memory of its source.

On the fourth day of his rest beneath those trees, Rulalin looked up into that sky and imagined the bright and shining sun far above the clouds, beyond what his eyes could see. As he did, for the first time since arriving in the Mountain, Rulalin found himself desperately hoping, even praying, for Malek's failure and defeat. He had realized the task of resisting and defeating Malek would not be easy. Even so, when he made his decision to leave Fel Edorath with Soran and Tashmiren and travel to the Mountain, he found the idea that Malek might fall (and Rulalin with him) distressing, if unlikely. At the same time, he was unable to embrace his new allegiance as readily as Soran apparently had, and the result was an almost unbearable tension. He wanted Malek to win so he could live. He wanted Malek to win so he could triumph over Aljeron and see his longtime enemy thrown down. He wanted Malek to win so he could behold Wylla again and deliver her from death at Malek's hand.

Now, though, he felt free. Free of what, exactly, he couldn't say, just free. He was no longer in the Mountain, entombed in the darkness of Malek's subterranean world. He was no longer pinned behind the walls of his city, watching his people starve while they waited for his death or capture. He was sitting beneath the trees, the cold rain dripping off the leaves and splattering upon his upturned face. He wasn't going back to Fel Edorath again. He wasn't going back to the Mountain again. He would fall on the battlefield or take Wylla north to Nolthanin with Farimaal, but he wouldn't ever go back to either of his former prisons.

He now felt free from any obligation to wish Malek or his cause well. Rulalin would do his part as faithfully as necessary in order to survive, but he would do no more. He had made his choice, and he needed to serve his new master. To fail Farimaal would be to risk Soran's life, and the lives of the men of Fel Edorath who followed him. Even worse, to fail Malek would mean to endanger his plan and hope to save Wylla. For her sake, if not for his own, he would not betray his odious allegiance. Even so, if defeat found Malek on the battlefield, Rulalin would not weep for his own ruin.

He was resigned. To live and survive and see Malek conquer all would be to see Wylla again. To die in defeat and see Malek thrown down once and for all would be to see the clouds parted and the sun restored, to see light and life return to Kirthanin. Those two things were all he now hoped for. To have both was more than he could imagine, but if things went very well, he might well see one or the other.

When the Malekim rejoined them and they set off for the northern border of the Erefen Marshes to pass through, he wondered if leaving the peaceful little grove would affect his newfound peace, but it didn't. For three days they traveled toward Erefen, and with each new day he found his frame of mind unchanged. Even Soran commented on his new attitude, expressing great relief that Rulalin had at last accepted and embraced their change of circumstance. Rulalin didn't bother to try to correct his young friend, for in a manner of speaking he had. It didn't matter if Soran didn't really understand what had happened within him, and the truth might have been alarming. So Rulalin rode on, to the marshland and into it, no longer fearing what tomorrow brought but simply rising to face it.

Four days in the Erefen Marshes, however, was sufficient to put Rulalin's happier outlook on hold. In ordinary weather, there would have been zigzags of dry ground running through the marshes, in many places wide enough for wagons to maneuver, though often long and circuitous. In these days of unending rain, however, these paths were all but hidden to the naked eye, and the long, slow train of giants, Malekim, wagons, and horses crawled at a snail's pace. They followed the careful leading of the giants, for whom a misstep into one of the deeper bogs or fens would not be fatal. Even so, many wagons and horses and not a few men were lost when a wrong step took them astray and swallowed them up. There was no place to sleep had they wanted to, and Rulalin was so bone weary that he began to believe that even death would be better than this if it would afford a bit of rest.

One of the things Rulalin most wanted to leave behind was the eerie nightlife. Erefen seemed to come alive after dark, as the pale forms of shimmering water snakes reflected the dim torchlight of the long, slow processional. It sometimes seemed to Rulalin that the surface of the marshes was but one large, slithering mass, but with each new morning, the evidence would disappear almost before First Hour. What's more, the deeper they moved into the heart of the marshes, the more the place came alive. By the second night, Rulalin was also keenly aware of strange, deep red, luminescent water bugs that scooted across the surface of the water like a thousand swarming flies on the carcass of a dead animal. They skated and slid across the surface in seemingly random patterns and dispersed only when the much larger water snakes glided through their midst. He imagined that in their own way they were perhaps beautiful, but they made his skin crawl as he rode through them. On the third night he scanned the marshland and saw untold millions of these swarming creatures illuminating every direction with an eerie red glow. He thought back to the night he had camped just south of Elnin Wood on his way to Sulare and the millions of Azaruul butterflies they had seen that night, their fragile green wings fluttering over the field. That was a grand display of delicacy and beauty. This, he thought, was a horrible place, and he wanted nothing more than to be out.

And then they were. They were out. Their sojourn in the marshes had come to an end over an hour ago, and though he longed to drop where he was and sleep, he knew that they would not stop until the hindmost part of their column had emerged onto solid ground. When that moment came, he would gladly slide down from his saddle and not care if he ever got up again.

The next evening, Rulalin's conversation with Soran was the most lively it had been since their brief reprieve following their departure from Col Marena. They talked about many things, and Rulalin even waxed philosophical on the particular effects on the psyche of being raised in Fel Edorath. Soran sat for most of the evening and listened, apparently enjoying Rulalin's uncharacteristic openness and transparency.

Still, Rulalin's character had not undergone a total transformation, and after a while, his own ruminations ended his willingness to talk about himself. He eventually laid down the topic and retreated into his more common contemplative silence. Soran, though, would not be deterred. He, like Rulalin, had been burdened by the long, slow drudgery of Erefen, and a question had burned in him for many days, a question he now put to his commanding officer.

"What do you make of this rain? I know we have talked about it before, but I was wondering if you've had any more ideas about its purpose?"

"No." Rulalin shook his head, tilting his face skyward as though to find a clue.

"All that time in Erefen, it felt like all I could think of was the water."

"And?"

"You remember how we wondered if it might have a military purpose of some kind?"

"Yes?"

"Well, I just can't see it. Every effect the rain has on our enemy, it also has on us, perhaps even more so since they slipped out to sea, and here we are having to make the trek overland."

"I know." Rulalin nodded. "It occurred to me that perhaps the purpose is more psychological than physical. Maybe all the darkness and gloom is supposed to wear down our resistance."

"Ours?"

"No, not as in you or me. You know what I mean. The resistance of all those who oppose him, of all the men in all the cities of Kirthanin, which included us and Fel Edorath until recently."

"Well," Soran said, "it certainly is depressing, all this rain and darkness."

Rulalin nodded. Soran said, "I hadn't considered that aspect, the psychological impact, but I did have a theory about the water."

"Yes?"

Soran sat forward, and Rulalin could see the eagerness on his face. "Maybe it isn't the rain that's so important. Maybe it's what the rain is supposed to do."

"Meaning?"

"Meaning this: We were wondering what direct impact all the rain might have on battle, on marching or trying to mount a defense against Malek. We were trying to figure out how the rain could advance Malek's immediate military cause. But maybe that isn't the point. Maybe the rain and all the mud and stuff is just the price we all have to pay to do something bigger."

"Soran," Rulalin said, "why don't you just tell me what you think all this rain is for."

"Water levels. Passing through Erefen gave me the idea. Maybe Malek wants to raise the water levels of Kirthanin. Maybe he means to destroy the coastal cities, places like Col

Marena, Cimaris Rul, and Kel Imlaris. I don't know, but that's what I was thinking."

Rulalin looked intently at Soran, who was watching him to see how he would react to this theory. He thought about the water covering even the dry ground in Erefen, and the increasing frequency with which they passed large and growing pools of water in depressions in the landscape. There might be something to the theory.

An image flashed through his head. A memory buried so deep, he hadn't thought of it in years, but he had a deep and unsettling feeling that there was a connection between the memory and Soran's theory.

"What is it?" Soran asked.

"Just a memory, but I don't know if it is important."

"What is it?"

"Years ago, when I was on the Forbidden Isle, we entered Nal Gildoroth. While we were there, some of our number descended into a deep, subterranean chamber. I stayed above with the others, but when they came up, they told us of an enormous room with a saltwater pool. Some dark creature, a creation of Malek's they thought, lived in that pool. Maybe that thing was made for this rain? Maybe it was a prototype of some new army he's been breeding to attack from the sea?"

Soran stared, taking in Rulalin's words. "Can you imagine?" he said. "Another creature, another weapon, another reason Malek won't be defeated and will rule over this world."

Rulalin shrugged. "I wouldn't take it too far; it's just a memory. There might be no connection between that and this at all."

"There might not be," Soran said. "Maybe we'll find out when we get to the coast."

"Maybe we will."

Rulalin looked across the open courtyard. To his surprise, the moon hung large and glorious on this clear, cloudless night, its rays illuminating everything. A large fountain dominated the courtyard, its water cast high into the warm summer night, each drop sparkling in the glow of the moonlight as it fell back into the fountain's pool. Rulalin smiled to see the young girl sitting beside it, dangling her legs in the water. Excited to see her, Rulalin crossed the courtyard to speak to her.

As he drew nearer, she looked up and smiled at him. Rulalin felt the flutter in his stomach that she had caused since the first time he saw her. Already at sixteen, she was breathtakingly beautiful. Her long, dark hair draped her shoulders, and her smile was as luminous as the moonlight. Despite the smile, her eyes betrayed a deep and piercing sadness. He felt stupid for forgetting that her father had only recently died, and he felt ghoulish for wearing such an eager smile in the time of her mourning. He tried to smile more soberly, but he did not know what to say.

A sound distracted him, and he turned away from Wylla and the pool. The courtyard bathed in moonlight vanished. Behind him now was a long and lovely stretch of snow trees, their full white blossoms dropping silky-soft petals to the ground in the late afternoon sun.

Wylla was also there. She stood in a long white dress with delicately embroidered sleeves and ornate cuffs that contrasted with the otherwise simple design of her clothing. The sides of her hair were pulled back around her head and tied over the remainder as it fell straight down her back between her shoulder blades. Her slender hands, clasped together, rested at her waist.

Again she smiled at him, and he adored her as the white petals fell in her hair and came to rest on her shoulders and smooth, bare neck. Rulalin checked himself to make sure there were no silly grins on his face this time and, trying to project a warm and friendly greeting, walked slowly through the snow trees toward her, ignoring the tickle of the petals as they fluttered against his face. Wylla waited, and as he approached, he was happy to see that the piercing sadness was gone.

There was kindness in those eyes, and he felt like a flower before the sun. And yet, even as he stopped before her, just an arm's reach away, he could see something else there. Not sadness, now, but something worse. Wariness. She was uncertain and wondering what he was going to say and do. He felt his attempt at a warm and friendly greeting failing. He felt desperation and deep need welling up within him. She had to see that there was no need to be wary and uncertain. She had to see how he saw her. She had to see him as he saw her.

Again, a sound behind him made him turn. The snowtrees were gone, and the newly rising sun hung low over the Southern Ocean. He stood at the top of the wide beach, smooth sand between him and the waves. Wylla stood down by the water. This time, though, she was not facing him, and she was not alone. Beside her stood Joraiem, the ocean breeze lifting his shoulder-length blond hair. They were barefooted, and the water washed in over their toes.

They held hands as they looked out to sea, but Rulalin started down the beach toward them anyway. It occurred to him that he would be interrupting, but he was drawn. He could not turn away.

As he drew nearer, they turned. To his surprise, there was no annoyance or anger at his intrusion, but both smiled broadly at his approach. Rulalin looked first at Wylla, whose smile was as warm as it had been by the fountain and under the snow trees, but it was different yet again. This time, it was distinguished by what it lacked. It was happy, only happy. There was no sadness and no uncertainty. There was only fulfillment and joy.

He blushed and looked from her to Joraiem, who likewise greeted him with a friendly smile. For a long time Rulalin stood there in the sand, looking almost blankly at Joraiem, whose smile did not waver and who did not move. When he could bear it no longer, Rulalin dropped his gaze and stared at his feet. He knew that they watched him, but he could not look up. He could not look up, because he knew the shame in his heart showed in his face. He could not bear for either of them to see it.

With under an hour of light left to march, they came upon a narrow east-west road stretching across the wide plain. Rulalin rode his horse up onto it, just to the west of the column, and stopped. Soran rode up beside him, but before he could ask what Rulalin was doing, Rulalin spoke. "I think this is the road to Dal Harat."

"Where?"

"Dal Harat. It's a small village in northwestern Suthanin. It is where Joraiem Andira came from."

Soran didn't say anything.

"He was a good man, Joraiem. I liked him almost instantly. One of the first nights we spent in each other's company, we were stuck in a terrible little inn in Vol Tumian, a small town on the Barunaan River where riverboat captains stop between Peris Mil and Cimaris Rul. We sat beside the river and talked.

"He had just suffered a loss. The girl he loved back home, who probably still lives down this road somewhere"—Rulalin pointed west—"had just told him she was promised to someone else."

Rulalin sat on his horse and stared. "I don't remember her name," he whispered. "I used to remember it."

Soran remained quiet.

"I thought he stole my love from me."

"Didn't he?"

"I thought so, and I hated him for it. I thought of all people, he should understand." Rulalin squinted westward through the steady rain. "But it was I who didn't understand. Wylla wasn't mine. I loved her, but I had no claim on her, except that which my heart fabricated. Joraiem stole nothing. I know that now. There was no malice in him, none."

Rulalin turned back to Soran. "Go on ahead. I'll catch up."

Soran obeyed. He crossed the road and rejoined the column, headed south across the wet, grassy plain.

Rulalin turned west again. "You were a good man, Joraiem, a better man than I." Looking over the opposite shoulder and gazing east over the heads of the marching men, he added, "I'll take care of her if I can and shelter her from the coming storm, but I'm sorry, Joraiem. I'm sorry."

HUNTED

THE HORSE ALJERON HAD BEEN riding since disembarking in Avram Gol was light grey with a whitish swirl around its neck and face. In the light flurries that had been with them over the last ten days or so, the horse seemed to melt into its surroundings. As Aljeron stood beside Evrim, who was kneeling in the snow perhaps half a hand thick, he gazed back at their two horses and contemplated again the extent to which his own horse blended in with the world. Evrim's horse was light brown with hints of red in his mane and tail, a stark juxtaposition against the snowy landscape.

"I don't know," Evrim said at last. He stood and shook his head. His eyes were still focused on the slight depression of snow at his feet. Aljeron had been stopping anytime he saw something that might constitute an animal track or some other evidence of life. This particular spot was so large that if it was a track of some kind, it belonged to something big. He wondered if it might represent something else. Maybe something heavy rested on the ground here for a time. He didn't know, but he took to heart both Cinjan's warnings and the universal testimony of those who had raised him that danger and death were what one could expect from a sojourn in Nolthanin.

"It might be evidence that something large passed this way; it might not. I can't read the ground here. If it's a track, the wind has blown loose snow over it for hours, smoothing out the ridges and imprints until nothing distinct remains. I'm sorry."

"No need to be sorry," Aljeron said. "All we can do is check. It isn't your fault there isn't anything here to tell us a story. Maybe that's a good thing anyway."

"Maybe it is."

They walked back toward their horses. Koshti, who had been sitting in the snow nearby, rose and trotted along beside them. Arintol and Erigan likewise sat, their hind legs drawn inward to balance themselves as they surveyed the wide, white plain that stretched to the horizon. Some distance away, Synoki and Cinjan remained in their saddles, having not bothered to dismount when Aljeron halted their progress a quarter of an hour ago.

Saegan, however, and the two younger men of Shalin Bel, Karras and Tornan, never failed to make the most of Aljeron's every pause. They always dismounted, always drew swords, and always drilled. They had been delighted to find that Saegan was willing to train and to teach them advanced lessons in swordsmanship. Fear at the prospect of a journey through the Nolthanin waste seemed to have dissipated with their peaceful exodus from Avram Gol two weeks ago and the beginning of their private lessons that same day.

Now they stood side by side, opposite Saegan, and Aljeron smiled to see Caan's former pupil assuming the role of master, passing on the same lessons they had learned side by side in the battle ring at Sulare. He paused beside his horse, watching the lesson, and noted that both Karras and Tornan showed marked signs of improvement. Saegan was a good teacher, very good. He would make an excellent instructor for the Summerland, should such a position ever be needed again.

That thought stayed with him as he swung up into his saddle. If things went badly in this war against Malek, there would of course be no Summerland left to go to, and no Novaana left to go. For surely if Malek conquered all Kirthanin, he would deal with the Novaana first. Why leave the authority structure intact? No, whatever might happen to the average citizen, the Novaana would not survive Malek's tyranny.

And yet, it occurred to him that if the war against Malek went well, so well that Malek was slain and his forces fully defeated, there might still be no need for the role that Caan had played in Sulare. If Malek were gone and the threat to Kirthanin removed, what need would there be for martial training at all? Learning the history and politics of Kirthanin might still be valuable, as studying the sea and stars would be, so Master Berin and Ulmindos and their successors might long have a place in Sulare, but why would Caan's services be necessary any longer?

It was odd to think of young men not learning the use of the blade, but it was also a little presumptuous to envision a world without Malek when Malek was still very much with them. There was plenty of work ahead for every man and sword in Kirthanin, whatever fancies he entertained to the contrary.

"Let's mount up, Saegan," Aljeron called.

The two young soldiers, their eagerness to practice their skills matched by their desire to earn Aljeron's good favor, sheathed their swords instantly and jogged to their horses. Tornan moved more slowly than Karras, still showing the tenderness of his wound, though it had been healing well. The two boys who had cowered in that burned-out building in Col Marena were growing up. They were becoming men and soldiers.

"So, we're ready to move out again, are we?" Cinjan said.

"Yes, we are," Aljeron answered. Though he ignored it, he could hear that faint tone in Cinjan's voice again. Perhaps it was irritation, perhaps condescension. Whatever it was, Aljeron didn't like it. He was used to being obeyed and respected, and his dislike for this friend of Synoki's grew.

With Cinjan and Synoki riding together at the fore, they set out, riding briskly through the early afternoon. It was only the eighteenth of Winter Rise, but the days were growing very short. Darkness fell now before the start of Twelfth Hour, and even if they rode hard, they would cover only a few more leagues before dark. They hadn't been able to find a place to camp last night that afforded them any shelter, and Aljeron knew they might not again. Still, as much as he preferred riding and sleeping in the snow to riding and sleeping in the rain, he wouldn't have minded finding somewhere even remotely dry that night.

He looked down at Koshti running through the snow. Flecks of white lodged in his orange and black fur. It appeared that the rate at which new flakes fell upon him was roughly equal to the rate his body heat melted away the ones already there. Even so, his long, powerful strides across the bare, white landscape were also beautiful. His coat was already thicker and fuller than it had been when they departed Col Marena. The difference was no doubt imperceptible to all eyes but his own, but he knew Koshti's fur as well as he knew his own skin. When he rubbed Koshti's back at night to please his battle-brother and warm his own hands, he felt the difference. They might run through snow all the way to Harak Andunin, but Koshti would remain to the end, warmer and more comfortable than them all.

The faster they rode, the faster the flurries seemed to swirl. Though Aljeron knew it was an illusion, he tried to focus on the fluttering flakes whirling around Synoki and Cinjan. The patterns of small white dots falling downward, only to swoop up into the air again as they swept by, was almost mesmerizing. He tipped his head back and looked at the snowflakes retreating into the sky as though to avoid being trampled by him and his horse, and he thought about how beautiful the snow was.

He had always thought snow beautiful, but it struck him now as an ironic reality. The rain that had blanketed them for weeks was a machination of the enemy, hurled at them somehow by that hammer-brandishing son of Vulsutyr. Presumably, this snowfall was connected to that same storm. And yet, even while they rode through this lonely, desolate, and cursed land, under a dark and foreboding sky, pursued every step of the way by this unnatural storm, he was surrounded by beauty. The loveliness of snow as Allfather had created it was not diminished by the fact it fell at the direction of the Bringer of Storms upon a long-forsaken land.

He looked over his shoulder at Saegan and Evrim riding side by side a few spans back. Slowing his pace, he fell in beside them. They slowed a bit as he did, both no doubt wondering if he was going to ask them to stop again. He leaned over toward Saegan, who was closest. "Even if Nolthanin is cursed, this place is beautiful in the snow."

Neither Evrim nor Saegan reacted visibly to his statement, but after a moment, Saegan said, "Indeed, but nature is always loveliest right before it tries to kill you."

There was no expression on Saegan's face and no emotion in his voice. "Yes, beauty and danger are not necessarily exclusive in the natural world," Aljeron answered, and he spurred his horse forward to resume its previous pace.

What evening light there was started to fade, and dusk crept over the fluttering white horizon. Aljeron halted the company, but he remained in the saddle, staring intently north. As far as he could see in every other direction there was nothing but snow, but there seemed to be something north. What it was, he could not tell, nor could Evrim, who also acknowledged the shape. Now he must decide whether to dismount and camp here or to push north in the hopes that they could reach the thing by nightfall, the thing that might provide some kind of shelter.

"I don't know," he said at last to Saegan and Evrim. "I really don't know what it is or how far away. We could spend a lot of precious energy for nothing."

"So we're staying?" Evrim asked.

"What do you think?" Aljeron asked.

Evrim shrugged. "I agree. It could be a lot of energy for nothing, but it would be nice to camp beneath some trees or with something to block the wind at our backs."

"Saegan?" Aljeron asked.

Saegan didn't answer. He was sitting on the other side of Evrim, but he was no longer looking their direction. He was looking south, watching the sky, and Aljeron followed his gaze. He saw a pair of large, dark birds flying rather low, moving very quickly, their black bodies starkly juxtaposed with the white ground and swirling snow.

"What kind of bird are they?" Aljeron asked.

Saegan shrugged. "I don't know."

"They look like crows, almost," Evrim said after he'd located the birds his friends were watching.

The two birds drew nearer, and as they did, they dropped steadily until they were flying not much higher off the ground than Aljeron was sitting. By this point, all the men, the Great Bear, and even Koshti were watching the incoming birds. As they flew overhead, Aljeron noticed that they were not entirely black, for the heads of both birds were a dark but unmistakable crimson.

As they passed, they screeched a hideously sharp cry that echoed in the gathering dark, and Aljeron winced as he raised his hands to cover his ears. Cinjan, some twenty spans away, was scrambling to remount his horse, as was Synoki, and in a moment, both men had joined him.

"Red Ravens," Cinjan said. "We must ride on."

"Why?" Aljeron said, bemused at the man's suddenly urgent tone and demeanor. This man who could barely restrain his mockery when Aljeron stopped to check tracks was now spooked by a couple of noisy birds. "They're just birds."

"Yes, but they're not alone. Red Ravens travel in flocks, large flocks. The main contingent is probably close by. They've been summoned now and will be on the way. We must ride!"

"Look!" Karras called, and all of them turned south again. Growing larger on the horizon was a great, dark cloud, sweeping northward.

Cinjan and Synoki spurred their horses northward without a word, and the others did likewise. Aljeron felt his weary horse respond to the urgency of his commands and soon they were riding harder than they'd ridden since coming ashore.

Even so, they lost ground. Aljeron kept checking the birds' progress with a slight turn of the head, and there was no doubt that the dark cloud of Red Ravens was closing the distance. The only good news was that the dark shape Aljeron had seen on the northern horizon was growing. He could only hope it would somehow prove a refuge and not a trap or dead end.

For several moments, maybe even a quarter an hour, they rode, until the sound of the birds grew almost deafening. The beating of a thousand wings and the shrieking calls of these creatures roared up behind them. Aljeron, whose eyes were fixed on the shape, realized it was a line of trees. But it was beyond reach. He suddenly pulled his horse up. They weren't going to outrun these birds. They were going to have to drive them off.

He pulled Daaltaran from his sheath and wheeled his horse around. Arintol and Erigan also stopped, stood, and in one smooth motion withdrew the long wooden poles that lay strapped upon their backs. Standing at their full height, they towered above Aljeron on horseback and presented such a formidable sight that the clouds of approaching Red Ravens divided east and west and wheeled around either side of them. The small company was now surrounded by birds crying out in savage, angry voices from all sides.

The others also drew their weapons, but they were more spread out than Aljeron liked. There was nothing to be done about that now. Hundreds of red-headed black birds swooped upon them with mouths open and talons spread wide.

Aljeron swung Daaltaran with wild abandon, feeling several of his strokes pass through birds, which screamed even louder as they fell fluttering to the snow and were trampled by the horses. Koshti was harassed by a dozen brazen birds, even though his massive claws swiped left and right above his head to protect his eyes. Through the mayhem, Aljeron saw Arintol and Erigan whirling their great staffs with incredible speed that created an almost completely bird-free zone around them.

Continuing to wave his sword, he pressed his horse in the direction of Karras and Tornan, who were flailing, almost in vain, to keep the Red Ravens off. Saegan and Evrim apparently had the same idea, for they also moved toward Karras and Tornan. Then all five of them, huddling together, moved toward Cinjan and Synoki, who were likewise struggling. A moment later, all seven men, Koshti, and both Great Bear had formed a close, tight circle, and with weapons still raised and wielded, managed to dissuade the Red Ravens from coming in low.

The ground was strewn with the writhing bodies of smashed and sliced birds, their dark blood seeping into the snow. Beyond the perimeter of their circle, Aljeron saw something curious beginning to happen. Healthy Red Ravens were alighting on the ground in the midst of their fallen fellows and pecking the flesh of the dead and dying.

"They're eating each other," Aljeron said, surprised.

"Yes, and while they're distracted, we should run for the trees," Cinjan said. "It will be dark soon."

The circle moved north, and the cloud of birds hesitated to follow. Once more they rode as fast as they could. The dark of night had almost surrounded them entirely when they reached the trees closest to the open plain. They rode into the small wood perhaps fifty spans before stopping and dismounting. None spoke, but all stood together with weapons still drawn.

A few minutes later, Aljeron was thinking about sheathing Daaltaran when the sound of the Red Ravens' beating wings suddenly swept over the trees. They could hear the rustling of the leafless branches as the birds lit upon them. The men stood very still, trying to see in the dark any signs of descending birds. Aljeron stared up at the trees, grateful that they were thick with plentiful boughs even if denuded by the cold of winter. Perhaps the interlacement of the branches would deter any attacks from above.

For several minutes, they listened to the birds flying and flapping, setting down in the trees and lifting into the air again. What light they had slipped away, and they continued to stand with weapons drawn in the darkness. For maybe an hour they stood this way, until at last the sound of the Red Ravens began to diminish. Some of the flock, at least, had flown away.

When at last quiet reigned above them, Aljeron put away Daaltaran and found Cinjan. "What was that all about?"

"What do you mean?"

"We were attacked by a flock of birds, that's what I mean! Don't they eat bugs and worms and things?"

"The birds of the north live off of whatever they can scavenge, like everything else in this land. All the weak and vulnerable creatures of Nolthanin have long since been eaten and purged away. Everything still here is both hunter and the hunted. That includes us."

"You're saying these Red Ravens were trying to make us dinner?" Evrim asked. "Seven men on horseback, a tiger, and two Great Bear?"

"Why not? They could live for weeks off us. They'd eat until they picked our bones clean, and then they'd move on looking for something else."

"That's why they ate their own," Aljeron finally said, thinking of the fierce red heads ripping into the black bodies, tearing at feathers to get to the food beneath.

"Well, they'll get nothing to eat from us," Saegan said. "Is everyone all right?"

Remarkably, there were no serious cuts among them. They had been aided by their heavy winter cloaks, and all of them could point to at least a few new rips and tears in their outer garments. Aljeron suspected they'd find some cuts on the horses in the morning, but given their successful ride to safety, he thought it likely that none of them was too badly off.

Grateful, he stretched out on the relatively dry ground beneath the trees and pulled his cloak tight around him. He had been about to give the order to set up camp when the first two Red Ravens flew overhead. Fortuitously, the birds compelled them to ride into the wood. Though he knew it could have gone worse, they were essentially unharmed and now enjoying the benefits of shelter. Despite the excitement of the day, he had much to be thankful for.

He closed his eyes, and images of dark wings flapping and white snow fluttering danced in his head. The snow was indeed beautiful, but Saegan's admonition rang in his head. *Nature is always loveliest right before it tries to kill you.* If the Red Ravens were a picture of what had become of the birds of Nolthanin since the First Age, what about the other animals that lived here? What else inhabited this place? What other creatures roamed this land, and how many more times would they flee for their lives across snowy plains on their way to Harak Andunin?

Harak Andunin. He had no idea exactly where it was, nor did he know what exactly he was supposed to do if and when he got there. "I sure hope this isn't all in vain, Valzaan," Aljeron muttered to himself. Soon he was fast asleep.

Aljeron awoke for the first time in days without a dusting of snow covering his body. The thickly interlaced branches above had not protected him entirely, though, for snow lay in patches on him, including a small and cold deposit on his scarred cheek. He brushed himself off as he sat up, stretched, and yawned.

It was later in the morning than he usually awoke, but no doubt the semidarkness created by the trees accounted for his sleeping in, and the others' too. All slept but Cinjan and Synoki, apparently both up and elsewhere.

He stood and shook the snow out of his hair. Looking around, he began to wonder where Cinjan and Synoki would be. Even if they had arisen earlier than the rest, why go off? Why not wake them all so they could be on their way? Where would they go, straying from the relative safety of the group? He was about to wake Evrim to join him in looking for the two men from Col Marena when he saw them coming through the trees.

He walked quietly around his sleeping companions and went to meet them, seeing as he did that their arms were full of branches. "Collecting wood this morning?"

"Yes," Synoki replied with a slight smile. "We thought we'd try a fire, since we had fuel handy and partial shelter."

"Well," Aljeron said, finding the idea of a warm fire appealing, even if part of him cautioned against staying put longer than necessary. "I don't see why we can't have a small fire, just to be warm for a little while. But—and I mean this—it will be a small fire. I don't know what other creatures we might attract with our fire and I don't want to, and I don't want our progress delayed too long, even for a little comfort. Understood?"

"Completely," Synoki said, and he brushed past with Cinjan. The rest of the group soon awakened, eager to sit around the small fire when it was going.

Aljeron's internal commitment to limit their time around the fire to no more than an hour was soon compromised. He found it more difficult than expected to give the command to pack up and go. Having come so far already and having so much farther to go, it seemed to him in the end to be quite unimportant if they lost a few hours today while enjoying the comforts of the fire. Besides, he could see already that it was good for morale. Tornan and Karras were talking quite comfortably with Arintol and Erigan, and it was good to see the Great Bear dealing so openly with the young soldiers. Also huddled together, and in seemingly better spirits than they had been since arriving in Avram Gol, Cinjan and Synoki chatted merrily away.

"Shouldn't we be getting on?" Saegan asked Aljeron quietly, and Evrim looked up from the fire.

"In a bit," Aljeron said, and he saw the relief in Evrim's face. "We've been cold for so long and will be cold again soon enough, it seems harmless to enjoy some more time by the fire."

Saegan shrugged. "I'm as happy as any to enjoy the fire. I just don't want to get too used to being warm, if you know what I'm saying."

Aljeron laughed. "I know what you're saying. The cold seems just that much colder for having been warm for a few hours."

"Yes, and more than that. Sitting here without rain falling on my face and with this fire to warm my hands stirs memories of life before everything fell apart. Maybe remembering those things isn't so helpful."

"Maybe it's hard to think about," Evrim joined in, "but I need moments of warmth like this. Otherwise, this whole venture is just too much. The dark, the wet, the cold, the gloom—it's overwhelming. For me, I need to remember sitting by a fire and feeling its warmth on my face and hands. It feels like home."

"Perspective is a curious thing," Aljeron said, looking at his friends. "As awful as the past weeks and months have been, I've found in this change of fortune a reminder of what is really important."

Evrim and Saegan looked at each other and both men, though normally reserved, smiled at each other. "What?" Aljeron said, surprised.

"Well," Evrim said, laughing a little bit, "a woman can do that for you."

"A woman?" Aljeron said, his eyes growing wide. Then recognition washed over him and he blushed. "Look, that's not what I meant. I meant that having been at war with Fel Edorath for so long, it was good to be reminded that Fel Edorath wasn't the real enemy."

"Sure you did," Saegan said, smirking. "The 'change of fortune' you mentioned had nothing to do with Aelwyn."

"I'm not going to argue the point," Aljeron said, almost sighing. "I won't lie to you and say she hasn't affected me and how I see things, but she honestly wasn't what I was thinking about when I said what I said."

"Fair enough," Saegan said.

"We've just been waiting for you to talk about her, but you haven't, so we wondered if at last the wall of silence was tumbling down."

"Wall of silence?"

"Yes, the wall of silence. You haven't said a word about her or what's going on with you two. We're in the middle of an expansive wilderness with nothing but snow and psychotic birds to keep us company. The least you could do is entertain us with your good fortune."

"I see," Aljeron answered, laughing. "How selfish of me."

"Quite."

"Well, there's not much to tell. Apparently, she's had crush on me since she was a little girl, and I've just not been around enough since she grew up to notice. In fact, if not for all this, I might never have noticed."

"What do you mean?"

"Just that if I'd met Aelwyn in different circumstances, this might not have happened."

"Why not?"

"I probably would have fixated on being so much older or something, but fleeing for my life from Malek did a wonderful job of stripping the superfluous concerns of life away. For her part, she might not have been emboldened to make her love known, and I might never have noticed more subtle interest. I'm not really in tune with the nuances of romance."

"Me neither," Saegan said, nodding. "Is it serious?"

"It is," Aljeron answered, and sober looks of reflection replaced Saegan's and Evrim's grins. "If Allfather should grant the opportunity, I will speak to her father, though at our age, that will be a formality."

"So we need to make sure that whatever happens between here and Harak Andunin, we keep you alive. You have unfinished business to attend to when we get back."

"Let's make sure we all stay alive."

"Hear! Hear!" Evrim chimed in. "If Aljeron is going to marry Aelwyn, I want to be there to see it. After all these years listening to his protests that he'd never marry, I want to be front and center when they're joined together."

"And I want to see what vocation Aljeron decides to take up if he's going to settle down and play the husband. Have you given any thought to that?"

"Sure," Aljeron said, laughing again. "I'm going to be a farmer."

With that, everyone chuckled. "Aljeron the married farmer—I'll believe it when I see it."

"Yes," Saegan said. "I suppose at least that way Daaltaran might still have a use. Will you use it to weed your fields?"

Aljeron pulled the long smooth blade from his sheath and rested it against his palm. The metal was cold to his touch and dark against the white snow and flickering firelight. He looked at the others, then back at Daaltaran and smiled. Reaching over, he scratched Koshti's head, but he did not reply to Saegan's question.

"Mindarin will be your sister-in-law, you know," Evrim said, a mischievous grin on his face.

"Indeed," Aljeron said, looking back at his friends. "Life with Mindarin as a sister-in-law may be many things, not all of them pleasant, but at least it won't be boring."

Late that afternoon, the open ground gave way to the first hilly stretch of land. As they passed between the first pair of hills, Aljeron drew Daaltaran and signaled to the others to be prepared. Slowing down and riding warily, Aljeron took turns watching both the hills and Koshti jogging along beside him. He knew that if there was trouble ahead, he would likely see it in Koshti's alertness before he saw it in reality.

For an hour or more they passed in and out of the hilly country, at times forced to ascend and descend through drifts of the still falling snow. There was no sign anywhere of anything amiss, so as they approached one final opening between the hills and saw open country beyond, Aljeron found himself lowering and sheathing Daaltaran in relief.

The Red Ravens from the previous night had him on edge. *They have everyone on edge,* he thought as he surveyed the relief in the others as they put their weapons away too. It was unpleasant being set upon by anything, especially by thousands of cackling and screeching birds that in another time and place might have been beautiful and harmless.

They rode forward across open ground once more. The wide open white of the plains stretched out before him, and Aljeron prepared to spur his horse on to a quicker pace. Before he did, though, he turned to look over his shoulder at the hills. They rose, white mounds against the grey sky, at uneven intervals above the white horizon.

Something moved against the near side of one of the hills. A Vulsutyrim, blanched white with snow that covered it from head to toe, detached itself from the hillside where it had stood hidden just moments ago as they passed by. Aljeron wheeled his horse and called out. Snow fell from the giant's head and shoulders as he shook himself free and started to run across the open ground, a mammoth blade raised high beside its head.

Koshti streaked across the snow like orange lightning hurled horizontally across the ground. The giant side-stepped the rushing tiger, swinging his sword in a vicious arc that would have sliced Koshti in half had the tiger not leapt to the side and rolled out of range in the snow.

Arintol and Erigan followed Koshti into the open space between the men and the giant with their great staffs ready. They approached more cautiously. Their staffs, though almost a span and half long, looked like mere sticks next to the long, slightly curved sword of the giant. The Vulsutyrim checked the pace of his advance, taking the threat of the Great Bear seriously as he took a second swipe at Koshti, who had tried to sneak in from behind and attack his heel. Now Saegan, still on his horse, moved around Arintol to present another threat to the giant, and the three pressed in, weapons raised.

Aljeron's own battle senses suddenly awoke, and he pushed his horse forward too, moving alongside Erigan to provide support on that side. On his shoulder, he saw Evrim approach, and for a moment he thought that despite the ferocity, size, and strength of the giant, it must see that it could not win this fight.

The thought was premature, for the giant lunged, dealing three quick strokes to both Great Bear, which they only just dodged and defended, and the last of which knocked Erigan's staff some ten spans through the air. It landed well outside the advancing arc of men and Great Bear. Arintol covered the defenseless Erigan, as did Saegan, who rode in, sword raised and furiously whirling in the hope that he might deal the giant's exposed arm a blow.

The giant, though, was too quick for Saegan. His sword swept in and before Saegan could move his horse out of the way, the giant's blade cut through the neck of the terrified creature. It collapsed beneath Saegan, throwing him sideways into the snow.

The giant raised his sword to finish Saegan, who scurried across the snow on his hands and knees, desperate to get out of the creature's reach. Karras rode in like a madman, his sword also raised and whirling. The giant, seemingly effortlessly, dodged the thundering horse and with a short, strong stroke, cut through Karras more completely than he had cut through Saegan's horse. Aljeron watched in horror as the two pieces of Karras's severed body slid off the horse, one on either side, and the frightened stallion ran off.

All at once, Koshti and the Great Bear, including Erigan, who had retrieved his staff, rushed in, claws and poles flying. Aljeron and Evrim, and even Saegan on foot, fell in close behind. For a moment, the giant gave up ground, using his great sword only on the defensive.

Aljeron was beginning to feel the battle fury, and he pushed in harder with Daaltaran. The giant's forearm and shoulder seemed almost within reach. Still, the creature defended himself with such speed and skill that Aljeron could not get close enough to draw blood. He grew frustrated and careless. He overreached in his stroke, and suddenly the right arm of the giant swung fast and furious in his direction, striking him across the chest and throwing him from the horse.

He landed none too gently in the snow, with Daaltaran nowhere to be seen. He leapt to his feet, and once he realized the giant's attention had been turned to the Great Bear, he began to search desperately in the snow for his sword. He found it in a matter of seconds, protruding from a drift. Sword in hand, he turned to face the son of Vulsutyr again.

As he spun, he saw Synoki's horse rear up, throwing its rider into the snow. Cinjan jumped from his horse to help Synoki, who winced as he stood.

The giant had driven the other men back and advanced directly at the Great Bear, who were falling back. With a swift and powerful stroke, he struck Arintol with his sword hilt and fists and sent the Great Bear sprawling. A lateral stroke directed at Erigan ensured that no help would come from that quarter, and before Arintol could pick himself up, the giant drove the point of his sword home, skewering Arintol upon the blade.

The stroke was sudden and vicious and the beginning of the end for the giant. As the slumping body of the Great Bear pulled the sword down and bent the giant over, Koshti leapt and landed on the Vulsutyrim. Sinking his claws into the giant's back and shoulders, Koshti held on somehow as the giant ripped his sword out of the Great Bear and stood, howling in pain.

As the giant tried to grab the tiger with his free hand, Erigan, fueled by rage, dealt the off-balance giant half a dozen swift, strong blows to the face, bloodying his nose and mouth with the end of his staff. As the giant was momentarily caught between the tearing claws of the tiger and the thunderous blows of the Great Bear, two things happened simultaneously. Koshti buried his jaws into the giant's neck, blood soaking Koshti's fur as he pulled his mouth free, and Erigan drove his great staff into the giant's groin with tremendous force, dropping the giant to his knees.

Aljeron drove Daaltaran into the exposed side under the giant's arm, sinking the sword to the hilt. On the other side, Saegan, drove his sword through the fleshy part of the giant's upper thigh, and now both men twisted their weapons with all their strength to make the wounds as grievous and gaping as their strength could manage.

Wrenching Daaltaran free, Aljeron stepped back from the giant, who knelt there in the snow, staring forward. The long curved sword dropped from his hand, and a small cloud of snowflakes swirled up around Erigan, who stood before the giant, his staff held firm, ready for anything. Koshti crouched on the giant's back and shoulder, blood dripping from his jaws on top of the giant's head. Saegan alone was still active. He pulled his sword out of the giant's leg and, reaching up, drove the blade into his throat.

As he did, Koshti leapt down. Saegan withdrew his sword and Erigan stepped back, allowing the giant to tumble forward, face down on the cold, wet ground.

8 THE FABRIC OF CREATION

ALJERON PLACED HIS FOOT on the giant's back and pressed hard. No reaction. With the tip of Daaltaran he lifted the hair off the back of the giant's neck and looked at the exit wound that Saegan's sword had made. Blood still seeped out of it, running down both sides of his thick neck, forming dark pools in the snow. Any lingering doubt was gone. The giant was dead.

Aljeron turned from the giant to see Tornan sitting beside the remains of Karras, desolate. He wasn't crying, and he wasn't speaking. He just sat, holding the upper torso of his fallen friend and staring out across the white plains. Karras had watched over him in that burned-out building in Col Marena, and now he was watching over Karras.

Several spans away, Erigan sat beside the still form of Arintol. Erigan's staff lay beside him, and both of his great paws rested on his friend's chest. Aljeron could see Erigan's mouth moving, though he seemed to be making no sound. Perhaps he was praying, or maybe he was mouthing the words to the song for the deceased, the same song Aljeron had heard Arintol sing with the Great Bear many years ago after the battle with the Malekim just north of Lindan Wood.

"Aljeron," Saegan said from close by. Like him, Saegan had not strayed far from the body of the Vulsutyrim and continued to poke it occasionally just to make sure it would move no more. "How do we know this giant was alone?"

"We don't." Aljeron shrugged, looking back toward the white hills. There were no signs of movement in that direction, or in any other as he turned slowly all the way around. There was only the horizon and the steadily falling snow.

"We shouldn't stay long, just in case."

"If there were more here, they would have fallen upon us too. We couldn't have handled more than one. We barely handled him." Aljeron gave the shoulder of the giant a light kick as he said this.

"More might be on their way. The sooner we get away from here, the better our chance of putting distance between us and whatever else is out there."

"If there are more coming, what chance do we have to outrun them?" Aljeron looked up at Saegan.

"I don't know, but waiting won't improve our chances."

"All right," Aljeron conceded, "but I won't leave Arintol and Karras to be food for Red Ravens or any other scavenger. We're going to bury them."

"Aljeron," Saegan said, "the ground is frozen; we'll never get them under the earth."

"Not beneath the ground, beneath the snow. There," Aljeron said, pointing at the hollowed out cleft in the hillside the giant had used for shelter. "We'll drag their bodies over and bury them under as much snow as we can. The carrion can feast on the giant and the horse. Maybe the snow will cover and protect our friends, at least until the spring thaw. It is the best we can do."

Saegan nodded, and they turned to Evrim, who had taken up a position not far from Tornan, watching over the young soldier from a respectful distance. They quickly explained their intent, and tenderly, Evrim guided the dazed Tornan away from the body as Saegan and Aljeron dragged Karras to the hill. They looked in at the place where the giant had burrowed in and set his trap. "Let's put Arintol in first, and then we'll put Karras in on top of him," Aljeron said.

They turned and walked back to Erigan, who was dragging Arintol in their direction. They took hold of his legs as well and helped pull the Great Bear to the cleft, where they settled the body as gently as they could. Placing Karras in on top of Arintol took only a moment, and they began to heap the snow on top of them. Erigan moved great piles of snow over to the bodies, and together they packed the snow around them and on them, until at last they were encased in a hard white tomb of compressed snow. The men and Great Bear stepped back from what they had done and turned to see the others watching silently. Tornan and Evrim, Cinjan and Synoki, all were on their feet just a few spans away. Even Koshti, who by now had licked most of the blood from the fur around his mouth, sat attentively in the snow not far from the rest.

Aljeron walked up to Synoki. "Are you hurt?"

"Just embarrassed, falling off my horse like that."

"Thanks for trying to help."

Synoki nodded. "Can you ride?" Aljeron asked.

"I think so."

"Good, then mount up with Cinjan and ride after Karras's horse. I don't think it will have gone far, and we will need it now that Saegan's horse is dead."

"All right." Synoki and Cinjan left, following the tracks of Karras's frightened horse. Aljeron approached Erigan, Evrim, and Saegan while Tornan stood quietly staring at the hill where they had buried Karras and Arintol. "There are questions we should ask before we ride on."

The men and Great Bear nodded and waited. "The questions before us are many, and I don't know where to begin. Where did the giant come from? Had he been tracking us? Was he here on a separate mission, or were we his mission? If so, how did he know to seek us here? How were we followed across the Bay of Thalasee? How does Malek know where we are? If he knows where we are, does he know where we are going? Will there be more attacks along the way? And, what's more, does any of this change what we are here to do?"

"To the last question first," Saegan said, simply, "no. We are bound for Harak Andunin just the same now as we were this morning. We knew we'd encounter danger and obstacles. This changes nothing."

"We cannot know the rest," Erigan began, "but it seems to me that it would be wise for us to plan for the worst. We must assume that Malek does know where we are, where we are headed, and why. We must also assume that having failed to kill us with this giant, he will try again. Where he gets his information, who can say? It may be that the birds of the air and the fish in the sea and the animals on the ground in this cursed land are his servants and spies, who knows? The only certainty before us is what Saegan has already affirmed. If you promised Valzaan to go to Harak Andunin, and if there is a chance that Sulmandir is there and the aid of the dragons may still be sought, then we must go forward, whoever or whatever might stand in our way."

Aljeron nodded. "Evrim or Saegan, anything to add?"

Evrim shook his head.

Aljeron surveyed their faces, and each displayed the resolve he had heard in their voices. "Very well then, as soon as Cinjan and Synoki are back, we move on."

"Aljeron," Evrim said. "Why did you send Cinjan and Synoki away before asking us the questions? Do you think they were involved in this?"

Aljeron looked over his shoulder in the direction the two men had ridden. "No," he answered thoughtfully. "I know you don't trust them, Evrim, but I can't see how they would be involved. They have been with us since Col Marena, and surely had the giant prevailed here today it would have taken their lives as well as our own. What's more, and you know this already, Saegan and I have already seen Synoki's valor in battle against the servants of Malek.

"However," Aljeron added, "I do not know this Cinjan, and I am not sure how much I trust him. I did think it prudent that we keep our own counsel on this matter, and I recommend that we continue to do so."

"Aljeron," Evrim said, stealing a glance at the young soldier a few spans away. "We should keep an eye on Tornan as the shock of this wears off."

"Yes, of course," Aljeron answered, turning also to look at the young man. They all started away from the hill, back in the direction of their horses, and Tornan silently followed with Koshti treading lightly beside him.

"Even if it takes longer than expected for Cinjan and Synoki to track down Karras's horse," Aljeron said as they walked, "we will ride from here today. It will be better for Tornan, and better for us all, not to sleep in this place. What's more, who knows what creatures of the wild the bodies of the horse and giant will attract. Agreed?"

"Agreed," they replied.

"Good, then may they return swiftly. The sooner we leave this place, the better."

Synoki slowed his horse to a walk as they approached the hill where the Great Bear and the boy soldier were interred, maintaining a tight grip on the reins of the retrieved horse. Cinjan likewise slowed down, and they eyed the others who stood at a distance with their horses at the ready.

"So now what?" Cinjan whispered.

"What do you mean, 'now what?'"

"Varatyr failed, that's what."

"True," Synoki replied, "but it wasn't a complete failure. There is one less Great Bear and one less man. If we have to take matters into our own hands, kill the others, and take possession of Balinor, the job won't be quite as hard as it would have been."

A dark glimmer flashed in Cinjan's eyes. "We've been out here for weeks. Why don't we kill him and be done?"

Synoki looked into Cinjan's dark and eager eyes. "Patience, Cinjan. Patience. You know as well as I do the answer to that. Aljeron and his secrets. I am not yet sure of their mission and therefore not yet sure if it poses a threat to us. We must wait until we know."

"Well, whatever we may find, I trust you will not forget your word. Promises have been made."

"Cinjan," Synoki said, almost laughing as they drew near to Varatyr's body. "You must have more faith in me than that."

Both men gazed down at the bloody form, now lightly covered with snow. "Such a magnificent creature," Synoki said. "What a pity."

"Are you coming?" Aljeron called.

"Yes," Synoki called back. He looked up. "Just taking a closer look at the giant. I haven't seen one since that day more than seventeen years ago. It brings back memories."

Aljeron did not reply, and Synoki drew closer to Cinjan to speak to him one more time before rejoining the others. "Your father and his father and their fathers on backward for almost a thousand years have come and gone, but not Farimaal, your great ancestor. You know the power of your Master, and he knows what it is you desire. Do your part and do not fail, and you will receive your reward."

Aelwyn gently stroked the side of the horse she would be riding. She didn't know what had become of the chestnut mare she had ridden from Shalin Bel, but since that horse wasn't hers to begin with, she didn't mind the change. This one was somewhere between a dark brown and black, though when she stood and looked closely as she was now, she could see lighter patches of grey hair on his neck and sides.

Her things were packed and stored in the bundle tied behind the horse's saddle, and she was ready to go, as were most of the women around her. Like them, she waited simply for the command. Also like them, she waited on her feet, realizing that as pleasant as it would feel today to get back up into the saddle, there was a long journey ahead, and she would likely enough soon wish to dismount.

"He seems like a gentle fellow," Mindarin said as she walked over to Aelwyn, leading her own horse.

"He does. And yours?"

"Yes, she seems rather docile too," Mindarin sighed.

"You seem disappointed."

"You know me, Sister, I like them feisty."

"We're not racing around the paddocks of our childhood home," Aelwyn answered, smiling. "We're undertaking a long and arduous march. A smooth and even temperament in both our horses and ourselves would seem advisable."

"I don't particularly care how arduous this march is, I want an animal with some spirit. If we're set upon by any creatures as cruel as they are fierce, I don't want to be sitting atop a glorified plow mule. Besides, hasn't it occurred to you yet that this might be it? If death on this march is my destiny, I'd like to go out lively, not clip-clopping dully along."

"Believe it or not, it has occurred to me that this might be it. It occurs to me every second of every day, but I'm not interested in spending my time thinking about how I want to 'go out,' as you put it. I'd rather focus on doing what I can to ensure our success and survival, since that is all that is in my power to do."

Mindarin looked closely at her sister, and she grew more serious. "You are right to do so, Aelwyn. I often do not because it is disheartening to see just how little I can do and just how much is not in my power."

"I know. I feel my limitations keenly too."

Mindarin put her arm around Aelwyn's shoulders. "You can't keep him alive by worrying, so just worry about keeping yourself alive for him."

Her sister's kind words somehow slipped past all the defenses Aelwyn had erected to keep her emotions under control, and tears began to flow quietly down her face. "It just doesn't seem fair," she said. "As if it isn't enough that the world is falling apart and we are all fleeing for our lives, why should he be the one who had to go north into that terrible wilderness? It just feels like I was given a glimpse of what we might have had together, even if only while we fled, only to have it taken away. I've been given a taste of what I can't have, and it is almost worse than if I'd had none at all."

"It might feel like that now, but it won't always. Besides, as dark as our future may appear, we should not give up. Aside from his promise to Valzaan, hope led Aljeron to go north. Hope that the dragons might be summoned to our aid. Hope that they might turn the tide of this war. Likewise, hope has led Sarneth and Benjiah into Taralin. Hope that the Great Bear might come forth from their draals and fight beside us. Hope that their strength and wisdom might be added to our own. We must not give up. You may live to see and hold him again."

"I know," Aelwyn said, trying to dry her eyes, though her cloak was soaked along with every layer she wore. "I've been doing all right with this, at least most of the time. I really have. It's just that every once in a while when I think of where he's headed with so little help, I just start worrying. Then, when the door is open, it all just seems to multiply, and pretty soon it seems overwhelming."

"It seems overwhelming because it is overwhelming. It is overwhelming because we have been overwhelmed. It is bigger than you and me and Aljeron and even this whole army, with or without the Great Bear. There's absolutely nothing wrong with feeling overwhelmed. If you didn't, I'd think you were in denial or something."

Aelwyn laughed. "I wish I could be in denial. It sounds lovely."

"No you don't," Mindarin answered. "Hiding from reality never makes anything better in the long run. I should know that as well as anyone."

From somewhere down the beach, a high-pitched whistle rang out. The same high-pitched sound enveloped the women, and they started to climb into their saddles.

"Well," Mindarin said, hugging Aelwyn and letting go. "It looks like it is time to go. I'd better get on my horse before she falls asleep standing up."

Aelwyn watched Mindarin walk away and then turned back to her own horse. "One foot in front of the other," she whispered into his ear. "I guess that's all we can do for now."

As he followed Sarneth's winding lead through Taralin, Benjiah gazed in awe at the splendor of the towering trees. The first half hour of their journey into Taralin led them through a full range of trees, foliage, and dense underbrush, some of which was prickly with nasty-looking, long, slender thorns. And yet, these outer defenses—for so they seemed to Benjiah as they picked their way through upon entering the forest—did not go on forever, and when they gave way to the inner world of the wood, Benjiah could not have been more overwhelmed by the beauty of Taralin.

It struck him as he rode that he hadn't seen a single tree all day that was crooked or forked, gnarled or bent. Every tree they passed seemed straight and strong and tall. The trees here were not especially thick, for most of them he could have wrapped his arms around. They were, however, exceedingly tall, with few branches and boughs less than twenty-five spans off the ground. The effect was a sensation of being in a large hall with a vaulted ceiling so astonishingly high that it could not be seen in any detail, supported by a myriad of pillars that looked almost spindly.

The farther in they rode, the more Benjiah had understood how much his joy at entering the wood was connected not just to the physical beauty of the place, but to the relative absence of rain. There was evidence all around of the perpetual pouring of the heavens upon the earth, for the ground was damp and the tree trunks were wet and dark, and upon closer examination Benjiah saw tiny but constant streams of water flowing down them. Even so, here beneath the widespread and still-green boughs of the trees, the water did not drench him as it had before. At one moment, a few hours into their ride, he raised a largely dry hand to his face and felt for the first time in days, his forehead, cheeks, nose, mouth and chin—all dry, all warm, or at least not as ice cold as they had been.

He was encouraged. Being dry, or relatively dry, was a big part of it, but there was more. The world here was green. The leaves in the branches above, the smaller trees, and even the thorn bushes through which they'd come were all green. He knew that in some places farther south in Suthanin, the world was basically green year round, though he'd never really been able to picture a place green in winter, or what winter would be if the world were still green. He didn't know if Taralin was such a place, or if the turning of the leaves normally came very late. It occurred to him that perhaps even this rain had somehow altered the normal cycle of things. There would be many questions to ask Sarneth when they stopped.

They did not stop for lunch until late afternoon, and Sarneth apologized to Benjiah. "I am sorry, Benjiah, but Great Bear do not need to eat with the same frequency that men do. I have been so preoccupied with our journey that I lost sight of your appetite. Rest for a moment, and eat, and then we will continue for a few more hours before dark."

Benjiah did not need to be asked twice. Opening his pack, he devoured the fruit that Mindarin and Aelwyn had forced upon him. It was the last of the stores of fresh fruit from their ship, and they insisted that he take it with him. When he declined, saying that the women should have it if anyone did, they insisted with all the maternal zeal of ten mothers, and Benjiah knew immediately that any further attempt to decline would only bring more of the same upon his head.

He was now grateful for their insistence, for the taste of the fruit was sweet and satisfying. He looked at Sarneth, who rested not far from him, and smiled.

"You are enjoying our journey?" Sarneth asked, his eyes suggesting something like a twinkle.

"Yes, very much."

"You have the look of one who enjoys the woods, is that not so?"

"Very much," Benjiah answered between bites. "Ever since I was a boy, I have sought opportunities to walk under the trees. Even in the smaller groves and woods north of Amaan Sul, I have found a peace, a tranquility, and a majesty that draws me. That's the main reason why I learned to hunt, because it gave me a good excuse to venture out of the city and into the woods."

"And what do you think of Taralin?"

"Taralin is beautiful. It is like no other wood or forest I have seen."

"It is not all like this," Sarneth answered, gesturing with a large paw to the trees. "As we go south, it will feel less open, and there will be more variety in the trees, but this area of the northern wood is indeed unlike any other forest in all of Kirthanin. It remains even now as it has been since the creation of the world."

"Having been through Gyrin, it is good to see a beautiful place like this unspoiled."

"Your time in Gyrin was dark?" Sarneth asked, looking at him intently.

"Yes. Even though we had only a few encounters with servants of Malek, the feel of the place is very different from this. There is a sense in Gyrin of something lost. I can't quite describe it."

Sarneth nodded. "Gyrin is dying, Benjiah, and it speaks to the truthfulness of your calling or to the giftedness of your woodcraft that you perceived it."

"Is it dying because of something Malek did?"

"Yes and no. It is not dying because Malek has done it harm, but because Malek drove away the Great Bear who lived there. There is no draal in Gyrin anymore."

"I don't understand, Sarneth, how are these things related?"

"I cannot fully explain the connection, for none of the Great Bear fully understand it; however, I will tell you what I know. There is something in the design of Great Bear that craves the shelter of the trees, much like the dragons crave the heights of the mountains and most men dwell in their towns and cities built in the open Kirthanin plains, usually by water. These things run deeper than preference, a desire for a certain environment; they reflect the fabric of creation itself, of creatures made for a world and a world made for its creatures.

"When Malek drove the Great Bear away from Gyrin, he stripped it of something elemental to its health and vitality, a crucial facet of its purpose. It was like tainting the water or soil, or shielding its leaves from the sunlight. Over the centuries of our exile, a slow and steady rot has eaten away at it. There is in Gyrin now a foulness, and no one knows if it is reversible."

"Surely," Benjiah said after a moment, "if Allfather can renew all things, He can heal Gyrin."

"I do not doubt that He can, but I do not know if He will. Perhaps Gyrin will be healed and restored when Kirthanin is made new; perhaps it will be razed and uprooted. That is not mine to decide.

"Come," Sarneth added, rising. "We will talk more at supper. Let us take advantage of what little light is left to us."

It was so dark by the time they stopped that Benjiah would have run into Sarneth when he halted had not Benjiah's horse drawn up suddenly, much to Benjiah's surprise. When he realized what had happened, he dismounted and followed Sarneth to the place where they would spend the night.

Sarneth bid Benjiah stay where he was while he disappeared into the trees. Being alone in the middle of this great wood in the dark did not frighten Benjiah, especially since he knew that Sarneth would be close by. Still, it had been a long time since he was so alone, and it felt strange to him not to be surrounded by more activity, all the more so since his uncles were not known for their quiet ways.

Sarneth soon returned bearing two long branches, both of which he broke into shorter pieces and used to construct a fire. The fire was not easy to light, because the wood was not entirely dry, but they managed, and soon it was burning brightly, casting flickering shadows across the soft forest floor and illuminating the closest trees.

They talked further of the ways of the Great Bear while they ate, and Benjiah listened, eager to learn whatever he could. He was struck by how little he really knew, and if he was to be granted permission to enter one of their draals as the representative of humanity, he wanted to be better prepared than he was to be a good ambassador.

As it grew late, though, weariness crept over Benjiah, and his yawns grew both more frequent and more pronounced. Despite his protests, Sarneth called a halt to their discussion, urging if not ordering Benjiah to get some sleep.

"And what about you?" Benjiah asked as he pulled his cloak tight and lay beside the fire. "Aren't you going to sleep too?"

"No," the Great Bear answered, "I am waiting for the patrol that will likely arrive some time in the night."

Benjiah sat up. "A patrol is coming? How do you know?"

"I have summoned them."

"How?"

"With this fire. Taralindraal, like all the draals of Kirthanin, is always keenly aware of the presence of fire within its borders. A fire up here, so far north and beyond the normal movements of the patrols, will not pass without notice. The Great Bear have read the change in the trees, and they knew not long after I lit this fire that someone is here. A patrol will be on its way to investigate, and I am waiting up to greet them."

"Then shouldn't I wait up too?"

"No, Benjiah, there will be nothing for you to do when they arrive. Sleep now, for your body requires rest."

Benjiah did not protest. He lay back down, and for a little while lay gazing at the fire and listening to the occasional pop of the wood, as ember by ember the stored energy within was released in light and smoke and heat. Slowly he drifted off to sleep.

When he found himself standing in the woods not far north of Amaan Sul, enjoying the shade of the trees from the bright sun, the thought that the scene wasn't real nagged at him. The thought that he was dreaming flitted through his mind and was soon lost again as he tried to pick up the spoor of the deer he had been hunting. Rarely had he pursued a quarry this elusive, but he was excited by the challenge. With Suruna ready in his hand, he continued through the undergrowth in search of his prey.

His frustration grew as the day wore on. There was absolutely no sign of the creatures, which he knew was impossible. He had known since he was a boy that every living creature left a trace of itself behind, whether seen or felt or smelled. And yet this deer had simply disappeared. Again and again he worked in widening arcs, reading the ground for clues he had perhaps missed, but he found nothing.

He looked up through the thick green canopy of the leaves. The sun had advanced much farther than it should have in the short time since he last checked. Something unnatural was going on. Suddenly, the light began to fade rapidly, as though something was sliding like an eclipse over the sun. Soon everything was dark, completely dark. There was no light of any kind, and Benjiah could not see anything in any direction. He felt around him with his hand, but there was nothing: no trees, no plants, no undergrowth of any kind. He was beginning to grow worried when suddenly he heard the sound of hushed voices, and reassurance washed over him.

Benjiah sat up. The fire beside him had burned down, but Sarneth had kept it stoked, and it was still going strong. The sound of voices was not part of the dream, for sitting around the fire now were four Great Bear. As he sat up, their conversation broke off, and they turned to look at him. It occurred to Benjiah that he should probably say something, but having just woken up, the words he wanted were jumbled in his head.

"Benjiah," Sarneth said, "this is the patrol I told you about. They are Trigan, Elmaaneth, and Kriegan, and I will introduce you more fully in the morning."

"Welcome to Taralin, Benjiah," one of the Great Bear beside Sarneth said as Benjiah surveyed them sleepily.

"Thank you," Benjiah answered. "It is a very beautiful place," he added, almost as an afterthought.

"We think so too," the Great Bear answered, something like a smile on his face evident in the firelight.

"Go back to sleep," Sarneth said. "There are still many hours until dawn."

9 TARALINDRAAL

ALL THAT DAY BENJIAH rode and the Great Bear ran, stopping only long enough for Benjiah to gulp down a snack at lunchtime. Barely did he have time to stretch his legs and eat before he was back on his horse and riding with all haste. The undergrowth thickened, and the difficulty of the path became even more marked. For all his training in the woods, Benjiah would never have been able to find his way along this intricate course or extricate himself once far along it.

His excitement following Trigan's announcement that he would be allowed inside the draal grew, even though the Great Bear's matter-of-fact tone had not exactly echoed with welcome. Whether he was welcomed with open arms or granted entry begrudgingly for purposes of their own, he didn't know. But he had not been turned away. Soon now, indeed very soon, for evening approached, he would pass inside the mysterious world of the draal. Though Valzaan was granted passage through Lindan with his uncles and father, he hadn't entered Lindandraal. In fact, he didn't even know if Valzaan had been inside a draal since Corindel's betrayal almost nine hundred years ago.

His anxiety returned. Was Valzaan's staff the reason the Taralindraal elders decided to allow him in? What would they expect of him? What if he disappointed them? He no longer doubted, even deep inside himself, that Allfather had summoned him to serve as a prophet, but what if the Great Bear found him wanting? What if they wanted a sign to verify his claim? He didn't want to let Sarneth and Caan and the others down. He didn't want to be seen as a pretender, a fraud, a child playing at a man's job and a man's role.

Peace. The voice from the other night in the storm resounded in his head. *You are not alone. I have called you, and I will equip you to do exactly what I have for you to do.*

As the dusky gloom of night descended all the more quickly, Benjiah felt the worry and fear slip away. He was neither anxious nor afraid of what lay ahead of him. He would speak as best as he was able to whatever issues were placed before him. That was all he could do. Other than that, he would stay close to Sarneth and follow his lead, for surely Sarneth had anticipated this eventuality and had a plan for the meeting.

Suddenly, just as the last light of day was seeping away, they rounded a corner and stopped. Benjiah reined his horse in, surprised to be face to face with an enormous tree. He looked around it, and as far as he could see, the way ahead was impassable. Much unlike the forest in the north, the tall thick trees of central Taralin were all but connected to one another by smaller bushes, shrubs, and lesser trees with wiry branches intricately interlaced. Benjiah couldn't imagine a hare or fox slipping through the dense undergrowth, let alone a Great Bear or a man on a horse.

That the Great Bear had lost their way returning to their own home was even more improbable to Benjiah than the possibility that there was some unseen way forward, so he remained seated on his horse, awaiting direction from his guides. A deep creaking and cracking in front of him drew his eyes to the enormous tree, and after staring at it for a minute or so, he began to see the outline of a large door swinging outward where the tree had appeared solid and seamless. The door was perhaps two-thirds the width of the entire tree, wide enough and tall enough to accommodate Benjiah on horseback and the Great Bear. When it had opened completely, revealing a Great Bear standing at the entrance to what now appeared to be a small tunnel, the Great Bear on guard stepped aside, and Elmaaneth led the way into the tree.

When Benjiah emerged from the tunnel, he gasped at the sight. Many more of these enormous trees dotted the largely open area. They rose, gigantic sentinels of the ancient wood, reaching high above even the tallest of the trees he had seen to this point on his journey in Taralin. What was even more remarkable than the trees was the presence of hundreds of Great Bear. They passed back and forth beneath the large trees like men and women walking along the streets of Amaan Sul.

The impenetrable line of large trees and undergrowth that he had observed from the outside appeared much the same on the inside and continued in either direction beyond what he could see. How large the draal was, he couldn't imagine, for nothing around him could provide him with a reference to the scale of the whole. The farther into the draal they moved, the farther away from this exterior boundary he was, and soon he lost sight of it altogether. At that point, there was only the draal itself and the comfort of spaciousness, filled with the magnificent trees and the equally magnificent Great Bear.

Most of the trees had large wooden structures built around their base. They were circular, like wheels lying flat around the end of an axle that stuck straight up into the sky. There didn't seem to be any windows in these structures, so at first Benjiah thought them solid, perhaps a sort of support or protection, but eventually he noticed doorways in some of them, and in a few cases Great Bear sitting or standing in them, watching the party as it moved through the draal.

Indeed, Benjiah was keenly aware all the way through that many sets of eyes followed them. This did not surprise him. He had expected to be something of an oddity. He at first tried to greet these spectators with a pleasant smile that would suggest his friendliness and gratitude for being there, but their impassive faces unnerved him. He began to feel uncomfortable, like he'd walked through the door to the wrong house and stumbled in on a family enjoying their evening meal. He looked down, watching the trodding feet of Sarneth and the others, and he did not look up again until they stopped moving altogether.

When he did, he was surprised to see a ring of smaller trees, the only ones he'd seen since entering the draal that were of "normal" size, though they were far from normal in appearance. The bark and leaves were both a white-grey, lined with a silver hue that shimmered like moonlight in the evening. In fact, to Benjiah, the circle of glistening trees appeared to be the closest thing to a night sky full of moon and stars that he had seen since the ever-present storm of the enemy began.

Sarneth turned around and came back to Benjiah. "You should dismount. This is the gathering place of the elders. When they summon us, you should appear before them on foot."

"Sure," Benjiah said, dropping down off his horse, savoring the solidity of the ground beneath his feet. "Do you think it will be long?"

"I don't know."

"Should I take my pack off the horse and bring it with me?"

"No. Take only Valzaan's staff."

"Just the staff?"

"Just the staff."

They did not wait long, perhaps no more than half an hour, but it seemed to Benjiah a long time indeed. Though many Great Bear had surrounded them upon their entrance to the draal, here, as they waited outside this ring of silvery trees, there were only two Great Bear in view, Sarneth and Elmaaneth. Where Trigan and Kriegan had gone, Benjiah did not know. As for Sarneth and Elmaaneth, they stood side by side but did not talk. They waited, motionless. If Sarneth was anxious, Benjiah couldn't see it. Perhaps in his own way, Sarneth had received the assurance of Allfather too, or perhaps his conviction that he was doing Allfather's will was enough to sustain him with or without such assurances. Standing beside these two Great Bear, alone with Valzaan's staff and no longer on horseback, Benjiah felt very small. He had been keenly aware of his youth and inexperience all the way here, and now he thought even his stature would argue against his credibility.

Emerging through a gap between two of the silvery trees, a Great Bear approached the three of them. "It is time, Elmaaneth. The clan summons you to appear before the elders, you and your guests."

Benjiah walked beside Sarneth as they followed Elmaaneth through the ring of trees. Inside, tall torches on slender poles illuminated the interior. Large stone benches framed the circle, and perhaps thirty Great Bear sat on these, watching their entrance. It occurred to Benjiah as they walked to an empty bench that this was the only stone he had seen since entering the draal, but he did not have long to contemplate the matter as he was faced with how to take a seat. The bench was as tall as his chest, and with his staff in his hand, he couldn't think of a dignified way to ascend. There seemed to be nothing else for it, so he set the staff upon the bench like he was placing it on a shelf, and with both hands palm down on the smooth stone, hoisted himself up onto it, none too gracefully. As quickly as he could, he righted himself and sat forward, his feet dangling like a child's from a grown-up's chair, and took Valzaan's staff back into hand.

Whether triggered by the ordeal of his achieving his seat or the comical sight of his legs dangling from it, a ripple of deep laughter spread around the watching circle. He flushed and looked down. Any hope he had for presenting a dignified face for the race of men disappeared. *At least if they were prone to view me with suspicion, they will be less likely to see me as a threat to their peace and safety, now that they've seen with their own eyes that I can barely function in their oversized world.*

The laughter quickly died down, though, and soon Benjiah noticed a Great Bear rise from his seat and amble into the center of the circle, facing the stone bench on which he was seated with Sarneth and Elmaaneth. The Great Bear had patches of grey hair around his eyes and mouth, much like Sarneth did, and he stood there for a moment, looking over the three of them.

"You are welcome within our circle, Sarneth," he said at last.

"Thank you, Parigan," Sarneth replied.

"It has been many years since last you sojourned with us in Taralindraal. Your clan is well, and the home of your fathers?"

"The clan is well and Lindandraal still lies at peace, at least for now."

"Lindandraal is threatened?"

"We are all threatened."

"Ah," Parigan answered, turning back to his vacated seat, though he remained standing. "I understand."

For a moment there was silence, but Parigan turned back toward them and addressed Sarneth once more from across the circle. "The elders of Taralindraal understand the concerns you have voiced for many years about the need to repair the divide between men and Great Bear, Sarneth, but why have you brought this boy into Taralin? Trigan brought word of Malek's attacks in Werthanin and of his likely entrance into Suthanin, but what news do you bring that you need help to convey? What can this boy's mouth say that yours cannot?"

"He was apprenticed to Valzaan before Valzaan's passing," Sarneth said, and a murmur ran around the circle.

"So Valzaan is dead then?" Parigan asked.

"Yes. He was cast into the ocean by a son of Vulsutyr traveling with Malek, the same Vulsutyrim who has summoned and sustained this storm that dominates our skies by day and by night."

Sarneth's answer was met by silence. Benjiah could tell that Parigan's gaze now rested upon him. "It is your claim, Sarneth, that this boy is a prophet of Allfather?"

"It is."

"What difference does it make if he is or isn't?" A Great Bear six or seven down from Parigan had risen to his feet. "Valzaan was known to our fathers and their fathers before them. This boy is known to no one. The clan should not have broken the tradition of the elders for him, even if he was an apprentice to Valzaan."

"That discussion is over, Kerentol," Parigan answered without hesitation. "Your thoughts on this matter were made clear enough when we discussed it the first time. The decision to allow the boy's entrance has been made, and while he is here, he is our guest."

"He does not belong," Kerentol growled.

"Enough," Parigan answered, the tone of his voice rising ever so slightly. Turning back to Sarneth, Parigan continued. "What purpose did you have for the boy when you requested his admission? If you wanted us to know that Valzaan has fallen but that an apprentice still rides with the army of men passing Taralin, you could have sent word or brought it yourself. Again, why are you here? And why have you brought him?"

"I have brought him," Sarneth said, rising to his full height on his powerful hind legs, "to remind the elders of Taralin of the face of men. He is a creation of Allfather, just as we are, as proud of his fathers and their fathers as we are of ours. He loves Allfather and is loved by Allfather, just as we do and are."

Sarneth started walking around the circle, addressing himself to the whole circle, taking in all of the elders of the clan. "The men of Kirthanin were ever our allies, and side by side we resisted the will of Malek together. Our allies of old have need of us again."

"Traitors of old, you mean."

"One of them, Kerentol, one of them. Would you like every Great Bear to be judged by the deeds of the worst of us? When will we acknowledge that Corindel's betrayal was the mistake of one man and not of all men?"

"And what of Andunin? Are we not all still paying for his mistake as well? Is it untrue that men are readily bent to Malek's will, while no Great Bear has ever entered into his service?"

To this Sarneth had no ready reply, and Parigan said, "You say they have need of us again, Sarneth, but why should we march forth now, leaving our draals unprotected?"

"They do have need of us," Sarneth said, "but I was not allowed to finish. We also have need of them. We must march forth and stand beside them now, because if we don't, there will be none of them left to stand beside us later. If Malek is allowed to break the will and armies of men, he will come when all else is his and destroy all the clans, one by one."

Again, murmurs spread around the circle. Sarneth did not wait for them to die down this time. "It has been almost nine hundred years since Corindel betrayed Gyrindraal. We have not forgotten, nor should we, but we must forgive. We must rejoin the world beyond our borders. We must send aid, and we must send it now. We are not safe any longer in our draals. Malek is on the move. I have seen his armies. They will overrun us and everything else in his path. He has Vulsutyrim, legions of Malekim, Black Wolves, and a host of men, and they are most likely headed south even now. They may already be in Suthanin, and they have already passed through Fel Edorath and Shalin Bel. What's more, a creature of the deep destroyed several ships in the convoy of men I sailed with from Col Marena. Some new terror has been unleashed upon us, and do not forget the manipulation of the weather we have already mentioned.

"The Mountain has been emptied. Malek is making his play for control of Kirthanin. Even if we stand beside the armies of men, we may not be strong enough to stop him. We may not have the strength. But, we have to go, don't we? We can't just sit here and let Malek take what he wants. If we did, would we not be as bad as Corindel?"

"How dare you?" Kerentol stepped forward into the circle, and the murmuring was renewed with growing intensity and volume.

Benjiah scanned the circle but could not read the passions of the elders. For a moment, chaos seemed to have taken over. Sarneth stood tall, saying nothing but holding his place, even as Kerentol surveyed the ring, no doubt also trying to gauge the reaction of his peers.

Suddenly, Benjiah felt Valzaan's staff warm in his hand, and a series of images flashed before his eyes. They came quickly and passed quickly, but each was as vivid as the one before, like a dream recalled in utter clarity upon the moment of waking. First came an image of night, the sky clear with a myriad of stars shining in the darkness. This picture faded and was replaced by an equally vivid image of day, a deep-blue sky without a trace of cloud, dominated by a bright and burning sun, hanging so close to Benjiah that he thought for a moment that if he but extended his hand, he could take hold of it. This gave way to an image of storm, the lightning and thunder flashing and rolling in the grey skies. A heavy bank of clouds boomed and flashed from horizon to horizon, and Benjiah clapped his hands over his ears to protect them from the din. This also passed, and the great and burning sun returned as the storm dissipated.

The next image was just as clear, if less coherent. A hundred moments of sadness flickered before Benjiah's eyes so rapidly that each disappeared as fast as his mind could recognize it, replaced by another and another and another. A crying child, a lonely woman, a sick animal lying stretched out in the mud. A decrepit house with its timbers cracked and bowed, an empty cradle beside a dead fireplace, a ship floating adrift and unmanned in a wide and fathomless sea. So many that Benjiah could not reckon their number. They flashed before him one after the other until he wanted to fall on his face and bury his eyes in the earth to make them go away.

They left him, and now a hundred moments of joy replaced them just as rapidly and relentlessly. A breeze rippled a field full of ripe grain, a pair of children holding hands waded into a stream, a man standing in the doorway to a shop threw his head back as he laughed and laughed and laughed. A cat nuzzled its head against an old woman's face, a fire roared in the great open hearth of a magnificent country house sitting snug and cozy in the middle of a winter storm, a flower opened and turned to face the rising sun. They each registered in his mind for a solitary instant, and though they filled him with wonder and delight, he felt relief wash over him when the last of them faded away and he was again cognizant of the circle of Great Bear.

He looked up. The circle had grown quiet, and Sarneth was looking at Benjiah. In fact, they were all looking at him.

Sweat had broken out across his forehead and was rolling down his face. His whole body was damp.

"Benjiah," Sarneth said gently and quietly, "Parigan has addressed you on behalf of the clan."

"I'm sorry," Benjiah said, turning to Parigan, "I don't know what just happened or what came over me, but I didn't hear you."

For a moment, Parigan looked at Benjiah, compassionately he thought. The Great Bear walked across the circle until he stood not five spans from him. "I simply asked if you, having come with Sarneth all this way to appear before us, had anything to say?"

Benjiah swallowed. The moment he had feared had come. Sarneth and all the elders of the Taralin clan were waiting for him to say something, but flushed and sweating from the overwhelming assault of images, he felt completely at a loss to say anything.

Almost involuntarily, he slid to the edge of the bench, then dropped to the ground. Walking forward, clutching Valzaan's staff in his hand, he passed between Sarneth and Parigan, moving into the center of the circle. He stopped there and turned slowly, looking from watching face to watching face. Then he realized why he was sweating. The staff was still glowing hot in his hand. He was not worried or anxious anymore, and when he opened his mouth, the words flowed evenly and clearly.

"So says Allfather.

"The sin of Corindel was very great. His refusal to heed the warning of Valzaan, my prophet, was not least among his offenses. Take heed, lest Corindel's failure become your own.

"The clan of Taralin has been faithful and true. You have protected your families and this forest with great care. You have kept the draal safe. You have discharged your duty with loyalty, and in this you have done well.

"You can hide in your draals no longer, however. It is time to come forth, to rejoin the world that was and is and will be again.

"Hear me. A dark storm lies over the land, and even now the true extent of the darkness is hidden from your eyes. The days ahead will be darker still, but you must not fear. My hand is not grown short, nor have I lost the power to save. Remember this, when all hope seems lost. Despair is a weapon of our enemy, and he will assault you with it in places where all other weapons cannot reach you.

"Malek's ultimate defeat will require the union of four great peoples. Then and only then will the last of his servants be defeated and the grip of his hand on Kirthanin be broken. The union of the Great Bear and men is the first step in that greater unity, and it must begin now.

"Even so, though man cannot stand alone and will not, it will be a man and his sacrifice that signals the end of Malek's oppression of my creation. As one man took up the blade, so another will lay it down, and the blade will pass from his hands and perish forever from the earth.

"This is what is and what will be. Know it as certainly as you know what has been. You are summoned now to come forth. The race of men does not call you. Sarneth does not call you. Your Maker calls you, the One who rules over the mountains and the forest, the land and the sea. It is He who calls you. It is time.

"So says Allfather."

For a long moment, no one in the circle moved or spoke. Benjiah remained where he was, the warm staff still glowing. At some level, in his mind, he was vaguely aware of the significance of what he had just done, prophesying in the name of Allfather, but he sensed no awe or wonder; rather, he felt only certainty that he had been what he was meant to be: Allfather's mouthpiece in this very place at this very time.

The silence was broken at last by Kerentol. "This is madness. What proof have we that this boy is speaking the words of Allfather? Are we to believe him because he carries Valzaan's staff, or a staff that looks like Valzaan's? Couldn't anyone have picked up Valzaan's staff after his demise? How do we know that he isn't speaking for himself, portraying as the will of Allfather his own desires and the desires of men?"

"And if he is speaking for Allfather?" Sarneth asked. "If the words just uttered here were not his voice or will, but the will of our Creator? Will you oppose them, Kerentol, simply because Allfather chooses to use as his instrument the mouth of a man? Will you reject your duty?"

"Enough," Parigan fairly shouted as he moved between Sarneth and Kerentol, both of whom had been drifting toward the other. Parigan stopped the movement of their bodies and silenced the movement of their tongues, likewise motioning to the circle to regain its composure, for murmurings and rumblings had again broken out. "What has happened here and what has been spoken must now be considered by the elders. No more will be said about it while our visitors remain in our presence. Elmaaneth, please look after our guests. We will send word when we've had time to consider what they said."

Elmaaneth rose and led the way out of the ring of silvery trees. Benjiah followed, holding Valzaan's staff firmly as he walked between Elmaaneth and Sarneth. As he retrieved his horse and walked away, he could hear the voices of the Great Bear taking up the matter.

They did not have to go far, for which Benjiah was grateful. Now that the intensity of the assembly had passed, he felt the weariness of the long day's ride wash over him. He was very tired, and the warmth that the staff had provided was gone. The cold of the night air returned with a vengeance. He pulled his damp cloak around his shoulders as tightly as he could, but it offered little comfort and less warmth.

They arrived shortly at one of the large round structures built around the base of the giant trees. A torch by the door illuminated the entryway, and after tying his horse to a post, he followed Elmaaneth and Sarneth through the doorway. Inside, it was large and open, with a simple dirt floor and little furniture. The roof was perhaps a span and a half or more above his head, allowing plenty of room for the Great Bear to stand comfortably at their full height. A large table stood against the side of the tree trunk, which served as the center of the room like the hub of a wheel.

In addition to this large, open, circular room, Benjiah saw a second, interior room built right into the tree. Indeed, as curious as it seemed, this hollowed-out place was where the Great Bear slept. They were in Elmaaneth's home, and this interior room was where Benjiah and Sarneth were to spend the night. With delight, Benjiah curled up on the wonderfully dry ground, as Sarneth likewise curled up, closer to the door. Elmaaneth remained a while in the larger outer room.

Sleep was not yet on Sarneth's mind, and he spoke to Benjiah quietly. "You did well before the elders, Benjiah. You have given the clan much to think about, and me as well. What did you mean about the union of the four peoples?"

"I don't know, Sarneth. I don't know what any of it meant."

"Has anything like that happened to you before?"

"Not like that."

"Can you describe it?"

"Well, while I was waiting, I felt warmth flow into me from Valzaan's staff. Then, a strange succession of images flashed before my eyes, and my senses were overloaded with them. When they had gone, my attention returned to the circle, and you were speaking to me. That's when I felt myself moving off the bench and into the circle. The words poured into my head and heart and out of my mouth. It was my mouth, but Allfather's voice that spoke." Benjiah looked over at Sarneth and added, "You believe that, don't you?"

"I do," Sarneth answered without hesitation. "Valzaan said you were called as a prophet, and if that were all the evidence I had, it would be enough. But there is more. I sense it in you, and I would likely believe even if Valzaan had not testified on your behalf."

"But will the clan?"

"That I don't know."

Benjiah pondered this. After a few moments, he said, "Sarneth?"

"Yes?"

"I've been very nervous, afraid of being seen as Valzaan's replacement. He was so remarkable, and I'm . . . well, I'm just me."

"And now? Do you feel different?"

"Yes, and no. I'm not as afraid in my heart, but I am still afraid in my head. I know what just happened was Allfather's doing. It was real, but I didn't control it. I don't know if I'm supposed to be able to. I wish Valzaan were here to explain it to me."

"Perhaps what happened tonight wouldn't have happened the same way if Valzaan were here. Maybe there is a connection between Valzaan's death and your prophetic birth, so to speak."

"Maybe, but I still wish he were here."

"So do I. He was a good friend, as well as a prophet."

"You knew him long ago, didn't you?"

"Yes, long ago. Now, let's try to sleep, Benjiah. The elders will not disband until they have reached a decision. We should sleep while we can, for what will happen when they have decided, I cannot say."

That night, Benjiah experienced a relentless flood of images like those that had come upon him earlier in the evening. He felt every emotion he had ever known in more ways than he thought possible. His felt the freezing cold wind cut through his cloak and flesh to chill his bones. He felt the searing heat of the sun burn his eyes and face and hands and any skin exposed to its punishing fury. He grieved the loss of a thousand innocent lives, swept away before a roiling flood that swept all things in its path utterly away. He celebrated a myriad of births as new life sprang irrepressibly from the mutual love of parents, who greeted each new arrival as though it were the firstborn of all Kirthanin. The images flowed into and out of his head, one after the other, one on top of the next, each vivid and strong, each gone in an instant.

He woke, damp with sweat that had soaked his clothes from head to toe, and sat up in the dark. Two large forms lay curled on the dirt floor nearby. Seeing no evidence of morning light beyond the door, Benjiah settled himself gently back onto the floor. He was almost afraid to close his eyes. He was physically and emotionally exhausted.

What's happening to me? Is all this from Allfather? What am I to learn from it? What is it preparing me for? With both hands he rubbed his eyes as he lay on his back, staring up into the dark. He was so young and knew so little of the world. Maybe that was it. Maybe Allfather was trying to show him the story of all things, of life itself. If he would speak for Allfather in this world, maybe he needed to understand the world to whom he was to speak.

He rolled onto his side. Whatever was going on, he wanted it to go away, at least for the rest of tonight. Here, for once, was real shelter over his head. He didn't want to waste it. Worn beyond resistance, he closed his eyes again.

Wide floodwaters stretched out before him. Beyond them, the dragon tower rose menacing against a grey and gloomy sky. The windhover flew above the water, headed for the far side. Not far away, caught in the top of a scraggly tree protruding out of the high waters, was a boat. Benjiah waded into the floodwater and over to the boat. Floating beside it was a broken oar, the narrow part of the shaft split in a long fracture that ran almost its entire length. In the bottom of the boat, though, a second oar lay intact. Pulling himself into the boat and freeing it from the treetop, Benjiah started to paddle across the wide, rolling river.

His passage complete, Benjiah stepped from the boat and walked toward the dragon tower. The stone was dark and smooth, the large iron door closed tightly shut. Peering up at the gyre far above, the windhover fluttered down and landed on his shoulder. "What's up there, I wonder?" Benjiah said under his breath.

Immediately, the windhover jumped from his shoulder and began to soar around and around, higher and higher. Benjiah closed his eyes, and as he did, he realized he could see what the windhover was seeing as it ascended. The earth fell quickly away, and his own form grew smaller and smaller as the windhover rose up the side of the tower toward the gyre. Benjiah gasped in anticipation as the bird rose above the edge and the gyre came into view.

It was large and open, and not especially wondrous. The curved stone on the topside was the mirror image of the underside, as one would expect, with a wide, flat floor about halfway down the open bowl. The large trapdoor that opened into the storeroom below was shut under the partial roof that once upon a time sheltered the dragons who slept there. Piled on one side of the sheltered portion of the gyre was a stack of firewood.

Light the beacon. Summon the dragons.

Benjiah opened his eyes, and the tower wall and door reappeared. He looked up into the sky, but the windhover was nowhere to be seen. He looked at the dragon tower door. There was nothing for it. He had to go in.

"Benjiah," Sarneth called softly as he shook the boy. "It is time to awake."

Benjiah sat up, looking sleepily at the large face of the Great Bear peering down at him. The light of morning was streaming into the interior room now, and Benjiah realized Elmaaneth was already up and out. "Has word come from the elders?" he asked, remembering suddenly what they were there waiting for.

"Elmaaneth has just been summoned. I expect him back soon. Did you sleep all right?"

Benjiah laughed. "No. It was a restless night."

"I could tell," Sarneth reported. "You rolled over and whacked me, twice."

Benjiah stifled another laugh. "Oh, Sarneth, I'm sorry."

"Don't worry about it. My own sleep was broken as well by many things and many thoughts."

"Maybe it's too dry in here."

It was Sarneth's turn to laugh, and the sound soothed Benjiah. By the light of day, the weight of the night's dreams didn't seem so heavy.

The sound of a door opening and closing drew their attention, and momentarily, Elmaaneth's form appeared. "Come, Sarneth and Benjiah, join me at the table. I have news."

Benjiah followed Sarneth out, and both took seats at the table opposite Elmaaneth.

"The elders have reached a decision. The clan will send aid to your friends south of Taralin, to march with them wherever their journey takes them, to Cimaris Rul and beyond if need be. What's more, messengers have already been dispatched to Elnindraal and Lindandraal to inform them of the clan's decision and to request their aid as well. Allfather's words are to be repeated in full at both places, and it is hoped that the full might of the Great Bear will be brought forth as soon as may be, perhaps before the end of winter."

"That's great news," Benjiah said, clapping his hands together. "Isn't it, Sarneth?"

"Great news indeed," Sarneth answered. "It is even better than I had dared to hope, though after your prophecy, I thought there might be a chance. I wondered if your words would not be the blow that broke the dam, and in so doing, release once and for all the power long held behind it. I don't know what strength still lies in the three remaining clans, but whatever happens now, we will stand together again at last, Great Bear and men."

"Two great peoples, unified," Elmaaneth added, excitement also evident in his voice, as it had been in Sarneth's own.

"The dragons!" Benjiah said, jumping down from his seat at the table. "They will be the third! That's what the dream means!"

"What dream?"

"Last night, I dreamt for the second time a strange dream about a dragon tower, and a voice told me to light the beacons and summon the dragons. I had the same dream on the *Silver Swan*. I wasn't sure what it meant then, but it is clearer now. I need to summon the dragons so they can join with men and Great Bear, the third great people united against Malek."

"And the fourth?" Elmaaneth asked.

Benjiah looked back at the table, then at the two Great Bear. "I have no idea."

"Well, we must trust that we will understand in time. More pressing matters lie before us."

"Yes," Elmaaneth said, nodding. "The elders would like me to guide the two of you as quickly as possible to the southern edge of the forest, so that you may prepare your friends for our arrival. As soon as the full measure of Taralin's strength is mustered, the rest will join us there."

"Then we must go. News like this should not wait."

“It can wait for breakfast, surely,” Benjiah said, realizing as he said so that he was very hungry.

“Take your breakfast with you,” Sarneth replied. “You can eat while we make our way through the draal. It will take a while to reach the southern exit, and we will only run once we have left the draal behind. Come, we have good news, and it begs to be told.”

A DIFFERENT ROAD

IN THE SUMMERTIME, when the cicadas were so numerous in the trees near her father's house that to disturb them was to be surrounded by a living, swarming fog, the baya-berry bushes would hang so heavy with great red berries the size of a man's thumb that Aelwyn could pick all morning and afternoon and not clear a single one. The blossoms on the bush would dangle, a delicate shade of light blue, emitting a scent so sweet it attracted every bee for leagues. On long summer days when the daylight lingered in the sky well past Twelfth Hour, she would walk barefoot in the tall, soft grass, feeling the tickly spears beneath her feet and the warm earth beneath her toes. She had to be careful not to disturb the black beetles' nests, but time and unfortunate experience had long since taught her the location of those, and she maintained a wide berth.

In the summertime, when at last the final rays of twilight had slipped away and the stars twinkled in the night sky, she would lie down in the lush grass and rest her hands behind her head as she stared up at the firmament. If she was very lucky, the Azaruul would come out in force, and the beaming lights of the heavens would be punctuated by the fluttering green stars of earth, her favorite creatures in the whole wide world.

The song of the swarming cicada, the smell of the baya-berry blossoms, the feel of the warm earth and soft grass, and the sight of the hovering Azaruul—these were the marks of summer. These were the happy symbols of her childhood, which strangely enough always felt like summer when she looked back at it. These were the things she most missed in the penetrating, ever-present, and seemingly endless rain.

It was not summer now, and happy memories of her father's country house, the home she had grown up in, were not easy to summon. There was something about this rain and this storm that discouraged her from even trying. The water fell hard now, not light and drizzly like before, and the heavy pattering of the drops upon the ground and the horses and their saddles and everything in the grass prevented her thoughts from roaming to happier times and happier places. She tried to summon the strength to make the vision of the baya-berries and blossoms stay, to hold onto the sound of the cicada above the sound of the turbulent rainfall, but they were all slipping away. Even the vision of the Azaruul gracefully floating between her and the welcoming night sky disappeared from view, and again everything was grey and wet and cold.

Aelwyn pulled her cloak tighter. She had almost grown used to the lighter rains that accompanied them for weeks, but this new, strong, pounding rain threatened to unnerve and unsettle her in less than a day. It had started to really pour during the previous day's supper, as they settled into camp just south of Taralin, and it had not slacked off since. Normally, she would have been comforted by the surety that such force in a downpour was unsustainable, but there was no comfort in such notions anymore. All conventional wisdom about how long a storm could last or how hard a storm could be had long since been overturned.

She looked at her sister, her legs drawn up under her dress with her arms clasped tightly around them, trying to stay somewhat warm, and she wondered how long they could hang on. The rain might be able to go on forever, but they could not. If the others were half as discouraged by this turn of events as Mindarin was, she wondered if Caan would ever get them up and moving again. It was tempting to slip into the shelter of Taralin's great, tall trees and simply hide and wait. Maybe she could find a dry hole in the ground where she could curl up and sleep. She wouldn't mind letting this whole war just pass her by, and she would accept with resignation any outcome, if only she could have some rest and warmth in the meantime. It was very tempting indeed.

She sighed as she watched the twins walking toward her. She knew she couldn't do that. Aljeron was out there somewhere, struggling toward Harak Andunin, and she needed to keep going too. It was the twenty-third day of Winter Rise now, and she wondered how far Aljeron had progressed into Nolthanin. Though it had been only three weeks since she'd bade him goodbye, it felt a good bit longer than that. She wondered, too, if he'd found any survivors in the ruined remains of Col Marena. He was unwavering in his commitment to go ashore and have a look, but it seemed to her like a futile exercise. Even so, she realized it was always possible he'd found men alive there, and she wished greatly that he found many and that they would be a great help to him.

"Hey," Pedraan said, looking down at Mindarin and Aelwyn.

Mindarin looked up but said nothing. The twins clutched their soaked cloaks so tightly their exposed hands were white at the knuckles.

"Hey," Aelwyn returned the greeting for both of them, though it sounded like an empty and hollow syllable.

Pedraal started to pace, and Mindarin looked over at his legs. "You've got to relax," she said without looking up at his face. "Benjiah is perfectly safe in Taralin with Sarneth."

"I know," Pedraal replied, looking not at Mindarin but at the forest. "Still, I don't think I'll be able to relax until he's back."

That was all either of them said. Pedraal kept right on pacing, and Mindarin kept right on clutching her knees up to her chin. Aelwyn took both of her hands and ran them through her long, wet hair, wringing out as much water as she could. She knew she'd never keep it dry, but it felt good if even for a moment to think she was pushing back the relentless tide of the pounding rains.

"What's next?" she asked out loud, though she didn't really mean to and didn't necessarily want to contemplate the question just then.

The others had heard, however, and there would be no dismissing the question now. Mindarin and the twins looked over at her, and Pedraal stopped pacing. "Well that depends, I suppose," he said.

"On what?" Mindarin asked tersely.

"On any number of things. It depends on what route to Cimaris Rul is the fastest and the best. It depends on what if anything we hear back from the scouts Caan sent out to explore the area east of Taralin. It even depends, I suppose, on what news Sarneth and Benjiah bring with them from Taralin, though I don't really know what news they could bring that would affect our plans. Still, if there is news of Malek's forces in Suthanin near Taralin, the Great Bear will have it before our scouts do."

"True," Pedraan said. "It could depend on any of those things, or something else entirely. Nothing is certain any more."

"The rain is certain," Aelwyn added softly, squinting as she looked up into the deluge.

The others didn't say anything to this. After a moment, Mindarin said just barely loud enough to be heard, "I don't know that it actually matters what comes next, really. I mean, we all keep telling each other that there's always hope, but what we're really doing is trying to convince ourselves that if we keep going we might just find a way out of this mess. Aren't we just delaying the inevitable? We're tired and cold, wet and miserable, and waiting for us at the end of this long and discouraging road is an army we can't really hope to defeat. We might as well just stay here."

"Even if there isn't any hope, I say we should still march on to Cimaris Rul," Caan said. All turned around to see him standing nearby beside a horse. Aelwyn had no idea how long he'd been standing there.

"Why?" Mindarin said, showing no embarrassment that she had been overheard.

"Because beyond hope there is fidelity, and even if I didn't think we could win this fight, I'd fight anyway, because it is the right thing to do. I'll not concede Kirthanin to Malek. He'll stake his claim to this world only after he's sent me back to my Maker, me and any man who will fight beside me."

"I hear that," Pedraan added, nodding in the rain. "And I'm not going down without taking my share of his hosts with me. Men, wolves, Malekim, even a giant, I don't really care. I'll kill anything that comes my way, and they'd better have armor made of iron, because my hammer's going to crush a few skulls before I die."

"Please," Mindarin groaned. "I can't take any more male bravado. So what if you die in a blaze of glory on the battlefield? Who'll remember when Malek wipes us all from the face of the earth? Who'll care then? What difference will it make if you died on your feet, wielding your axe, or in the comfort of your house, under a solid roof and in a dry bed? What difference will it make if you spend your last days marching and riding in this nightmarish rain, or if you spend your last days in peace, curled up beside a roaring fire? What difference?"

"Maybe it won't matter to anyone else," Pedraan answered, "but it'll matter to me."

"It matters to more than just you, Pedraan. It matters to every creature of Allfather's in Kirthanin." Caan grew more animated. "Malek has tried twice before to seize control of this world, and he didn't succeed either time. He can be beaten. We know this. History proves it."

"Maybe so," Mindarin said begrudgingly with a shrug of her shoulders. "But history only tells us what was. It doesn't say a thing about what will be."

"I think you're wrong," Aelwyn said, uncharacteristically contradicting her sister in front of others. "History does tell us about what will be. The prophecies of Allfather are part of history, and they tell us that sooner or later, Malek will be defeated, once and for all. Maybe not now, maybe not in our lifetime, but it will happen. That's why we have to fight, because Allfather calls us to and because one day we're going to win, us or our children, or our children's children."

"So may it be," Caan said, looking gratefully at Aelwyn. "For now, though, we need to consider some of the options before us. I've called a meeting to discuss our plans for the near future, even if the distant future is beyond our reckoning—"

A growing commotion in the direction of Taralin interrupted their conversation, and each of them turned to see what the noise and excitement were about. At first, none of them could see anything, for hundreds of men had risen to their feet and were staring in the direction of the forest, but eventually, the figure of a man on a horse and a Great Bear passing through the ranks became clear. At last, Benjiah and Sarneth had returned.

When Benjiah and Sarneth saw Caan and the others, they headed straight to the group. Benjiah, who had been in great spirits ever since the draal's decision had been announced two days ago, had a huge smile on his face as he dismounted from his horse.

"Nephew!" Pedraan called out, grabbing Benjiah in an excited hug and lifting the boy off the ground.

Pedraal slapped him on the back and laughed as soon as Pedraan dropped him. "Good to see you, my boy. We knew you'd be fine, of course, but it is still good to see you."

"Yes, and it is good to see you," Benjiah answered when he regained his breath, his back smarting from the blow. At moments like these he was keenly aware that his uncles didn't fully understand their own strength.

Before he could say anything else, Mindarin and Aelwyn came around him too. "Good to see you returned safely," Aelwyn said with a warm smile.

"Thanks," Benjiah answered, blushing.

"You look none the worse for wear," Mindarin added loudly, looking him up and down. "I suppose you've had a lovely week, riding in relative peace and shelter. We should all have cut through the forest."

"That might not have been wise," Pedraan said, throwing Mindarin an annoyed look.

"By the Mountain!" Caan's voice interrupted their greetings, and the group turned to Caan, whose hand rested on Sarneth's shoulder. Caan clapped his hands together and smiled.

"What's this?" Pedraal asked, looking at Sarneth and Caan and then back to Benjiah. "What's going on?"

"Yes," Benjiah said, his own smile returning now, even bigger. "I had meant to tell you before Uncle Pedraan almost crushed me with his greeting, but we have big news. The Great Bear are coming."

"What?" Pedraal asked. "Where?" He looked back at Taralin.

"How many?" Mindarin put in at almost the same time.

"When?" Pedraan asked.

Benjiah laughed at the mix of excitement, eagerness, incredulity, and wonder in their faces, and again he was speechless. Impatient, they all turned to Sarneth for the answers. The Great Bear returned their looks with his deep, dark eyes.

Sarneth quickly summarized the decision of the Taralindraal elders, saying in conclusion, "The Great Bear have decided at last to renew their old alliance with men."

There was a long moment of silence as Sarneth's words sunk in, and then finally Pedraal said to Sarneth and Benjiah, "You have both been to the draal?"

"Yes," Sarneth answered. "Benjiah was admitted with me, and he also joined the elders in their council."

Benjiah flushed crimson again as the eyes of all rested intently upon him again. "And how long were you there?" Pedraal continued.

"From sunset to just after sunrise, two and a half days ago."

"So, all this is the result of your half-day visit," Pedraal said, his head shaking in disbelief.

"That is too great a claim for the role we have played," Sarneth answered. "The history of the fellowship between men and Great Bear is long, and the severing of that connection was grievous for many. For hundreds of years, many, including Valzaan and me, have argued that restoring the ties is essential. No doubt many of those discussions and arguments, though they seemed fruitless at the time, were seeds that have grown toward this decision. The Great Bear are not a hasty people, and this would not have been possible had not the hearts of many in the draal already been convinced that the time was come to lay aside the past in order to face the future."

"Yes," Caan said, nodding as he looked up into Sarneth's face. "You have long been our ally and supporter in the draals, whose doors were closed to us. We have much to thank you for."

"No thanks are necessary. What is best in this case for men is also best for the Great Bear. We must stand together, or we will none of us stand for long."

After a moment's pause, Caan said, "Well, I had come to notify everyone of a meeting to be held about our next step. Given this news, there are some things I need to see to first. If possible, I'd like some time with you, Sarneth. Could you come with me now?"

"Certainly."

"Good." Caan looked at the rest of them. "We will assemble to talk over dinner. Catch up with one another, only be discreet about what exactly you say and to whom until we have discussed these matters at more length."

Caan and Sarneth started away, and the three men and two women watched them go. Mindful of Caan's charge to be prudent, they stepped a little farther away from the Werthanim camp and sat in a small circle in the wet grass.

"My, my," Pedraal said as they settled in. "You've had yourself quite an adventure now, haven't you?"

"Indeed," Benjiah answered. "And what of your journey along the coast? Any more sightings of the creature in the water?"

"None."

"So your march was uneventful?"

"Yes, uneventful and wet," Mindarin replied. "There was water in the sky, water in the sea, and water pooling on me and under me when we'd stop to sleep. That was the story of our week."

"But you," Pedraal put in, "you've been where no man has been in almost a thousand years, except for Valzaan, perhaps. What was it like?"

"Do you mean Taralin, or just the draal?"

"I meant the draal, but Taralin too."

"It was beautiful. They were both beautiful. The northern realm of Taralin is one of the most majestic things I've ever seen."

"See," Pedraan said to his brother. "I told you he went just to get back inside the woods."

"Yeah," Pedraal added. "You probably took your time sightseeing while we struggled under the full fury of the storm."

"I did no such thing. Sarneth set a brisk pace, and after we met up with the patrol, we moved even faster. It was almost a blur."

Pedraal nodded. "I know what you mean. We tried to follow Sarneth and some of his cronies along the secret ways of the Great Bear in Elnin, and it wasn't easy. Go on."

"Well, which part do you want me to tell?"

"All of it," Aelwyn said happily. "We have all afternoon."

Caan took the meeting quickly to the matter of the Great Bear. "Give me your best guess as to what kind of strength the draal could muster quickly to meet us here."

"I would say, and I will be conservative, that the Taralindraal should be able to bring a thousand Great Bear without too much difficulty."

"So many?" Aelwyn said, excited.

"So few," Brenim said, disappointed.

"A thousand Great Bear aren't like a thousand men, you know," Caan said before anyone else could say anything. "We don't think of a thousand as a strong fighting force, but think of a thousand Sarneths, shoulder to shoulder in the line, wielding their staffs with might and power. They could engage five times their number of Malekim, something that even the full force of our current army, some eight thousand men, probably could not. While we can fight and hope to hold our own with the men and Black Wolves, the Great Bear will bring real options for defeating the Malekim."

"But what about the giants?"

Caan shrugged and smiled. "One thing at a time. We'll figure out a way."

"It is possible," Sarneth said, "that the draal will send more. If this were the Elnindraal, I would have said that we could reasonably expect two thousand Great Bear, but Taralin is a smaller clan."

"Two thousand!" Pedraan said. "Let's hope those messengers get there quick. Will the elders of the Elnindraal send aid to Cimaris Rul, do you think?"

"I don't know what they'll do."

"Sarneth," Caan interjected, taking control of the discussion again, "how are the Great Bear organized, militarily? Will there be an appointed commander?"

"Of course. Every time a clan goes to war, two of the elders are appointed to lead the army. However many Great Bear come, there will be two elders from Taralindraal with them."

"Will they allow themselves to be counseled by you, do you think?"

"Counseled, certainly," Sarneth said, "but not directed. They are responsible to the clan for the army, not me. Still, if you treat them equitably as you would any other ally, if you listen to as well as speak with them, you will find them almost certainly willing to help you in any way they can. They know where we are going and why we are going there, and they have agreed to go too, even though that means leaving the draal almost defenseless. They are counting on the assumption we have all made that Malek will try to defeat the human cities first. So, they know that they need to help you stand and fight, for if they let you fall, then Malek will come for them next and there will be no one to stand with them."

Caan nodded. "The Great Bear will need to travel at some distance, for I don't know what the horses will do if a thousand Great Bear filter through our ranks."

"Yes, they will understand that. They will probably form a rear guard for our column and come behind. They can move very quickly over long distances, so they won't worry about keeping up. They would worry about leaving this army behind, though, if they were to take the lead, and they know that between here and Cimaris Rul, at least, we will be in danger from behind."

"We will press on with all speed as soon as they arrive. I want to have the city prepared for Malek's arrival. With the Great Bear at our side," Caan said, his fist clenched tightly, "we'll give him something to think about when he gets there."

That night was one of the most dismal of Benjiah's life. He had been so full of excitement since the meeting with the elders in the draal that went through three whole days at something of an emotional peak. After the initial excitement of the news was the excitement of riding back to the others to share it, which was followed by the excitement of actually sharing it. Now all those things had passed, and with his emotional high waning, he found himself exhausted but unable to sleep.

While Taralin had not provided complete shelter from the rain by any means, the trees afforded some shelter from the lighter rains, meaning that for more than a week he was spared the difficulties of sleeping in the complete open. What's more, the rain fell so heavily these last two days that the conditions in the camp were far worse than at any time since their emergence from Gyrin weeks and weeks ago. Now, the ground was so saturated that large pools of water overflowed every depression and dip in the terrain. Benjiah couldn't find a spot where he could keep his whole body out of one of these growing puddles. The place where he eventually settled turned out to be especially inopportune, since the spot where he laid his head was on something of a slope. It proved to be the location of a small but growing rivulet that fed a large pool of water.

All attempts to seek relative comfort in the total dark of the moonless and starless night only led to further soaking. He rolled or crawled through half a dozen growing pools before finding a place where a small tuft of grass kept his face out of the muddy soil. There he curled up, trying to keep the cold out, but he lay most of the night shivering in the dark. His senses seemed heightened in those dark watches of the night, as they sometimes are when sleep eludes, and he was suddenly aware of how frequently the coughs and sneezes of others echoed through the dark. He was not surprised at these signs of human frailty so much as he was surprised not to have heard them before. It was a wonder that they weren't all sick by now, and he wondered how long they could go on like this before they were. Perhaps their passage aboard the ships had delayed the full impact of being exposed to all this rain.

Benjiah shivered, clasping his cloak tightly around him. The night was interminable, though he was sure morning could not be far away. At about the moment that he gave up on getting the rest he so desperately desired, he fell asleep.

He woke with a start at the sound of a horse, whinnying not far away. He sat up, wondering where he was. The sight of his uncles, their faces appearing to him haggard, more so than he had ever seen before, staring absently straight ahead as they sat side by side, brought reality back to him. He could tell by the light that it was still early morning, and he looked around at the men moving about, wondering how many of them had barely slept, if at all.

He crawled across the wet, muddy ground and sat up beside his uncles, who watched him blankly. "I had the dream again. That makes three times."

"The tower?"

"Yes."

Neither Pedraal nor Pedraan betrayed any emotion. They simply continued to stare at Benjiah. "So what now, do you think?" Pedraan asked at last.

"I have to go."

"We're going with you."

"I just need to figure out which way to go."

"Well," Pedraal said, "while you were with Sarneth in Taralin, Pedraan and I discussed this possibility. We're not sure which one is closer, the dragon tower north of here along the coast, not far from your father's home town of Dal Harat, or the one east of here on the other side of the Barunaan. But, even though we're not sure, we thought that we should head to the tower by the Barunaan, because it would put us closer to Cimaris Rul when we have done what we're going there to do."

Benjiah looked closely at his uncles. "You've discussed this already?"

"We had a lot of time together on horseback, riding south along the wood. Yes, we've discussed it."

"Well," Benjiah said after a moment, "the dragon tower that I've visited in my dream is by a river, I think, so I would have said that we should go to the one by the Barunaan whether it was the more logical choice or not. That it is also closer to Cimaris Rul, and your thinking it is better, confirms for me that we should go there."

"Then we're agreed?"

"We are, so now what?"

"We should go to Caan," Pedraal said. "We should see what he says."

"What if he doesn't want us to go?" Benjiah asked. "I don't want to disobey his orders, but I have to go."

"Patience, Benjiah. No need to fight that battle yet. We don't know what he'll say or how he'll react. Let's go to him first."

They all three stood and stretched, and Benjiah realized for the first time that the rain was not falling as heavily today. "It has slowed down," he said. Then looking at his uncles, he added, "The rain."

"Yes," they answered together, and Pedraan added, "Finally."

They walked through the camp, making a straight line to the place where they had dined with Caan and the others the night before. They found him sitting alone with Gilion, talking quietly together. When they had secured Caan's attention and made clear their desire to speak with him alone, Gilion graciously excused himself with a formal bow.

"Yes?" Caan asked, eyeing the three of them curiously.

"The time has come for us to travel by another road," Benjiah said, and he could see from the looks on their faces that his firm tone had surprised not only Caan but his uncles.

"What do you mean?"

"I have had a dream from Allfather," Benjiah began. "In fact, I have had it three times, and it calls me to a dragon tower. I have work to do there, work that cannot wait. I am going with all speed to the dragon tower east of here, across the Barunaan."

"The journey there will take you across the open Suthanin plains, and we do not know of the movement of Malek and his hosts. If they have made better time than we expect, you could ride right into his company."

"That is all the more reason we must make all haste."

Caan looked from the determined face of Benjiah to Pedraal and Pedraan. "The two of you are planning to go as well?"

"We promised Wylla to take care of him, and even though he may not need our care so much as we had once thought, we will go with him wherever his road leads us."

Caan nodded. "Even if you make good time and get across the plains before Malek's hosts come down from the north, he will almost certainly come down between you and us. It may be hard, if not impossible, for you to rejoin us there, if that was your plan."

"It was," Pedraal conceded, "and we will deal with what we find after the tower when we get there."

"Caan," Benjiah said, "it may not make any sense to you, but we need to go. In addition to the dream, I had a prophecy while in the assembly of elders in Taralindraal."

"Sarneth mentioned it."

"Then he has told you of the call for union among the four peoples of Kirthanin?"

"He has, though we don't know what that means."

"Nor do I, but it seems to me logical that if the healing of the age-old rift between the Great Bear and men is part of what Allfather intends, then why not the healing of the even older rift between men and the dragons? It is time a man ascended to the gyre of a dragon tower and lit a beacon once more."

"If that is so, then who is the fourth? Perhaps the four peoples mean not four different races, but rather the three faithful nations of men, the Werthanim, Suthanim, and Enthanim, along with the Great Bear."

"Or," Pedraan said, "maybe the prophecy speaks of the Werthanim, Suthanim, Great Bear, and dragons. If so, then their summoning and our convening in Cimaris Rul would fulfill the conditions for the prophecy to be completed and for Malek to be defeated."

"I don't know what to say to any of these theories," Benjiah said, "but I know I am summoned to the tower, even if this summons is not connected to the prophecy, though in my heart I believe it is."

"And what of the Grendolai? Do you not believe in them? For my part, I believe the Grendolai were real, and I believe they might just be alive and well, lying in darkness in their new homes."

"That may be," Benjiah answered, "and if it is, then I will trust Allfather to guide me inside the tower as clearly as He has guided me to the tower. All I know now is that I must go."

Caan put his strong hand on Benjiah's shoulder. "It sounds like you must. I will not try to stop you or tell you not to go where you believe Allfather is leading you. Valzaan believed in you, and I believe too. And yet, if I may counsel you: The road to the dragon tower beyond the Barunaan does not diverge from our route for many leagues. You should travel with us to Hol Oradin at least. There, where the coast breaks more inland and southerly to Cimaris Rul, you should strike out across the plains. It will be a much shorter trip, leaving you less exposed in open land. At least do this for me. Ride with us that far, and ride with what protection our army and the Great Bear can afford."

"That is a sensible suggestion, except that I don't want to lose too much time waiting here. We don't know when the Great Bear are coming, and if Malek is moving down through central Suthanin as you suggest, delay could be costly."

"Sarneth does not think it will be long. Give us a day, and if there is no word from our scouts or any sign of the Great Bear, go with my blessing."

Benjiah turned to his uncles, who nodded. "All right, then," Benjiah said at last. "We will wait for one day. But if there is no sign of the Great Bear by first light tomorrow, we will ride on alone."

"Fair enough," Caan replied, "though I hope to have sight of them long before then. Indeed, I hope very much to see them before noon today, that we may be on our way this very afternoon."

"Let us hope so," Benjiah answered, and all four men turned to look at the border of Taralin not two hundred spans away.

It was only midmorning when Caan's hopes were realized. The travelers were finishing their meager breakfasts when all through the ranks a collective gasp arose as men and women sprang to their feet with an energy that had left them days if not weeks ago. Filtering through the trees along the border of the forest for as far as the eye could see were hundreds and hundreds of Great Bear. They walked, majestic and powerful, each with his staff strapped to his back, now crossing the broad open stretch of land between Taralin and the camp.

The foremost Great Bear stopped some fifty spans away. Even at that distance, it was easy to see the agitation of the horses. Behind these, the Great Bear continued to pour out of the wood. On and on they came, and the people stared in wonder. At last, no more came out from the wood, but there was no more room. An enormous line of Great Bear, thirty or forty deep, stretched out before them.

Benjiah noticed Sarneth walking out to meet with some of the Great Bear in the center of the forward line. Benjiah could not be sure, but it looked to him as though Elmaaneth was among those that Sarneth conversed with. No one moved, and both the Great Bear and hosts of men silently considered one another.

At last Sarneth turned and reapproached the camp. Benjiah ran out to meet him, and Caan walked out as well. "Was that Elmaaneth?" he asked, excited.

"Yes," Sarneth said as he continued on to Caan. "He is with them, as is Kriegan."

"And which of the elders have come?"

"Parigan has come—"

"I knew it!" Benjiah said, delighted.

"And so has Kerentol," Sarneth finished.

"What?" Benjiah said, his smile vanishing. "But he hates us."

"He doesn't hate you," Sarneth said evenly, for by now, Caan and several of the other captains had arrived and were listening to their exchange. "You should understand, Benjiah, and all of you, that it is the custom of the Great Bear to send two elders with any army it deploys, because we believe it is wisdom for representatives of our most divergent beliefs to share leadership of our armies. This is not seen to be conflict, but balance. You should also understand, that as adamantly as Kerentol might have opposed Parigan in the assembly, having now been outvoted by the assembly of elders, he will support the will of the draal. Kerentol will fight as hard as any in the battles that are to come, and he may well give up his life for you or for me."

Benjiah did not speak, and Sarneth turned his focus to Caan. "The elders of the draal send word to you, Caan, that they would be pleased to speak with you if you would be willing to go with me before them."

"I am honored," Caan said. "Lead on."

The meeting between the Great Bear and Caan took but a few moments, and soon Caan returned with Sarneth. He looked to his captains, who waited with expectant eagerness in their faces. "They are ready to march. It is time to mount up and ride."

Word of their imminent departure shot through the camp, and a flurry of activity swept through the same men and women who had but lately rested lethargically in the muck and mire, too weary and dispirited to even rise. Benjiah turned to Sarneth before heading back to his horse. "How many, Sarneth? How many have come?"

"Parigan says there are a little more than fifteen hundred Great Bear under his command."

Benjiah smiled in reply, then raced back through the camp to his horse, where Pedraal and Pedraan were already mounted and waiting. As he reached out to take his horse's reins, he felt the pull of *torrim redara* upon him.

The voice that had spoken to him in the storm and in his dream spoke to him again. *This is the beginning, but there is more to be done. The full might of the Great Bear and men, even were it assembled here, would not be enough to win this war. Remember, Benjiah, and do what I have called you to do.*

Benjiah scanned the immobile men and the frozen Great Bear. There seemed to be so much power and strength assembled here. Were it not for the clarity of the warning, Benjiah would be tempted to think this force strong enough to hold its ground against the Bringer of Storms. But he had been warned, and the warning was clear.

Just like that, he slid out of *torrim redara* and back into real time. But before he could catch his breath, the scene around him disappeared, and he found himself gazing down on the men and Great Bear from far above. He blinked and the view changed; now the wood was down below. He blinked again, and as far as he could see, there was open ground, green with grass and pools of murky water. Twice, three more times, the view changed, and each time he saw nothing but open grassland.

He had not been able to see through the eyes of a windhover in weeks, and now, out of nowhere, the ability had returned. Even as the thought occurred to him, the view changed once more, and he saw hundreds and thousands of Black Wolves, running. Behind them, thousands upon thousands of Malekim ran too. Benjiah had not seen them so clearly at Zul Arnoth, and the Malekim were not on the beach above Col Marena. He had not realized how many there really were. In their midst, running in great strides, were hundreds of Vulsutyrim, their faces hard as stone as the water ran down their long wet hair and fell from their faces onto their broad chests. Benjiah didn't know if he could feel the windhover shuddering or he quaked himself, but a chill ran through him. Last, behind all the others, what looked like perhaps twenty thousand men on horseback rode hard, the great puddles on the ground splashing up under their hooves. This great sea of soldiers was moving south, and quickly.

Benjiah blinked again, and the men and Great Bear were moving all around him. His uncles stared at him.

"Are you all right, Benjiah?"

He secured his hold of the reins. "Yes, but even with our newfound aid, we are greatly outnumbered and time is short. We must ride."

"We're waiting on you, Nephew."

Benjiah climbed up on his horse. "Let's go."

11
THE DRAGON TOWER

RULALIN SAT UNCOMFORTABLY upon the bench again. This time, he was alone in Farimaal's tent. He had been nervous, asking for an audience with Farimaal, and Tashmiren made the most of the opportunity to remind him of his subordinate position among Malek's hosts. Even so, the message was relayed, and eventually he was summoned. He went quickly behind the messenger through the dark camp to Farimaal's tent and was admitted by Farimaal only to be interrupted before he could speak. A second messenger, sticking his head inside the tent, called Farimaal out, speaking only vaguely of "news from the north." Farimaal, for all of his unhurried demeanor, slipped outside quickly, and now Rulalin sat upon the wooden bench alone.

Farimaal did not keep him waiting long, and soon the brooding captain of Malek's hosts returned, his gait unhurried. He slouched in his chair sideways, as was his custom, and leaning his head back so that he appeared to be staring at the roof, addressed Rulalin. "Speak."

"It's about the rain," Rulalin said. When Farimaal neither spoke nor moved, he continued. "Aside from a few bridges across the Barunaan in the south, near the Southern Ocean, river crossings are dependent upon a system of ferries, which are strewn unevenly up and down the river. My guess is that the flooding will wipe out most of these vessels, if it hasn't already. Even if it doesn't, they will not easily accommodate an army in a river crossing."

Farimaal looked from the ceiling to Rulalin's bench. "All this I know," Farimaal said. "What is your point?"

"My point is this: If the Werthanim sail past Cimaris Rul and don't come ashore west of the Barunaan in Suthanin, we may be cut off with no easy way across, especially if the bridges in the south are washed away."

"They will not bypass Suthanin west of the Barunaan."

With Farimaal's assurance that the fleet would not sail beyond Cimaris Rul, Rulalin could think of nothing to say.

"If that is all," Farimaal added, "you may be dismissed."

Rulalin rose, bowed slightly toward Farimaal, who was again contemplating the ceiling of the tent, and slipped outside into the darkness.

Benjiah sat astride his tired horse, gazing down the gradual descent of the hill at the northern gate of Hol Oradin. It was the third day of Full Winter, and since midmorning of the previous day, it had been obvious that they were close to the town. A few days prior, the army struck a small road that wound south along the coast, and every so often they passed a farmhouse with standing fields on the inland side. As of the day before, those houses grew more frequent and those fields more compact.

Benjiah pitied the owners of these soggy fields, their winter grain stunted and struggling to grow in fields covered with standing water several hands deep. He pitied them not only because of the bad yield their spring harvest would provide, but because he knew they were likely unaware of the mighty foe that was even now rolling southward, ever closer. They were unaware, and Benjiah could not warn them. Caan forbade the men to speak of Malek and his army to any farmers outside Hol Oradin or to any merchants within, for the news should go first to the town elders, who could decide for themselves in what manner the news should be broken to the inhabitants.

The farmers, invariably, gathered at their windows or fences to stare at the great host of men, entranced by them and mystified by the wondrous sight of fifteen hundred Great Bear. He doubted very much whether the town elders would have to send any messengers north with Caan's news, for he believed most of these families would be in Hol Oradin by nightfall to see for themselves what was going on.

When he had reached the crest of this hill and seen Hol Oradin no more than a hundred spans away, Caan gave orders to halt the column while a messenger was sent into the town to communicate their friendly intentions. While not really worried about their reception, Caan believed it only right when bringing an army almost entirely devoid of Suthanim to the town. They would acquire any supplies Hol Oradin could afford to part with on their way to Cimaris Rul. Hol Oradin represented the first chance since their brief stay in Shalin Bel to supplement their almost exhausted food supply, and their last chance before Cimaris Rul to bring something in with them if they were in fact marching toward a siege.

Benjiah looked at Pedraal and Pedraan, sitting nearby on their horses, and when they nodded almost in unison to him, he spurred his horse and rode up to Caan. Caan looked over at Benjiah, then turned back to the town. "So, the time for your departure has come?"

"It has. Here, our roads diverge."

Caan didn't answer, but they were not left in silence for long. Mindarin and Aelwyn, who had been riding some distance behind, arrived after riding hard. "Not so fast," Mindarin said as they reined in their horses.

"When the column stopped, we knew you three would be making your move to head off," Aelwyn added while Mindarin caught her breath.

"Without saying goodbye to us."

"We didn't want to make a fuss about going," Pedraal answered.

"We don't want a fuss either," Mindarin echoed matter-of-factly, "only a chance to wish you well and see you on your way."

"Glad to be rid of us, are you?" Pedraan said, smirking.

"Immensely," Mindarin said, without skipping a beat, "except for young Benjiah. He's a comfort to have along. We'll be sorry to see him go, but it may be worth it, since he's taking the two of you with him."

"And here I thought we were growing on you," Pedraan said, pretending to be hurt.

"The sky may be falling and the world may be ending, but things will have to get a whole lot worse before that happens."

"Hush," Caan said, scowling. "No talk of the world ending, even in jest. There is too much at stake here. I won't have it."

"Sorry, Caan," Mindarin said, truly apologetic.

"It's all right. I am glad you all haven't lost your good spirits to this infernal rain, but I'm not in the mood for your play fighting right now." Turning to Benjiah, he added, "None of our scouts has brought back any word of Malek's movement. That may indicate good news, if they are still well north of here, or it may just mean they're farther east than the scouts have gone. Ride hard and keep your eyes open. If you are spotted, outrunning the Black Wolves will not be easy."

"We'll move as fast as we can. I am as eager to reach the tower as I am to avoid being caught in the open plains by Malek."

Caan studied Benjiah's face. "I hope you are right about the dragon tower. It still sounds like folly and madness to me."

"I know what it sounds like," Benjiah answered. "Don't worry about us. You have enough to worry about."

"We do indeed."

"Look for us in Cimaris Rul," Pedraal added. "We will come to you there if we can."

They led their horses down the side of the hill that faced inland.

"Take care of yourselves," Aelwyn called as they rode down the hill.

"We will," Benjiah called back, and soon they were hastening away, pushing their horses to a run through the steady rain.

For more than ten days they rode, rising before dawn and stopping only after dark, when it was simply too dangerous to go forward. Though the land was open and spacious, large pools of standing water had risen so high they formed interlocking networks of shallow but growing waterways. Some of these were deeper than they first appeared, and the three men discovered the first day that these must be taken with care, and in some cases bypassed, because the water was too deep and the footing for their horses too soft and treacherous. A few of the pools plunged their horses in up to their necks, and Benjiah marveled to think of so much water so far inland. This made movement in the dark especially tricky, as the shallow puddle and deep pool were impossible to tell apart after the last light of evening slipped away.

Where the terrain allowed, though, they pressed as fast as their horses could go, pushing the boundaries of their own endurance. They were driven by the deep and unsettling fear of being caught in this open grassland alone, but also, at least for Benjiah, by the urgent desire to reach the Barunaan. He had not had the dream since the third time on the southern border of Taralin, and he was beginning to wonder if he had misread the sign or answered the summons too late.

On the morning of the fourteenth day of Full Winter, Benjiah drew his horse up to a standstill, and the twins rode up beside him.

"What is it?"

"Down there, can you see something?" Benjiah asked, pointing southeast over the open ground.

Pedraal and Pedraan peered in that direction. After a moment, they turned back to him.

"I don't know if there's anything there," Pedraal said.

"I don't know either."

"Hold on," Benjiah said, closing his eyes. A few times during their ride, he had tried to summon a windhover so he could scout around for signs of the enemy or guidance to the tower, but he came up empty each time. *Don't fail me now. I need to see!* He pressed his eyes closed even tighter, but still there was only darkness. Then, almost as he was about to give up, he saw the ground rushing by beneath him. *Southeast. Show me if what I thought I saw was the tower.*

The King Falcon swung around, and as he turned southeast, Benjiah could see the rising form of a dragon tower in the distance. He was right.

Benjiah opened his eyes and the tower disappeared. "It's the tower. We need to go this way."

"If you say so," Pedraan said, looking at his brother, "but I can't make out a thing."

"Trust me," Benjiah answered, pushing his horse forward.

Onward they rode, picking their way through the pools and rivulets, which were growing more numerous and in many places, deeper.

"It would make sense that the runoff would be even more dramatic closer to the Barunaan," Pedraal said.

"Yeah, though with all these little rivers around, we may miss it."

"I doubt it," Benjiah said.

"It was a joke, Nephew," Pedraan scoffed.

"Oh."

Late in the evening, Benjiah slowed to a halt again. The tower loomed now; they had found the Barunaan at last. The flooded river swelled before them, stretching so wide that it looked to be a half a league across. The surface seemed so calm that at first Benjiah couldn't detect a current, and he began to wonder if this was really the Barunaan after all. But, as he continued to examine the water, he saw what must have been a large riverboat overturned, gliding downstream, its long keel exposed to the falling rain and its prow now pointing haphazardly into the gloomy sky.

"This is unbelievable," Pedraal said, reminding Benjiah that he was neither alone nor visiting this time in a dream.

"Yeah, I've never seen floodwaters like this," Pedraan echoed.

Benjiah did not join their conversation, for he turned his attention to the near banks, searching carefully up and down the edge of the floodwaters. After a moment, he saw what he was looking for, and murmured out loud, "There it is."

"There what is?" Pedraal asked.

"The tree," Benjiah answered, not taking his eyes off it for fear it might disappear if he looked away. "The scraggly treetop, in my dream. Each time I dreamt of this, there was a boat with a broken oar caught in the branches of a scraggly tree. I can see the tree, but from here, I can't see if there's a boat."

Benjiah started south along the water's edge, keeping the tree in view. As he drew up alongside of it, he began to make out the presence of the boat from his dreams, caught exactly where he had dreamed it, in the branches of the downstream side of the tree. "There," Benjiah said, stopping and pointing the boat out. "Can you see it?"

"Plain as day," Pedraan answered. Benjiah turned to look at his uncle with a smile, and he saw the wonder in his eyes as his uncle looked not at the boat but at him. He looked from Pedraan to Pedraal, and the same look was in his eyes too. He blushed. "It was a dream, you know."

"A vision, more like."

"Either way, Allfather showed me. That's how I knew."

"We know," Pedraal said quietly. "So what's next? We cross in the boat?"

"Each time in my dream, I got into the boat and paddled across. I suppose we can all get in."

"It looks big enough to carry all three of us."

Benjiah looked from them back at the boat, and it did look large enough to hold all three of them comfortably. If there was just the one unbroken paddle, it would be a nuisance for rowing all the way across. Still, glancing once more at the size of the flood-broadened river, he knew it was fortunate that there was any transportation at all. It would have been a very long and hard swim.

"What about our horses?" Pedraal asked, and the question caught Benjiah by surprise. He looked down at his own mount, standing patiently beside the water. "I don't know. I was never on horseback in any of my dreams."

"We'll have to leave them, obviously," Pedraan said. "They can't cross in the boat."

"Of course," Pedraal answered, "but we'll have to tie them up. We'll need them for the ride to Cimaris Rul."

"Sure, and it makes sense to leave them over here, since we'll need to come back across the river. Cimaris Rul is on this side of the Barunaan, after all."

"So is Malek's army," Pedraal replied. "I'd hoped to use the river as a shield between us and him on the journey south, just in case our time spent here allowed him to catch up. It will be very frustrating indeed if we follow the river down only to be caught before Cimaris Rul by some of his army, cut off from escape by these floodwaters."

"Frustrating is one way to put it," Pedraan answered with a humorless laugh. "Still, even if the river could shield us all the way down, what if the flooding is even worse down there and we reach Cimaris Rul but can't cross over to it? That would be frustrating too."

"There are bridges, Brother, remember?"

"Yes, if they survive the rising waters."

"We can decide what to do after we've been inside the tower," Benjiah said. "The bottom line is, we need to tie the horses up in case we need them later. Let's find a place for them that won't be too uncomfortable if they're left on their own for a couple of days."

"Speaking of that," Pedraal said, "maybe we should wait to cross until first light. It may be almost dark by the time we get over there, and I don't want to go in at night, do you?"

"No," Benjiah answered, "though once we're inside it won't matter. It will probably be dark as night inside, no matter when we enter. Still, even if we don't go in tonight, I want to cross tonight. If we spend the night on that side of the Barunaan, then we can enter as soon after dawn as we like. Let's put the river crossing behind us. Ascending the tower will be excitement enough for tomorrow."

Neither Pedraal nor Pedraan argued, though Benjiah could see they weren't exactly crazy about the idea. They seemed to have conceded to him leadership of their venture, and they did not second-guess his wishes. They spent a few minutes finding a suitable tree to tie their horses to, and it was trickier than they first thought. Several trees grew in the shallow water on the banks of the flooded river, but Benjiah fretted that to tie them in such a place would both deprive them of adequate food and leave them vulnerable if the river continued to rise. After a while, though, they did find a good spot, well back from the water's edge, where grass still grew through the mud and muck. They tied their horses and walked with their packs back to the boat.

"Well," Pedraan said when they reached the water's edge, "I suppose there is nothing else for it but to wade out to the boat." As he said this, he hoisted his pack onto his shoulder and started out, holding his war hammer firmly in his other hand. Pedraal followed, and Benjiah came after. He'd entrusted what food he had in his own pack to his uncles, and he carried only Valzaan's staff, Suruna, and a quiver full of arrows.

The boat was precisely as Benjiah had dreamed of it. Both the functional and fractured oar were right where they were supposed to be, and Benjiah felt a strong sense of déjà vu as he pulled himself into the firm but weathered boat. Unlike his dream, he didn't do any rowing, for Pedraal and Pedraan both insisted that because Benjiah was the brains of the mission, they could at least serve as the brawn. They proceeded to tease each other most of the way across that they were always reduced to their muscles, and that to be taken seriously as thinkers and leaders they'd need to starve themselves and take to using longer words when shorter ones would do.

"The sword must be a thinking man's weapon," Pedraan said after several moments of this. "They always trust armies into the hands of a man with a sword. It's never the warhammer guy or the battle-axe guy, like us. It's never even a spearman or an archer. Why all this prejudice in favor of men with swords? What makes them so special?"

"Envy," Pedraal answered. "Most people can't wield a war hammer or a battle-axe, so they're jealous of us."

"That must be it."

"Of course," Benjiah chimed in, "it must be jealousy. I'm sure it has nothing to do with the fact that most Kirthanim soldiers carry swords. Nor could it have anything to do with the fact that some people who carry war hammers and battle-axes come across like lug heads who just like to smash things. It can't be anything like that."

"No," Pedraan said, shaking his head, "surely it can't be that."

Pedraal laughed as he rowed, and they proceeded across the Barunaan in silence. Except for the center where the current was strong, they had an easy passage. The water was almost glassy smooth, except for the falling raindrops, which made interlacing circles ripple outward in repetitive but beautiful patterns that absorbed Benjiah's attention for much of the journey. When he looked up from the water, the far side of the river was much closer than he had expected, and he noted immediately a windhover sitting on the ground not far from the water's edge. The King Falcon rested in the grass, perhaps fifty spans away, watching them approach.

"I had forgotten about you," Benjiah said under his breath.

"What's that?" Pedraal asked as he rubbed his arms after passing the paddle to Pedraan to take them the rest of the way.

"The windhover, just ahead. He was in each of my dreams too. I had forgotten that."

"What part does he play in all this?"

"I don't know. In my first dream, he led me to the boat, and in the later ones, to the tower."

"Maybe his job's over, then."

"Maybe."

While Pedraal and Pedraan pulled the boat out of the shallow water, Benjiah watched the windhover leap into the air and fly to the dragon tower. Benjiah started after it without waiting for his uncles.

"Hey, what are you doing?" one of them called, and he could hear them running across the sloppy ground to catch up.

"Couldn't wait for us?" Pedraal asked as he came up beside Benjiah.

"Nope," Benjiah answered, keeping his eyes on the windhover, which had landed in the grass beside the door of the tower.

Benjiah did not walk up to the door, but he did cross over to stand beside the tower. He reached out with his hand and felt the stone. When his fingers touched the wet, smooth wall, unimaginably bright, searing light flashed before him, and he winced at the shock of it. It was the light of the visions he'd been having for so long, before the dreams of this tower, before Valzaan's death. The light always followed the images of pouring rain and preceded the images of himself in a wooden cage. But as soon as it had come, it had gone, and he opened his eyes to the dark, smooth stone of the tower wall. Leaning back, he gazed up the side at the curved bottom of the gyre so far above. He hadn't realized how big the gyre was, but it extended quite a ways out from the tower's side.

"All this used to be fields of grain, I think," Pedraal said, and Benjiah turned around. His uncles weren't examining the tower as much as the ground around it.

Pedraan saw Benjiah look over and explained. "This is where we met Valzaan, your father, and the rest as we were traveling to Sulare."

"Indeed, when he shut Mindarin up, remember?"

"Of course." Pedraan laughed. "There was no doubting that he was a prophet when he did that. Nothing short of a miracle could have made her close her mouth so long."

"The rain has beaten down the grain," Benjiah said.

"Looks that way."

Benjiah looked back up at the gyre. "That is where I must go."

"Yes, but not tonight."

"No, not tonight."

They retraced their steps toward the river, none of them really eager to spend the night right beside the tower, even if it would have afforded them a little bit of shelter, nor did they want to go inside until they had to. They preferred the dampness they knew to the darkness they did not. After a small supper, Pedraal and Pedraan worked out a plan to alternate keeping watch, absolutely refusing to allow Benjiah to take a shift.

"You think we're doing this to protect you," Pedraal said after several minutes of fruitless arguing. "Really, though, we just don't trust our safety to the likes of you."

Benjiah laughed. "Then you'd better stay down below when I go up the tower tomorrow."

"Oh no," Pedraal came back. "We're going up to keep you safe."

"Is that so? Then I hope you have something more than that axe and hammer with you, because if there really is a Grendolai in that tower, I'm not sure they will be sufficient."

"We'll see," Pedraal answered.

"That we will," Benjiah said, lying back to go to sleep. His uncles sat up together, whispering together about which of them was most likely to smash the head of the Grendolai should it threaten them the next day.

Benjiah looked from the high place where he was standing, and all around him was darkness. Above, it was dark and below, it was dark, but somehow he knew he was high, very high. In his hands was the staff, and he clasped it tightly. Already, in such a short time, the feel of the staff was quite comforting.

A flash of lightning far above split open the sky, and he saw for the first time the earth. As quickly as it had come the flash was gone, but the image it revealed remained with him. It was all wrong, now that he had a moment to think about it. He saw the grass and flowers and fields of grain, but they were rolling and rippling like waves in the sea. They were surging and swelling as though fluid, and now he began to wonder if he had seen it at all, or if his eyes were playing tricks in the darkness.

Boom. Boom. Boom. Three quick, loud thunderclaps echoed around him, and he tried as best he could to cover his ears. The lightning returned, and again he searched the ground so far beneath him. Sure enough, it was rising and falling in rhythmic motion. The light disappeared again, and now he wondered why the thunder preceded the lightning.

A long, low laugh sounded far away in the darkness, not below or above, just far away. He felt a chill and shivered. The laugh made him uneasy. He thought about calling out in answer, but he didn't know what to say. He gripped the staff tighter, wondering where he was and what he was supposed to be doing.

And then, suddenly, the staff began to glow. At first the faint and gentle light illuminated a small circle around him, but the light grew and grew in intensity. Soon it was so bright and so hot that he wanted to let go of the staff, but he couldn't. The brightness became so strong that, rather than illuminating the surrounding world, it washed it out. He couldn't keep his eyes open for longer than a few seconds, and when he did he could see nothing around him, only brightness. Soon he couldn't open his eyes at all, but even then the brightness was all around. His eyelids weren't much protection, and searing, bright light dazzled his eyes even as he squeezed them tighter and tighter.

Benjiah opened his eyes. The rain was still falling steadily, and the morning was not far away. He looked over at Pedraan, sleeping curled up in a ball, and then over at Pedraal. He was supposed to be on watch, for he was sitting upright, but he was asleep. His face was resting on his big open hand, and his elbow dug into his crossed leg. It didn't look especially comfortable.

With both of his uncles sleeping, Benjiah rose quietly, staff in hand, and made his way through the semidarkness to the dragon tower. He stopped before the door, and this time he did reach out to feel it. The metal was cold and smooth, and he traced it lightly with his fingertips. Of all the adventures in the world that little boys dreamed of, opening the door to a dragon tower to see what was inside was both the most desirable and the most feared. Nothing could rival the mystery that the tall, ancient structures inspired, and nothing could rival the dread they produced either. And here he was, called by Allfather to open and go in.

Benjiah realized it was the fifteenth day of Full Winter, the last day of the year. Tomorrow was Midwinter, and back home, as well as in towns and villages and cities all across Kirthanin, they would be celebrating the Feast of the New Year after the Mound rites. He wondered if there was anyplace in Kirthanin where the sun was shining and where the New Year would be greeted with any semblance of cheer. For him the thought of the feast and the New Year was almost disheartening. There was so little reason to rejoice.

"Trying to slip off without us, eh?" Pedraal asked as his uncles appeared, one on either side of him.

"I didn't try to; I did."

"Only because Pedraal couldn't keep his eyes open," Pedraan mumbled.

"I noticed," Benjiah answered. "Good thing the watch wasn't left to the likes of me, right?"

"I was only resting my eyes."

"Your eyes and everything else."

"Anyway," Pedraal said, stepping up to the door, "Is it time to get this out of the way and go on in?"

"I suppose it is," Benjiah said, noticing for the first time a slight trickle of water seeping through the grass right before the door. He peered more carefully down, and sure enough, water appeared to be flowing out from the tower through the grass.

"Pedraal, I might be careful if I were you—"

Benjiah's words were too soft and too late. Pedraal gave a mighty tug on the great iron ring on the dragon tower door, which slid outward a few feet. As it did, a massive wall of water came crashing out upon Pedraan. The water fell like a cascading river that has burst a dam and struck Pedraan so hard it sent him skidding across the soggy ground for several spans.

Pedraal scrambled over to help his brother, who rose, utterly soaked and dripping and looking wide-eyed at the now open door. "What was that?" he mumbled as he regained his feet.

"Looks like water's been getting inside the tower, somehow," Benjiah said, "and it's been collecting faster than it's been able to trickle out."

"That's a strong door, and well made," Pedraal said, feeling the inside of it as it stood open.

"Great," Pedraan muttered.

Benjiah stepped into the dark doorway, looking at the small space just inside the door where the spiral staircase began to ascend not even a span away. The air was close and musty, old and stale.

"It stinks," Pedraan said from right behind him. "Which means I'm going to stink now that I've been bathed in the water that collected here."

"Don't worry, Pedraan," his brother said. "With all the rain we've been having, you'll only need to spend a few hours outside to get yourself clean again."

Benjiah stepped inside, and his foot splashed in a small puddle on the stone floor. As he stepped all the way inside, so that Pedraal and Pedraan could come in too, Valzaan's staff began to glow. A soft, gentle light began to shine out, mostly from the carved windhover at the top, but also from the handle of the staff as well.

"That's a neat trick," Pedraal said, staring at the staff in Benjiah's hands. "I was wondering what we were going to do for light in here with nothing dry to set on fire or use as a torch. How'd you do it?"

"It's not a trick," Benjiah said, looking at the staff quizzically. "I didn't make this happen."

"Well, however it's working, I'm glad for the light."

"Me too. Now are we going to go up or what?" Pedraan added.

"We're going up," Benjiah answered, and, setting his foot lightly upon the first step, he began to ascend.

At the top of the spiral staircase, Benjiah paused for a moment to catch his breath. The twins, behind him, stopped, and Benjiah could hear them taking deep breaths as well. It was quite a climb.

Pedraal had tried to take the lead, but on the narrow, winding stair, the light from Valzaan's staff was needed in front. Eventually both uncles were forced to concede that Benjiah would lead the way as long as he was the one to light it. And so he went first, step by step, up and up. They climbed in silence, for instinctively, without ever discussing it before entering the dragon tower or saying anything on the stair, they slipped into a quiet mode where even their footsteps were carefully placed so as to produce a minimum of noise.

Now they stood before the final stair, and the light from the windhover revealed a short hall or landing that led through an open doorway into a much larger room. Benjiah peered down the hall, wondering if a Grendolai indeed lived within, but his concentration was broken by a tug on the back of his cloak.

He turned, and Pedraal and Pedraan both motioned him to head back down. He frowned. Their eyes grew more intense as their hand gestures grew more insistent. He nodded, reluctantly, turned from the top, and followed them twenty or thirty stairs down. There, Pedraal and Pedraan crouched on a stair below Benjiah. He sat down too.

"Shouldn't we talk about what's up there?" Pedraal asked, whispering so quietly that Benjiah had to lean in very close to hear.

"You mean the Grendolai?"

"Yes, and the room. What is beyond that hallway? Have you seen it in your dreams?"

Benjiah slowly nodded. "I have."

"Well, describe it to us."

"Picture the outside of the tower," Benjiah started, "where the walls suddenly curve way out, far above the ground. Now, imagine that curved thing up top is a large bowl. The dragon gyre is the top third of that bowl, with a flat floor of mostly stone stretching all the way across, except for a large, wooden trapdoor that leads down into the bottom two thirds, which is a large storage room. That's what the large room at the top of the stair is—the storage room."

"And that's where the Grendolai set their traps for the dragons," Pedraal said, exchanging nods with Pedraan. "We should have paid more attention to Master Berin's history lessons."

"If there is still a Grendolai here, that's where he'll be," Benjiah added.

"Only one way to find out."

"Follow us," Pedraal said as he and his brother started to rise.

Benjiah set the staff down and placed a firm hand on both their shoulders, and they looked at him in surprise. "I know you think you need to protect me, but here, I need to protect you. Follow me."

Without waiting for a reply, Benjiah took the staff and started back up the stairs. Once more he hesitated on the brink of the upper landing. He gripped the staff and finally stepped up and started forward, Pedraal and Pedraan close behind.

When he reached the door into the big chamber, he paused and peered in. He could see a faint stream of light falling like a spotlight on one narrow patch of floor less than twenty spans away. Looking up to the ceiling, he could make out a small hole in the wooden door that led to the gyre. So this was the answer to the water riddle. He'd noticed the slight trickle along the interior wall of the winding stair, but it had been hard to believe that so small stream could have fed so large a reservoir as Pedraal had unleashed. Given time and a constant supply of water, however, Benjiah imagined a lot of strange things would be possible.

Well, we're standing in the doorway with a light. There's no way to hide our presence now. It is forward and in or back down, and we can't do that. Benjiah, gripping the staff, stepped in.

Immediately, the light from the staff grew stronger, flaring up enough to illuminate the curved exterior walls sloping gently upward. Directly ahead, perhaps seven spans away, against the opposite wall, in the shadowy edge of the light, something moved on a large dais, withdrawing into what little shadow remained.

"I would welcome you as a host, but you do not enter as a guest," a low, soft voice spoke from the shadows. The words were calm, almost soothing, but the hair on Benjiah's neck tingled, and he gripped Valzaan's staff still tighter. Staring as intently as he could in the direction of the voice, he could make out an odd assembly of something like crates or stones rising up off the floor. He took a few steps closer, and the light from the staff brought them more clearly into view, even as the large dark form on top of them was silhouetted more fully. He stopped, for he knew now what he was looking at. The Grendolai had built for himself a throne.

"I am not disposed to deal graciously with visitors who intrude upon my peace, but put away that light and I will consider whether to spare your miserable lives." This time Benjiah heard agitation in the voice. Agitation, but no fear.

"So, you are still here, ancient usurper," Benjiah called out as the words flooded from his mind to his tongue. His own voice sounded steady, far more so than he felt. "Still squatting as an uninvited guest in a house not built for you."

"I claimed this place by the strength and power of my own two hands. I did what you could not do, Kirthanim. I killed a dragon to stake my claim. You could not do the same, for you are but flesh and bone. And it is such soft flesh, isn't it?"

"I did not come to contest the strength of your hands, only the validity of your claim. You have no place here. You are a servant of Malek, and this tower was built by servants of Allfather to honor the dragons. I am here to reclaim it for them."

"I am no one's servant."

"Are you not? Are you not here at the behest of your maker and your master, the Master of the Forge?"

"I am here because I like it here, and no man is going to drive me away. I grow weary of your visit, and if you don't have the sense to leave, I will come down from here and rip you in half to teach you about the validity of my claim."

"I will leave when I'm ready."

"You will never leave here alive!" Benjiah saw the massive form step down from the crude throne. The Grendolai was truly impressive. He was easily twice as wide as any giant, though not nearly as tall. His arms were thick and long, and the hands cast giant shadows against the wall behind him as he raised them to step off the dais.

It only took a second for the Grendolai to descend and take a single step in their direction, and in that second, Benjiah raised Valzaan's staff high above his head. "Enough!" he called out, his voice loud and booming in the hollow stone room. "You cannot threaten me! I am a prophet of Allfather and I speak for Him and wield His power. Hear now the judgment Allfather passes upon you. Your wickedness has long risen up before Allfather's throne, and He will tolerate neither it nor you any longer. Your dominion in this place is over. Your time and the time of your brothers is over. I will listen no longer to the sound of your voice. I have spoken. So says Allfather."

As soon as the last syllable of Allfather's name died away, the staff began to glow white-hot and as dazzlingly bright as it had in the dream. The light grew and grew in intensity, and the staff was so hot, Benjiah was sure he would find his hand burned beyond repair. Benjiah shut his eyes as tightly as he could to keep them from being seared by the brilliance, but still the whiteness of the light was inescapable.

A moment later, the heat and light were gone, and the staff glowed as it had before. Benjiah opened his eyes. The first thing he saw was Pedraal and Pedraan, face down on the ground, covering their eyes and heads. The second thing he saw was that there was more light in the room, though his staff appeared to be glowing more faintly. He peered up, and the mystery was quickly solved. Where before there had been a small patch of light falling in from the trapdoor, now there was an enormous hole. The heat from the flash of light had burned away the wood in its entirety.

The twins were beginning to draw themselves up off the floor, looking in wonder at Benjiah. Benjiah did not wait for them to say anything but started toward the far end of the room. The sight that awaited him was gruesome. The various pieces of wood and stone that had formed the throne were scattered around the floor. As for the Grendolai, it had been burned into the wall of the dragon tower. A dark, smoldering outline of its body remained, still smoking.

"You destroyed it," Pedraal said in awe, coming up behind Benjiah.

"Allfather destroyed it."

"How did we survive? It was so bright, so hot," Pedraan murmured.

"We survived because Allfather's judgment was not meant for us. Not this judgment, anyway." Benjiah turned and looked back at the center of the large storage room. Water from the gyre was pouring into the now gaping hole, some four or five spans above the floor. The beacon was up there, under the partial roof that covered the center of the gyre, but how were they to get up there?

"We need to search this room. There must have been a ladder once, for those who kept this room supplied and used the beacon. If we're fortunate, it will still be here, somewhere."

They spread out, and it did not take long to find the ladder, lying along the outer wall, with some other ancient relics of the Second Age that were not of any use to the Grendolai's throne-building venture. It was old but sturdy, and before long all three of them had ascended out of the darkness of the tower onto the gyre.

The large gyre spread out around them, most of it uncovered, except for the central portion with its small roof just big enough to provide cover where the dragon would have slept, as well as to cover the trap door and beacon. The beacon was still there, raised up off of the floor of the gyre, so that the rain water had not soaked it but passed underneath it. "I'm glad whoever designed this place thought to keep the beacon off the ground," Pedraal said. "Or this would have been really frustrating. To get up here and not be able to light the beacon."

"Before we light this, Benjiah, let's go out and see what we can see from the edge of the gyre. I want to see this view."

"Sure, we have plenty of time. I don't want to light it until this evening anyway, just to make sure it is visible a long way away." They started away, moving out from the covered part of the gyre, and making their way to the edge of the flat bottom of the gyre to the place where the outer wall sloped upward to the rim.

"It only really matters if someone, or something, is looking for it."

"We'll light this thing, but will anyone see it, and will anyone come?"

"We'll see," Benjiah answered, looking out at the broad river and broad plains, stretching far away below. "We'll see."

FLOOD

1 MIDWINTER

WYLLA WALKED THROUGH THE WET streets, the gutters running with water deeper than she'd ever seen. All the drains out of the city gushed with it, and water puddled in even the smallest of depressions in the paving stones. At times in her life water had been rationed during drought, but she could not recall a time when the city had suffered from too much.

Allfather shall make all things new, so be it? The words of the chief elder echoed inside her as she walked. The words of the mound rite always brought to mind memories of chief elders of the past pouring water upon the mound to symbolize the cleansing of the Mountain. This year, the bowl of water that the chief elder took with him to the top of the mound seemed superfluous, for water was streaming down all sides before he ever ascended it.

Still, she cherished the words of the rite and the promises of cleansing and renewal, perhaps now more than ever. The dark skies persisted week after week, bringing a dark mood to dark days, full of doubt and fear. The gate in the northern wall of the palace courtyard and city wall had been repaired and replaced, but the presence of a thousand soldiers in tents outside the city served as a constant reminder of the raid on the palace in Autumn Wane. Life in the palace resumed, but Elnah's death and the loss of her infant son still weighed heavily on Wylla's heart. Her own little boy, no longer so little, was out there somewhere, and she wanted very much to see his face and know that he was well.

Allfather shall make all things new. There were days when she didn't know if she really believed that the darkness would be dispelled and that Kirthanin would be healed of its many wounds, that Malek would be finally and completely defeated, but that was their hope. It was the hope of all hopes, the lingering dream that kept her placing one foot after the other. The Midwinter rites renewed her trust in Allfather. There would be a day when Kirthanin would know joy without sorrow, rest without weariness, and peace without war.

But not yet. She did not know when it would be or if it would come in her lifetime, but it wasn't here yet. Even so, it would come. Allfather would not leave them in darkness forever. A new dawn was coming, and with it the remaking of the world. The renewal of all. The restoration. All things new. Were there any words in the world more beautiful than those?

The festivities of Midwinter were underway. The day advanced steadily toward evening, and the people of Amaan Sul prepared to welcome a New Year despite the fears and uncertainties that had fallen upon the city like all this rain. She looked around at them, bundled up against the elements, but not depressed or downhearted. Nearby, a man sat in the doorway to a shop with a fiddle, and his fingers slid along the strings as he played a merry jig. Close by, a woman danced in the rain, her long hair soaked with water, alternatively sticking to her neck and face as it whirled through the air.

Wylla smiled at the free-spirited expression. As they left the music and solitary dancer, she turned to Yorek beside her and said, "It's been a long time since I felt like dancing. I miss it."

"You miss dancing, or the desire to dance?"

"Both."

"Well, it is Midwinter. With the New Year's celebration just getting underway, there should be several opportunities to dance."

"But how, Yorek?" Wylla stopped and looked at him. "How can people dance in the midst of the storm?"

Yorek ran his fingers through his grey beard. "Dancing in the storm isn't any different from dancing in the sun. It's just damper."

Wylla frowned at him. He could be deliberately obtuse at times. "I don't mean the rain. I mean the storm. Malek's loose. Gone from the Mountain and roaming the world. How can people dance?"

"They dance because they can. They can't hold back the storm. They can't stop Malek. They never really could. Deep down they knew, we all knew, that Malek would come when he was ready, that our defenses without dragons or Great Bear would be inadequate. They've been dancing under the shadow of the Mountain all their lives; why stop now?"

"Because time may be so short."

"Exactly. How precious then is this day? This opportunity?"

Wylla didn't answer. She looked back down the street at the woman, still dancing in the rain. The man had begun a new song, slower but beautiful, and she turned gracefully in step with the rhythm. "I don't begrudge them the dance, Yorek. You're right. There might not be many more opportunities. I just wish my feet were as light."

"You carry the weight of responsibilities that they do not."

"I know, but I used to dance anyway."

"Then maybe you should, even if you don't feel like it. Maybe your feet just need to be reminded what it feels like."

"Maybe."

"Aunt Wylla!" Wylla turned to see Roslin running up the street toward her, followed by Kyril and Halina, walking more sedately. She splashed in the puddles as she came, seemingly unconcerned about the wet trail she was blazing. "We've been out walking ever since the Mound rites, and we're having such a good time even though we all wish it would just stop raining, but still, it is exciting to be celebrating the New Year. The New Year always makes me think of my birthday even though it isn't until Summer Rise. Still, a New Year is a New Year and that means a new birthday, and I'll be twelve, and being twelve means a lot more responsibility than being eleven."

"Roslin," Kyril said, putting her hand on her daughter's shoulder as she came up alongside them. "Didn't you have something you wanted to show Yorek?"

"Oh yes, Master Yorek. Halina and I have been practicing and wanted you to see how much we've progressed. We thought today would be appropriate, being a day of celebration and all." Roslin reached down into a pair of deep pockets in her heavy cloak and pulled out three small balls. They were brightly colored and fit well in her small hands. Halina produced three balls as well, and despite the rain, they both began to juggle. Roslin dropped a ball but picked it back up and, smiling, quickly started again. Soon, both girls had all three rotating smoothly, flying in even arcs through the air, their hands deftly working. After a few moments, a ball slipped from Roslin's hand and fell to the ground again.

"That's very good, Roslin and Halina," Yorek said as Roslin retrieved the ball that had rolled a few spans away. "I'm very impressed with both of you."

Halina caught her balls and smiled, having maintained the juggling without a hitch. "Thank you," she said.

"Master Yorek," Roslin started as she ran back to him, bouncing with every step, "would you juggle for us? You're so good at it, but it's been so very long since you've juggled. At least, I haven't seen you juggle for ages and ages, and even though everybody is so busy these days, it is a night for celebration. Surely today is a day for juggling."

"Yes," Yorek said, stooping before the girl. "I'll juggle for you. This is indeed a day for juggling."

He took the balls Roslin held out to him as well as the three in Halina's hand. He turned and leaned in close to Wylla, whispering in her ear. "Now I juggle; later you dance."

As he straightened back up, Wylla smiled. "All right," she said. "Later on, I'll do it."

A large crowd moved in and out of a line of inns that bordered the great city square of Amaan Sul. As darkness fell on the city, the light from the open doors and windows spilled out onto the streets, where revelers and merrymakers ignored the rain that had now turned to snow and danced to the tunes that floated upon the wintry air. Wylla sat beside a fireplace inside the private parlor of one of these, looking out the window at her people, smiling. She turned to Yorek, "I think it is time. Come with me?"

"Sure," Yorek replied, and rising, followed her outside.

As they stepped out into the crowd, the sound of horses clopping along the busy streets greeted their ears, and Wylla looked up to see Captain Merias and several men come to a halt before them.

"Your Majesty," Merias began.

"Captain?"

"Forgive this intrusion on your celebration, but we have need of you at the south gate."

"What is it, Captain?"

"Refugees, Your Majesty. Come from Werthanin by way of Garring Pul. Lots of them."

"A horse," Wylla said simply, and one of the soldiers dismounted and helped her up into his saddle. "Yorek, find a horse and follow after. I may need you."

"Yes, Your Majesty."

Wylla turned toward Merias. "Lead on, Captain."

They rode through the dark evening, the snow falling thickly around them. The going was slow, for the crowds were dense and all the streets were full of people preparing to welcome the New Year. As they approached the extreme southern portions of the city, the crowds thinned out somewhat, and they were able to trot at a quicker pace to the large southern gate.

Over the gate a gilded dragon was perched, his mighty wings outstretched. Even in the darkness, the form of the dragon gleamed, a golden beacon of hope and welcome for all who passed underneath, either into or out of the city. As Wylla rode under the gate, she turned her eyes from the dragon above to the sight before her, a small host of travelers standing and sitting all around the gate. Many soldiers of Amaan Sul were there, holding torches, and in the flickering light, she could see the ragged clothes and weary faces, dirty from so many days on the road, camping in the mud and mire.

Her heart raced as she looked at them, men both young and old, women and children of all ages. They were castaways, afloat in the waves of a world where the waters of both sea and sky had drowned their boundaries. They washed up on her shore, and she had no idea how many more were coming.

She dropped down off her horse, and Merias dismounted as well, standing close beside her. "I am Wylla Someris, Queen of Enthanin, and I welcome you, all of you, to Amaan Sul."

A man of perhaps fifty sitting nearby rose and walked slowly to her, nursing something of a limp as he came. "Your Majesty, I am Derran, and we are all farmers from Werthanin. We have come seeking refuge inside your walls."

"Derran, you and yours are welcome here. What news do you bring?"

"News, Your Majesty?"

"Yes, of Werthanin and the wider world."

"I don't know about wider world, but Werthanin is overrun. Through seven long years of civil war, we clung tenaciously to our farms north of Erefen, but when Malek came, we had no choice but to leave."

"You saw Malek's hosts?"

"Some of us did. A great throng, too great to be numbered, swept across the land like clouds across the sky. We had no choice but to flee, and we rode to the Kellisor Sea, which we crossed though many were lost in the crossing, for the strange winds and storm have made the journey perilous."

"You made for Garring Pul?"

"Not at first. We crossed to Peris Mil, but when news came that Malek had traversed the Erefen marshes and was headed south, we set sail again and made for Enthanin, though it may only be a matter of time before Malek comes here."

"I see. Malek is definitely headed south through Suthanin?"

"Yes, Your Majesty. Many refugees and pilgrims came both to Peris Mil and to Garring Pul while we were there, all with the same story."

Wylla nodded, looking at Merias. "Master Derran, I would question you further on what you know of matters beyond our borders, but for now let us look to your shelter and care."

"We would be grateful, Your Majesty."

"What do you suggest, Your Majesty?" Merias asked quietly as Derran turned back to his fellow pilgrims.

"The inns are full for the celebration," Wylla said, thinking out loud.

"They are. The city is teeming with people."

"They must be taken to the palace."

"The palace?"

"Yes, we will take as many into the halls and open rooms on the first floor as we can, and we will erect spare tents in the courtyards for the rest. It will be tight, but we must provide these people with shelter."

"But, Your Majesty," Merias began.

"There is no time, Captain. These people are drenched, freezing, and no doubt starving. It will take an hour to lead them north through the city, so start organizing it. I will head back in advance of you to start making preparations."

"Yes, Your Majesty." Merias nodded and called several of his soldiers to himself. Wylla mounted her horse and was about to ride back into the city when Yorek emerged through the gate.

"My queen?" Yorek asked as he came upon her.

"These are refugees from Werthanin."

"Yes."

"They have nowhere to stay and the city is full of people celebrating the rites of Midwinter and the coming of the New Year. Captain Merias is preparing to move them all to the palace."

Yorek looked closely at Wylla's face, and she tried her best to set it with hardened finality. Eventually, Yorek nodded. "Yes, Your Majesty. Very good. I'll come with you."

Relieved, Wylla whispered, "Thank you," and rode back into the city.

A few hours later, the palace was full to bursting. Refugees were claiming areas of cold stone floor all over the first level, in the main hall, the kitchen and dining room, the queen's first-floor parlor, everywhere. Another small crowd moved into the stables off the main courtyard, and still more waited while soldiers put up tents in the courtyard by the northern gate and also in the large open area surrounding the fountain.

"I think there shall be enough room, barely," Wylla said as she stood in the doorway, looking out over the courtyard from the wall above.

"Yes, Your Majesty, though we will need to find more permanent lodgings tomorrow. These may be but the first wave of refugees we will see in these troubled times."

I know, Wylla thought, and suddenly she smiled. "I have felt so helpless these past couple months since Valzaan rode forth with Benjiah and my brothers, but now at last I can see where I can reach out and alleviate some of the sorrow that is creeping over our world."

"Yes. It was nobly done, offering the palace. Many would not have done so."

"You don't think me foolish for taking in these strangers?"

"No, my queen. Malek has reached out his hand for you, and we know what that looks like. These are not assassins. They are people like us, seeking shelter from the storm. I can see that as clearly as you."

"They seek a shelter, but how long will Amaan Sul be a safe harbor? How long will we be a refuge?"

"I don't know, Your Majesty."

"We should press our guests further, to see what else they can tell us."

They came down off the wall and entered the crowded palace. Stewards of the house were busy moving among the refugees, seeing that everyone had a blanket or cloak or towel. Big fires were being stoked in every fireplace, and several kitchen stewards were hard at work on a stew that would feed a small army.

After searching the main hall for a few moments, Wylla saw Merias with the man named Derran, and she moved through the crowd to summon him. Merias turned and followed her with Derran and a second man, this one younger, perhaps only thirty. The five of them passed out of the large open hall and soon ascended a stair to the second story, where they entered a smaller parlor. Yorek joined them and sat beside Wylla, and Merias remained standing as Derran and the second man took seats facing them.

"Your Majesty," Derran began, "this is Carses, a soldier of Fel Edorath who has helped to guide us in our travels."

Wylla's heart pounded as she looked at the young man. Fel Edorath. It was logical that people of Fel Edorath would flee before Malek too, but she had not been prepared to hear that a soldier of the city would come here. She was surprised that mention of that city agitated her, but she could not deny that this was indeed her reaction.

"Your Majesty," the man named Carses began, "I know that Amaan Sul supported Shalin Bel in its grievance against Fel Edorath, but even so, I thank you for the refuge you have granted us tonight."

"You are welcome," Wylla said, looking intently into the young man's face. "The grievance of Shalin Bel and the Assembly was not with Fel Edorath, but with Rulalin Tarasir. I have no reason to have a grievance with you, have I?"

"No, Your Majesty. I was just a scout in the army. I have nothing against Amaan Sul. Not when I served in the army, and certainly not now."

"Certainly not now?"

"No, Your Majesty, my allegiance to Fel Edorath is broken for good. I will follow her captains no more."

"Why is that?"

"They have betrayed us all."

"Ah, that."

"You know already?"

"Yes, word has reached here of Rulalin's betrayal. It is true?"

Carses hung his head, looking at the floor. "It's true. When Corlas Valon marched out with his men to join Aljeron Balinor, I stood beside the road and cursed him as a traitor to abandon our city in her time of need. I thought we were staying behind to defend Fel Edorath against Malek, but when I learned that we would march forth under Malek's banner, I was ashamed. Our lives had been purchased but our honor had been forfeited. I rode south during the confusion of the muster, and I never looked back."

"You are not responsible for the decision of your superiors," Yorek said kindly. "By refusing to join in their mission, you have not forfeited your honor; you have preserved it. What's more, if Derran is correct, you have helped to preserve the lives of these who travel with you. That is a choice worthy of praise."

"Yes," Wylla added, smiling at the young man. "There is no need to hang your head here. I will not hold Rulalin's choices against you if you will not hold my allegiance with Shalin Bel in opposing Rulalin against me. Agreed?"

"Yes, Your Majesty." Carses looked up, gratitude in his face. "And thank you."

"There is no need. Now, tell me, what else do you know? If Malek has headed south through the Erefen Marshes into Suthanin, what of Shalin Bel? What of Aljeron's army and your men that marched with him?"

"I don't know much, only that shortly before we left Peris Mil for Garring Pul, pilgrims from Shalin Bel arrived. They said that messengers had come to the city in advance of Aljeron Balinor, warning them they were coming with Malek hard on their heels. It seems a battle was fought at Zul Arnoth, but Aljeron and those with him were pushed back with ease."

"There was a battle at Zul Arnoth?" Wylla asked, thinking of Benjiah, bow in hand and determination on his face.

"Yes, though I don't know much about it."

"You say Aljeron was on his way to Shalin Bel, and yet there are reports of Malek passing south through the Erefen Marshes. What does that mean, I wonder?" Wylla asked, looking as much to Yorek as to the other men in the room. "Surely if Aljeron was holding the city, he could not have been overrun so quickly."

"I don't know, Your Majesty, how long anyone could hold out against the full might of Malek's hosts," Yorek said quietly, "but you may be right. Perhaps Malek has moved south because Aljeron has moved south."

"I think that must be it," Derran said. "If Malek's intent had been to go south from the beginning, why leave Fel Edorath and move west to Zul Arnoth and Shalin Bel? Why not just head south to start with? He probably changed directions because his quarry has changed directions."

"Unless he has already concluded the conquest of Werthanin and is simply moving south to subdue Suthanin," Carses said. "Fel Edorath didn't fight; maybe Shalin Bel didn't either. Maybe they did, but maybe there wasn't much fight left in them."

"It's all speculation," Merias said abruptly. "All we really know is that Fel Edorath and Shalin Bel have been emptied of their citizens, and Shalin Bel was likely overrun or abandoned. Nothing else makes sense. Malek wouldn't leave Werthanin before he had subdued it, and he certainly is the hunter and not the hunted. He is taking the war south, whatever his goal might be."

"Have you any other news?" Wylla asked.

"Not of Malek," Carses answered.

"Of anything?"

"Only that the Kellisor Sea rises daily with the waters of this unceasing storm and that the rivers and streams of Kirthanin are so swollen they have burst their bonds and seep across the land. Peris Mil and Garring Pul are both in danger of being swallowed up by the sea, and every day the morning brings more clouds and more rain."

"This, too, we knew," Wylla answered, rubbing her forehead gently with her fingers. Indeed, she knew all too well, for every messenger that came to Captain Merias from the detachment at the Kellisor brought some new tale of wonder of the sea's remarkable growth and expansion.

"I think," Yorek said, "unless there is more that Derran or Carses has for us, that we should let them rejoin their friends and families and enjoy what is left of the celebration, and perhaps we could remain and reflect for a moment on their news?" He ended with just the slightest inflection to indicate he was asking, though with a clear expectation that the answer was not in doubt.

"Yes, good idea," Wylla said, rising. "I am sorry to detain you tonight. You are no doubt weary from your travels. Please, enjoy the hospitality of my house, such that it is, and we will talk further tomorrow."

Carses and Derran both rose and bowed slightly. "We are most indebted to Your Majesty," Derran said.

"Yes," Carses added. "We have been long in the rain. Shelter is a gift of immeasurable worth. Thank you."

"You're welcome, and we will see what we can do about making more permanent arrangements, that is, if you think you will stay in Amaan Sul."

"We hadn't looked any further down the road that led us here," Derran answered. "For my part, I've had enough of the road for a while."

"Then stay as long as you like," Wylla replied. She walked to the door and opened it, summoning a steward from the hall. When she had given the man instructions to lead their guests back downstairs, she bid them both a good evening.

Closing the door behind her, she leaned back against it wearily. "Are you all right, Your Majesty?" Merias asked.

"Yes, I'm just tired," she said, and both men remained quiet. "So what have we learned tonight?"

"We know Malek has moved south, and that the people of Shalin Bel who fled before Malek came there. I think"—Yorek paused—"if Aljeron expected to succeed in defending the city, he would not have sent messengers telling the people to flee. I think he knew before he ever returned that he couldn't hold it. Whether he tried or not, that's what we don't know."

"And if he didn't," Merias said, "what did he do, and where did he go?"

"Where could he have gone but west, to the sea?" Wylla mused out loud. She looked up, realization dawning on her, but Merias spoke first.

"Col Marena."

"Yes," she nodded, walking over to a small cabinet in the room. She opened it and withdrew a map of Kirthanin. She placed it on a small table nearby, and all three drew close around it.

"If he didn't defend Shalin Bel, he must have gone there," Merias said, putting his finger on Col Marena. "That's what I would have done. If I couldn't hope to win by fighting, then my only options for retreat would be south by land, which would take me to Erefen and perhaps leave me exposed, or by sea. If I could outrun my enemy to the sea and take all the ships, he'd have to double back and take the longer route by land."

"So he's gone to Cimaris Rul?" Wylla asked.

"That would make sense," Yorek added. "Whatever fighting strength he still has under his command, it can't be much. He'd need a strong city and fresh army."

"So, the war remains far away, at least for the moment," Wylla said.

"For the moment."

"But now we know what's happening, we don't have to wait for it to come to us. We can go to it," Merias said, almost imploringly.

"If we're right, then we know where the next big battle is likely to take place," Wylla conceded.

"Then let me go. If I muster our full strength, I could take twenty thousand men with me. The united forces of Enthanin could join both Aljeron and the Suthanim and stand together!"

"I think we should be more cautious, choose a middle road."

"There is no middle road," Merias protested. "We move or we don't."

"There is a middle road. We know that Malek's main force has moved south. Let's recall the twenty-five hundred men watching Gyrin for an attack from the Mountain. They can fall back and set up defenses here around the city. The rest we can send to set up a defense south of the Kalamin, though I would suggest they not move farther south than Elnin, in order that they not be caught too far from the river should a return crossing be necessary. From there, riders should be sent out in all directions to watch for signs of retreat from the south."

For a while the men debated, Merias growing more heated in his insistence that they must send their full strength south, as quickly as possible, to aid the Kirthanim in their defense of Cimaris Rul. Yorek resisted, less insistently, but was no less committed to his own position. After a while, Wylla had heard all that she could bear.

"I think," Wylla said, "we should lay this aside for now. Let's go back downstairs and see what our guests may need."

"Your Majesty," Merias said impatiently, "this is no time for delay."

"You forget yourself, Captain," Wylla said.

"My apologies," Merias said softly.

"I have heard you both and will weigh your counsel. I will make a decision tomorrow. Maybe the beginning of a new year will inspire me."

They left the parlor and headed downstairs. Merias took his leave to make sure the Amaan Sul soldiers had finished their work on the tents in the courtyard. Many of the Werthanim were already bedded down for the night, though others stood and sat in small clusters. It was a subdued assembly, but Wylla was everywhere greeted with warm smiles that betrayed both the gratitude of her guests and the spirit of Midwinter.

She moved among the groups and exchanged pleasant greetings and words of welcome, all the while checking on the stewards to see that all the needs of the Werthanim were being met. When word came from Merias that all were sheltered, either in the palace, the stables, or the tents, Wylla sighed in relief. She could rest now, knowing that at least for the time being, they were settled and taken care of.

It was late now. A few were still talking, and many were trying to sleep. The big fires burned low, and the rooms were darker with just the glowing embers and the few torches. She passed out of the big hall where most of the Werthanim were and stepped into the long, narrow hall that would take her to the stairs up to her apartment. Just inside the hall, sitting in a large, comfortable chair, was Yorek. His eyes were shut and his face seemed to Wylla very peaceful. He was slumped slightly to the side, snoring quietly.

Wylla reached down and touched his arm gently. His eyes opened suddenly, and he looked up at Wylla, for a moment confused, but then he smiled. "You should go get some sleep in your own bed, Yorek."

"Yes, Your Majesty. And you?"

"I'm headed to bed too."

"Very well," Yorek said, yawning as he stood up.

"I'm sorry I didn't keep my word."

"What's that?"

"Dancing. I didn't dance."

"Oh," Yorek said, looking down at Wylla. "I wouldn't worry too much about that. Dancing is wonderful, to be sure, but you chose to shelter the homeless and feed the hungry. You chose what was needful. You can always dance tomorrow."

"It isn't Midwinter tomorrow."

"True, but unless I am mistaken, dancing is allowed year round."

"It is, Yorek." Wylla sighed. "But I am sorry to have missed this opportunity to dance with the celebrants of Midwinter, who welcome with their songs and their dances the coming of the New Year."

Yorek rested his big hand on Wylla's shoulder. "Your heart will summon your feet to dance again when it is ready. Don't worry."

"I hope so."

"Good night, Your Majesty."

"Good night, Yorek."

The palace was alive when Wylla went down in the morning. Children were laughing and playing in the various open rooms, their mothers and fathers talking happily among themselves. Wylla was again greeted with warmth and cheer as she passed through their midst. She was polite and welcoming, but she was looking for Yorek and didn't want to put this off any longer.

When at last she found him, he was sitting on a bench in the kitchen before the fire, eating breakfast. He finished hastily while Wylla sent a steward to retrieve Merias. "I have decided," she said to Yorek, "and I want to go over things with both of you at once."

They waited in her private parlor upstairs, talking about inconsequential things to pass the time, but it seemed like ages before Merias arrived at last.

"You sent for me, Your Majesty?"

"I did.

"I want you to recall the men from outside Gyrin. These you will bring here to guard the city. Just enough to hold the gates should any more raiding parties come our way from the west while our eyes are turned south. Then take your whole strength south across the Kalamin."

"Yes, Your Majesty," Captain Merias said, nodding. If it was less than he had hoped for, he hid his disappointment. Wylla could see nothing but excitement in his eyes.

"When you have established a strong forward position, send detachments out in every logical direction. Post men west of the Barunaan near Peris Mil. Post men south toward the gap between the Barunaan and Lindan Wood. Post men north of Lindan. Post men near the gap between Lindan and the Arimaar Mountains. Even post men north of the Arimaar Mountains in the plains east of Kel Imlaris. Watch every passage north. You are to guard and aid in any retreat that might come your way. See any and all men of Kirthanin fleeing before the enemy back safely across the river into Enthanin. If we are to be the final battlefield, so be it."

"Yes, Your Majesty."

"What's more, I entrust you with full authority to order whatever march or maneuvers you see fit to best aid our Kirthanim brethren against the enemy. If you have opportunity to press the attack or aid, then do so. We must strike the most effective blow against the enemy we can with our full strength. This will not work if you have to check with me. Captain Merias, you are to go and do whatever Allfather lays before you to do, do you understand?"

"I do."

"Good, then go and begin making preparations immediately. I will expect to be briefed in full before the army departs and to be made fully aware of the chain of command you establish for Amaan Sul's defenses."

"Of course, Your Majesty." Merias rose, bowed, and quickly exited.

"Well," Wylla said when he had gone, "it is done."

"Yes, and done well."

"We shall see. I hope to keep the war from coming to Amaan Sul, Yorek, but I fear that the war is coming and cannot be kept away."

It took Benjiah a while to realize he was underwater, but underwater he was. The ground was soft and sandy, and here and there, sea plants with long, bright-green tendrils swayed as they rose from the sea floor. He was suddenly self-conscious about the fact he was underwater and wondered if he shouldn't be heading up to the surface for air. But he was breathing normally through his mouth and nose. Slowly, he opened his mouth and inhaled. Air, not water, filled his lungs, and his anxiety disappeared.

Looking around him, he saw various plants and growths on the sea floor, and schools of fish swimming around and above him. A large green-and-blue fish with a gaping mouth passed directly overhead, seemingly unaware of the visitor. Nearby, moving in and out of one of the large sea plants, was a school of bright-yellow fish, so bright they almost seemed to cast off light. Benjiah watched them swim out of the plant and into the distance, thinking he could see their yellow glow long after he couldn't see them.

He looked down at his feet, half covered in sand. He wasn't trying to stay anchored there, so why wasn't he floating away? Maybe he was stuck. The thought was alarming. Perhaps he should push off and see if he could float up. He did. He floated up a span or so and stopped, waving his arms in a circular pattern to keep him suspended above the sea floor. He smiled. It felt great. He felt free. He closed his eyes and leaned back, his body slowly floating backward as if he were reclining on air. He stopped moving his arms, and he couldn't tell if he was sinking slowly downward or hovering where he was. A moment or two later, his question was answered. He felt himself land gently on the sea floor as his body nestled softly into the sand.

For a long time he lay there. It was peaceful and carefree. At the moment he wasn't sure why, but he seemed sure that this was a rest he badly needed. Here, he would not be disturbed. After a while, though, he sat back up and opened his eyes. He must have rotated slightly as he floated downward, because the vista before him had changed slightly, in the distance if not in the foreground. He could see, though it appeared to be a long way off, something large and white gleaming as though resting upon some distant ridge.

He pushed off the ground and started swimming. He looked up and had no idea how far up the surface was, assuming there was a surface somewhere. He was down deep. He rose, higher and higher, so that the sandy sea bottom dropped out of view. When he looked down, he saw shining colors swimming through the dark waters: yellow, red, blue, green, and even purple. He was getting closer, and the white object, whatever it was, no longer appeared to be above him.

Benjiah was close enough now to see that the white object was even more expansive than he had thought. It looked like a wall of sorts, running some distance in both directions, to his right and to his left. The closer he drew, the more certain he was that he looked at a wall. Not a strange wall-like formation, but a wall. It wasn't completely solid; he noticed a wide gap to the right, and toward the gap he headed.

He paused at the gap. It was not part of the original design, as a gate or door might have been, for the edges were rough and uneven. What had caused the hole was a mystery, for even a cursory survey of the cross-section revealed that the wall itself had been a sizable undertaking. It was broad and densely packed, and as he reached out and ran his fingers over the cool stone, he began to wonder who could have built such a thing down here, so deep in the ocean.

He pushed off from the wall and swam through the opening. Benjiah almost stopped where he was, for what he saw on the other side was almost certainly impossible. Beyond this great wall lay a mighty city. Buildings—houses, shops, even towers—stretched up above the subaquatic skyline. Perhaps he shouldn't be surprised. Whoever was capable of building that massive wall down here was no doubt capable of building the city within it. With Benjiah's every stroke, however, the scale of this undertaking grew all the more impressive.

In all his days, he never heard tell of a city at the bottom of the sea, from the Great Northern Sea to the Southern Ocean. Was this a great accomplishment of some past age? Was it symbolic? Surely it didn't have any real purpose or use. Unless—and now he felt himself growing excited—unless this city had not been made by men or Great Bear or dragons at all. Maybe this city belonged to a great race of the ocean, a race unknown to men. Maybe this was the city of the fourth people prophesied to bring about Malek's fall. Maybe Allfather was granting him a vision of where to go after he succeeded in contacting the dragons.

The farther he swam, though, the less likely this possibility seemed. Aside from the fantastic nature of the idea that an undiscovered race inhabited the bottom of the ocean, there was no sign of life—at least, no sign of life outside of the occasional fish. He paused, floating in the middle of what he would have called a street, which ran like an ordinary city street between two long rows of tall buildings, wondering what this all was for. He looked more carefully at the building closest to him and saw a door half open, swaying ever so slightly, no doubt moved by the rhythmic pulsations of the current that ebbed and flowed. One way to get to the bottom of this would be to go inside and see what he could find.

He swam to the door. He grasped it firmly and pulled it wide open. The interior was nearly dark, with only a limited amount of light coming through the open door. He hesitated to swim into the deeper darkness, but as he floated there, a couple of large, luminescent green eels swam past him into the room, taking their faint green light with them. He followed.

It appeared to be the front room of a house. A couple of wooden chairs and other smaller pieces of furniture floated up near the ceiling. Other smaller trinkets, like candles, a pair of boots, and a thin wisp of cloth likewise floated up and down in the room. He moved into what appeared to be a kitchen, and here the water was even more littered with kitchen implements and crockery. Swimming up the stairs at the rear in the house, he examined a series of bedrooms. Waterlogged mattresses hovered just above the floor, and smaller wooden pieces floated near the ceiling.

He didn't understand. Whoever had built this city was capable of a remarkable feat, the construction of a life-size city underwater. Why would such people then fill the houses with wooden implements and furniture that clearly didn't belong underwater? Could it be that this city had once been above the ocean, on an island or something? Had the land beneath it crumbled and given way so that it fell into the depths of the sea?

He swam out of the house. Something wasn't right here, and he needed to know what. He swam down the street, past more houses and shops, all dark within and bearing no sign of life or even death, except the fish that kept him company. He reached a tall, cylindrical building that he guessed must be a tower, because it rose high above the other buildings. He looked up and saw that many spans up, the tower seemed to shift sideways. It occurred to him that this might be the surface of the water. Maybe the dark above was the nighttime sky.

Upward he swam, following the solid wall of the tower. About fifteen spans up, he paused and looked down. It was like looking through the eyes of a windhover. Everywhere he looked were the streets and houses and buildings of a great city. All quiet, all empty. He resumed his journey, and after a moment, he had, sure enough, reached the surface. As he broke through the water, he felt himself instinctively open his mouth and gasp as he took a deep breath. Rain was falling gently, and he treaded water as he looked around. It was dark and cold up here, and he could see perhaps a dozen more spires protruding out of the water.

In that moment, he understood. This was not a city built by a missing or unknown people. It was not a city designed to exist underwater. It was an ordinary human city, buried under span after span of water. A chill rippled through him, and he turned around and around in the water, faster and faster. He knew where he was. He hadn't swum from some deep portion of the ocean floor up onto a shallow ridge, he had swum from the ocean floor up onto land. These white spires were the towers of a coastal city, and he knew which one.

2

CIMARIS RUL

AELWYN PICKED HORSEHAIR OFF the palm of her hand and tried to drop them on the ground, but the wet hairs clung tenaciously. She shook her hand violently and managed to get most of them off, but she sighed as she looked at those that remained. Reluctantly, she wiped her hand on her cloak, which oozed water as she applied the pressure.

Unexpectedly, tears welled up in her eyes. It wasn't the hair, or the wet cloak, or any one of the myriad of daily inconveniences. It was the sheer relentlessness of it all. Always on the road. Always in the saddle. Always wet. All these dark clouds. All this rain. All this water.

She knew it was time to mount up and ride, but she couldn't muster the strength to climb into the saddle. She leaned in and rested her forehead against the smooth, damp side of her horse. She stroked his flank with her hand, aware that the hair she had wrestled to remove had now been replaced, but she didn't care. It was soothing to feel the solidity of her quiet, patient horse. Every day, he submitted obediently to her leading and did all she asked of him. Did he understand the unnaturalness of the weather? Did he sense the urgency of their flight?

Perhaps for the horse, obedience was simply a matter of trust. As a domesticated animal, he went where he was led. He ate what he was given. He walked and ran when directed and halted when commanded. She continued to stroke him lovingly. The horse was not panicked by the rain because he still had a master he could rely upon to give him the directions he needed, a master he trusted to take care of him in the midst of the storm. So did she. She stepped into the stirrup and climbed up into the saddle.

Mindarin pulled up alongside her. "You all right?"

"Yes," Aelwyn said, wiping tears from her cheeks, though they were likely hidden by the rain. "Sort of. I mean, I don't know. I'm just . . . not coping well this morning."

"We had a late night. Squeezing a short march in after honoring the rites of Midwinter and then staying up late to greet the New Year was perhaps inadvisable."

"It isn't the weariness. At least, it isn't that alone. It's the weariness and the rain. It's the flooding. Being forced off the coastal road because it's under water. Riding all day with the rain in our faces. Always soaked and miserable. All this gloom. I just wonder sometimes how much more I can take."

Prompting her horse alongside Aelwyn, Mindarin reached down and placed her hand gently on her sister's knee. "It's all right, Aelwyn. We're all just barely hanging on. At least we're almost there."

Aelwyn nodded.

"Caan says today."

"I can't wait. Just to be dry. I don't care what else happens. I just want to be dry."

"Me too."

"It's unlikely there will be shelter enough for all of us in Cimaris Rul."

"Yes, that's true, but I'm sure we'll receive first accommodations."

Aelwyn grinned mischievously through the rain at Mindarin. "Really? I thought I heard you telling Caan the other day when he suggested slowing the pace for the sake of the women that the women were just as tough as the men and that no special allowances needed to be made."

"That's right."

"Well?"

"Well what?"

"Don't you see the inconsistency?"

"There's no inconsistency. I didn't say the women needed first consideration for accommodations, just that we'd get them."

"I see."

"It'll do the morale of the men good to let them think they're sacrificing for us. We can't take that from them. They've lost so much already."

"How generous of you."

"I do what I can."

All around them, the ranks and ranks of horsemen were moving into formation for the day's ride. Aelwyn urged her horse forward, looking over her shoulder at her older sister. "Well, the sooner we get back on the road, the sooner you can boost the morale of the troops."

"Then what are we waiting for?"

Mindarin spurred her horse past Aelwyn and joined the column already underway. Aelwyn rode after her, ignoring the looks of surprise from the other women and soldiers that they passed. Every day they trotted along, so as not to leave those forced to walk behind, and it felt good to let the horse run. She knew the front of the column wasn't far ahead, but she was tempted not to stop. She'd love to just go, ride until she reached the gates of Cimaris Rul. Then she would rest, really rest.

Aelwyn looked up at the great white walls of Cimaris Rul. It was only midmorning, and the city was already within view. They had departed the coast, for they encountered flooding and water almost waist deep in places there the last couple of days, and cut across the grassy plains. From this direction, there was no entrance to be seen in the wall before them. Despite the overcast weather, the white stone of the city walls gleamed. They exuded strength, and Aelwyn sat tall in the saddle as she rode behind Caan and the other captains.

Riders were coming out from the city to meet them, and as Aelwyn looked closely, he could see that one of them was Bryar, whom Caan had sent ahead that morning. The other three were dressed in red and gold, which Aelwyn gathered was the livery of soldiers from Cimaris Rul, or at least of the gate wardens. They rode hard, then slowed to a stop before Caan.

"Caan," Bryar said as the captains veered aside so that the column could continue moving toward the city. "These men are sent to escort us into the city."

"Very good," Caan said, looking the three men over. "Is Talis Fein still in command of the army of Cimaris Rul?"

"He is," one of the young men answered.

"And you are?"

"Barune, Master Caan," the man replied. "My name is Erril Barune. I am in charge of the gate patrol."

"You are aware in the city, Erril, of Malek's departure from the Mountain and invasion of Suthanin?"

"We are. Riders from the north brought word less than a week ago. His arrival is expected in the next three or four days."

Caan nodded, looking at Sarneth and Elmaaneth, who were close beside him. "That fits with our understanding of his location and progress. It doesn't give us much time."

"No, sir, it doesn't," Erril answered.

"You don't seem unduly concerned," Caan said, looking at the three men closely. "I'm not sure if I should be impressed or worried."

"We are greatly concerned, Master Caan," Erril again answered. "But as you'll see soon enough, there are other matters that at the moment are more pressing."

"More pressing? More pressing than the imminent arrival of Malek with hordes of men, Black Wolves, Voiceless, and Vulsutyrim?"

Erril's face turned red again. "I know it sounds strange, but while Malek will likely be here in a couple of days, the rain has already been here much longer. While many eyes look to the north, we look to the Southern Ocean, for its assault on our walls has already begun."

Aelwyn felt her stomach tighten. There had been some speculation about the danger all this rain might pose to Cimaris Rul if sea levels rose high enough, fast enough. Most who had seen Cimaris Rul, like Caan, thought it unlikely that the enormous walls would be in any danger, at least not yet. Aelwyn, who had been clinging to the hope that Cimaris Rul would be their refuge against both the rain and Malek, was suddenly confronted by the prospect that it would soon be assaulted by both.

"What do you mean?" Caan asked calmly. "Has the sea wall been breached?"

"Not yet, but the water is rolling in higher and harder all the time. When last I looked, it seemed the highest waves would soon roll in over the top of the walls."

"And when did you last look?"

"Just before I took my place at the north gate at the end of Fourth Watch."

Caan nodded. "If the water is as high as you say, then there must be fear that the walls won't hold."

"There is, all who aren't involved with the evacuation are busy trying to reinforce the south wall."

"Evacuation?" Caan exclaimed, his voice finally betraying surprise.

"Yes, the army of Cimaris Rul has been overseeing the evacuation of the city for the last five days. It is almost complete."

"Is it?" Caan said, not so much asking as murmuring to himself. "If you don't mind, Erril, I think I need to see Talis Fein as soon as possible. All right?"

"That's why I'm here, Master Caan. I am ready when you are."

The small cluster began moving instantly, and Aelwyn rode hard after them. The excitement of the ride was gone now, and the towering white walls were not as comforting as they had been just moments before.

Riding into Cimaris Rul wasn't like Aelwyn had expected it would be. She thought there might be fear, of course, for their arrival would signal the battle to come. Yes, she expected fear, and she saw some as the gatekeepers in red and gold stood to either side while they rode quietly in.

She also expected there would be joy, for while they were bringing dark news, they were also bringing hope, with thousands of men and a large force of Great Bear. She had envisioned cheers from the crowds lining the streets and hanging out their windows to greet their Werthanim brethren. But there were no cheers and no crowds. Had she not heard the young officer telling Caan about the evacuation, she would have been stunned not to see the great buildings of Cimaris Rul full of people seeking shelter from the rain and sea.

Cimaris Rul, though, did not disappoint. She had heard about it, and now she was finally seeing it with her own eyes. Cimaris Rul, city of the tall buildings and taller towers. Its reputation preceded it. Not nearly as large in land area as Shalin Bel or Amaan Sul, Cimaris Rul had grown up rather than out. Most buildings were at least three stories tall and towered over the narrow streets. Watchtowers reached high above the rest of the city into the sky. Most of these buildings appeared to be built of the same white stone as the walls, and she imagined that nearby must be a great quarry that had given birth to the city and sustained its growth over the long years.

Ahead, Caan and the men from Cimaris Rul slowed. She looked past them and could see men on horseback coming down the street to meet them. She glanced at Mindarin, who seemed to understand instantly, and they led their own horses closer to the front so as to be able to observe the exchange.

"Master Caan," said a bearded man with a gold chain hanging over his simple red cloak. He rode out to where Caan's horse was stopped and swung down out of his seat. "Neighbor, it has been too long since you were our guest. Much has happened since last the summer breeze brought you here on business from Sulare, but we will aid you in whatever way we can, though I imagine we will both be in need of aid before long."

"We may indeed," Caan answered, dropping from his horse and embracing the other man. "Talis, it is good to see you."

"And you."

"It is true then; you have evacuated the people?"

"Yes. With Malek's approach from the north and the sea's growing fury, we couldn't stay. We have waited and waited for some break in the rain so that the tide might go down, but there has been none. We have given up on waiting."

"The rain has followed us from Fel Edorath to Shalin Bel, and all the way down the coast of Suthanin," Caan answered. "It is a device of our enemy, for what ultimate purpose we do not know."

Talis looked from Caan to the faces of the others assembled. He nodded. "I have not been far from the wall since the rain started, so I didn't know how extensive the storm was. Your news is disheartening. If our enemy can make it rain the length and breadth of Kirthanin, what else can he do?"

Caan shrugged. "His power is great, that much is true. Still, we must resist him as best as we are able."

"Indeed we must, which is why we have been preparing to leave. Though it was unimaginable even up to ten days ago, most here now believe the southern wall will be breached, perhaps soon. As strong as it is, it was not designed to hold off the full force and might of the Southern Ocean."

"Where have you sent the people? Southeast across the Barunaan to Sulare?"

"No. I fear that if the rain has been as constant there as it has here, Sulare is likely under assault from the ocean as well. Besides, we couldn't have taken that road even if we wanted to. Both of the great bridges across the Barunaan just east of the city have been washed away by the rising water."

"What? Both gone?"

"Yes, the rising tide has washed over the Barunaan delta and swept away the low-lying bridges."

"So where have the people gone?"

"The High Bridge, half a day's ride north and east, still stands. They have gone that way."

"The High Bridge? You mean the high, narrow bridge at the gorge?"

"Yes, its height alone has saved it, for though the river continues to rise in the gorge, it has not overflowed."

"But it is narrow. The whole city is crossing the Barunaan there?"

"That's why it has taken almost a week. Still, the first ranks of our army have already crossed, and this very day I was planning on emptying the city entirely."

"There are no ships that could be used?" Caan asked, looking wistfully past Talis in the direction of the tumultuous Southern Ocean.

"No. All the ships that were in our harbor perished weeks ago as the water battered them into pieces."

Caan ran his fingers though his hair and for a moment stroked one of his long grey braids. "Talis, I know that there is precious little time for delay, but could we take a few minutes, preferably somewhere inside, out of this rain? It may be that there is nothing for it but to march to this High Bridge, but now that we're here, perhaps we could discover alternatives."

"I don't know what alternatives there could be, but we will certainly get you out of this rain. I will send word to my wife, who has stubbornly remained in the city with me, to have refreshment brought to us at the center tower. I will take you and your officers there that you might see for yourselves the fury of the sea against our southern wall. Then you will realize that our choices are few."

The tower that Caan referred to was not far away, and Aelwyn was glad to dismount and get inside. They passed through several rooms to a stair that wound steadily up and around. Every so often, small windows opened out on the grey afternoon and the white city farther and farther below them.

The stair emptied out into a large, circular room at the top of the tower with great wide windows all around it. Looking straight out, Aelwyn could see well beyond the city into the soaked grasslands they had crossed. In fact, the rear ranks of their army were still coming in through the gates, and behind them came the Great Bear, a solid line of brown and grey coming along behind the soldiers from Shalin Bel.

Aelwyn turned to see the others following Caan and Talis Fein toward the opposite wall, and she walked along behind them. When she got close enough to look out over the southern half of the city, she gasped. In the distance, great waves were slopping over the top of the thick white wall, which ran around the city in a complete ring. Beyond the wall, the water was choppy, surging up and down constantly and spraying water high up into the sky. She couldn't imagine how the walls were holding up now, let alone how they could do so much longer.

"You see now why we must go," Talis said to Caan, who was staring out as soberly as the rest. "The water will win its unrelenting battle against our walls, and when it does, we should be as far away as possible."

"Unless we fight instead of flee."

"March out to meet Malek?" Talis asked.

"Yes." Caan turned away from the window to face his host. "How many men do you have?"

"Twelve thousand," Fein asked, "if I recall those who have already set up camp on the other side of the High Bridge."

"That means we could put twenty thousand in the field, along with fifteen hundred Great Bear."

"Do you think that is enough? What news of our enemy do you have?"

"He has more than that," Gilion spoke up, meticulously straightening his mustache with his fingers. "Our enemy has hosts of both men and Malekim, with a large advance force of Black Wolves and hundreds of Vulsutyrim. Caan, you know we can't hope to defeat them in open battle. Our only hope is to stand behind strong walls in a well-provisioned city."

"Which can't happen here," Talis added.

Caan looked at Gilion, annoyed. "I know this isn't what we hoped for, but we are weary and only grow wearier each passing day. We have sailed and marched all the way here, and for what? To march across the Barunaan? And where will we go from there? If we can't go to Sulare, then there is only the long trek to Amaan Sul or Kel Imlaris. But if all the coastal cities are being assaulted by the very waters of the sea, what hope is there that Kel Imlaris will be much better?"

"I don't know if there is much hope in Kel Imlaris, but there is little hope here," Talis answered quietly.

Movement from the top of the stair caught Aelwyn's eye, and she turned to see a woman with some men in red and gold emerge from the tower stair. "Nyan," Talis called, starting across the room toward her. "That was fast. Have you brought food for our guests?"

"What we have I have brought," she answered, smiling.

"Nyan?" Mindarin said, walking from Aelwyn's side toward the woman.

"Mindarin?" the woman answered, then she smiled and opened her arms wide to give Mindarin a hug.

Soon Bryar and Caan also embraced her. Excited, Mindarin introduced Nyan to Aelwyn, and Aelwyn gathered that Nyan had been at Sulare with Mindarin and the others. Then a light seemed to dawn on Mindarin's face. She pointed at Talis. "Is this the young man Calissa told us about who escorted you so romantically all the way from Cimaris Rul to Sulare?"

"It is indeed."

"I see," Mindarin said knowingly, giving Talis a good once-over. "You were the subject of much speculation, I can tell you that. Calissa would be absolutely green with envy if she knew I'd met you at last."

"Calissa has met Talis, Mindarin," Nyan said. "She and Darias were here visiting about twelve years ago."

"Ah well," Mindarin said, shrugging her shoulders. "At least now I've met him too."

Mindarin walked over to Nyan and a second time embraced her. Aelwyn could see how tightly she held her, and she looked away. Mindarin had talked of the ordeal she faced when captured on the Forbidden Isle, but Aelwyn knew it could never be fully understood by those who weren't there.

For a time, the question of what should be done was dropped, as the men with Nyan placed food and drink on the sparse tables. Aelwyn wasn't hungry, but she took a cup of cider and walked back to the window that overlooked the Southern Ocean.

Behind her, she could hear Mindarin and Bryar trying to catch up with Nyan, attempting to cram seventeen years into a few moments. In normal circumstances, their paths would have crossed in the Assembly, but Nyan had been to only one Assembly since their time together in the Summerland, and only Wylla of all their old friends was there that year.

No one spoke of Werthanim's civil war overtly, but Aelwyn could hear it being carefully avoided in the things that weren't said. Now that Malek had come forth, the war was old news, but it was like an old wound to those who had been in the Summerland when the murder happened. The happiness at being reunited was evidence of the Summerland's success in bringing them together, but the circumstances that reunited them were evidence of its failure.

Aelwyn looked back over the city toward the Southern Ocean and gasped, dropping her wooden cup onto the stone floor, where it bounced loudly. A great, dark form rose out of the swirling sea and towered over the distant wall, resting two immense, webbed hands on top of the thick, white stone.

"Aelwyn, what is it?" Mindarin called out, and she could hear the sound of many feet crossing the floor quickly.

"There." She stretched out her arm to point out the menacing form.

"By the Mountain!" Talis said. "What is that?"

"The creature from the deep that sunk our ships," Caan said. "Talis, this is the answer to all the questions about the lost ships from Sulare and Cimaris Rul. It is what sunk several of our ships while we were on our way here from Col Marena. It is why we had to finish that journey on foot."

"What's it doing?"

No one answered, and no one moved. Aelwyn felt frozen, rooted to that very spot. The creature hadn't moved, and she half expected that in a moment she would blink and it would disappear, slipping back below the waves of the tempestuous sea. But she was wrong.

The great form hunched over the wall, and the two webbed hands wrenched huge chunks of stone from the top of the wall. As the hands flung the stone pieces into the water, waves washed in through the gap, spilling into the streets.

They all stared, stunned in disbelief, as the creature, hovering some four spans higher than the wall, proceeded to rip the section to pieces. Though it was a long way off, they could hear the echoing sound of stone cracking and splitting. They could also see water pouring in through the growing hole.

Talis recovered from the shock first.

"Flee! Flee now! There is no more time for debate. Everyone out of the city. The wall is breached, and with or without this creature's help, the Southern Ocean will finish the job he's begun. We have to go!"

There was no argument, and soon they were all flying as fast as they could down the long, winding stair. The next thing Aelwyn knew, she was stepping out from the shelter of the tower into the rain-soaked streets, preparing to mount her horse again. As she did, she looked back at the entrance to the tower. Her heart sank. She had tasted shelter, even if only briefly, and now they were leaving the city. It was too cruel. It would have been better if they'd never entered the city and the tower at all.

It was late afternoon before they finally rode away from Cimaris Rul. They had halted the column and redirected the Great Bear bringing up the rear to follow troops to the High Bridge, several leagues northeast. Aelwyn waited with Caan and the others by the gate, watching soldiers from three of the great cities of Kirthanin march out together. Some wore the red and gold of Cimaris Rul, others the purple and grey of Shalin Bel, and still others the black and white of Fel Edorath. All wore looks of dejection, bracing themselves against the wind and rain as they marched into the fading daylight.

As the last of the soldiers exited, Talis and Nyan Fein rode out, motioning for Caan and the others to follow. Aelwyn reluctantly nudged her horse forward, looking back over her shoulder at the beautiful buildings. She sighed at the thought of all that empty shelter going unused. She was about to turn forward when a steady stream of water came pouring out the gate. It was only perhaps a hand deep, but it moved quickly and swirled around the hooves of her horse. She looked back up, searching the street for signs of anything amiss, but it was empty. She spurred her horse and rode on.

Nighttime descended over the countryside, and Aelwyn rode in silence. Images flashed through her head of the creature from the sea ripping the wall into pieces. Dark webbed hands clasped the white stone and threw the severed chunks into the churning water. She envisioned the streets of Cimaris Rul filling with water and the great scaly creature squeezing through the breach and swimming through the empty city. The image was suddenly very real, and almost involuntarily, she spurred her horse on faster.

The night passed slowly. They hadn't ridden many nights during their trek south, and Aelwyn was surprised at the bite in the cold night air. *I thought the south was supposed to be warm,* she thought as she held her cloak tight against herself. *This rain would be a lot easier to take if it fell on a warm summer evening.*

Not long before morning, the soldiers ahead stopped moving. She drew her horse up alongside the others. Talis and Nyan had dismounted. "We're not far from the High Bridge, but the crossing will be slow in the dark," Talis explained. "Might as well get down for a while."

Soon they were all down, holding the reins of their horses, moving forward in fits and starts. "So," Caan said to Talis. "What was your plan before we got here?"

"Our plan was simple, really. Put the rising floodwaters of the Barunaan between us and Malek. Get across while we could."

Caan nodded. "And then?"

"Head north. I figured we had some time to decide whether to head for the gap between Elnin and Lindan."

"Were you thinking Amaan Sul or Kel Imlaris, or something else entirely?"

Talis looked at Nyan, and she smiled. "We hadn't decided. I wanted to head to Kel Imlaris, because it wasn't quite as far, but Nyan was worried about heading toward a coastal city. I found it hard to believe that a storm like this could be universal, and I still do, but after hearing from you all, I guess she was right."

"Impressive, a man who can admit he's wrong," Mindarin joked. "You really did get yourself a good one, Nyan."

"I don't think any of us know what the weather is like at Kel Imlaris," Caan said, "but it would seem the road to Amaan Sul might be better."

"But if we assume that the rain has been falling like this all over Kirthanin," Corlas Valon put in, "we will have the Kalamin to deal with. It may be flooding as well, and I don't know of any easy passages close to the Kellisor Sea."

Silence fell as they all shuffled forward again. "Well, as I said," Talis eventually said, "we have some time to decide. Kel Imlaris could be underwater by the time we get there if this rain has been falling off her shores too, and the road to Amaan Sul could dead-end in an impassable, flooded river. We may decide to flee into the Elnin or Lindan, or perhaps seek refuge in the peaks of the Arimaar Mountains. Who knows? Right now, what matters is getting across the High Bridge."

"Talis," Gilion said, "if the river is as bad as you say, it would be great if we could keep Malek on this side of it. This High Bridge—any chance we could take it down after we cross?"

"Well, the idea has been discussed," Talis said. "The High Bridge is narrow, but it is solid stone. I don't know how it was built across such a high gorge, suspended like it is in midair, but it is very strong. We haven't brought anything with us that would be very effective in destroying it, mostly because we didn't think we could."

"We do have fifteen hundred Great Bear," Gilion added.

"What are they going to do," Brenim said, "jump up and down until it falls away underneath them?"

"They might be able to knock it down with your head. It's hard enough," Gilion retorted.

"Sarneth?" Caan asked.

"I will speak to Elmaaneth and Kerentol on the other side, but I have crossed the High Bridge before, many years ago. If my memory serves me well, its destruction is an unlikely proposition. The bridge is very solid indeed."

Later that morning, with the earliest rays of dawn illuminating the bridge, Aelwyn understood Sarneth's doubt. The High Bridge seemed to her to be an impossibility, a bridge made from what appeared to be a single piece of stone arcing over the narrow gorge. What's more, it boasted no supports of any kind, at least none that she could see. The bridge seemed simply to have grown over the gap, like an outgrowth of rock extruded from the gorge in some century or millennia past. The High Bridge was perhaps a span and a half wide, with only some ancient rope looped through small posts to serve as rails. They didn't look strong enough to withstand her own weight, let alone a misstep from her horse, so she felt very glad that she had not needed to cross the bridge in the dark. She understood now why she had felt they were all but crawling this last half a league.

"I see what you mean," Gilion said to Talis as they stood on the strong stone. "How would we shatter this? Sarneth, do you think there is any way?"

"There might be, with enough time and the right tools, but I fear that we have neither."

"Well," Gilion said with a sigh, "it was a good idea anyway."

"There is still hope," Talis said, motioning them to the edge of the gorge. "How far down from here would you say the water level is?"

"Four spans, perhaps, maybe less," Brenim said as they all peered down.

"I think less," Talis answered. "Normally, the surface of the Barunaan should be ten spans below us."

"The water has risen so far, this far inland?"

"Yes," Nyan said. "Elsewhere, where there are no strong walls like this gorge to contain it, the waters of the Barunaan have flooded fields and roads. Here though, the water has nowhere to go but up. It has risen almost three spans in the last six days."

"Three spans!" Aelwyn marveled.

"Even so," Mindarin added, "what good does it do us?"

"Perhaps the water will do to this bridge what we cannot: wash it away or cover it over; in short, render it unusable."

"But if Malek was only three or four days away yesterday, " Mindarin replied, "he is only two or three days away now.

Surely he will discover where we've gone and be here before the water can rise another four spans."

"Maybe," Talis responded, "but remember how long it has taken us to cross, and he is leading a mighty host. If he decides to follow us across this bridge, it will slow him down considerably. I would say that it will take him at least a week, if the water doesn't prevent him from using this crossing."

"Caan," Talis continued, looking up from the gorge and into the grim eyes of the former combat instructor, now commander of the combined forces of Shalin Bel and Fel Edorath. Aelwyn could hear excitement in his voice. "What about here? Why not take our stand on the other side of the bridge? I had almost dismissed the idea, thinking that my men alone were too few, but with your men and the Great Bear, this narrow confine might serve us well."

Caan looked up from the gorge. Sadness seemed to fill his eyes. "Yes, the narrow passage would help," he conceded, "but I just don't know, Talis. A Vulsutyrim who wields a great hammer marches with our enemy. Valzaan, who was with us in Werthanin, called him the Bringer of Storms. I saw him summon lightning from the sky at Zul Arnoth and blow holes through the stone walls. I just don't see how we could stand against him here, without cover. We would expose row after row of men and Great Bear. If he still commands the same power, and I have no reason to think he doesn't, this divide would prove little barrier to him. He would rip us to pieces."

"If stone walls and narrow bridges provide no defense against him, then where are we to turn?" Talis asked, looking back over the bridge.

"I don't know," Caan answered.

They fell quiet again, and Aelwyn gazed down the sheer side of the gorge to the rushing water. The sight of it whirling so rapidly made her think of the images that had plagued her all night of the Southern Ocean breaking through the wall at

Cimaris Rul and flooding the empty streets. She shuddered and pushed the picture away, not wanting to see the creature again in her mind's eye. She was relieved when Talis eventually said, "Well, let's cross over. Whatever we are going to do, it isn't going to be on this side of the Barunaan."

Slowly they started across the bridge. Some remounted and rode, but Aelwyn felt more comfortable walking on her own two feet and leading her horse. She was an able rider, but even if being thrown from her horse was unlikely, she didn't want to risk it.

At the highest point of the bridge's arc, she looked back. Though she knew that Aljeron was on the other side of the world, this bridge placed yet another divide between them. It had been so long since she felt the warmth of his touch, and with every step, it seemed to her that he was fading farther and farther away.

3
SNOW SERPENT

ALJERON'S HORSE LABORED through the waist-high snow. He felt the surge and struggle of every step. Lather, white like the snow that surrounded them, was thick on the horse's hide. They would have to stop soon. There wasn't enough food, so hunger compounded the weariness. He hated to go so slow and stop so soon each day, but they'd already lost one horse, and if the others died from overexertion, then where would they be? Stuck in the Nolthanin waste with nothing but mountains of snow in any direction, that's where. Aljeron shuddered to think what that would mean for their prospects of ever seeing this journey through. He'd begun to wonder about their prospects as it was.

He looked down at Koshti, dappled with large streaks and patches of white, padding along as if above the snow. Though Koshti weighed a good bit more than Aljeron, he somehow managed to stay almost completely aloft as he deftly and tirelessly trotted along. Aljeron wondered how he did it. It couldn't be the distribution of his body weight over four feet, because that certainly didn't help the horses. Their hooves sunk like stones through the dense snow. Koshti's paws, though, so wide and furry, seemed to dip only slightly, grip the snow, and refuse to sink. It was as if they were natural snowshoes.

Yesterday or the day before had been Midwinter, but he wasn't sure. He thought he lost a day somewhere, so even though he guessed it was the first day of the New Year, he couldn't really be sure. For the last ten days at least, every day was the same. When the snow came up above the horse's knees, their pace slowed and they traveled less, stopping earlier each day. What's more, even though they were riding, he felt the weariness growing as well. Whatever day it actually was, they had not celebrated the New Year. Synoki mocked the suggestion that they at least briefly observe the rites of Midwinter, and none of the others expressed interest in any formal observation. In the end, he simply encouraged them to meditate on the words of the rite as they rode. Even for him, though, it was hard to focus on the Mound rite for long, for the weariness of each day shortened his attention span, mercifully driving away thoughts of despair, but also keeping him from concentrating on things he wanted to contemplate.

He couldn't imagine how tiring each day had become for Erigan, who, unlike Koshti, didn't glide along on top of the snow. The Great Bear labored, burrowing a wide swath through the endless sea of snow. He kept pace and never complained, but Aljeron could see him breathing heavily as his frosty exhalation came sometimes smooth and steady, and sometimes in a rush that worried him.

Erigan had been very quiet since Arintol's death, speaking only when addressed. Having not ventured far from the Lindandraal, he probably had never seen one of his own die in battle. Aljeron had, far too many times. He grieved the deaths of Karras and Arintol, but along with the sadness, he felt that the group was fortunate. Allfather had saved them from what could have been a disastrous surprise attack. Had Aljeron not seen the giant step out from his hiding place, the Vulsutyrim could easily have killed two or three of them in his first charge before they'd known what was going on, and the surviving men or Great Bear would have been hard pressed to take him down. As it was, they succeeded only through sheer force of numbers.

His horse shuddered and hesitated as it took its next step. Aljeron stroked its neck and whispered, "Soon, we'll stop soon."

The thought of stopping was disheartening, not only because it was only midafternoon, but because stopping meant he'd have to prepare a small snow shelter to sleep in. They all carved out tiny, curved niches in the snow like miniature caves, where they were warmer than when on horseback and exposed to the falling snow and biting wind. Even so, he hated the daily ritual of shoveling and packing and creating his, in part because it took time to do well, and in part because he never seemed to be able to do the work without thinking of his cozy rooms in Shalin Bel, especially his favorite chair in the parlor nestled up close to the large, open fireplace. Sometimes, he almost thought he could feel the soft cushioned seat and the warm glow of the crackling fire, but as quickly as it would come, it would go.

He looked up into the grey expanse that met the white on the horizon. It was a boring perspective in every direction. Endless white capped by endless grey. The only variation was the steadily drifting snow. Some days it fell slowly and lazily, like blossoms from snow trees floating merrily to the ground. Other days, it fell thick and fast, straight down like rain. Either way, there was always the white snow. Always the grey skies.

His stomach rumbled. The small piece of dried meat they'd all shared that morning hadn't gone very far. He'd been hungry by Fourth Hour, but the hunger pains went away until now. Despite their severe rationing, he just didn't know if they'd make it. He had counted on some wildlife, some game along the way. Cinjan confirmed there were creatures that could be eaten, though like the Red Ravens some of them were entirely likely to try to eat them too. Cinjan admitted, however, that he hadn't considered the effect the snow would have on their hunting. Aljeron didn't know where any creatures could go to hide from the snow, but they had gone there. He understood now, much better than he would have liked, the frenzied attack of the Red Ravens. This place made anyone and anything willing to risk its life for the possibility of eating well. He feared the feverish hunger would be theirs before long, and it made him very afraid.

At just that moment, when he felt his morale slipping and the despair rising, Aelwyn's face rose up out of the great white expanse before him and hung warm and welcoming in the air. He smiled and closed his eyes. The endless white disappeared, but she did not. She did not because he held onto her and compelled her to remain. He could see her, standing on deck beside him, smiling at him. He could feel her, her fingers lightly tracing his own as he held her hand in his. In this cold, dreary place, even the thought of her bright smile and warm touch revived him.

He was just imagining himself reaching out to stroke her soft, silky hair, when a sudden thought, an intruder, pushed into his make-believe world. *Is she still well? Is she all right?* His eyes popped open and the glare of the white expanse made him squint.

He pulled his thoughts back to Aelwyn. Since the Vulsutyrim, they had seen no more evidence of Malek's interest in or knowledge of their journey. He doubted very much that

Malek would spare much strength to pursue them into this barren wilderness. It was entirely likely that the journey itself would kill them, so why waste anyone or anything to do it? No, Aljeron was as convinced as ever that despite the attack, Malek would probably turn his attention south. If he did, then that would mean that Aelwyn and the others were still in the path of the storm. Of course, if Malek and the Bringer of Storms were both moving south and the snow here was as constant as the rain had been in Werthanin, then maybe everyone was in the path of the storm.

Yes, but not everyone was in the path of the storm of men, Malekim, and others that came from the Mountain. He remembered the growing anxiety he felt as he led his men across the breadth of Werthanin to escape that storm, and despite all his troubles now, a part of him was relieved that this particular storm no longer pursued him. But it was likely chasing her, and he felt disquieted to think of what would happen when she ran out of places to run.

He had thought in Col Marena that he might not survive this quest and that she might lose him, but he hadn't given much thought to the possibility that he might survive but lose her. He couldn't lose her. In the short time they'd had together, he realized that Aelwyn was home to him, every bit as much as Werthanin or Shalin Bel was. She was home, and if he came through this and she did not, where would he go? What would he do? He would have no home to go back to.

As he thought of Malek and his hosts pursuing the weary and bedraggled Werthanim survivors, the earnest and eager young face of Benjiah popped into his vision. *So much like his father.* At least in appearance. Aljeron hadn't spent enough time around Benjiah to know how far the likeness extended. He had been amused to see Benjiah running his fingers through his hair as they prepared for battle in Zul Arnoth. How funny nature was that even such a small thing as a tic like that could be passed down from father to son. *What must it be like for Wylla to see her son doing that?*

Aljeron hoped Benjiah was all right. Furthermore, he hoped that with the need of Kirthanin so great, Benjiah would learn quickly his prophetic place and role. It was a lot to ask of someone who had the body of a man but was still but a boy, but it seemed to be the will of Allfather that this boy become a man with all speed. He didn't know if Benjiah would be sufficient for the task, but he certainly hoped so.

His horse shuddered again, stumbling slightly in the snow. Aljeron patted him gently and pulled back ever so slightly on the reins. "Easy, rest now."

After whispering to his own horse, he turned to look at the others. "I think that's all for today. We need to give the horses their rest."

He dismounted and began to dig out a hole big enough for him to kneel in. He sighed. Another night, another snow shelter to make.

The next morning Aljeron rolled out of his snow bunk, stood, and stretched. Grey skies. White snow. Both as far as his eyes could see. Right now the snow was falling slowly, softly, lazily. He was glad, not so much because it was a little easier to ride in, but because the lighter snow would bury them a little more slowly. He didn't know what they would do if they didn't reach Harak Andunin before the snow was over the horses' heads.

Cinjan was also awake and standing. Aljeron looked at him, at the same grim face that never gave anything away, ever. Not even first thing in the morning. Something had hardened this man, whether life on the sea or previous trips into Nolthanin or something else. Whatever it was, he stood impassive and unmoved.

"Cinjan," Aljeron called, and the man turned to look at him. "Where are we?"

"A little south of the center of the Andunin Plateau, I think."

"Are we ready to turn north yet?"

"We might as well. That will lead us to some steep approaches, but once we sight the plateau, we can travel along at its base until we find a more welcoming way up."

"I wonder what the snow will be like there?"

"I have no idea, but I imagine a lot like it is here."

Synoki rose and nodded with his smile, which to Aljeron was barely distinguishable from a smirk. Evrim and Saegan were both soon on their feet, though Aljeron could tell by looking at Evrim that he had only just awakened, probably at the sound of their voices.

He was glad to think they'd head north again. Getting up and over the plateau would put them at the Great Northern Sea. For some reason, he hoped that getting to the coast would mean easier going, that maybe the snow wouldn't be quite so high at the water's edge. Harak Andunin was visible from the Great Northern Sea, or so it was said. If they could cross the plateau, get to the sea, and follow it to the mountains, then maybe they would succeed after all.

"Once we're up," Aljeron said, "how much time do you think we'll need to get across?"

"Don't know. In ordinary conditions, we could ride across the narrower parts of the plateau in about three days, but in this?"

"And how far beyond the other side to the Great Northern Sea?"

"Not far."

"I still think we should hug the coastline until we see the mountains and Harak Andunin from there."

Cinjan shrugged. "It isn't the most direct route, but it'll work."

"Don't mention Andunin," Evrim grumbled, clearing his throat.

"Why not?"

"Because right about now I'm pretty annoyed with him."

Synoki laughed. "I think a bit of snow madness has come over you, Evrim. You're upset with a dead man."

"I am. What was he thinking? Why did he accept Malek's offer? If he hadn't, then maybe when Alazare threw Malek from the Mountain, it would have ended."

"Maybe it would have." Aljeron nodded.

Tornan rose, making himself visible above the snow. His hair was disheveled, and ice crystals clung to the ends.

"I find it difficult to be so hard on Andunin," Saegan said.

"What?" Evrim said, looking at Saegan in consternation. "You agree with what he did?"

"Of course not," Saegan said. "Don't be absurd. I just find it hard to judge him, because we aren't in his shoes."

"It isn't hard at all," Evrim shot back. "One of the Twelve comes along and says Kirthanin needs a new boss, and he plans to be it, you stay out of it. Or you say you'd be glad to help, and as soon as he's gone, you go find one of the other Titans. You don't accept the offer and join the rebellion."

Saegan rolled his eyes. "Is anything ever that simple? What if Malek had caught him being faithless? What would have happened to him? His family? If the lives of Kyril and your girls were at risk, what would you do?"

"My wife and my girls are at risk now because of what he did."

"I know," Saegan said, his voice softening. "I don't want to argue. It just seems to me that Andunin was in a rough spot. I don't think we should underestimate how hard it would be to say no when he had his family's safety to think about."

"And not only that," Synoki said, "don't forget how alluring the power must have been. The appeal of power is another strong motivator. It would have been hard for anyone to say no to that."

"I would have said no," Evrim insisted, his voice firm but calm.

"Are you so sure?" Synoki replied, sounding intrigued. Aljeron felt a chill, and not from the snow.

"The most powerful being in the world offers you a chance to share the rule of Kirthanin," Synoki persisted. "He makes for you the tools of conquest, hands you the keys to power and glory beyond imagining, and you'd just say no?"

"Yup, I'd say no."

"A true answer is hard to come by, since we have a little hindsight," Aljeron said. "But Evrim's answer seems all the more reasonable when we consider that allying himself with Malek certainly didn't do Andunin any good. He lost his home, didn't get any of the power promised him, and left a legacy of ruin for the world."

Synoki scowled at Aljeron. "Easy for you to say, knowing what happened. But how was Andunin, a mere man, to know what Malek himself could not foresee?" Synoki's voice softened, and the smirk-smile returned. "Anyway, who knows if any of it is really true? They're all just stories to me."

Now Aljeron frowned. "What do you mean? Are you saying that you don't believe Malek seduced Andunin and created weapons for their rebellion?"

Synoki shrugged his shoulders. "There might have been an Andunin. There probably was, but you know how stories get distorted and exaggerated from one teller to the next. Besides, what makes you so sure about Andunin? How do you know what happened? You weren't there. You never met him."

"I haven't met Malek either, but I don't really need to, do I? I know enough. Anybody with any sense knows enough about him without meeting him."

"Really? Are you sure? I find it quite remarkable that everyone knows so much from stories alone about people they have never seen. As for me, I'll reserve my judgment. I don't believe everything I hear, and I think you'd be wise to do the same."

The conversation didn't go any further than that, and Aljeron was glad. Synoki said things like this now and then, and part of Aljeron thought the man just liked to stir people up, but part of him wasn't sure. Synoki acted as though he didn't believe any of it, but he'd been on the Forbidden Isle. He'd seen Malek's forge beneath Nal Gildoroth and even carried one of Malek's hammers. Did he not believe in Vulsutyr, the Fire Giant? He'd seen the towering statue of him in the center of Nal Gildoroth. Did he not believe the stories of dragons and garrion? He'd been carried in a garrion many leagues across the Southern Ocean. Surely if anyone had seen enough evidence to believe in the old stories from the First and Second Ages, those who had been with Synoki on the Forbidden Isle had.

At last it was time to ride, and Aljeron pushed the unpleasant exchange out of his mind. He shared both Evrim's annoyance at Andunin and Saegan's empathy for Andunin's dilemma. He had been in a few tough spots, including this one, but to have Malek at the height of his glory and power pressure him into betraying the world, well that would be quite another thing indeed.

"Are we ready?" he asked as he surveyed Erigan, Koshti, and the others on horseback.

"We are," came the response.

"Then, Cinjan, take us due north."

The downside of the lighter snow was that the cloud cover seemed lighter too. It wasn't that Aljeron liked the grey skies, but the darker they were, the more they took the edge off the glare. Today, Aljeron would have to resort frequently to rubbing his eyes or shutting them to give them relief, but every time he did, opening them again was a brutal experience. After craving the sun constantly for weeks, he found himself in the strange position of wishing he could crawl into a cave to give his eyes a rest.

Despite his struggle with the glare, it was his eyes that gave him the happiest moment he'd had in days. Just after Eighth Hour, he saw rising in the distance the southern edge of the Andunin Plateau. "Is that it, Cinjan?" he asked, wanting to make sure his eyes weren't deceiving him.

"It is."

"How far do you think?"

"Far enough we won't make it today, but if we can press on a few hours and have a good day tomorrow, we should reach the base of the southern wall."

"Sounds good to me," Aljeron replied, allowing himself to smile broadly as he looked at Evrim and Saegan.

"We will need to be careful as we proceed," Cinjan said.

"What do you mean?"

"I mean that the terrain around the plateau is full of dried stream and river beds that are likely both empty and covered with snow. Depending on how the wind has blown snow drifts, we may not always be able to see them before our horses' hooves find them."

"We'll take it a little slower, then," Aljeron responded, hoping that slowing the pace wouldn't keep them from reaching the plateau the next day.

They started out again, but he checked the pace of his horse and tried to show restraint even though everything within him wanted to move faster, not slower. Even so, their spirits were high; he could tell because the relative silence that had accompanied them the past week or so was broken by intermittent comments and a real if scattered conversation. The Andunin Plateau might be a formidable obstacle in its own right, but as a landmark it also represented real progress, proof that they had almost reached the next stage in the journey. They might not anticipate ascending and crossing it, but they all looked forward to seeing what lay on the other side.

Almost an hour after spotting the plateau, he saw a second sight almost as welcome as the first. A large snow rabbit was running in their direction. It was almost completely white, and only its motion made it visible. Koshti had also seen it, and the tiger bolted, an orange and black streak flashing across the snow to intercept the animal. Aljeron watched, expecting the rabbit to double back, but though it veered to avoid the tiger, it kept coming more or less in their direction, undeterred by Koshti. Aljeron didn't understand the creature's odd behavior, but at this point, he didn't really care if the animal's stupidity meant fresh meat. Koshti quickly overtook the rabbit and snatched it up in his jaws, snapping the creature's neck. At first, the others had been leery of letting Koshti run down what few animals they had seen, but they learned soon enough that Koshti would bring any prey to Aljeron. To be sure, Aljeron kept the biggest piece for the tiger, but the rest was always shared equally among them.

"Well done," Aljeron called as Koshti trotted across the surface of the snow back toward them. He turned to Evrim. "That'll make a nice if small dinner."

Evrim was frowning. "What was it doing? I've never seen anything like that. Why didn't it turn around?"

"I don't know. Maybe this storm is driving more than just us crazy."

"I guess, but it doesn't sit right."

No sooner had he stopped speaking than Evrim's eyes grew wide, and he motioned to Aljeron to turn around. "Aljeron, look!"

Aljeron turned and immediately saw what caused Evrim such wonder. Not one, not two, but perhaps twenty or thirty snow rabbits were running at great speed across the distant snowscape. They were not headed directly for the travelers, but if they kept on at their current trajectory, they would pass just ahead.

Koshti moved out a few steps in front of the horses but stopped, moving side to side and pausing every few seconds to stand absolutely still and stare at the rabbits. Aljeron looked down at his battle brother. He sensed bewilderment, and Koshti was never bewildered.

"Evrim, even Koshti is confused by this. Do you have any idea what's going on?"

"None. I've never seen anything like it."

"Cinjan?" Aljeron asked, looking down the line of horses at their guide. "We're open to suggestions."

Cinjan stared at the running rabbits, now perhaps only thirty spans away and cutting the distance rapidly. He shook his head slowly. "I don't know what this is."

"Who cares what's going on, this is food for weeks. We should get as many as we can," Tornan called out as he pushed his horse forward, lurching through the snow.

For a brief moment, the others stared at the young man and his horse as they gradually accelerated, kicking up a small snowstorm in their wake. Then Evrim seemed to shake off the passive daze as though waking from a dream. He called out, "Tornan, stop, you don't know why—"

Tornan's horse, one moment plunging boldly ahead, disappeared headfirst as though falling into a hole. Tornan's head snapped back wildly, and Aljeron caught a brief glimpse of terror before he too vanished beneath the snow.

"Tornan!" Aljeron cried out, pushing his own horse forward.

"Aljeron, stop!"

Aljeron halted and looked back at Evrim, who had called his name, only to see his friend pointing once more. Aljeron turned, but it wasn't snow rabbits that he saw. They were still running, seemingly unaware of the man and horse who had just disappeared. What Aljeron saw was not something he could easily describe or understand. It was like a rolling wall of snow, a rippling wave in the snowscape. Snow sprayed up and out as a large, white, endless ridge a couple of spans in diameter sped through the open terrain. It had been perhaps thirty spans away when Aljeron first looked up; it was now only twenty.

A muffled call from the snow pulled his attention back to the place where Tornan and the horse had disappeared. "Aljeron?" Tornan's terrified voice called. "Someone? Get me out of here."

The rolling ridge was only fifteen spans away. Without any command, Aljeron's horse started backing away through the snow. "Get out of there, Tornan. Climb up if you can!"

Ten spans. There was no answer from Tornan, and the rolling ridge came within a stone's throw.

"What is it?" Evrim called out.

As though in answer, a giant, white, serpentine head rose briefly above the spraying snow. It was fantastically large, with gleaming dark eyes in the white scaly face, and it disappeared as quickly as it had risen, plunging deep below the surface. A moment later, it burst through the hole made by Tornan and his horse.

"What is that?" Aljeron shouted, turning to look Cinjan in the eye.

"Snow Serpent," Cinjan called back, his eyes wide. "I thought they were extinct!"

"Evidently not!" The Snow Serpent's head reemerged, a horse head and foreleg protruding from its enormous mouth.

"By the Mountain," Aljeron gasped quietly as he watched the great white head rise two or three spans above the ground. The jaws of the Snow Serpent opened a little wider, and the head and foreleg disappeared, sliding down the creature's throat.

No sooner had the creature finished swallowing his meal than he turned and faced them. It slid forward, and its head and body seemed to rise, like it was climbing a ridge, and then Aljeron understood what had happened to Tornan and the horse. They hadn't fallen into a hole but had gone over the edge of something. The Snow Serpent was rising up out of it and coming their way.

He drew Daaltaran and heard the sound of other blades being unsheathed. He saw a brown flash as Erigan rushed past him, his great staff whirling in his strong claws. As the Snow Serpent drew near, Erigan swung mightily to hit its head and struck a fierce blow. The serpent hissed loudly and with a quick strike used the side of its head to knock Erigan several spans sideways into the snow.

Koshti was next, covering the distance between them and the Snow Serpent in a flash. He dodged the open mouth as it shot down to grab him in its powerful jaws. Having ducked underneath its head, Koshti leapt up on its scaly back and started scaling the back of its neck just as he had climbed the giant. This time, however, he wasn't so fortunate, and the icy scales were no doubt more slippery. The Snow Serpent gave his head a violent shake and Koshti lost his grip, sliding sideways and tumbling off. The fall was more than two spans, and on normal terrain could have broken the tiger, but he fell in a crouch into half a span of snow.

To give Koshti time to get a safe distance away and take advantage of the Snow Serpent's distraction, Aljeron moved in. Saegan and Evrim had the same idea and approached, one on either side of Aljeron. He rode hard and thrust Daaltaran at the scales. The tip of his sword penetrated, and he felt the instantaneous reaction of the Snow Serpent as it whirled in their direction. The great head came upon Evrim first, and it opened its jaws wide and hissed right in his face as Aljeron withdrew the sword.

Evrim, who was now staring straight into the mouth of the Snow Serpent, suddenly lunged and thrust his own sword into the great, gaping hole. Aljeron heard the blade sink into what must have been the back of the creature's throat, and Evrim began to withdraw his arm immediately. Evrim was agile and quick, one of the quickest men Aljeron knew, but he wasn't quick enough. The great mouth closed fast on Evrim's arm, and the next thing Aljeron knew, he was staring at Evrim, sitting still on his horse's back with his whole arm gone, blood seeping down the side of his cloak. It was a surreal moment, like a bad dream, for as the great white head rose again for a moment above them, with blood dripping down the underside of his frosty white scales, Evrim slipped sideways out of the saddle, his eyes rolling back in his head, and dropped into the snow.

There was no time to think of helping him, for the Snow Serpent was not done. He lowered his head and came at them again. Aljeron prepared to strike, but he never got the chance. Erigan's staff came rushing into the corner of his vision, and he watched as the Great Bear, with a mighty growl that was almost a roar, buried the staff deep in the Snow Serpent's eye. The head jerked up, wrenching the staff out of Erigan's paws. Swinging back and forth and hissing in agony, its underside was exposed to them all. Aljeron rode in with Saegan beside him, and dropping quickly from his horse, drove in Daaltaran with all his weight up to the hilt. The hiss in the sky turned into a scream. He pulled Daaltaran out none too gently and drove it in again. Beside him, Saegan was also punching holes through the tough scales. The great body shuddered, wavered, and fell into the snow.

Again, Koshti landed on it, this time running to the head. Aljeron looked as Koshti used his powerful jaws to rip out the other eye. If the Snow Serpent wasn't dead, at least he would never see again, Aljeron thought as he pulled his sword out and drove it in again.

After he had pierced the Snow Serpent almost a dozen times, he looked at the blood pouring out all of the holes, he looked at Koshti, who continued to rip scales and skin off of the serpent's face, and he looked at the body lying still in the snow. He stopped. The creature was probably dead, but Evrim might not be.

He pushed through the snow to where his friend lay, still at the feet of his horse who had not moved since the fall. He reached down and gently pulled him to a sitting position. He was barely conscious, but he wasn't dead. Saegan joined him, and together, with spare clothes from their packs, did their best to bandage the open wound where the limb had been severed from Evrim's body. He had lost a lot of blood, but if Allfather smiled upon him, he might live.

Aljeron stood up, leaving Saegan to watch over Evrim. He saw that Cinjan and Synoki had approached, and both looked down at Saegan and Evrim with impassive faces. A sudden, overwhelming rage boiled in Aljeron's blood. Almost without thinking, he stepped over to Synoki's horse, reached up with his powerful hand, grabbed Synoki by the front of his cloak, and pulled him off the horse. In a single fluid motion, he had Synoki down in the snow, half buried and bewildered. In the same fluid motion, his free hand brought Daaltaran none too gently against Synoki's throat.

He saw Cinjan drop to his feet, holding a sword in one hand and a long, nasty-looking dagger in the other. He didn't draw near, however, because one end of Erigan's staff, still dripping with serpent blood, was planted firmly in his chest. Cinjan had one eye on Aljeron and the other on the fierce gaze of the Great Bear.

Aljeron turned his attention back to Synoki. "Now look, you, this is the second time we've fought for our lives since leaving Avram Gol, and while you might have fallen from your horse and been unable to help last time, neither you nor your friend here lifted a hand to help us this time. You have some explaining to do, old friend. So you'd better start talking and it had better be good, or the life I helped save from the Forbidden Isle is going to end here at the end of my sword. Speak."

"It would be easier to speak," Synoki said with some effort, "if your knee wasn't crushing my chest and if your sword wasn't pressed quite so tightly against my neck."

"I'm running out of patience," Aljeron said, not moving.

"You remember that I am crippled," Synoki said, a glint of anger flashing through his eyes.

"That didn't stop you from fighting beside us in Nal Gildoroth and above Lindan Wood."

"That was seventeen years ago when I was younger—"

"Not good enough."

"You didn't let me finish! I was younger, and the foes I fought were more my own size—Malekim and Black Wolves. The giant frightened me as much as it did my horse, and this Snow Serpent even more so."

"Were you not on horseback? Are you not as nimble as any of us in the saddle?"

"You're a soldier," Synoki said fiercely. "You're trained to do these things. I'm a sailor and a merchant. I have no idea what to do in moments like this."

"You are carrying a sword."

"It's for show, a social sign that I'm not mere sailor anymore. It's not like I've ever used it."

Aljeron had no ready answer to his. He'd been trained in the use of the sword of course, but he had to admit many men in this world were unlearned in the arts of war. He remembered the Synoki of his youth, lean and sinewy, and carrying nothing but the hammer he had found beneath the city of Nal Gildoroth. He wielded that hammer in battle more like a blacksmith than a warrior.

"What would you have done if the Vulsutyrim or the Snow Serpent killed us all? Where would you be then?"

"Dead, probably."

Aljeron couldn't think of another question for Synoki. He looked from Synoki to Cinjan, still frozen in his tracks. "And him," Aljeron motioned at Cinjan, returning his steady gaze to Synoki. "Your friend seems to know how to use a sword. Why is he so ready to draw his sword against me when he's yet to draw it beside me?"

Synoki looked up at him, and for a long moment he was silent. Eventually he said, "Maybe he's just protective of his friend."

"Well, next time there will be no excuses. You two had better prove beyond any shadow of my doubt that you're willing to die that the rest of us might live."

"We'll do what is needed," Synoki replied quietly.

"Indeed you will, and right now you will look for Tornan in case he's still alive under all that snow. Understood?"

"Perfectly."

Aljeron let Synoki up and watched him start off through the snow, his hobbled walk more pronounced than usual. Cinjan sheathed his sword, and the dagger disappeared beneath his cloak. Erigan withdrew the staff, and Cinjan started after Synoki. Aljeron halted his progress by raising his blood-soaked sword and holding it in front of his chest. Cinjan stopped but didn't turn to look at Aljeron, keeping his eyes on Synoki.

"Next time you draw a blade on me, you die."

Cinjan didn't reply and didn't look, and eventually Aljeron lowered his sword and watched them both trudge past the fallen Snow Serpent.

Eventually Aljeron joined them, but the search for Tornan turned up nothing. The body of the Snow Serpent lay with its head nestled in the snow. The body, almost ten spans long, extended back as far as the ridge that Tornan had plummeted over, and down into the depressed area at the bottom, likely a riverbed. The place where the Snow Serpent came to rest covered part of the area that Tornan's fall had disturbed. All their efforts to excavate that area turned up nothing. There was no evidence of either the horse or his rider, only snow churned by the passage of the Snow Serpent.

The sun was beginning to set when Aljeron called Synoki and Cinjan to climb back up the embankment. He had little doubt that Tornan was anywhere other than in the belly of the dead Snow Serpent.

Weary almost beyond comprehension, Aljeron struggled out of the snowy riverbed. He returned to the place where Saegan was giving a now conscious but obviously feverish Evrim a drink, placing snow in his open mouth. Aljeron stooped beside them and looked from Evrim to Saegan.

"How is he?"

Saegan shrugged.

Evrim looked over at Aljeron. "Aljeron?"

"It's me."

"Am I dying, Aljeron?"

"No," Aljeron said firmly. Then he added, "I sure hope not."

"I want to go home," Evrim said, closing his eyes.

"Me too."

Aljeron looked back across the wide, snowy expanse at the now-distant body of the Snow Serpent, its great, menacing form now just a white ridge running along a white horizon. He was glad to leave it behind at last.

For a day and a half Evrim teetered on the border of reality, on the border between life and death. The fever persisted despite the cold, despite the snow, despite all they tried to do. As the second day dawned, Aljeron despaired of his life. That despair seemed confirmed by the fact that his burning forehead was cooling to the touch.

But Evrim was not dead. His fever had broken. He awoke weak and hungry, but alive. They gave him what remained of the snow rabbit that Koshti had killed, and he was able to eat some of it. Knowing that Evrim should not be moved, but that they might all die if they delayed much longer, Aljeron gave the order to move out.

Cinjan and Synoki rode in front, for Cinjan was still their guide, despite Aljeron's misgivings. At least in things geographical he had not yet proved false. His knowledge of the landscape seemed to match both what they had encountered and what little Aljeron knew about Nolthanin. Even so, Aljeron insisted Cinjan guide from the front. Inwardly he vowed never to turn his back on him again, and that included while they were riding. Evrim was weak, and with only Saegan and Erigan left, one or two intent on causing mischief would have more opportunity now than before.

Aljeron's misgivings only deepened following the attack. When not consumed by worry over whether Evrim would live, or debating whether they should try to harvest meat from the Snow Serpent, all he could think of was that image of Cinjan with sword and dagger in hand, held at bay by the Great Bear's staff but coming for him.

Why the concealed weapon? For weeks they had traveled together, and he had never seen the blade. It was a long dagger and would have required some concealing. What's more, it wasn't a weapon that seemed to have any legitimate use. It wasn't a hunting knife. You couldn't kill or skin an animal with it. Long and dull on the sides, with a supersharp point, it was an instrument designed to kill motionless or defenseless prey. It wasn't a combat weapon either. Aljeron would laugh at a man who stood face-to-face with him with only that in hand. So why? Such weapon would be effective only if unexpected.

Aljeron looked at Cinjan, riding a few spans ahead of him. *Whoever you are, I'll be watching you.*

4 THE TOWER RECLAIMED

BENJIAH WATCHED THE FLOATING EMBERS of the beacon fire rise up, get caught by the wind, and whirl out over the top of the tower and into the darkness. The dancing flames of the beacon entranced his sleepy eyes, and he found himself mesmerized, now and then realizing he'd been staring for some time at the beacon aware of nothing except the wild rhythm of the flickering fire.

It wasn't that he minded the absence of thought. In many ways it was a relief. After the tumult of the last few months, and after all the miles—through Gyrin, across Werthanin, down the coast, through Taralin, across the plains of Suthanin—he didn't rest his mind as well as his body. However, he was in theory at least supposed to be a watchman.

He was supposed to be watchman in case the beacon drew trouble, whatever that might be. If trouble was to come, they believed it would come through the inside of the tower, though that would be tough. Pedraal had found a long metal shaft in the storage room and jammed it through the handle of the door at the foot of the stairs. It was pinned against the stone wall on either side of the door. Pedraal reckoned enough force from the outside might snap it, but it would require an impressive feat of strength. Coming from Pedraal, that was saying something.

If someone did get in, then the second major obstacle would be getting up through the big storage room onto the concave platform where the beacon was. They pulled the ladder up with them every night, and any attempt to enter the trapdoor from below would almost certainly raise the alarm.

Still, watching for trouble was only part of his duty. They had agreed to make sure someone was always awake and alert, just in case the beacon actually summoned some dragons. Of course, Benjiah didn't expect all the dragons to just show up, but he hoped that at least one might take notice, flying high above the earth beyond the sight of man, or perhaps gazing from the top of one of the distant Arimaar Mountains with eyes that were said to see for leagues and leagues.

But now, after the beacon had burned for six days and nights, he was beginning to doubt. Either they hadn't seen it or they just weren't interested, and the men were running out of things to burn. Benjiah drew his knees up close and rested his chin. He had not mistaken the call of Allfather. He was meant to come here to light the beacon and summon the dragons. He didn't doubt that, but why weren't they coming? Perhaps he'd been summoned to light the beacon, not because the dragons would come now, but merely to let them know that the tower was reclaimed. Maybe it would take time to rouse them, and they would come forth at some future point.

Maybe, he thought, reclaiming of the tower was the point. Maybe Allfather called him to light the beacon because He knew that Benjiah would have to face the Grendolai. Now he had, and the Grendolai was reduced by the power of Allfather to a charred outline fused with the stone wall of the tower. Not only had Kirthanin been freed of one of its most terrible enemies, but Benjiah had been convinced that Allfather really could display immense power through him.

He stood and stretched. He looked on the other side of the beacon, where the floor began to slope up more severely, at his uncles sleeping on the stone. He thought about the real if subtle change in their relationship. They had always been more like older cousins than uncles, friendly and affable and rarely paternal, but a shift had occurred. A distance separated them now. Not a lot, and not always noticeable, but real distance. There was also, at times, deference. Sometimes they looked at him as if he were a soldier to size up. That was it. Ever since the incident with the Grendolai, they had been sizing him up.

The explosion of light. The remarkable inner flood of lightness and joy. The surge of power. He walked out from under the roof and felt the cold drizzle on his face. He was getting spoiled by the dry life here under cover. When the time came to leave, and he knew it must be soon, it would be very hard.

He scaled the sloping wall as far as he could, and it was as far as he needed to go. He could lean his elbows on the top of the curve to anchor him so he didn't slide back down. The starless night meant that even this close to morning, he could see very little of the surrounding countryside. He had seen it by daylight, though, and knew there wasn't much to see.

I can't see the things I want to see, and I keep seeing things I don't know that I want to see. He stroked his hair. He thought again of the dreams. First, there were the dreams he'd been having for years. The rain, the light, the wooden cage, the great city. They had appeared less frequently since the flight through Gyrin, but they began again in earnest after the forced landing by Taralin. He realized not long after the destruction of the Grendolai that the awesome explosion of light in the tower was the flash of light he had dreamed of for years, even as the constant rainfall they had been subjected to for months was also the rain of his dreams. It was very eerie to know that two images that had haunted his dreams had appeared in reality. Now he wondered about the other images, and if they were things to come. The image of the cage, or wooden box, or whatever it was. The image of the great white city square, empty and enormous. Were they also scenes from his life yet to be? Were they images of things that might be, or images of things that were set, as sure and as settled as the things of his past?

He felt strange to suspect that he stored glimpses of his future in his visual memory. It moved Benjiah to reverence and contemplation. Why had Allfather shown him the rain and the light? Was it so these strange and wondrous things could be understood and accepted by him after the fact? Was it so Benjiah would understand that neither event had caught Allfather unaware, that as much as he and everyone else might reel in the face of the inexplicable, it was known to Him as surely as yesterday? If that was so, then what did this cage and city portend? What would happen to set them alongside this storm to end all storms, and the wielding of divine power in his dreams? He didn't know, but he suspected he would one day find out.

Beyond these recurrent dreams was the new dream that had twice now come to him since the lighting of the beacon, the dream of the city underwater. He was as sure the second time as he had been the first that it was Cimaris Rul. He'd never been there, so he couldn't explain this certainty, even as he couldn't explain whether he was dreaming of something already come to pass or something that was coming. He was quite certain, however, that this great storm could bury Cimaris Rul under an overwhelming mass of water.

He let go of the slope and slid back down. Walking out into the cold rain helped him to stay awake, but he had little tolerance for staying in the wet long. Back under cover, he flapped his cloak to shed the excess water, then shook his head.

Out of the corner of his eye he saw one of his uncles stirring, and shortly, Pedraan appeared at his side, rubbing the sleep from his eyes.

"Up a little early," Benjiah greeted him.

"I know, but I might as well take over."

"Are you sure?"

"Yes. Go get some sleep."

"All right, I will." Benjiah was very tired and had no interest in sticking out the rest of his watch if Pedraan was up anyway. He walked around the beacon and curled up on the stone not far from Pedraal. If he was lucky, he would fall asleep before the sun began to rise and sleep well into the day.

When Benjiah awoke, it was late morning. Benjiah sat up, rubbed his eyes, and looked around. The flame of the beacon was less impressive by day, especially as it was clearly dwindling in size. Without more fuel—and he had no idea where they'd get dry wood near here—they'd have to let it die soon. He looked across the way and saw Pedraal and Pedraan standing, their broad backs to him, looking across the top of the tower and out over the broad expanse beyond. They were laughing, and it was good to see their humor undeterred by the apparent failure of their mission.

He rose to walk toward them, though slowly and awkwardly, for his foot was asleep. Pedraan turned and watched him half dragging his right leg behind him, and he laughed. "Nephew, most people have to be awake to injure themselves, what have you done?"

"It's asleep," Benjiah answered.

Both of his uncles were looking at him now, and the merriment had slipped from their faces. He wondered what about his appearance had given him away, but they were suddenly very sober too.

"What is it, Benjiah?" Pedraan asked, stepping closer and taking him by the shoulder. "The dream again?"

"Yes."

"What did you see?"

"The same thing all over," Benjiah said, the image of the white towers emerging out of the dark waters coming back to him. "I think Cimaris Rul is underwater."

"Already? Now?" they both replied, looking both at each other and at him. Pedraal led him toward the beacon, and they all sat near its warmth. "You've never suggested that this dream is a vision of something already come to pass. Are you sure?"

"No. I was sure about coming to signal the dragons, but they haven't come, and we're about out of wood and time. But as I woke from this dream for the third time, I felt a conviction that the sea wall is breached, and that the Southern Ocean has swallowed the city."

"Well," Pedraal said at last, "I suppose it's possible. If the flooding in the south has continued, Cimaris Rul could be underwater."

"If it is," Pedraan added, "what of Caan and the others? Where will they go? Were they trapped there when the floodwaters rolled in?"

"I saw no evidence of death in the city, no bodies in buildings or anything like that. The city looked empty and deserted."

"Maybe they found it empty."

"Maybe," Benjiah added. "Then what would they have done?"

Pedraal shrugged. "Who can say?"

"Certainly they wouldn't turn back," Pedraan said confidently. "With Malek driving south, they would still need to find a defensible place. Almost surely that means they would have fled across the Barunaan."

"If they could cross the Barunaan," Benjiah said. "You saw how flooded it is here. If the Southern Ocean has broken its bonds and come inland far enough to cover Cimaris Rul, the Barunaan may no longer be passable."

"It may not. On the other hand, Cimaris Rul does occupy the lowest land in all Kirthanin. It is right on the beach, and that southern wall has been battered by many a storm before this."

"But it has never broken, Brother," Pedraal replied. "Benjiah's right, we have no idea which side of the river Caan and his armies are on."

"I think I need to try again," Benjiah whispered. His uncles looked at him closely.

"You mean the King Falcon?" asked Pedraan.

"Do you think it might work?" asked Pedraal.

"I don't know, but I have to try." Inwardly, he had his doubts. He'd been trying to make contact with a windhover since they reached the dragon tower, but he had yet to be successful. Each day since the death of the Grendolai, he searched the skies for a King Falcon to bring a glimpse of their companions to his eyes, but it was all for nothing. Now such information was imperative, but he didn't know how to get it. He needed Valzaan. He needed Valzaan to tell him what he was doing wrong and what to do differently. He needed someone to talk to about a lot of things, and Pedraal and Pedraan just weren't the people he needed.

They watched him rise and walk back around the beacon to the place where he had slept. He didn't know that he needed to be alone for this to work, but it felt strange trying too close to the others. What's more, he'd just had a vision here, and he thought that maybe returning to this spot would help.

He settled in on the sloping floor and tried to relax, closing his eyes, but as he did so, he heard Pedraal's voice across the silence of the moment. "Uh, Benjiah, maybe you'd better try that later. We have company."

At first, Benjiah didn't understand. He looked instinctively toward the hole that led down into the large storage chamber. There was nothing there. He looked then at his uncles, who were turned east, looking off into the sky. The beacon roof obscured his view, so he rose and walked back around to them and immediately saw what they were looking at. Two large, golden forms were flying toward them at great speed, clearly visible against the grey horizon.

"Dragons!" Benjiah exclaimed.

"It would seem so," Pedraan answered.

"It's worked after all," Benjiah added, almost as an afterthought. "They're coming here. They've seen the signal."

"Yes, now what?"

"What do you mean?"

"I mean we're about to have a couple dragons as guests. What are we going to say? As I recall, they're none too patient and more than a little intimidating."

"We tell them our story, that's what."

Even though they were still a fair bit a way, Benjiah thought he could see the slightest hue of red around one, and the slightest hue of blue around the other.

"One is a red dragon, the other is a blue," Benjiah said.

Pedraal laughed. "Funny, Benjiah."

"I'm serious."

Pedraal looked at him. "You can see that from here?"

"Yes."

Pedraal looked at Pedraan. "Can you tell?"

"No, not at all."

They turned from him back to the sky and watched the dragons. Pedraal said, "Whatever color they are, they'll be here soon. Look how big they're getting how quickly. I wish I could go so far so fast."

The dragons began to circle in a wide arc above the top of the tower, closing the circle gradually and coming lower and lower with each pass. They both alighted on the tower at almost exactly the same moment, the red dragon to their left and the blue dragon to their right, on opposite edges of the tower roof. The three men had stepped out from under the small roof so that they could be clearly seen.

The red dragon leaned in low until the great golden head was almost within reach, its great dark eyes blinking as it looked them over. "I know you," it said with a deep voice that sounded like the rumbling of thunder.

"Eliandir?" Pedraal said, very uncertainly.

"You two were with Valzaan when I carried him from the Forbidden Isle."

"We were. It is good to see you again after—"

"Why are you here?" Eliandir said, his voice gruff and impatient. "And what means your lighting of the beacon?"

The blue dragon had stepped closer from the opposite edge, and he looked down from his full height, towering over them all. "What of the usurper below? How have you bypassed him?"

"You mean the Grendolai?"

"Yes, the Dark Thief."

"We didn't bypass him," Pedraal answered. "He's dead."

"Dead?" the blue dragon echoed, then turned to face the opening that led down into the great storage room. One of the great wooden doors was gone entirely, burned away by the explosion of light and heat that had come from Valzaan's staff. The other was shut, flat with the rest of the floor, closed after the men emerged from below. With a single deft motion, the blue dragon threw it open, and, leaning his head down over the hole, blew an impressive stream of fire down into the darkness. Then he dropped down inside, and Benjiah could see by the flashes of light and hear by the sound of it, several more explosions of flame below. After a moment, the blue dragon rose out of the hole, wings flapping, and came to a rest once more beside them.

"How came he dead?" the blue asked.

"Benjiah," Pedraal said, pointing to his nephew, who as yet had said nothing and had not really been noted by the dragons.

Both dragons lowered their heads and peered intently at Benjiah, and though he tried to keep still, his knees quivered at the sight of two enormous dragon faces with gazes fixed steadily upon him.

"You carry Valzaan's staff, boy," Eliandir said. "How so? What is the meaning of this?"

"He left it with me."

"Left it with you? Why? When was he here? Where has he gone? I would like to speak with him if he is near."

"He is not near," Benjiah said, looking down, unable to keep his own eyes fixed on the dragon under the heat of his stare. "He is no more."

"Valzaan is dead?" Eliandir said, and for the first time since they landed, he heard a change in the dragon's voice. It might have been surprise, but Benjiah was only guessing.

"Yes, he was killed at the end of Autumn Wane on the beach north of Col Marena. One of Malek's captains, a great Vulsutyrim who wields a terrible hammer and is called the Bringer of Storms because he has been manipulating the weather and causing this rain, he cast Valzaan into the sea."

At the mention of the Vulsutyrim, Eliandir and the blue dragon both got a fierce and burning look in their eyes, and when Eliandir spoke next, there was an angry edge to his words.

"Yes, I know him. We have seen him from above. His name is Cheimontyr, and he was first among Vulsutyr's sons when we engaged Malek at the end of the Second Age. It seems that rule of Vulsutyr's children has passed to him."

"Cheimontyr," Benjiah repeated, as though trying the name out. "He is the Bringer of Storms."

"It would seem so, though it is a gift that must have come from Malek in the long years since, for he brought neither that ability nor that hammer with him from the Forbidden Isle."

Eliandir raised his head back up to a normal height, but the blue remained where he was, gazing at Benjiah. "If Valzaan passed, why did he give his staff to you? You are only a boy, even by the reckoning of men."

"He gave it to me because I am a prophet of Allfather," Benjiah said, trying to sound as confident as he could.

"A prophet of Allfather?" Eliandir said, coming in for another close look.

Both gazed at him for a few more moments, and eventually they raised their heads and said, though more to each other than to him, "Yes, he is telling the truth, he is Allfather's chosen vessel."

For a long moment, the dragons stood at their full height, and for the first time, Benjiah had a chance to look at them side by side. While both at first glance looked the same, great golden dragons, the glint of red on Eliandir and the blue on the other were particularly visible up close. He could also see that Eliandir was a head taller than the blue, and more sleek and slender. The blue was shorter but looked thicker, wider. His great head was broader than Eliandir's and his feet larger with longer talons. They both looked frightening enough to put terror in the heart of any living creature, but for some reason, the blue looked even stronger than Eliandir.

Eliandir broke the silence. "All right, you have slain the Dark Thief, but why have you lit the beacon? Why have you summoned us from our mountain homes and our peace above the clouds?"

"We have summoned you because Kirthanin has need of you. If you have seen the one you call Cheimontyr, then you know Malek has come forth. Can you not see the peril that Kirthanin is in?"

"We have seen the hosts of Malek, even as we saw the infighting of men that so weakened Werthanin as to invite his coming. A thousand years have passed, but nothing has changed. The affairs of men are not our business. If this is why you have summoned us, we have no more to discuss."

"Wait," Benjiah called as both dragons began to turn away. "We have reclaimed this tower for you as an offering for the dragons, as a sign of our desire to repair the divide between us."

They turned back, and Eliandir spoke. "For the killing of the Dark Thief, we thank you, but the faithfulness of a few men can hardly repair the damage done by the whole race in this world."

"That's true," Benjiah answered, his mind scrambling for some way to convince the dragons to help. He had assumed that lighting the beacons would be enough. "But Malek's treachery is not the fault of man, nor is it man's responsibility alone to oppose him. All loyal creatures of Allfather are needed if Malek will be overcome."

Neither Eliandir nor the blue responded to this, but they did not move to leave either. Benjiah knew he was going in the right direction. "I am Allfather's prophet, and according to His word revealed to me at the Taralindraal—"

"Taralindraal?" the blue dragon said. "The Great Bear do not allow humans inside their draals anymore."

"They allowed me," Benjiah replied. "I was taken there by Sarneth, an elder of Lindandraal. What's more, they have sent fifteen hundred Great Bear to aid the armies of Werthanin, which have fled before Malek and Cheimontyr."

The dragons looked at each other, and the blue said to Eliandir, "The rumors then are true; Great Bear have come forth from Taralin."

"They have," Benjiah picked up excitedly, "in part because of the prophecy that Allfather gave me, that Malek would not be defeated and Kirthanin would not be free until the union of four great peoples. Allfather told me then that the union of the Great Bear and men was the first step in that larger call for union."

"Allfather has told you that summoning the dragons was to follow the union of men and Great Bear?" Eliandir asked.

"Not in so many words," Benjiah began, "but in a series of dreams and visions He showed me this tower and directed me here. Why else would He bring me to a dragon tower? You have seen for yourself the charred remains of the Grendolai. Allfather brought me here to slay him and light the beacon that you might come, and you have. Surely you can see as well as I that Allfather meant for you to come to me and hear His call."

Eliandir leaned into Benjiah's face, and his deep gaze again made Benjiah tremble. "That you have been called by Allfather I can see, and that you have reclaimed this tower from its usurper we can see as well. That we have no choice but to do as you say is not so obvious, lacking an explicit direction from Allfather to do so."

"But . . ." Benjiah began, frustrated.

"However," Eliandir raised his head back up to his full height, so that he stood there looking down over all three men. "Your words make it clear that what you say must be considered. If the Great Bear have decided the time has come to aid the world of men once more, we cannot overlook it."

"And," the blue added, "the death of the Dark Thief after he has lurked in the darkness below for almost a thousand years is evidence of your credibility."

"What's more," Pedraal said, looking at their visitors with grim determination, "the children of Vulsutyr are abroad. This Cheimontyr threatens to drown the world, and his children are a force that none of us can stop without you."

A deep rumbling from the dragons was followed by their increased agitation. Benjiah could see their massive talons protract and retract as Pedraal spoke of the Vulsutyrim. He had heard of the hate between the races, of course, but he could see it now visibly in the reactions of these two.

"You see," Benjiah continued, "we have need of you. Without your power and your strength, we will not stand. Malek will destroy the armies of men and Great Bear, and then you will be all that remains. Perhaps you can withstand him alone, but surely our best chance for survival is to come together, whether you believe the words of my prophecy or not."

"Believing your prophecy and interpreting it aright are two different things," Eliandir said. "Even Valzaan was cautious about assuming that he knew the meaning of everything Allfather directed him to say. Even so, we will take your message to as many of our brothers as we can, though the number of Sulmandir's children who still venture out of their lairs is few. What are your names, young prophet?"

"I am Benjiah, and I am the son of two of the people you rescued from the Forbidden Isle seventeen years ago. I owe my existence at least in part to you. These are my uncles, Pedraal and Pedraan. They were among those you rescued."

"I am Eliandir, and this is Dravendir."

The blue snorted and ducked his head just the slightest, as though in a small bow, though still high above them.

"If you please," Benjiah continued. "I have been trying to see where our friends have gone. They were headed for

Cimaris Rul, but I am afraid the city is now under the waters of the Southern Ocean."

"You must be a prophet indeed, for this is recent news. The city is under water. We have no news of a host in Suthanin near Cimaris Rul, but we know that before the city was destroyed, an evacuation had already begun."

"Where were the evacuees headed?"

"They were crossing the High Bridge over the Barunaan."

"Over the Barunaan?" Pedraal said. "So they'd be on the eastern side of the river?"

"Yes," Dravendir answered, "if your friends got to Cimaris Rul in time to join the evacuation, they'd be on this side of the river."

"Are they headed north?"

"That we could not say."

"And Malek? Have you seen him recently?"

"We have not, but last we knew, his hosts were moving rapidly south across the plains of Suthanin between the Barunaan and the Taralin Forest, though that was over a week ago. When we return to the Arimaar Mountains, we will see if there is more recent word of him."

"You are going to the mountains now?"

"Yes."

"You will come back, and help?"

"We will help as we are able. We cannot promise more aid than our own, for since the fall of our great father, every child of Sulmandir has followed his own course. Take the road south, and you are likely to meet those who have left the city. We will look for you on that road."

"Thank you," Benjiah called after them, as the dragons rose from the tower and moved in ever-widening arcs higher and higher.

For a long while they stood and watched the dragons fly away, their great golden forms getting smaller and smaller until they were little more than two golden specks against the immense grey sky. Benjiah felt goosebumps on his arms, and he couldn't believe he had just been in a conversation with dragons.

"I can't believe it," he said to his uncle.

"Can't believe what?" Pedraan said.

"I can't believe it worked," he answered, smiling. "They're the third, I know it. The Great Bear have come forth, and the dragons have answered the beacon. The prophecy is being fulfilled."

"Then who is the fourth great people?"

Benjiah shrugged. "That I don't know, but right now, I don't really care. At least two dragons have pledged their aid to us, and if Allfather smiles upon us, who knows how many more will come?"

Caan threw his wooden cup through the darkness, past Gilion's head at the tree they were arguing underneath. Gilion was an old friend, to be sure, but he could still drive Caan as crazy as he always had. "Why is all your counsel only of marching and retreating and running away," Caan said angrily.

Gilion smoothed his cloak and tried to look like someone who hadn't just had a cup go sailing past his head. "I give the counsel that I think is wisest, and right now marching and retreating seem wisest."

"Well," Caan said, "have you ever tried to picture a scenario where we turn and fight, where we take a stand? I'm so tired of all this running. There aren't going to be any scenarios where things look favorable, so if you're waiting for one, you'll need to get over it."

"If they catch us, the fight will be forced upon us. If they don't, then we still have one choice left: to pick the ground on which we stand. We are right to be patient and keep looking until we find the ground we want. Besides, we have hope of finding reinforcements in the north."

"If we can get far enough to find some," Caan said, his anger dissipating. For all his impatience, he knew Gilion was talking sense.

"Yes, if we can make it far enough to find some," Gilion echoed.

Caan looked up at Gilion, his face impassive but wary after Caan's flash of temper. "I'm sorry, Gilion. I'm frustrated with the situation and I took it out on you. I shouldn't have."

"We're old friends," Gilion said quietly. "Don't let it trouble you."

Caan smiled. His mind looked back over the long years that he and Gilion had known each other, remembering a particular day long ago. "Gilion, do you remember that night we spent in Garring Pul almost fifty years ago, on our way through to Amaan Sul? The night we stayed at that inn, The Old Blue?"

"You mean in the stable of The Old Blue," Gilion replied, laughing. "All the real rooms were taken."

"Yes, that night."

"Of course," Gilion said. "I remember it for the same reason you do."

Caan smiled. "She was beautiful, wasn't she?"

Gilion nodded. "She was indeed."

"We wasted half the night just sipping our ale as slowly as possible, just so she'd keep coming back to our table to ask if we needed anything else."

"That we did, and when we finally went back to the stable, it was with great reluctance."

Caan walked over to Gilion and put his hands on his friend's shoulders. "Gilion, there's something I never told you."

"Oh?"

"Well, you fell asleep pretty quickly, and when you did, I snuck out of the stable and went back inside."

"You did?"

"I did. They were just closing but let me in, and I found her cleaning up. I tried to find out if I could look her up on our way back through, but she told me that it was you, not I who had caught her fancy. I'm sorry I never told you."

Gilion was wide-eyed. "She told you that?"

"Yes, and I was jealous, so I kept it from you. I probably would have broken down and mentioned it if you'd ever said anything about her, but you never did, so I didn't either."

"Remarkable."

"You're not mad?"

"No, just confused."

"Why?"

Gilion looked at Caan. "The next morning, I woke before you. You were snoring steadily, so I snuck out and went back inside. They had just started serving breakfast, and she was there. I approached her as well, with the same intent, to see if I could call upon her on our way back through, but she told me that she had eyes only for you."

"For me!" Caan said, astonished.

"Yes," Gilion confirmed it. "Like you, I was jealous and said nothing, and like me, you never said another word about it."

Caan threw his head back and laughed, slapping Gilion on the back. "What a clever woman. She disposed of us both in short order, and for fifty years we've carried our guilty secrets."

"Yes," Gilion said, blushing. "Sorry, old friend."

"No," Caan said, "don't be. We were young and foolish. Now we're just foolish."

"Yes, sometimes we are."

"Gilion," Caan said, looking his old friend in his eyes. "Always give me the counsel you think is wise, whether I like it or not. Agreed?"

"Agreed."

BATTLE BY THE BARUNAAN

RULALIN STOPPED HIS HORSE on the great stone bridge and looked down at the rushing waters of the Barunaan below. They swirled less than a span beneath the bottom of the bridge. He didn't know how far down in the gorge the waters of the river normally ran, but he suspected that water had never before come so close to sweeping over the bridge itself. The two main bridges from Cimaris Rul across the Barunaan farther downstream had been washed away.

He tried not to be amazed anymore at the power of the storm that Cheimontyr had summoned and maintained, but even though the rain had noticeably slackened of late, its cumulative damage had become clearer in the last week than ever before. The extensive pools of knee-deep water they'd ridden through on their way to Cimaris Rul were evidence, but more than that, the complete submersion of the city signaled destruction by water to an unparalleled degree. He had never expected to find one of the great cities of Kirthanin sunk below the incursive waters of the Southern Ocean. But there it was, sitting in the distance, beneath the water. The hosts of Malek moved on quickly once they discovered the trail of those fleeing the city, so there was no time to stop and stare.

Now Rulalin was here, atop this great bridge, Soran behind him as they moved silently to the eastern side of the Barunaan. As their horses stepped onto dry land, Rulalin turned to look at Cheimontyr, standing no more than five or six spans upriver. He was overseeing the crossing of Malek's hosts. Rulalin had never been so close to the giant, and he flinched at the sight of his odd skin. Unlike the other giants' skin, his appeared dark from a distance, but now that Rulalin was close, he could see the skin was itself very pale and appeared to be stretched thin over something black and deep blue. This blue-black hue showed through the taut surface and especially in the giant's face produced an eerie and unsettling look. Rulalin stored the image away and then turned back to the road and kept riding.

"I think the rain's slowing down," Soran said as he drew up even with Rulalin.

"I think so too."

"There's been less, definitely less, the last week at least."

"I know."

"Any ideas?"

"Maybe Malek's or Cheimontyr's or whoever's purpose for it is accomplished. Maybe the waters have risen high enough. Maybe the destruction of Cimaris Rul was the goal. Maybe he doesn't intend to destroy all things with water. Maybe all of the above. Of course, he can't be completely finished with it yet."

"Why not?"

"It's still raining."

"True." Soran smiled. "Maybe he can't turn it off."

"That would be ironic," Rulalin replied. "Cheimontyr conquers the world for Malek but is drowned in the flood he created."

"If that didn't mean we'd be dead too, it wouldn't be the worst outcome in the world," Soran said, looking back over his shoulder. "He scares me."

When Soran turned back around, Rulalin looked him in the eye and after a moment added, "He should."

Benjiah dropped from his saddle, exhausted. Three days out from the dragon tower, he was missing the sedentary life beside the beacon more than ever. After helping to retrieve the horses for the trip south, it seemed he had never dried out. He was sore, soaked, and cold, and the memory of the big, bright beacon on the dry stone was torturous. He coughed. On top of it all, he was feeling sick. He'd weathered the rain all right until now, but he felt as if he might have a fever coming on and there was nothing to be done about it. He tried to console himself by recalling it was already the twenty-third day of Full Winter, and that he'd been lucky not to come down with something sooner, but it was a hollow comfort. He coughed some more.

Pedraal was standing beside his horse, watching Benjiah with concern on his face. "You all right?"

"Yeah," Benjiah said, smiling, "just have a little cough, that's all. Got used to the warm and dry, I guess."

"That makes three of us," Pedraal answered. "If we were all we had to worry about, I'd say we should just hold the dragon tower. The three of us up there, it would take an awful lot to get us down. They'd have to get in through the door, first of all, and we had that jammed up pretty good. After that, they'd have to figure out a way up onto the roof without us cutting them down. We could hold that tower a long time."

"Sure, until they starved us," Pedraan said.

"Granted, we would run out of food eventually."

Benjiah coughed again as he took his pack and moved off toward the small clump of trees they'd decided to take shelter under for the night. "Sure you're all right?" Pedraan asked as he walked past.

"I'm sure," Benjiah answered, then added as he set his stuff down on the ground, "I'm going to try again."

He didn't really want to try, but he knew that if he said he would, they'd leave him alone. He didn't feel well, and their constant inquiries, as if all of a sudden he was frail as a newborn, didn't make him feel any better.

As he settled in, though, he sighed and capitulated that he really did need to try again. They were three days out from the tower, and they hadn't seen the dragons again. Without word from them, and without being able to see anything through the windhovers yet, he and his uncles were moving blind down the Barunaan. They had no idea how far away their friends were or how close behind them Malek might be.

He closed his eyes. In his mind, he reached out, looking for a King Falcon who might be nearby. Immediately he felt the sensation of flying, the darkening daylight below him now as well as above. He felt the giddiness of making contact at last and focused the eyes of the windhover downward. The wide Barunaan, well past ordinary flood stage, was right below. He directed the bird to move out over the eastern side, and it did. He saw nothing that would answer his questions, and he was about to try to make contact with another windhover when the bird flew over what looked like a patrol of human soldiers. He directed the bird to look forward, and as the creature's eyes swept upward, he saw something he had not expected. A mass of people was gathered below, but they weren't soldiers.

They were men and women and children, grouped in families and other small clusters all over the ground.

The windhover flew farther, and eventually flew over what appeared to be soldiers, men camped in more orderly units in a wide variety of uniforms. A little farther on, he began to see the Great Bear as well, and seeing them was vaguely reassuring. He understood now why they hadn't yet met up with Caan and the others. They must be traveling with much of if not all of the civilian population of Cimaris Rul. And yet, even as the understanding dawned on him, he grew concerned. They were traveling much more slowly than he would have expected, but surely Malek's host was not.

Instantly, he started to reach out for a falcon that might be farther south, and he felt the change. He adjusted to the new bird and directed him to make for the Barunaan. After a few moments, he saw the river come within view and realized the windhover had been flying over the plains on the western side. He directed the windhover to keep going straight ahead, and once across the river, turned it south as well. Again, he was about to look for another bird farther south when he caught sight of something unexpected.

Several Vulsutyrim, with Cheimontyr at the front, were running together in a dense cluster, surrounded by a sea of Black Wolves. There were more than he could reckon, all moving at great speed. Behind them, he saw men on horseback and Malekim, also moving quickly, and he felt his heart sink as he was reminded of the sheer magnitude of Malek's forces.

In a heartbeat, the windhover doubled back and soared north, and Benjiah focused intently to note what landmarks he could, as well as the distance between the two groups. After a little while, he opened his eyes and stood up suddenly.

"We have to go, now!" he said, his voice betraying his anxiety.

Pedraal and Pedraan looked up at him, surprised. "What do you mean? We just stopped for the night."

"It doesn't matter. Pack up. We have to ride."

"Benjiah," Pedraan said, "there's at least time for you to explain what's going on."

"Not really. Caan and the others have been slowed down by the large civilian population they evacuated from Cimaris Rul. They aren't moving fast enough. Malek's army has not only crossed the Barunaan; they are flying at great speed and will overtake them in perhaps as little as a day. Battle is inevitable, and we need to be there when it comes."

Pedraal and Pedraan obeyed. They stood, moved quickly to their horses, and reattached the things they had just untied. Before long they were back in the saddle, and Benjiah's weary body groaned louder than it had when he dismounted. He ignored it and secured Valzaan's staff in his hand as he spurred his horse on. There wasn't time to think about the aching. The Bringer of Storms was coming, and this time there was no Valzaan, only Benjiah, to stand against him.

Aelwyn closed her eyes and felt the rain that today was so light it was like a gentle mist. Were it a hot summer afternoon, it would have been pleasant. She opened her eyes and looked at the faces of her sister, Nyan Fein, and the gathering captains. There was disappointment, fatigue, and fear in their eyes.

Caan and Talis Fein stood a short distance away, talking quietly. She knew from things Nyan had said that Talis was taking the debacle of their flight very hard. He knew the citizens of Cimaris Rul were slowing the army down, but he had no good answer to the question of what to do with them. Some believed that if they sent the civilians east while the army continued north, that Malek's army would let the civilians be, but no one could say with complete confidence that this was so. In the end, lacking a clear plan for their safety, Talis and Caan were unable to cut them loose. Consequently, they were all keenly aware that they now faced a serious predicament.

Caan and Talis turned toward them, and Aelwyn rubbed her arms to hold out the morning chill. All eyes were on Caan as he broke the silence. "I think we are out of choices."

"So we're not moving out?" Bryar asked.

"Not us," Caan answered. "Talis will leave here when we're finished, to oversee the departure of the citizens of Cimaris Rul. The rest of us will examine the ground and do our best to set up a plan of defense."

"Are we sure?" Corlas asked.

"Pretty much," Talis answered.

"Sarneth," Caan said, "how far would you say we are from the southern edge of Elnin Wood?"

The Great Bear paused before saying, "Six days if we were moving quickly. At the pace we've been maintaining, more."

"More than six days," Mindarin moaned.

Caan shook his head. "I'm sorry Corlas, sorry everybody, I just don't think there is any other way. We'd never make it."

"How close do we think they are?" Gilion asked.

"Bryar?"

She shrugged. "Hard to say. Our scouts in the rear have skirmished twice with Black Wolves. We assume they were a fair distance in advance of the main force, because they quickly disengaged both times. Even so, they can't be too far away."

"At this point, it doesn't really matter if they're a day behind, or three," Caan said. "The point is, we're not going to make Elnin Wood or the gap between Elnin and Lindan or any place else that might be remotely safe before they overtake us. We need to stand and fight, and this place is as good as any."

Caan looked at Gilion. "Do you agree?"

Gilion returned the look. "Yes, battle is upon us."

There were nods of reluctant agreement, and Caan continued. "Sarneth, we'll need your counsel now more than ever. When Elmaaneth and Kerentol arrive, we'll need your help staging the troops for battle. It has been a long time since an army of men and Great Bear fought side by side."

"I will help as I am able," Sarneth answered.

"Good, then we should get about our business today, for it may well decide our fate tomorrow."

"Caan," Sarneth said as they prepared to break.

"Yes?"

"Though Elnin is beyond reach, I would still suggest sending a pair of Great Bear there for aid. Even though help will not reach us before this battle, we may survive to see another day, and their help could be timely."

"We could," Caan said grimly. "Do you think we will? Survive, I mean?"

"I hope so."

"Then send the messengers. Send them and pray that our hope is not in vain."

Aelwyn sat up with a start. Mindarin placed a steadying hand on her shoulder and looked at her sister in the dark. "Bad dream?" Mindarin asked.

"Something like that."

The dream had begun well enough. She was standing on the deck of the *Summer Sun* again, but this time, the day was bright and sunny, so bright that to look across the sparkling sea she had to use both hands to shield her eyes. She turned from the rail, hoping to see Aljeron, but she could not find him. In fact she could not find anyone, and that alarmed her.

There was no one in the rigging, no one before or aft. The sails were up and the ship was moving, but there was no pilot that she could see. She stopped over the stairs that led down into the dark hold, and for some reason, she hesitated. She had been down there many times, of course, and so she knew she had no reason to be afraid, but the shadows spooked her. Instead of going down, she called, "Hello? Anyone?"

There was no answer, except for the echo of her own voice. She decided it was silly to let her misgivings keep her from going down, so she set her foot on the top stair and descended.

The rooms below were as empty as the deck above. She moved from one to the next, her panic increasing. The large room with the table around which they held their council the night before setting sail for Cimaris Rul was the last room she checked, and there was no one at the table, under it, or anywhere else. Suddenly, the ship lurched, and she was thrown back against a wooden support beam rising out of the floor. She struck her head hard and lay dazed for a moment. By sheer strength of will, she picked herself up and staggered to the door. She ran as best as she was able back down the long hall that led to the stairs and quickly ascended. She burst out from below, back onto the deck, and stood open-mouthed.

The sky was cloudy and grey, and the sun was no longer visible in any way. Even so, the dramatic change in the weather was not what arrested her attention. The gigantic black form of the creature she had seen looming above the walls of Cimaris Rul rose above the deck. The massive body, rising easily five spans above the ship, ended in a giant head, sleek and slimy. Two great webbed hands rested on the sides of the ship, several spans back from the prow. She was alone on the deck, and the creature's deep, black eyes were trained upon her.

For a long moment, neither she nor the creature moved. A chill wind blew across the deck, and the day was unnaturally silent. Then, after a moment, a creaking drew her eyes to the creature's hands. The boards under what looked like the thumbs began to shatter, and shards of wood popped into the air. Soon, the creature ripped two sizeable holes right out of the ship itself. Then, in one swift motion, one of the great black hands was raised high into the air, balled into a fist, and lowered with remarkable speed and power squarely in the center of the deck. She screamed, and that was the end of her dream.

Now she drew her knees up under her chin and tried to warm up. Despite the fact the rain was lighter, it was still late Full Winter, and at night, the bitter cold returned.

"It sounds like a terrible dream," Mindarin said, consoling her after she described it.

"Yes, that creature," Aelwyn said, struggling for words. "He's so awful."

"Don't worry about him," Mindarin said. "He's in the ocean, and we're headed deeper and deeper inland. We've seen the last of him."

Aelwyn nodded. "Is there any news?"

"Yes," Mindarin answered. "Word came back from the front lines about the start of Fourth Watch that dark forms have begun to assemble in battle formation opposite our lines."

"About the start of Fourth Watch?" Aelwyn asked, surprised.

"Yes, you've been asleep for hours."

"Hours," Aelwyn echoed, finding it hard to believe. "Then it is almost morning."

"Yes, the dawn should come soon."

"The twenty-fifth of Full Winter," Aelwyn said absentmindedly, looking out at the great dark Barunaan in the distance. Caan had set up their defenses with the river on their right to limit their exposure, and the Great Bear were heaviest on the left in case Malek tried to flank them. Aelwyn and Mindarin had arranged the women behind the side by the river, where the men from Shalin Bel were thickest. There they prepared to bring water and what medical aid they could once the battle began. Caan tried to urge them to continue north with the citizens of Cimaris Rul, but Mindarin refused. She argued convincingly that this was precisely what they told Aljeron they would do when he granted them permission to come along, and this was what they intended to do. In fact, seeing their resolve, Nyan recruited some of the women of Cimaris Rul to stay behind and aid the men of their city in much the same way, despite her own husband's pleadings.

"I wonder if this is the day we die."

"It is likely enough, Sister," Mindarin answered matter-of-factly. "And if it is, so be it. I will die doing something useful, and that isn't all bad. So much wasted time in my life . . ."

Her voice trailed off, and Aelwyn thought about answering but knew that even if she protested it wouldn't do any good. It was not a time for false cheer. "We've all wasted our fair share of time, Mindarin. You're not alone there."

The sound of approaching riders startled them both, mainly because the horses came from the north, behind them. Mindarin withdrew the long knife she carried and stood to see who it might be, and Aelwyn stood beside her, bewildered.

"Who is it?" Mindarin called out as the form of the horses became clearer.

"Benjiah," came the first reply, followed by another. "And us."

Aelwyn exhaled, relieved, and smiled as the blond boy rode out of the gloom and came to a stop before her. He was such a handsome young man and, everyone said, the spitting image of his father. His face bore concern, and she could see in his eyes that he was anxious. Perhaps they were flying from some trouble of their own, or perhaps they somehow had intelligence of the pending battle.

"Where are Caan and the others?" he asked, looking down at her.

"They are up at the battle line," she answered, gesturing in that direction.

"That way?" He motioned, pointing with Valzaan's staff, which she noticed was gripped tightly in his hand. She was struck by the way he wielded it and was taken aback for a moment. Mindarin answered the question.

"Yes, they are all up that way."

"You said battle line," one of the twins said, but in the darkness, Aelwyn didn't know which had spoken. "Caan is aware of the approach of Malek's army?"

"He is," Aelwyn answered. "He decided yesterday that because we couldn't outrun him, we needed to prepare for battle. The people of Cimaris Rul who have been marching with us were sent on ahead."

"Yes," Benjiah continued. "We passed some of them earlier in the night."

"How far did they get?"

"They are a good way from here, but if we are overrun, they aren't far enough to get anywhere safe, if there is such a place anymore."

"Is that how you knew we were here," Aelwyn asked, "and not in Cimaris Rul?"

"Not really. The dragons told us."

"Dragons!" they both exclaimed. Aelwyn felt hope surge within. "You mean to say they came? What happened at the tower?"

Benjiah looked down at them from his horse. "I will gladly tell you, but now is not the time. I must find Caan quickly. I may not be able to tell him anything he doesn't know already, but I should find him nonetheless."

"Benjiah." Mindarin stopped him before he spurred his horse on. "Are dragons coming?"

"I hope so," Benjiah answered, but Aelwyn could hear the uncertainty in his voice, and she felt some of her excitement slip away. They had perhaps talked to dragons at some point, but they were not with dragons now and had no guarantee that dragons were coming to help them. Their trek across Suthanin had perhaps been in vain.

Benjiah and the twins said farewell and moved on through the dark, and both Aelwyn and Mindarin turned to watch them ride away. After a moment, Aelwyn said, "I'm glad they're back, but it is disappointing."

"About the dragons?"

"Yes."

"Don't give up, he didn't have time to tell us everything. They may be coming."

"I hope so."

"And anyway," Mindarin added, "Benjiah is a prophet, like Valzaan. His coming alone might help."

"We'll need whatever we can get," Aelwyn said. Again she looked into the darkness and pictured the boy who didn't seem any longer like a boy. *May Allfather speak and act through you today indeed, and may Allfather protect both you and us.*

Benjiah stood beside his uncles, not far from Caan at the fore of deployed troops of Shalin Bel. At Zul Arnoth he'd been relegated to the back where he would most likely be safe, and on the beach by the Bay of Thalasee he'd been sent on ahead so as to be out of harm's way. Here though, at last, Caan and the other captains were forced to grant him permission to stay up front. There was no Valzaan. There was only Benjiah. He held Suruna in his hand, and would use it when the enemy came, but Valzaan's staff lay beside his feet where he could pick it up with ease. If Allfather led as He had in the tower, he would sling Suruna over his back beside his quiver and pick up the staff. Even so, he did not wish to presume that Allfather would necessarily visit him with power in the coming battle. Should He not, Benjiah was ready with Suruna to fight the way he knew best.

Benjiah looked out over the nearby Barunaan, its waters as wide as a fair-sized lake. Caan had stationed the soldiers from Shalin Bel beside the river, forming the extreme right of their line. On the far left were most of the Great Bear, though others appeared all along the line. In the middle, Talis Fein had stationed the men of Cimaris Rul, as they were the freshest. Even so, the couple thousand men from Fel Edorath lined up behind these in reserve, under the command of Corlas Valon, just in case the middle buckled.

The water of the Barunaan looked peaceful. Small delicate circles from the lightly falling raindrops expanded across its surface. The light of morning was bright enough now that he could see clearly the patterns interlacing far down the river. It was a beautiful image and really, all things considered, a beautiful morning.

"Look lively now," Pedraal said, nudging Benjiah. "Here they come."

Benjiah turned to look across the open field, and sure enough, a mass of Black Wolves and men on horseback were charging their way. Benjiah thought he could see a great horde of Malekim behind them. "The Malekim are coming along behind this time."

"Yes," Pedraal replied without looking. "They are effectively shielded against our cyranic arrows by their own advance forces. They know our archers won't waste their cyranis against men and wolves, and by the time we have clear shots, they will be almost here."

Benjiah reached back and grabbed a non-cyranic arrow himself. He nocked it and took aim. He scanned the approaching hosts and picked out a wolf a little ahead of the others. He let his arrow fly. It struck the wolf in the chest, and it stumbled and fell. At that moment, a great swarm of arrows flew, and many dozen men and wolves went down. Still, the charging line came on, and the gaps that had been opened quickly closed.

Benjiah fired again, as did the other archers. Still more men and wolves fell, and still the line came on. "Stand back, Benjiah," Pedraal said, his voice escalating, and suddenly his uncles and the soldiers advanced, their weapons readied. He watched as Pedraal and Pedraan cut down several men and wolves each, with battle-axe and war hammer flying. Pedraan wielded the war hammer with such fury that he even crushed the head of a horse in the fore of the charge. The creature's skull caved in completely and its forelegs crumpled as it pitched its rider into the waiting soldiers, where he was quickly dispatched. Then all became confused to Benjiah. The galloping line clashed with the men of Shalin Bel and the others down the line. Benjiah could feel the surge and saw the strain as everyone fought desperately not to give ground, but as rank upon rank came up behind them, give ground they did.

And then the forms of the Voiceless appeared, visible among the men on horseback and towering over the wolves, and Benjiah grabbed a cyranic arrow and shot one of them in the neck. He saw it fall, but so many flooded in from behind that he didn't bother to nock another. He slung Suruna on his back and took up Valzaan's staff, which lay half a span or so in front of him, almost under his uncle Pedraan's feet. The smooth, cool wood was reassuring in his hands, but though he hoped for some sudden surge of power, there was none.

The Great Bear rose onto their hind legs all along the line, and they towered over all the others. They moved forward with staffs raised high and began slowly but surely to push back the approaching foe. If he thought Pedraal and Pedraan had wielded their hammer and axe with devastating effect, he hadn't seen anything yet. The Great Bear swept two and three men from their horses at a time and sent shattered wolves flying through the air. They pushed on through the crowd to reach the lines of Malekim, and then they unleashed their full fury. Some Great Bear went down as Silent Ones with cruel, curved blades swarmed them, but far more Malekim fell as the Great Bear showed why they were known as the bane of the Voiceless.

The battle raged on, and though many fell on both sides, their line did not give up any more ground. After the short-lived defense of Zul Arnoth, Benjiah had not known if they could hold their ground here for long. Perhaps with the aid of the Great Bear, this outcome would be different.

Just then, as hope was rising inside him, he saw the approaching forms of perhaps fifty Vulsutyrim. They strode across the battlefield more than a span higher than the mass of Malekim, which parted before them like stalks of grain. At the front was Cheimontyr, carrying his dread hammer high and rallying the others with it.

Right before Benjiah's eyes, the tenor of the battle changed. The giants began to devastate the Great Bear even as the Great Bear had devastated the Malekim. He watched in horror as the Vulsutyrim slew men and Great Bear alike, their powerful bodies and arms almost impossible to withstand.

One of the giants was working his way toward Benjiah, who found himself with a closer view than he either wanted or expected. The grim face of the Vulsutyrim showed neither pleasure nor hate, only concentration. He was now at the front of the line of men and Black Wolves, facing the soldiers from Shalin Bel. Pedraal and Pedraan had split up and were trying to slip around behind him, but they were having to contend with Malekim as well as the giant's great strokes with his sword. Benjiah saw Pedraal decapitate a Black Wolf that leaped at him and, in a single, fluid motion, whirl with all his might and drive the same blade of his battle-axe deep into the Vulsutyrim's leg, right behind his knee.

The giant howled with pain. Blood, perhaps from a severed artery, sprayed Pedraal, and the giant's leg buckled as he dropped to one knee. Nearby, a pair of Great Bear and Pedraan seized the opportunity to move in for the kill as Pedraal tried to wrench his axe free. The giant's arm was raised, but a Great Bear's staff slammed against the Vulsutyrim's elbow, and the blade dropped heavily to the ground. From the other side, Pedraan broke the giant's arm at the shoulder with a crushing swing of his war hammer. Soon the giant was down, an unmoving mass in the battlefield.

Even as Benjiah watched this Vulsutyrim fall, he felt the line of men and Great Bear breaking. The fury of the Vulsutyrim was too much. They could not hold. Benjiah looked down the line at Cheimontyr, who was leading the charge deep into the center of their line. *Allfather, here I am! I am ready. Deliver your people through me. As you struck down the Grendolai by my hand, use me to strike down this Cheimontyr. Let me end his storm forever.*

There was nothing. Benjiah felt no surge of power. No sensation of light or heat rippled through his body, no change affected the staff gripped tightly in his hands. Disappointment washed over him instead, and he began to fall back with the soldiers all around him.

Look up and see.

Benjiah stopped as men continued their retreat. The whole battlefield was seething with energy, with fear and panic, but a sudden and overwhelming peace fell upon him as he heard the voice that had spoken to him before out of the storm. He looked up into the sky, and there, high above the battlefield, rushing in from the east, were the golden forms of several dragons.

As they grew nearer, he was able to distinguish five dragons. Their powerful wings sent gusts of wind across the battlefield, drawing the attention of others, even though most had not yet thought to look up.

"Dragons!" he screamed, hoping to rally the morale and hope of the men who were falling back in dismay. "The dragons have come!"

As if on cue, the dragons swooped down from their heights, and fire exploded across the field in the face of their enemy. The backward motion of their own line stopped and suddenly reversed itself. He looked at the startled faces of the Nolthanim on horseback, who looked shocked as whole ranks of Malekim were set ablaze by the swooping dragons. Close by, a dragon focused in on a Vulsutyrim, and the bewildered giant, after feebly trying to strike the soaring dragon, was set afire. The smell of burning flesh drifted across the battlefield on the wind generated by the dragons' wings. Benjiah watched the giant who, howling with pain, trampled a handful of Malekim as he ran screaming into the waters of the Barunaan.

The dragons ascended back into the sky to regroup, and for a moment, the storm of fire and chaos brought by their surprise descent broke. Almost instantly, the Vulsutyrim began to regroup, falling back from the front lines and turning their attention to the skies. They clustered in defensive formations, and several produced long, slender spears that shone as though made of some kind of metal. The others, though, were far less organized. Malekim and Black Wolves alike panicked at the sudden arrival of this ancient adversary. Disorder reigned among their ranks. Only a few horseman in the distance, opposite the far left of their own line, seemed to be rallying the men to prepare for the next attack of the dragons.

The next thing Benjiah knew, the line all around him was surging forward, pressing back the hosts of the enemy. The dragons came again, and though the Vulsutyrim did a better job of defending themselves, the very presence of the dragons had utterly dismayed the forces of Malek.

We can win this battle, and perhaps, we can end this war. Right here. Today. Benjiah felt excitement exploding within him. A few hours ago he had wondered if any of them would survive the day, and now, it looked like they would do far more than survive.

Just then, a swirl of dark clouds seemed to drop from the sky, and a roll of thunder as deep as any Benjiah had ever heard rumbled across the field. Benjiah's eyes were drawn to a lone Vulsutyrim standing in the middle of the battlefield. Cheimontyr. His right arm held the hammer aloft, and Benjiah could see lightning running along the hammer and down his arm and also upward into the swirl of dark cloud. The giant's face was contorted with rage, and a chill seized Benjiah's heart.

The dragons seemed to falter, losing speed and dropping slightly as though fighting a strong headwind. Then, as Benjiah watched in disbelief, a sudden surge of power and light burst from Cheimontyr's hammer and struck the dragon closest to him. It struck with such force that the great golden wings fell limp almost instantly and the huge form of the dragon plummeted to the earth and lay smoldering in the field.

Cries of rage and anger erupted from the other four dragons, as they quickly descended around their fallen brother. Flame once more erupted from their mouths in wild, erratic bursts as they cleared a sizeable space around the motionless body. Having secured the site of his fall, two of the four rose once more into the air and renewed their attack on their enemy.

Now, however, the advantage of the dragons had been somewhat neutralized. Not only were they necessarily wary of Cheimontyr, still wielding his great hammer, but with only two of them airborne, they were increasingly harassed by the Vulsutyrim, who sensed an improvement in their chance to take control of the day. The battle on the ground between the Voiceless, wolves, and Nolthanim on the one hand, and the Great Bear and men on the other, had not been fully rejoined. Despite the fall of the dragon, the enemy seemed reluctant to engage and instead fell back. What remained was a showdown between the dragons and Vulsutyrim.

Perhaps sensing this, or perhaps simply acknowledging their brother was dead, the two dragons watching over the body of their brother returned to the air. Once more the tide of battle changed, and even with the threat of Cheimontyr, the remaining Vulsutyrim were harried by the four. It was an amazing spectacle, and all Benjiah could do was watch.

"The river!" A shout from one of the soldiers rose on the far right of the line.

Benjiah turned to look, and it did not take long to figure out what the shout had been about. A great black form was speeding upriver in the center of the swollen Barunaan. As it approached, a great head and arms and body seemed to erupt from the water. It was enormous, standing at least seven or eight spans above the surface of the river, with great long arms and massive webbed hands. Cries of terror rippled throughout their own line as the creature reared back his head and sent a shrill, high-pitched shriek across the battlefield.

"Kumatin! Kumatin! Kumatin!" shouted the Vulsutyrim, who sensed in the arrival of the creature yet another shift in the battle.

Two dragons swooped down to unleash two streams of flame in the direction of the creature. Despite his massive size, the creature proved nimble as he dove under the water to avoid the flame and then shot out again. His great hand clasped the neck of one of the dragons, and with a single jerking motion he pulled the dragon with him down under the floodwaters. Benjiah, not far from the river, could see some flashing and roiling below the surface, and at one point thought he saw a golden talon poke out of the river. It quickly disappeared as both the creature and the dragon remained underwater for several minutes.

Stunned silence blanketed the field. The three remaining dragons were still airborne, now shying away from the river as well as from Cheimontyr. It was almost as though the giants and dragons were simply watching each other, waiting for the next surprise.

A horn sounded down the line, and Pedraal and Pedraan turned and started calling out orders for retreat. Similar calls echoed down the line, and quickly, with as much order as was possible, men and Great Bear began to withdraw.

Benjiah followed his uncles through the mass of soldiers to the place where Caan was already addressing some of his officers. "We must fall back. North and inland, away from the river. We must put distance between us and that thing, as well as distance between us and them. I think the dragons will understand and help guard our retreat."

There was little else said, for there seemed no other choice. The weariness of the day settled heavily on Benjiah. By now it was early afternoon. He had gone from complete despair to the pinnacle of elation to a deep confusion. Was this a defeat or a victory? Was that creature in the river the thing that had sunk their ships? Had it come inland all this way up the Barunaan? Where would they go now, and what would they do?

He looked back over his shoulder at the battlefield, where the dragons and giants were still at their odd dance of defensive maneuvers. He saw the great black creature rise out of the river and stand again, towering over the proceedings. His heart sank. Here was yet another foe seemingly beyond their strength. *How can we win this war?*

6
HIS REWARD

RULALIN DROPPED WEARILY from his horse. The dragons seemed finally to be gone, and around the battlefield he sensed a general letdown in the defensive positions of not only the Vulsutyrim but of all Malek's hosts. No one moved to pursue the enemy immediately, and for that he was grateful. After the fight today, he would relish a slow evening and hopefully, a good night's sleep.

Farimaal seemed to be the lone man still on horseback, dressed in his Grendolai-hide armor that made him appear less a man and more a creature of legend. Even though his human eyes were visible beneath the burnt-black helmet, he was most unsettling. Rulalin still wasn't comfortable seeing him ride to battle in this way, and though he had been for a time almost right alongside him, trying to rally the men when the panic from the dragons set in, he was ill at ease even now.

Farimaal, though, showed no awareness of any of the activity immediately around him. Rather he sat, gazing northward in the direction of the enemy's retreat. Rulalin wondered what was going through his mind. Was Farimaal taken aback by the sudden and surprising appearance of the dragons? Was he brooding over the fact that once more the enemy had slipped from his hands? Was he simply contemplating their next steps? Information about what exactly the armies were doing and why was never readily forthcoming, so Rulalin doubted he ever would know what Farimaal was thinking.

He heard a crack and looked down to see the broken shaft of an arrow underfoot. He should pay more attention to where he was going and what he was doing. He didn't think much cyranis had been used in the fight, but he didn't want to find out otherwise by stepping on an arrow that pierced his boot, as improbable as that might be.

As he looked at some of the fallen on both sides, he noted the colors of Shalin Bel, Fel Edorath, and Cimaris Rul among the slain. Soldiers from three great cities standing shoulder to shoulder. He felt a momentary twinge of envy. He'd like to have known such camaraderie and single-minded purpose, though serving under Aljeron would have taken much of the pleasure out of it.

He thought of Aljeron, his primary foe and opponent these last seven years, though only rarely glimpsed, and usually from afar, across a battlefield. He hadn't seen Aljeron since that strange day by the Bay of Thalasee when Cheimontyr hurled Valzaan into the sea, though. He had hoped to see Aljeron today, especially when he pressed his own men into the center of the enemy line. Likely, Aljeron was on the right, where most of the men of Shalin Bel were arrayed, instead of in the center with the soldiers from Cimaris Rul. Rulalin didn't know how to describe it, but it had been strange to press the attack only to see someone he didn't know commanding the enemy. The personal antipathy between him and Aljeron did not apply to this unknown captain of Cimaris Rul, and he felt cold at the prospect of destroying rank upon rank of soldiers who were not his personal enemies.

He picked his way across a few more fallen men and Black Wolves. Of course, they hadn't destroyed rank upon rank of the enemy after all. The surge of the Great Bear halted that, and even the aid of the Vulsutyrim was thwarted by the appearance of the dragons. He was still processing all that he had seen that day, and he knew that whenever he found Soran in all this mess, they'd have much to talk about.

He hoped Soran was all right. They had been separated in the confusion. Men under his command from Fel Edorath were scattered by the very first strike of the dragons, as bursts of flame struck all around them. He did his best to hold them together, but by the time any kind of order was restored, he'd lost track of Soran. That, too, was an odd experience, as he could not remember the last time he rode into open combat without Soran sticking closer to his side than his own shadow. He didn't know if Soran was alive or dead, but so far, none of the faces of the dead soldiers belonged to him.

Rulalin led his horse slowly, carefully through the battlefield, but he stopped. A man in Fel Edorath garb lay groaning at his feet, facedown in the mud. Rulalin stooped and rolled him over. Under the blood and mire, he recognized the face of one of the men who had accompanied them, but it wasn't Soran, and he didn't know the man's name. Gently, he wiped mud from the man's face and, cupping his hand, brought some water to his lips.

"Tell me," Rulalin said softly, "where are you hurt?"

The man moved his right hand from the ground to his side. Leaning over, Rulalin saw the gaping hole through the man's right side. It was a fatal wound. There was no doubt. "It's a good one. How'd you come by that?" Rulalin asked, trying to sound as though it wasn't serious.

"My brother," the man said, short of breath. "He fell. I turned to look. As I did, I was hit. The dragons came. Everything fell apart."

"It did indeed," Rulalin answered. "Is your brother nearby?"

"Don't know. Don't think so. Had to move to avoid being trampled. Think he's that way." The man tried to point, but his trembling hand dropped into the grass.

"Do you want me to help you find him?" Rulalin asked.

"Don't think I can get up." Then the man looked up at Rulalin, almost as though seeing him for the first time. "Captain Tarasir?"

"Yes."

"We fought Great Bear today. Dragons. Not just Aljeron."

"We did," Rulalin answered, uneasy.

"I never thought I'd fight against dragons."

"Neither did I."

"Will Allfather forgive us?"

Rulalin looked silently down at the man, his face white as snow and his hair matted on his forehead. He recognized the hunger for absolution in his eyes. Still, he couldn't just say yes. "You were following your general and watching the back of your brother and kinsmen."

"Is that enough?"

Rulalin did not answer. He took the man's hand. It was cold and slick from the water and mud. The man watched him for a moment longer, then looked away.

He did not live long. Shortly thereafter, he closed his eyes, and the labored breathing slowed, then stopped. Rulalin did not let go and did not move. He remained, stooped, his legs cramped and uncomfortable, looking at the man. Eventually, he lowered the man's hand to his chest, rose, and stood looking down. This man's guilt was his guilt.

"Forgiveness isn't mine to grant," Rulalin said quietly, "but I'm sorry."

He turned and walked away.

Soran was using a fallen Malekim as a stool when Rulalin found him. He'd been slashed across his upper arm and managed to bandage the wound himself. Even so, the knot was awkward, and Rulalin removed the wrapping to retie it properly. Rulalin again marveled at Soran's tolerance for pain. The wound was raw and oozing and had already begun sticking to the bandage, but Soran didn't wince or groan as Rulalin removed and reapplied it. Rulalin thought that perhaps it was a trait of youth, but he doubted it. He didn't remember being so unaffected by his own aches and pains when he was Soran's age.

When Soran was ready to walk, they rose to go. Rulalin helped Soran to his feet. "Where's your horse?"

"He's dinner for the birds, if all the meat hasn't been burned off the bones," Soran answered.

"You mean a dragon burned up your horse?"

"I do."

"How'd you escape then?"

"Luck. Pure, blind luck."

"Well?" Rulalin said, holding the halter of his own horse but waiting for Soran to speak before they moved into the dusk.

"Well," Soran said, "you remember the chaos that accompanied the arrival of the dragons?"

"Could I forget it?" Rulalin laughed.

"They came out of the sky like golden stars falling to earth, and all was terror and confusion. All around us, men and wolves and Malekim scrambled in every direction to avoid the bursts of flame. I saw you were trying to hold a sense of order, and so wheeled my horse around to bark commands to the retreating men, but it bolted."

"You lost control of your horse? You're a better rider than I am."

"I guess my horse feared the dragons more than it feared me, because it took off at a dead run, galloping toward the river, cutting across the retreating line of our own forces. So, there I was, the dragons above and behind and the enemy not twenty spans away on my right, and I was most in danger from our own men and allies. The horse kept right on running until a pair of retreating Malekim stopped right in front of us to check the sky for dragons. The horse stopped, and I flew over the Malekim and landed in the grass several spans away. I rolled out of the way of another galloping horse and looked up just in time to see flame envelop everything—my horse, the Silent Ones, and the horse and rider that had almost trampled me. I was getting up to my feet when I took my wound, a careless cut from one of our own soldiers running with his sword unsheathed."

"And here I thought you'd taken a wound nobly in battle."

"No, I'm afraid not."

Rulalin nodded and gripped him on the shoulder of the uninjured arm. "I'm glad you got lucky. I'd hate to be out here without you."

"Thanks," Soran said, blushing. "I'm glad I got lucky too. Those dragons were something, weren't they?"

"They were," Rulalin answered, searching the darkening horizon as though to make sure they weren't around. "They were magnificent. Remarkable creatures, the dragons. So powerful, so fast, so much to be feared. I mean, when they first appeared, even the Vulsutyrim seemed overwhelmed. Could you have imagined yesterday that anything could throw the Vulsutyrim into disarray?"

"No."

"Now, it's true that not all the Vulsutyrim were engaged."

"That's right," Soran agreed, "and they were caught by surprise. That could disorient anyone."

"True, the giants regrouped pretty quickly, all things considered."

"They did."

"At the same time," Rulalin began, looking at Soran with his eyes wide, "remember, there were only five dragons here today. Only five!"

Soran shook his head. "Just five."

"Can you imagine the power of a hundred? Even just fifty? Fifty dragons in the sky! Wheeling and diving from above the clouds. That would be something to see, wouldn't it?"

"It would, but it would likely be the last thing we ever saw, because they'd be fighting against us."

"They would, wouldn't they?" Rulalin answered, musing out loud. "Didn't think we were signing up to fight against dragons, did we?"

"No," Soran said.

"Have I ever told you about flying in the garrion?" Rulalin said abruptly.

"No."

"Well," Rulalin said, looking back to the sky. "It was amazing. It was smooth, like you'd imagine a bird gliding on the wind, but you could still sense the dragon's power as his great wings beat rhythmically. To look through the window at the sky, and the ocean so far below, was one of the most remarkable sensations I've ever felt. I'd love to feel that again."

"Not likely now."

"No," Rulalin admitted, "not unless the dragon has me in his talons and is carrying me up to dash me on the ground."

"That's a pleasant thought."

"There are worse ways to die."

"Worse than being dropped from the sky?"

"Sure. At least on the way up, you'd have the sensation of flying. And then, when he dropped you, there'd be the calm of falling."

"Calm? That's a strange way to put it."

"I'd rather go that way than get incinerated by the dragon's fire, or be impaled on an enemy sword, or have my head crushed by a Great Bear's staff."

"Well," Soran conceded after a moment, "I guess they're none of them very pleasant options."

"No, not very."

They walked on for a while, quietly. "Rulalin?"

"Yes?"

"Did you think they had us?"

"For a little bit, sure, I did."

Soran nodded. "It was the first time since we left the Mountain that I thought we might lose a battle."

"You weren't worried beside the Bay of Thalasee, when Valzaan cooked up that little sandstorm?"

"Dumbfounded, maybe, but that happened so fast I didn't really have time to think we might lose. Today, though, I thought the battle might end with us in retreat. I thought they might take the field and start moving us back. It wasn't something I'd ever expected to feel again."

"Me neither."

"Then Cheimontyr took one of the dragons down. That seemed to change the course of the battle."

"It did, but it still seemed to me we were in jeopardy. It was that great black thing from the river that saved us."

"Yes," Soran said, nodding again, "you're probably right. That was when I knew we'd hold the field."

"Did you hear what all the Vulsutyrim said when he appeared?" Rulalin asked.

"Kumatin, wasn't it?"

"Yes, Kumatin. What's that mean, I wonder?"

"I don't know. We'll have to ask Tashmiren."

"Tashmiren," Rulalin sneered. "He'll enjoy that.

"What?" Rulalin said, mimicking Tashmiren's condescending mockery. "All this time in the rain and on the road and you still haven't figured out the reason for the storm? You still don't understand the greatness of our master's plan?"

Soran laughed. "You do that a little too well, and now when he says something like that when you ask, I'm going to laugh and he's going to yell at me."

"You find your ignorance amusing, underling? At least your master has enough sense not to applaud his own stupidity," Rulalin continued.

"Stop it," Soran finally said when he stopped laughing again. "I'm serious. I won't even be able to look him in the face."

"True," Rulalin sighed, "that is hard enough."

"You will have to ask."

"I know."

"I wonder if Kumatin is his name."

"Could be, or some kind of greeting or command. I don't know."

"Where'd he come from?"

"One of Malek's creations, I'd guess."

"Yes but how? When? Where? Malek's been living under the Mountain. We were there together. There wasn't much water, remember?"

"I do, but he's been away from the Mountain before, right?"

Soran looked at Rulalin for a few minutes, then light dawned in his eyes. "Of course. Your visit to the Forbidden Isle. You said you were there because Malek had been there, right?"

"Yes, and as far as I know, he was frequently away from the Mountain. Valzaan suggested as much."

"That pretty much means it could have been anytime, anywhere."

"I guess so."

Soran looked at Rulalin closely. "What? What are you thinking?"

Rulalin shrugged. "Well, I don't know. It's nothing."

Soran let it go. "And the rain. You think this creature's the answer?"

"Yes. It seems clear enough now. The destruction at Cimaris Rul. The appearance of that thing when the battle was turning against us. The storm has opened the door and created a road from the sea into the very heart of Kirthanin. Without the rain, it could terrorize ships at sea and small coastal towns, but the flooding gave it access to Cimaris Rul and now to inland Suthanin. Who knows where else it can go?"

"Yes, that's right. Malek made it for a reason, but if the dragons were a surprise to it as much as they were to us, this wasn't the thing. So what was it made for, and why has the Barunaan been made into a road for it?"

"I don't know, but I'm guessing that before long we will."

"Whatever the reason, today that thing saved us."

"It sure did."

They walked on, approaching the camp. Soran stopped and surveyed the activity, the men of the Nolthanim milling around the tents. "Don't you ever wonder, Rulalin?"

"Wonder what?"

"Where is Malek in all this? You went to him in the Mountain, but no one ever sees him. No one ever talks about him as though he's around, as though he's here. He's never visible, looking over the battlefield. There is no tent or pavilion with giants standing watch at the doors. Where is he?"

Rulalin scanned the sight in front of him. He had wondered about that more than once. "I don't know, Soran. I don't think a big pavilion or tent would be his style, though. I imagine he'd move imperceptibly through his own host. Perhaps in disguise, almost invisible to watching eyes."

"But why? Wouldn't the sight of Malek sitting astride his horse rally the troops and boost their morale?"

Rulalin shrugged. "Cheimontyr and Farimaal do that well enough. If Malek was broken in his fall from the Mountain, he might not be so imposing to look at. The mystery he can create by being invisible is perhaps more effective. You know, like when you were a kid and your room was dark at night; the things you imagined were lurking in the corridors and under your covers were always more terrifying because you didn't really know what might be there. Maybe the idea of Malek is more frightening than the reality, or at least the appearance."

"Maybe," Soran answered, still scanning the camp. "But someone must see him, mustn't they? I mean, Farimaal and Cheimontyr at least. After all, they have to get their orders somehow."

"I guess, though I heard from Malek clearly enough without seeing his true form. I'm not sure it is necessary to see him to obey him."

"But how does he know what's going on? How does he command without firsthand knowledge of the situation? You'd never try to fight a battle, much less a war, without being involved."

"No, I wouldn't, but I'm not Malek. I doubt my limitations are his. Besides, if he can move about all of Kirthanin unnoticed and unknown, who's to say he can't move around our camp or the battlefield similarly? He may be right here in front of us somewhere, watching us."

Soran didn't answer, and Rulalin felt the hair on his arms stand up as he remembered sitting in Malek's chamber and swearing allegiance. The idea that he had perhaps been in

Malek's presence since without knowing it was more than a little disconcerting.

"Of course," Rulalin continued, "it could be that Malek isn't here at all."

"You mean he might still be in the Mountain?"

"It's possible."

"But what of all this talk of Malek coming forth?"

"That could be figurative, you know. If this army conquers Kirthanin, it's Malek who has conquered, isn't it?"

"Sure, I guess so."

"But Malek might be outside the Mountain without being here, couldn't he? If he can travel to the Forbidden Isle and back, he could be anywhere and up to anything. Perhaps he is personally controlling that thing in the river. Maybe he's overseeing the movement of the army but doesn't move with the army. I don't know. Nobody has offered me that information, and I'm not about to ask. I don't even want to think about what Tashmiren would say if I tried to ask him where Malek was and what he was doing."

"You're right, we can't ask. Unless they choose to tell us, we just aren't going to know."

"Which means we aren't going to know, right? You don't think Tashmiren would just choose to tell us something like that, do you?"

"No, not really."

They started into the camp, and Soran said, "I guess, in a weird kind of way, it would be comforting to know that he was here. All that power behind us when we go into battle, watching over us as it were."

"I guess."

Soran looked at Rulalin. "You said it yourself, Rulalin. What if a hundred dragons came? What if even fifty dragons show up next time? What would we do then?"

"I don't know."

"Could we win that battle?"

Rulalin shrugged. "With all the giants, with the beast from the sea? With all of us prepared for their coming? Maybe."

"Yes, with all of that, maybe."

"I don't know what you want me to say. Fifty dragons would change things a bit."

"I guess nothing is guaranteed in this war any more than it is in any other, except that people are going to die, and we don't want to be among those who do."

Rulalin and Soran were huddled in the darkness, for the cold that came after dark reminded them that even a little drizzle was still a far cry from dry. A man they didn't know came straight toward them out of the gloom, much to their surprise, for Tashmiren was about the only man in the entire camp not from Fel Edorath who ever spoke to them, and this stranger was definitely one of the Nolthanim.

"You are Rulalin Tarasir?" he asked, looking straight at Rulalin.

"I am."

"Farimaal has summoned you."

Rulalin stood. "I am at his disposal."

The man turned back into the darkness, and Rulalin scrambled to keep up with him. They made their way quickly across the camp to Farimaal's tent, and Rulalin waited while the man disappeared inside. He wasn't gone long before the flaps swished aside once more, and he returned. "He'll see you now."

Rulalin nodded and ducked inside the tent. It was dim, lit by a solitary torch on the far side. Farimaal, as usual, was slouched in his wooden chair, and though a rough bench sat not far away, Farimaal didn't tell him to sit, so he did not.

After a while, Farimaal looked up from his seat. "You did well today."

Taken aback, Rulalin wasn't sure if he'd heard correctly. "Pardon?"

"You kept your head and kept order among your men as well as one could expect, given the circumstances."

Rulalin felt himself blushing. "Thank you, sir, I tried to do what I could."

"One of the seven captains of the Nolthanim fell today," Farimaal said. "He served me many years."

"I'm sorry," Rulalin said. He didn't know how the Nolthanim army was organized or who the seven captains were, but he gathered the man had been important.

"He was slain by a Great Bear. I saw it with my own eyes. The Great Bear crushed his chest like you or I would crush the shell of a locust. It angered me. After I killed the Great Bear who killed him, I cut his head from his shoulders and stuck it on his own staff."

Rulalin shuddered. He could envision the head of a Great Bear shoved down onto the blunt end of the Great Bear's staff, its lifeless eyes open and staring.

"His division needs a captain. He lost many men because he was deployed at the front of the attack, but those who survived now need a captain. I'm appointing you to take over his command. His men will fight along with your own, under you."

"Under me?" Rulalin almost stuttered. If he was surprised before, he was bewildered now.

Farimaal gazed at him. "Your response doesn't beget confidence. Do you or don't you understand what I'm telling you?"

"I do," Rulalin said quickly. "I'm sorry, sir. I will do what you wish."

"Better," Farimaal said, then looked away.

The gravity of both the offer and the responsibility was dawning on Rulalin. As pleasant as it was to be commended by Farimaal, Rulalin didn't imagine he would broach failure well.

"There are benefits that go with being a captain, as well as responsibilities," Farimaal said after a few moments, looking back at Rulalin. "You'll be given his captain's tent, which you can share with your young friend if you wish. It is a visible sign of your rank, and you must remember whenever a man under your command is inside it with you, that he is under you much like he is under your roof. Do you understand?"

"I think so."

"Your men will follow you on the battlefield because of who you are off the battlefield. You are always a captain, always in command, even when there is nothing to command."

"I will remember that."

"And," Farimaal continued as though Rulalin had said nothing, "you answer now to no one but me."

"No one?" Rulalin asked, his excitement rising.

"No one. I answer to Malek. You answer to me."

"That includes Tashmiren?" Rulalin asked, realizing as he did it might be a mistake to be so obvious.

From where he was, he couldn't tell if Farimaal reacted adversely to his question. "It includes Tashmiren. He is not a captain of the Nolthanim under my command. He is a personal emissary and servant of Malek, and as such should be afforded respect, but as peer, not a superior."

Rulalin considered this newfound freedom. How he'd enjoy the next time he saw Tashmiren. As the good news sank in, he toyed for a moment with asking Farimaal about Malek and his whereabouts. He abandoned the idea, however, on further thought that seeking information about Malek when none had been offered would not be so well received as his boldness with reference to Tashmiren.

Instead, he decided that as a captain under Farimaal, he might well have permission, even a duty, to ask more basic questions about their immediate goals and purposes.

"Farimaal, if I may?"

"Ask."

"If I'm to serve as one of your captains, I feel there is much I need to know."

"You will be told what you need to know when you need to know it. We will pursue our enemies as before. The dragons have set us back temporarily, true, but we will regroup and move out when we're ready."

"And that thing in the river."

"The Kumatin."

"That's its name?"

"Yes."

"What is it?"

"Another of Malek's creations, spawned for this day. The day of Malek's coming."

"Cheimontyr's storm, it has all been for this Kumatin."

"That was the foremost of all its purposes."

Rulalin nodded, wondering if he should proceed. Farimaal had been candid and forthcoming, and he didn't know how long his newfound favor would last, so he decided he might as well. "The Kumatin, do you know of its origin?"

"Of course."

There was an edge in Farimaal's voice, and Rulalin took a note of it. *Always assume that Farimaal knows. Let him say when something is unknown to him.* "Was it created on the Forbidden Isle, by any chance?"

"I'm not sure 'on' would be the correct answer."

"Under?"

"That might be more accurate."

"About seventeen years ago?"

Farimaal smiled. Even from across the tent, Rulalin could see the glint of his teeth. "Yes, about seventeen years ago."

All the way back across the camp, Rulalin walked with an unusual spring in his step. It had been a long time since he felt this good about something. Not in recent memory had he felt like whistling. Not that he did; it would not have been warmly received in a military camp the night after what some might call a defeat. Still, he couldn't disguise the bounce in his gait. Not answerable to Tashmiren. Not beholden to Malek's lackey. That was indeed a beautiful thing.

He thought back to the first time Tashmiren had come to Fel Edorath from the Mountain. So smug. So condescending. He strutted into Rulalin's room like a visiting dignitary. Even as he extended Malek's offer of amnesty, refuge, and aid, he made it clear by his tone and his body language that he couldn't fathom why Malek would waste his time with Rulalin and Fel Edorath. When that visit ended, and Rulalin sent him off with his initial rebuff, Tashmiren left with a gleam positively sparkling in his eyes, all over the prospect that now Malek would raze Fel Edorath rather than spare it.

After leaving Farimaal's tent, Rulalin realized that this promotion was a good sign for his future hopes. He had asked Malek for a share in the Nolthanim's inheritance, life in Nolthanin without interference from Vulsutyrim, Malekim, or Black Wolves. Life in a world governed by men, presumably Farimaal and his captains, which now included him. Surely this promotion meant that if he served well, his request to take Wylla there when the conquest was complete would be granted.

He could see Soran sitting alone in the wet grass. He smiled at the thought of letting his young friend know the good news. Looking back, he saw the young Nolthanim soldier who had escorted Rulalin back to his horse. He would guide Rulalin to his new tent.

"Soran," Rulalin said as he approached.

"Yes?" Soran said, standing up suddenly as Rulalin come to a halt with the Nolthanim beside him.

"Get your stuff and follow me. We're not staying here tonight."

"We're moving out now?"

"No, we're not leaving the camp, we're just not staying here in the camp."

"Oh, all right," Soran said, collecting his belongings. Rulalin did the same, and soon they started out through the camp behind the soldier.

In the hour or so since Rulalin was summoned to Farimaal's tent, the activity in the camp had settled considerably. Men who milled around, taking care of their weapons and checking on their friends, now sat in small circles and in some cases were already asleep or trying. Despite his elation, Rulalin could feel the weariness of the day in his bones, and the memory of readying for battle that morning seemed very distant indeed.

The soldier in front of them stopped, and Rulalin looked up to see a sizeable tent, obviously prepared for their arrival, for one of the flaps was tied back, and an invitingly bright torch was mounted on a post inside.

"Is this it?" Rulalin said, realizing as he did it was an obvious and stupid question.

"Yes," the young soldier answered.

Rulalin looked with a grin at Soran, who looked puzzled.

"What?" Soran asked.

"Let's go in." Rulalin started ahead and ducked inside.

"Sure," Soran answered, following Rulalin.

"Isn't it great?" Rulalin said, looking around at the tent, which was bare except for a couple of mats unrolled on the relatively dry grass and a small wooden table that looked like it might fold down for easy moving. Two small barrels sat by the table, serving as chairs.

"Sure. Whose tent is it, and why are we here?"

Rulalin, seeing that the young soldier had not come in after them but was standing with his back to the open flap, stepped up close to Soran and whispered, "It's my tent, and we're here because we're through sleeping out in the open."

"Your tent?" Soran asked. "How's that?"

"I've been promoted. Apparently, the Nolthanim serve under seven captains, all answerable directly to Farimaal. One of them died in the battle today, and Farimaal's appointed me to assume that command."

Excitement and confusion appeared on Soran's face. "That's great, but what about the men from Fel Edorath?"

"They'll be under my command as well. The men of this unit will be joined with our boys, all under me."

Soran looked around, the joy of it really hitting now. "So this is yours."

"Ours," Rulalin corrected. "You'll share it with me. My promotion is your promotion. As my right-hand man, the more responsibility I have, the more you have as well."

Soran nodded, grinning. "This is really good. After a day like today, I could use a night's sleep in here."

"Yes, and not just tonight, every night."

"Hey," Soran said, getting really excited. "If you're a captain of the Nolthanim, it shouldn't be too hard for you to procure a horse for me, should it? I had this vision of walking the rest of the way, all over Kirthanin and back again."

"I would think that shouldn't be too hard. No doubt more horses lost riders today than riders lost horses."

"That's great," Soran answered.

"You know what's better?"

"What?"

"Farimaal says I answer directly to him. That means Tashmiren has no direct authority over me."

"Really?" Soran's eyes grew even wider with delight. "We don't have to take orders from him?"

"Well, technically I guess I don't, but I would assume that means you're pretty safe too. Farimaal said I should consider him a peer, but if you are my attaché, then he should respect your position as well as mine."

"Should, but you know him. He doesn't respect much of anything."

"True, but even if he's still mocking and rude, he has no real power over us. Before, the hardest part was having to listen to him. As far as we knew, he could just have us killed if he liked. It isn't that way anymore. He's not my boss now; Farimaal is."

"Well, well," Soran said, walking over to the table and sitting down. "You are full of good news tonight. Are there any other surprises?"

"Maybe not any surprises, but some news." He joined Soran at the table and in short order filled Soran in on all he had discussed with Farimaal, especially the Kumatin.

"So, Kumatin is its name."

"A strange name for a strange creature."

"And now we know the reason for all this rain."

"Looks like it."

"Well, if the rivers are swollen enough to allow this creature passage, then maybe the rain will stop soon. They can't want to flood everything, can they?"

"I wouldn't think so."

"This Kumatin might like that, but no one else in this army would."

"No, I wouldn't think so."

"Good news from you tonight indeed." Soran leaned across the table and whispered with a glance at the flaps of the tent. "Especially about Tashmiren. I'd love to see his face when he finds out you're a captain of the Nolthanim now."

"He may know already."

As though drawn by the mention of his name, the closed flap of the tent was thrown open, and Tashmiren strode boldly in.

Rulalin thought about looking at Soran to gauge the reaction on his face before greeting Tashmiren, but thought better of it. "You're welcome to my tent, Tashmiren, but in the future, it would be appropriate for you to seek permission before barging in."

Rulalin spoke softly, almost gently, but he saw that the words cut. Tashmiren flinched but held his tongue. When he did speak, his words were strained. "I see you've started to make yourself at home. Like a pair of dogs thrown a bone, eh?"

Rulalin ignored the remark. It was easier to do, knowing that he was safe from more serious reprisal. "What brings you here at this hour? I'm tired. I was in the fight, after all."

"I merely came to congratulate you on your good fortune. It's refreshing to see how nicely things have turned out for you. Not so long ago besieged and near defeat, now a captain in the mightiest army ever to walk Kirthanin. I guess being in the right place at the right time has its advantages."

"Well, I would say my ascendance has very little to do with fortune. I've earned my position in battle. How'd you come by your post, I wonder?"

"Careful," Tashmiren said, the veneer of smug politeness lowered for just an instant. "You may be under Farimaal's command now, but my master is his master. Don't forget it."

Not waiting for reply, Tashmiren wheeled and exited, and none too soon. Before the flap had fallen shut, Soran started snickering uncontrollably. As Rulalin turned to see what was going on, Soran struggled for control, eventually managing to say in a squeaky voice, "Don't forget it."

They were just beginning to laugh together when the Nolthanim guide stuck his head in. "Captain Tarasir?"

"Yes?"

"There's food and water here, sent by Farimaal. Should I send it in?"

"Yes, by all means," Rulalin answered, slapping Soran on the back.

"Farimaal also wants to know if you'd like to meet with the other officers of your unit tonight or tomorrow morning."

"Tomorrow morning would be fine. Let them sleep. I suspect they've earned it today."

"Yes, sir."

The man's head disappeared out of the doorway, and another man entered carrying a pitcher of water and a tray of bread and cooked meat.

After the man had left, Soran raised his cup. "Here's to putting Tashmiren in his place."

Rulalin raised his cup as well. "I'll drink to that."

A few hours later, Rulalin lay awake on his mat, listening to Soran snoring lightly. For a day that had begun with battle and near incineration by dragons, it had turned out pretty well.

The events of the day swirled in his head—his conversation with Farimaal as a captain of the Nolthanim, images of the Kumatin towering over the Barunaan and the battlefield, dragons swooping out of the sky with flames shooting out of their mouths. On top of all that, he'd been given a tent and engaged in a pointed conversation with Tashmiren, saying what he wanted to say, at least much of it.

Suddenly, a different image rose up before him—the dying soldier on the battlefield. *Will Allfather forgive us?* The question hit home with renewed power. The tent, the meal sent by Farimaal, the comfortable mat. He had seen them as his reward for valor, but as he lay there, he knew them for what they were. They were his reward for betrayal and treachery.

THE PLATEAU

RULALIN'S FIRST MEETING with the Nolthanim officers under his command was just ending when a soldier appeared, again summoning him to Farimaal's tent. Rulalin went immediately, doubts and worries whirling inside him. Had Farimaal thought better of the promotion? Had he been too aggressive in his dealings with Tashmiren? Was he not as protected as he thought?

Arriving at Farimaal's tent, he was shown in to find six other men standing in Farimaal's presence, and his suspicion as to their identity was soon confirmed as they were introduced to him. They were the other captains of the Nolthanim, and though he was an outsider, they treated him with respect. His fears of dismissal and censure abated.

Farimaal, dressed in the Grendolai-hide armor that was his trademark in battle, held the fearful helmet under his arm. Rulalin was a bit taken aback. The enemy had withdrawn from the field and was retreating northward; he couldn't imagine any further combat this day.

"The appearance of the dragons has made a short side trip necessary. You will prepare the officers under you to oversee the march north. We will be away from the camp a few days but will rejoin the main host before there is further action."

The captains looked at one another, and Rulalin could see that he wasn't the only one in the dark. Confusion was in their faces.

"We have yet another weapon at our disposal to use against the dragons that we have not yet utilized. You and I ride now to secure that weapon."

"Captain Farimaal," one of the Nolthanim captains spoke up. "We're in the middle of Suthanin. Where is this weapon?"

"In the dragon tower north of here, not far from the Barunaan."

Rulalin shuddered. He understood the armor now. Farimaal would ride to the dragon tower to reassert his authority over the Grendolai, the bane of the dragons since the Second Age, and Rulalin would go with him.

In the late afternoon of their fourth day on the plateau, Aljeron and the others found a deep depression. A ridge of rock had protected the southern side from snow drifts, so they decided to camp there for the night and to do their best to sleep on the steep slope. Aljeron spent a good amount of time clearing out loose rocks under the snow in the place where he wanted to settle in. Still, to have to clear snow only a couple hands deep was nice.

Synoki and Cinjan settled in a bit farther down, as Aljeron directed. He and Saegan helped Evrim down from the surface of the plateau, and after getting him settled in, took their own places, where they could keep their eyes on Cinjan and Synoki without difficulty. Koshti, beside Aljeron, would likewise help with the surveillance. Ever since Cinjan had drawn his weapon on Aljeron, Koshti kept his eyes glued to the man. In retrospect, Aljeron marveled at Koshti's restraint at the time, because he expected Koshti to take Cinjan's throat out. He figured that Koshti saw Erigan's staff planted firmly between Cinjan and Aljeron and realized the situation was under control.

Erigan offered to stay up on the surface of the plateau. He didn't mind the snow quite as much as the others, and he thought it prudent in case trouble came in the night. Aljeron agreed to the plan, because he knew that his own watchfulness as well as Saegan's would be occupied with Cinjan and Synoki.

Next to him, Evrim held Saegan's sword. Since eating their meager meal, his attention had been fixed on the blade. "I wonder if I'll ever really be able to use this thing with my left hand," Evrim said.

"With practice, you can learn anything," Saegan said, watching Evrim's awkward attempts to thrust the sword into the air effectively.

"I guess so," Evrim said, sighing as he lowered the sword and sat looking at it.

"It'll take a while to feel right," Aljeron said, wishing he knew how to help. Evrim had borne the physical pain bravely, but Aljeron sensed the finality of his loss was beginning to set in, and it was the pain in Evrim's mind that worried him.

"It'll take a while for what to feel right? The sword in my left hand, or the absence of my right?"

"Both."

Evrim didn't say anything, and Saegan, who had discussed with Aljeron at length their need to boost Evrim's spirits, stepped in. "The big obstacle for you will be balance. You'll need to learn to compensate for the absence of your right arm as you balance yourself."

"Balance is everything," Evrim said.

"Balance is everything," Saegan agreed.

"And if there is no way to compensate?" Evrim asked, turning to look at Saegan so that Aljeron couldn't see his face.

"There is a way," Saegan persisted. "With practice, you can learn anything."

Evrim sat for a moment, then reached out his hand, extending the sword to Saegan, who took it carefully. "Thanks," Evrim said.

"Anytime."

"I guess it doesn't matter right now anyway," Evrim laughed, though Aljeron knew it was forced. "Too bad we couldn't recover my sword from the back of the Snow Serpent's throat. I rather liked that blade."

"We tried to pry that mouth open," Aljeron said, "but even Erigan with his staff couldn't get it to budge. The jaws must have locked somehow."

"I know," Evrim said. "I'm not blaming anybody."

He reached down and pulled his hunting knife from its sheath. It was about a hand and a half long, with a curved tip and an extremely sharp edge. Aljeron had seen him skin and gut a large pig with that knife in less than an hour, though granted, that was a few years ago and with his right hand. "I guess I'll just have to hope that either no trouble finds us at all, or that it comes right up close so I can use this. Otherwise, I'm in trouble," Evrim joked. Nobody laughed.

"Let's hope for the former. We've had trouble enough," Aljeron said, looking at Cinjan and Synoki, closer to the bottom of the depression where the snow was deeper but the slope wasn't so steep. He wondered what they were talking about, but he didn't care so long as they continued to do what they were told.

"All right," Aljeron said, redirecting the conversation. "Let's have a look at your arm."

"It won't be any different than it was last night."

"Still," Aljeron persisted. "Let's have a look."

Evrim slid the cloak off his shoulder so Aljeron could examine the wound. It was continuing to heal well, without infection, and Aljeron was relieved. He remembered the infection that seemed to take over Caan's leg on the Forbidden Isle, and that had been his biggest fear after Evrim survived the initial loss. Aljeron slid the cloak back on and nodded to Evrim silently. "Well?" Evrim said. "How does it look?"

"I think it looks better," Aljeron said. "But every time I say it looks better, you scoff at me."

"Maybe I do," Evrim said, "but that doesn't mean I don't still want you to tell me it looks better."

"It looks better."

"Good, then maybe it will become bearable to look at after all, so Kyril won't be repulsed by the sight of me, if we get back."

"Kyril won't be repulsed," Aljeron said gently. "She'll just be glad to see you, especially when she finds out all you've faced since you parted."

"I hope so."

"You know so. Kyril's love is constant. Just focus on staying alive long enough to see her again."

"Do you think we will?" Evrim asked, gazing up at the sky.

"I don't know," Aljeron said. "I've given up trying to think beyond the next step."

Evrim didn't say anything else, and Saegan sat silently too. Movement below them drew Aljeron's attention, and Koshti's too. He rose to all four feet and stood alert, watching Synoki and Cinjan begin to make their way up the side of the depression.

A growl from Koshti's throat drew the attention of the two men moving up the slick slope, and they turned to see Daaltaran extended in their direction.

"What do the two of you think you're doing?" Aljeron asked.

"I'm growing tired of this treatment—" Synoki began.

Aljeron stood, his anger flaring. “I don’t especially care, Synoki. I asked you a question.”

For a moment, Synoki glared at Aljeron, but then his face softened. “We were going up to the surface to examine the sky before sunset.”

“Why?”

“Because it is impossible to see the horizon in any direction from the bottom of this depression. While it’s true that the storm seems to have lessened a good bit, and that the snow is light, there’s no guarantee it will keep on like this. I’d like to know if heavy weather is coming our direction. I’d hate to find out by waking up buried under a mountain of snow when we could have taken precautions.”

“The weather hasn’t changed in a week.”

“That doesn’t mean it won’t.”

“Erigan will tell us if he sees a change in the sky,” Aljeron retorted.

“Maybe he isn’t looking.”

“Enough. You don’t need to go up.”

“Maybe we don’t need to, but I want to.”

Aljeron stared at them both. They remained where they were on the slope, watching him. He tried to avoid confrontations like this as much as possible. “All right,” Aljeron began, and the two of them started onward. “One of you can go,” he added.

They stopped, and if they were annoyed by his decision, they kept it to themselves. Cinjan went back down the slope while Synoki continued up. Aljeron watched Synoki, who went up to the top of the depression but didn’t climb all the way out. He surveyed the sky for a few moments, then turned to come back down.

“Well?” Aljeron asked as Synoki passed their place on the slope.

“There doesn’t appear to be any change coming.”

"Surprise, that," Aljeron answered. Synoki, ignoring him, returned to his place near Cinjan.

"Aljeron," Evrim said, and Aljeron peeled his attention away from the men and looked at his friend.

"Yes?"

"What do you make of the change in the weather?"

"I don't know, but I like it. Maybe one of these days it will stop snowing altogether."

"Wouldn't that be great," Evrim said.

"It would indeed."

"I used to love snow," Saegan spoke up, "until this."

"I know what you mean."

Aljeron realized sunset couldn't be far away. Less than an hour, he thought, perhaps much less.

"There was a song my mother used to sing us," Saegan said, "all about winter and snow."

"Sing it," Evrim said. "I could use a song."

"I'm not much of a singer, and given the circumstances, it may not bring much cheer."

"I don't care, it's music, isn't it?"

"It is. Well, what do you think Aljeron?"

"I'd love to hear it," Aljeron said.

Saegan nodded. "All right, I might speak it more than sing it, but I'll try to do it justice."

When the north wind blows
Then come the snows
And starlit skies
Their windows close.
And all that's bright
Is clothed in night
As winter swallows
The morning light.
And all that's warm

Is lost in storm
As cold winds howl
And snowflakes swarm.

But though it's stark
And the world grows dark
There is beauty still
In winter's heart.
When the clouds away
The light of day
Reveals white fields
A dazzling display.
And when stars return
Then children learn
That still their fires
As brightly burn.
For winter is
As all things are
Here for today
And gone tomorrow.
A season of cold
From times of old
To balance summer
The season of gold.

Saegan, who spoke as much as sang, stopped there and looked up at the darkening sky. "Well, I think that was basically it. I don't know if I remembered all the words just right, but that's the gist of it."

"I liked it," Evrim said, "even if it is a little melancholy. The idea of being here today and gone tomorrow hits close to home. I'm here today but was almost gone a few days ago."

"Yes," Saegan said, "it puts things in perspective. We are all always just a short step from death, and we should bear in mind our frailty."

"True," Aljeron agreed, "but I found the song encouraging. In the long history of the world, winter has always given way eventually to spring, and spring eventually to summer. It's only four days to Winter Wane. The season of gold will return."

Early afternoon the following day, Aljeron called a halt to their steady progression across the plateau. The snow had indeed been lighter this past week and more, but the wind up here on top of the plateau was brutal, and today was no exception. Freezing temperatures replaced the damp as the primary assaulting sensation. Aljeron was not surprised, really, since the time from Midwinter until about the middle of Winter Wane was always the coldest time of the year, but now that the snow was not their principle concern, there was nothing to distract him from the true depth of the cold.

"Why have we stopped?" Saegan whispered.

Aljeron pointed east across the plateau. Saegan turned to look, and after a moment turned back. "Any ideas?"

"None," Aljeron replied, fixing his gaze on the distant dark spot in the middle of the white horizon.

"Should we ask?" Saegan queried.

"Not sure what good it'll do, but I guess so." Aljeron leaned forward in his horse and called to Cinjan and Synoki, who had stopped a short distance ahead. "There is something on the plateau to the east. Do you have any idea what it is?"

Cinjan and Synoki both turned and looked, and now Evrim also searched the eastern horizon. Koshti jogged lightly along the snow a few spans away from the horses and faced that direction eagerly as well.

Cinjan turned to them after a few moments. "I don't know what it might be, but I'm sure it is nothing of importance."

"How do you know?"

"Because it isn't moving and therefore isn't a threat. The plateau is barren, so the only thing that would be important to note is the approach of something hostile."

Aljeron turned from Cinjan again to the object in the distance. Despite the likelihood that Cinjan was right, Aljeron felt drawn to examine it.

"I think we'll go and check it out, all the same," he said at last, turning his horse to the east.

"Did you hear what I said?" Cinjan said, almost angrily, staring at Aljeron.

"I heard you," Aljeron answered coolly. "You may be right and it may be nothing, but I'd like to see for myself."

"I thought crossing the plateau and finding the Great Northern Sea as quickly as possible was our objective," Synoki said, gazing blankly at him.

"It is," Aljeron answered, shifting a little uncomfortably in his saddle. He had hammered away at the need to plow ahead and keep up the pace, and now he was suggesting a diversion that could consume the rest of the day without providing any useful information or taking them any closer to the Great Northern Sea.

"Then why don't we just keep moving?" Synoki replied. "Why waste the couple hours or so it will take to get over there and back?"

"There's no need to come back," Aljeron replied. "We have to move east eventually. We can head due east to whatever it is, and once we've examined it, resume our journey north. It won't be a total waste of time and effort."

Cinjan and Synoki grumbled but did not protest further. Soon, the whole company had turned east, heading toward the dark object in the distance.

They traveled for perhaps an hour, and as they drew closer, Aljeron felt his disappointment growing. It appeared to be nothing more than a great rock, confirming Cinjan's contention that it would not be anything of significance. He began to dread arriving at it, for he didn't want to listen to Cinjan and Synoki rebuke him.

And yet, as they did grow closer, his disappointment was mitigated somewhat by the realization that it wasn't just any large stone, but a Water Stone. The smooth sides and worn grooves that wound down the exposed surfaces were unmistakable. Snow had collected on top and in the grooves and ledges, but the sheer sides were grey and dark against the white snowscape.

"A Water Stone," Evrim said as they drew to a halt beside it.

"Yes," Cinjan said. "All this way for a Water Stone."

"The largest Water Stone I've ever seen," Saegan answered him. "It's enormous. Can you imagine the explosion of water that must have created this one? Can you imagine this Water Stone when the water flowed from within and ran swirling down its sides?"

"Yes, that's all well and good," Synoki replied, "but when it comes right down to it, we've come here for nothing."

"Perhaps," Saegan said, backing his horse up a span or so. "Aljeron, come back here, see what you make of this."

Aljeron backed up beside Saegan, as did the others. Aljeron looked again at the stone, but didn't see anything of note.

"What am I looking at?" he asked Saegan.

"There," Saegan replied, pointing to the snow-covered top. "In the middle, back a ways, can you see it?"

Aljeron looked and at first saw nothing. But then he understood what Saegan had been trying to show him. A black ridge of stone protruded above the half span of snow piled on the rock.

"I see it," Aljeron said.

"It's a different color than the Water Stone."

"It is indeed," Aljeron said, "I want to go up there."

Aljeron dropped from his horse and shuffled through snow to the Water Stone. The side was smooth and slick from the snow and ice, and he had little success scaling the side. It took some time, walking around the Water Stone, for Aljeron to realize he was not going to be able to get up.

"I think I can get up there," Saegan said after Aljeron had circled the stone, "if you give me a boost from your shoulder."

"All right," Aljeron said, helping Saegan until his feet rested squarely on Aljeron's broad shoulders. Reaching up, Aljeron grabbed Saegan's ankles and held him steady as Saegan started up. Using his fingertips and tiptoes, moving from thin groove to thin groove, Saegan soon ascended well above Aljeron's reach. A few times, it looked like he might come tumbling down, but he kept his hold and nimbly made the top, clearing off snow, which fell like a miniature avalanche.

Aljeron had moved back from the base of the Water Stone and stood beside the horses of the others. Saegan stooped, moving snow away from the black protrusion. Aljeron could see furrows growing on Saegan's forehead as he piled the displaced snow on either side.

"Anything?" Aljeron called up.

"There's writing carved on it," Saegan called down.

"Writing?" Aljeron called back, exchanging glances with Evrim. "What does it say?"

"Hold on," Saegan called back. "I'm just getting the last bit of snow cleared away."

They only had to wait a moment before Saegan called down to them, but Aljeron could feel the tension growing inside him. Someone had placed a message here, who knew how many years ago, to stand on top of this Water Stone. But what message, and for whom?

"You won't believe this," Saegan said.

Aljeron felt a chill. "Maybe not, but read it anyway."

"All right.

"Placed here by the clans of the Nolthanim,
To bear witness, both now and hereafter.
Summoned here by Andunin and confronted with
The choice that is not a choice, we are agreed.
We will march as one, to our glory or our doom.
If Malek is true, we will rule with him.
If he is false, then we will fall with him.
This stone is our witness,
That we do what we feel we must.
This stone is our witness,
That we can see no other way.
This stone is our witness,
Whether for us or against us,
No one knows."

"We know now, don't we?" Aljeron murmured.

The wind whistled across the plateau, whisking a light dusting of snow off the Water Stone and spraying Aljeron and the others in the face. Aljeron looked at Cinjan and Synoki, who appeared to be bored. He turned back to Saegan, who was looking down at them.

"What a terrible place to be," Evrim said at last. "You were right, Saegan, I'd hate to be faced with their alternatives."

"Indeed," Aljeron added. "An unenviable dilemma. You can hear their uncertainty in the inscription."

"No," Saegan said. "There is no uncertainty here. They know what they're doing is wrong. They knew. This witness stone is a plea for forgiveness. It is a witness to their shame."

Aljeron opened his eyes to see Saegan looking down at him, his hand gently shaking his shoulder.

"I'm sorry, Aljeron," Saegan whispered, "I can't stay awake any longer."

"That's all right," Aljeron said, sitting up and rubbing his eyes. "What time is it anyway?"

"Only Second Watch, about midway through."

"All right."

Saegan hesitated before lying down. "Wake me when you need to. I don't expect you to go all the way to dawn."

"I'll wake you if I need to," Aljeron assured him.

Saegan nodded, moved a few steps away, and wasted no time making himself comfortable. Aljeron leaned back until he rested against the north face of the Water Stone. They had decided to camp there for the night because the northern side angled just enough to afford what might generously be called shelter from the snow. Feeling the cold stone against his back was at first a shock. Aljeron realized that while it was nice to sit watch with something to lean against, he'd have to be careful. Being more comfortable meant it would be easier for him to fall asleep.

He glanced in the direction of Synoki and Cinjan, both apparently fast asleep. Not for the first time he wondered if all this vigil was really worth it. He'd never even seen them stir in the nights he and Saegan shared the watch, and the two of them were growing more and more weary.

Koshti stirred, raising his head and looking at Aljeron in the dark, his tiger eyes bright in the gloom. Somehow Koshti seemed always to know when it was Aljeron's turn to keep watch. At least he would have some company during the long night. Koshti moved closer, treading quietly in the dark, and lay down with his long back nestled up against the Water Stone. Aljeron stroked Koshti's warm, soft fur, at any time a pleasant texture, but never more so than in this wintry wasteland. As he glided his hands through Koshti's winter coat, the tiger leaned down and rubbed the top of his great head along Aljeron's right leg, between his hip and his knee. It was an atypical display of affection from his battle brother with others nearby, but Aljeron was glad of it all the same. The warmth of Koshti's fur was encouraging, and as he continued to stroke the tiger's soft side, he contemplated just how much he needed encouragement.

He gazed northward across the wide plateau. All this endless plain, covered with this endless snow—just the latest obstacle in what seemed to be an endless journey. He had begun to realize, perhaps for the first time in his life, that there might be an end to his willpower. There might be a limit to the number of days he could convince himself to go on, to keep getting up on his horse's back and keep moving forward. There might just come a day when daylight came and he didn't move, didn't speak, didn't do anything.

He needed to reach the other side of the plateau, and soon. He needed to stand on the edge and look down at the Great Northern Sea. He needed to see something other than endless snow-covered terrain spanning the horizon. He needed to see the waves rolling in and hear the sighs and murmurs of the reliable tide.

Even more than he needed to reach the Great Northern Sea, he needed to find the northern end of the Tajira Mountains. He needed to see them looming in the distance and know that Harak Andunin was there, waiting. Regardless of what awaited them, they just needed to get there.

As he thought of the Great Northern Sea and the Tajira Mountains, the same doubt that had plagued him since setting out for Avram Gol returned. What if Sulmandir wasn't there? What if they found the Mountain but nothing else? He pushed the thought away, as he always did, but it was increasingly hard to do. The farther they came and the more they paid for only possibly achieving their goal, the more he worried that it was all for naught. Surely, he thought as he looked up to the cloudy skies, Allfather would not bring them so far through so much only to find Sulmandir wasn't there. He wouldn't do that would He?

But even as Aljeron tried to comfort himself with that line of reasoning, his heart sank. He knew he couldn't define Allfather's purposes or plans. Surely loyal servants of Allfather throughout the history of Kirthanin had set out hoping and praying for something only to find their hopes denied. Why should he assume that just because he had traveled and labored and sacrificed that Allfather would be obligated to satisfy his hopes? Sulmandir might be in that mountain. Sulmandir might not be in that mountain. Valzaan had not promised that he was. If even Allfather's prophet knew it was not a certainty, Aljeron had to acknowledge it as well.

All Aljeron could do now was keep going. They had come much too far and paid much too high a price not to see it through. When the dawn came, and it would, they would saddle their horses and set out. They would continue through the endless snow across the endless plateau. And, when they reached the other side, they would see the Great Northern Sea. From there they would head east toward the Tajira Mountains, and once there, they would look for Harak Andunin. Once there, well, they would see what they would see.

Their third day out from the Water Stone, which was the last day of Full Winter, Aljeron noticed a change in the horizon. While the grey above the white was still grey, at moments the grey seemed to sparkle. Aljeron motioned to Evrim, Saegan, and Erigan to come up next to him.

"I keep seeing something shining in the distance, just above the horizon. Have any of you seen it?"

"Yes," Saegan answered, and Erigan likewise confirmed it.

"My first thought was that it might be the glint of weapons, but who would be riding out there with swords or spears drawn?"

"That was my first thought too," Saegan said, still peering ahead, "but then I noticed the same sparkle all along the horizon. I don't think it's people at all."

"It isn't," Erigan said. "It is the sea."

"Are you sure?" Aljeron asked, looking from the horizon to the Great Bear.

"I am sure."

Aljeron smiled. "Then let's not waste any more time talking about it, let's keep going."

Aljeron bid Cinjan and Synoki pick up the pace, and they rode harder than they had in a quite a while. Aljeron realized that it was perhaps unwise to be careless when the terrain remained potentially hazardous beneath the snow, but he couldn't bear the thought of slowing. His heart was bursting to reach the end of the plateau.

As the morning passed, the sparkling intensified until they could see all along the distant white horizon a different kind of grey above the snow and below the sky. It was a grey that surged and swelled and shone even in the half light of the cloudy winter day. It was water, lots of water, as far as the eye could see, and Aljeron thought it was every bit as beautiful as the wide blue Southern Ocean as he had seen it from the sandy beach of Sulare.

By midafternoon, they were sitting at the edge of the plateau. The side fell steeply away many spans to the plain below. Beyond that, the shores of the Great Northern Sea were visible. They sat, all of them, gazing out at the undulating expanse.

"We've made it," Evrim said, his voice trembling. He turned to Aljeron, a tear in his eye. "I have to admit, for a while there I didn't think we'd ever get here. At least, I didn't think I'd ever get here."

"But here we are, and you are here with us," Aljeron said, smiling.

"Yes," Evrim said, turning back to the sea. "Here we are."

"So what now?" Saegan said. "Do we try to find our way down today? Or do we start looking for a way down in the morning?"

"I want to start looking for a way down tonight," Aljeron replied.

"We don't have much daylight left," Cinjan said, but Aljeron cut him off.

"We may not find a way down tonight, be we're going to start looking tonight. As far as I'm concerned, we've spent enough time up on this plateau."

At first the search yielded nothing. There were a few places where the men, on foot, might have been able to climb down, but they could find no path suitable for horses. It was growing dark and Aljeron was growing frustrated, when suddenly Koshti darted a little way off along the edge and then disappeared over it. Aljeron rode behind him swiftly until he came to the place where Koshti waited on a wide ledge a span below. Though the initial drop looked difficult, Aljeron could see why Koshti had gone down—a narrow but passable path wound all the way down to the bottom.

"Careful with the first step, but there is a way down here," Aljeron said, turning back to the others. "Tonight the bottom of the plateau, tomorrow the sea."

8

THE FORGE AND THE BLADE

ALJERON DROPPED EAGERLY from his horse's back. Ice and frost lined the edge of the beach where the water from the Great Northern Sea rolled in, and they crunched under his feet as he stepped to the very edge. Stooping, he cupped his hand and dipped it in the remarkably cold water. With all the snow, they had not been at a loss for water, but finally being here made the water precious all the same.

Aljeron stood and gazed east along the shoreline. As far as he could see, the snow tapered off as the land descended gently to meet the sea. He was delighted to have been right about the lack of snow, for if it was really like this all the way east to the Tajira Mountains, they should be able to move at a better pace, no longer worried about their horses laboring through the snow, and no longer needing to dig snow burrows to sleep in at night.

He could feel that the balance had tipped in their favor. They had crossed the plateau. They had reached the Great Northern Sea. They had come so far, and now it was the first day of Winter Wane, which meant cold weather in their immediate future but also that Spring Rise was only thirty days away. He peered above the shoreline at the grey horizon and wondered how far beyond the limits of what his eyes could see the Tajira Mountains lay. In the end, it didn't really matter, because he knew they were there. He knew they were there, and even if he couldn't see them with his eyes, he could see them in his mind, and he would hold their image before him every moment of every day.

"Well," he said, turning to take in the rest of the company, "we've made it to the Great Northern Sea at last."

There was some celebration, but more than that was an eagerness to be on their way. He wondered if the others, like him, had only one thought in their minds now: to ride until the mountains were in view.

"We'll ride along the coast all the way to the Tajira Mountains," Aljeron said, reiterating what had been discussed more than a few times since leaving Avram Gol. It seemed right to verbalize their goal once more.

"Do you have any idea how far from here?" Evrim asked.

"Cinjan?" Aljeron asked, looking up at their guide.

Cinjan shrugged. "From the Simmok River, I believe the distance to the Tajira Mountains is probably ten days to two weeks, depending on our pace. I'm not sure though, I have only once been east of the Simmok River."

"And the Simmok," Saegan asked, "do you know how far that is?"

"Not far. I wouldn't be surprised if we got there in the next couple of days."

A couple days to the Simmok, and beyond that, perhaps less than two weeks, and they'd arrive. After almost two months on the way, he couldn't believe they were finally so close.

"If we ride single file, close to the water's edge, the snow will provide next to no hindrance for our horses," Aljeron said. "We should be able to set and maintain a good pace."

"Then what are we waiting for?" Evrim said. "The sooner we start, the sooner we get there."

"I'm all for it," Aljeron replied. "Cinjan, Synoki, lead the way."

Cinjan turned his horse eastward along the coast, and Synoki turned after him. They set off quickly and though Aljeron usually followed them, he motioned to Saegan to go next, and for Evrim to follow him. Today he wanted to ride in the rear.

Koshti looked up at him as the others started off, and Aljeron thought he could sense disappointment, though he wasn't sure why. Perhaps the tiger was eager to be off and running along the Great Northern Sea, or perhaps he was unhappy having Cinjan and Synoki virtually out of view. Either way, when Aljeron at last spurred his horse on, Koshti leapt up and ran gracefully along on the inland side, keeping Aljeron and his horse between him and rolling waves.

As Aljeron rode, reflecting on the many weeks since he bid farewell to Aelwyn, he wondered what was happening down south. Despite this group's early fears that Malek had sent perhaps a sizeable contingent of his forces after them, it now appeared that he had not. This meant, most likely, that the Werthanim and any help they had managed to procure in Suthanin were almost certainly the object of Malek's full attention. He couldn't help but worry for Aelwyn, and he found himself once more hoping and praying that they had not come all this way in vain. He needed to find Harak Andunin, and fast, because all Kirthanin desperately needed the help that might wait there.

On the morning of the third day of Winter Wane, they reached the Simmok delta, where the river emptied out into the Great

Northern Sea. As they approached it, Aljeron's heart sank. It was so broad that the beach on the other side was almost out of sight, and he could tell that the water ran deep.

"How are we going to cross this?" he said, half to himself and half to the others. "Is the delta normally this broad?" he added, turning to Cinjan, "or is this just the result of all the rain that fell before the snow?"

"I don't remember the delta being this wide."

"So what do we do?" Aljeron asked.

Cinjan shrugged. "I don't know."

"We swim it," Saegan said, determined. "We'll swim across, and our horses can swim too."

"Koshti won't like that plan," Aljeron said grimly, looking down at his battle brother.

"That water will be freezing," Evrim said.

"We can't let this deter us," Saegan replied. "We've come too far. It's just cold water."

"Too much time in too much cold water will kill you," Erigan said, uncharacteristically stepping into one of their debates. "I have a higher tolerance for cold than any of you, and even I can see that the distance is possibly too far for me. This water is as cold as water can be without being ice, and almost certainly some of you would not see the other side if we did this."

"Then what do you suggest?" Saegan asked.

"I suggest that we head upstream. The waters upstream should be narrower, even if the Simmok is flooded. What's more, it is even possible that farther in, the river may be frozen. It has been cold enough, long enough, that we may find ice thick enough to cross on foot. I would prefer that to swimming this wide and dangerous passage."

"And if there is no ice?" Aljeron asked. "Or if the ice we find is not thick enough to support our weight?"

"Then we will find the narrowest place we can and swim. Even if we lose a day scouting the river, if it cuts the distance we have to swim in half or limits the danger to ourselves, it will be worth it, will it not?"

The others discussed this for a few minutes, and as they did, Aljeron felt relief at Erigan's suggestion. He was an adequate swimmer, though by no means proficient, and he felt weary beyond reckoning. The elation of having crossed the plateau and reached the Great Northern Sea had worn off somewhat, and the deep fatigue that accompanied them these many leagues returned. While he felt the force of Saegan's urgency, he had gauged the distance across the delta as Saegan and Erigan spoke, and he truthfully didn't know if he could make it. They could lose a day or more if they went upstream, and as much returning to the sea on the other side. Even so, it seemed to him better than crossing the Simmok here.

"I say we go upstream," Aljeron said as the discussion died down. "Erigan is right. If we can find a better way across the Simmok, even if we lose some time, we should."

Saegan did not protest, and there was no further debate. Cinjan and Synoki, without needing to be told or prodded, turned immediately south along the Simmok. Saegan and Evrim turned after them, but Aljeron hesitated. He looked out over the grey expanse that stretched as far as he could see to the north. He had been so happy to get here, to look out over this horizon, and now, in a few hours, it would be lost from view again. He knew it was the right thing to do, but it was hard to let it go.

All day their horses waded through the snow, but the Simmok beside them didn't look promising. Immediately upstream the breadth of the river decreased, but it was still swollen and wide. They forged on, hoping that it would continue to narrow, but for several hours there was no change. At midday, they took a break to rest their horses, and the discouragement Aljeron felt was evident in the others as well. The prospect that maybe they would spend a whole day trudging through the snow and still not find a way across the Simmok seemed increasingly likely.

However, by late afternoon, their fortune changed. Not only did the river begin to narrow, but they saw ice formations over long stretches of the river's surface. They had only now to find a place where the river was frozen over from bank to bank, and they might be able to cross without swimming at all. Hope rose in Aljeron, and he like the others paid scant attention to the land before them. All of them watched the Simmok, hoping for a crossing point around the next bend.

Late in the afternoon, they did round a bend and find their crossing point. The river was narrower here than anywhere else along the way, though Aljeron imagined it was still broader than it would have been before the storm. More importantly, the surface of the river was coated with ice, as far upstream as they could see from the bend.

"This is it," Aljeron said, and they stopped. "If the ice is thick enough, this is where we cross."

"How do we know if it is?" Evrim asked.

"One of us will have to test it, I guess," Aljeron replied. "I'll go down on foot. If it supports me, I'll come back and try to lead my horse across. If it supports us both, then the rest of you will come."

"That will be unnecessary," Erigan said. "I will go across now. If the ice holds me, it will hold all of you."

"And if it doesn't?"

"I'll fall in," Erigan said.

"If you get pulled under the ice, you will drown," Saegan said.

"I might, but I doubt it," Erigan answered. "If the ice can't hold me while I'm on it, it isn't going to hold me while I'm under it."

Aljeron thought he heard a hint of eagerness in Erigan's voice, as though he was daring the river to try to swallow him.

Aljeron dropped off his horse and stood on the riverbank in the snow. Erigan started down to the river, and all eyes were on him. He stood beside the river for a moment on all fours, and then reached out with one great paw. He set it down on the ice, and the ice held. He reached out with his other front paw, and again the ice held. In a moment, he was out on the ice completely. He no longer hesitated between steps, but kept moving, slowly and surely, not wanting to rest too long in any one place. Soon he was halfway across, and shortly thereafter, he ascended the bank on the other side. The ice had held, all the way across.

"Well, he made it," Evrim said.

"He did indeed," Aljeron answered. "Let's not waste any time following him."

Aljeron started down the bank, leading his horse, then he waited at the riverside for the others to catch up. "All right, Synoki and Cinjan, lead the way. We'll be right behind you."

"Not too right behind us," Synoki said dryly. "Let's try to keep the weight of the company evenly distributed, with decent intervals between us. The Great Bear might not care if he falls through the ice, but I do."

Synoki stepped out first, cautiously, testing the ice with his foot. Then, when he was out on the ice a few steps, he pulled the reins, coaxing his reluctant horse none too gently to come after him. This the horse did, though by his gait Aljeron could see the animal was not pleased at this turn of events. When Synoki had moved a small distance from the shore, Cinjan started out after him.

"I'll go next," Aljeron said, stepping onto the ice. There was a layer of snow on top, perhaps half a hand thick, so it wasn't nearly as slippery as he thought it might be. Even so, he took small steps, lifting his feet and setting them back down as lightly as he could. Sometimes he shuffled across the ice, not lifting them at all. "Come on now," he whispered to his reticent horse. "We'll be across in no time."

The distance seemed longer than it appeared, now that he was out on the ice. He looked at the far bank and saw that Erigan had returned to the river's edge. He didn't know if Erigan or anything else would be able to save him if he fell through, but it was some comfort to know the Great Bear was watching over them.

He looked back over his shoulder, and he could see that both Evrim and Saegan had started out onto the river as well now. Turning back around, he saw Synoki only a couple of spans from the far bank. It must feel good to see land so close again, Aljeron thought.

As he did, a loud cracking ripped through the wintry stillness. The sound came from up ahead, and Aljeron looked up to see Cinjan's arm flail as the ice below him gave way and he fell into the freezing waters of the Simmok River. Almost without thinking, Aljeron ran forward, letting go of the reins of his horse. Synoki started to turn around, and Aljeron called out, "Get off the river! Don't come back!"

Aljeron lowered himself to his stomach so that his whole body lay across the ice near the hole, distributing his weight as much as was possible. The fragments of broken ice floated in the hole, but there was no sign of Cinjan. Koshti, who had been a couple of spans ahead, returned and stood on the other side of the hole. "You too, Koshti. Get off the river."

Koshti didn't move.

"Can we help?" Saegan called out from a short distance behind.

"No," Aljeron called back. "Get Evrim and the horses to the far side. Steer clear of me!"

Still there was no sign of Cinjan, and Aljeron began to fear that he was already many spans downstream under the ice. He took a big breath and plunged his head into the freezing water. The shock was beyond startling. He almost gasped, which would have brought the ice water into his mouth and lungs, but through sheer strength of will he managed to hold on. His eyes stung with the cold, but he made them search for a sign of Cinjan.

The waters of the Simmok were dark and murky, and he couldn't see much. Suddenly, a hand flashed through the water not far below him. For a split second, he hesitated. *Why save him?* The thought echoed in his head. He didn't trust Cinjan, and with the man dead, it would be much easier to keep an eye on Synoki. Besides, no one would know that he had a chance to grab him. If he told the others there was no sign of Cinjan, they would have no reason to think otherwise.

But that's as good as murder. His own hand shot down through the cold water. He couldn't leave a man to die here, not like this. He felt Cinjan's icy hand and wrestled for a firm grasp of Cinjan's wrist. He pulled with all his strength.

His own head shot up out of the water and was greeted by the cold air. In the hole before him, Cinjan appeared, his free hand reaching desperately for the edge of the hole. With his fingers numb and nearly useless, Aljeron could see him unable to grab hold. He started to scoot back, pulling even harder, when the ice under his own chest cracked. He felt himself sliding headfirst into the freezing water.

Suddenly, something took a remarkably strong hold on his ankles and had halted his descent. He began to slide quickly backward along the solid ice, and Cinjan came up out of the water. Soaked from the waist up, Aljeron rolled over, gasping, to see who had saved them. Standing there on all fours was Erigan, looking down quietly on the both of them.

Aljeron smiled slightly, then lay his head back down on the ice and closed his eyes. He was exhausted, and the water that soaked him was so cold that his chest hurt when he breathed.

"Let's not delay here," Erigan said. "The break might expand, and we are not yet safe."

Slowly, Aljeron crawled onto his hands and knees, and with Erigan's help, stood up. Cinjan, completely drenched, also needed a hand to regain his feet. When Aljeron offered assistance, though, Cinjan looked up at him with pure hate in his eyes. Aljeron hadn't expected a warm thank-you, but the intensity of the man's loathing caught him by surprise. He was about to withdraw the proffered hand when the look passed and Cinjan reached out for him. "Thank you," Cinjan said as he stood, "for saving my life."

"You're welcome," Aljeron said. "But without Erigan, we both would have drowned. Let's get off the river."

They shuffled the rest of the way across, and only when he was sitting in the snow on the far bank did Aljeron pause to look back at the hole in the ice. It was at least twice as big now as it was when Cinjan went in, and he knew that the whole section on which he lay must have given way. He had no idea if he would have been able to get back out on his own, but the image of Cinjan's stiff and frozen hands powerless to grasp the side of the ice haunted him. *Without Erigan, we both would have drowned.*

"Did all the horses make it over?" he asked at last.

"All present and accounted for," Saegan said. "All we nearly lost were the two of you."

"Do you think you can keep going?" Evrim asked.

Aljeron nodded. "Let's go downstream a little, see if we can find a better place to camp. We'll never get back to the sea tonight. We'll strike out for it in the morning."

"Let's not go far," Saegan said. "I'll need time to clear a place for a fire."

"We only have wood for a couple more," Aljeron protested. "We shouldn't waste it here where the wind is likely to blow snow on it all night. Let's save it."

"We're not going to save it," Saegan said, almost disdainfully. "Don't be foolish. You're half-soaked, and Cinjan is completely soaked. We need the fire tonight."

Aljeron conceded, and they moved on for less than an hour before finally stopping for the night. When they burrowed in and Saegan eventually got the fire going, Aljeron was very glad that Saegan had won that dispute. The heat from the fire was initially painful to Aljeron's numb hands, but it became more soothing as his fingers thawed. Koshti came and settled in beside him. He had stayed within a span of Aljeron every step of the way from the river.

"I'm all right, Koshti," Aljeron said softly, stroking the tiger's fur.

Saegan offered to take the first watch, and Aljeron again did not protest. He knew Saegan was likely going to watch all night, and ordinarily he would have objected, but tonight he was too weary. He would make it up to Saegan later. As he lay down, the vivid image of Cinjan falling through the ice came to mind. As he replayed the scene and the rescue, he wondered if Cinjan would have rushed to his aid had their places been reversed. Would he have reached down to grab his hand? Would he have even looked for it? Thinking of the look of hate Cinjan gave him, he felt pretty sure he knew.

Aljeron pushed that away for now. Despite the mishap, their mission for the day had been successful. They had crossed the Simmok. They had only now to head northward again and return to the Great Northern Sea. From there it should be a straight shot to the Tajira Mountains. It was at last the final leg of the journey.

The way north seemed both easier and quicker than the way south had been the previous day, perhaps because the weight of worry was behind them, or perhaps because they were about to leave the deep snow once more, or perhaps because the return always seems shorter after a successful going out. Whatever the reason, Aljeron found himself pleasantly surprised when, shortly after midday, the Great Northern Sea appeared on the horizon.

That night they camped once more beside the sea, and Aljeron took the lion's share of the watch, giving Saegan a chance to make up some lost sleep. The following day was the lightest day yet for snow, as the merest sprinkling fell out of what seemed to Aljeron to be an even darker sky.

As Aljeron mounted his horse after another scant breakfast, he turned to Evrim and Saegan. "The snow has slowed almost to a stop, yet the sky seems darker than ever."

"I'll take the gloom over the wet," Evrim replied.

"Me too," Saegan said, nodding.

"I don't disagree, but we're not well equipped to journey in the dark, so I hope this isn't a foreshadowing of things to come. If the rain and snow go away only to be replaced by an endless night, we may find ourselves yearning for the cold and damp before long."

"That's a pleasant thought," Saegan said sarcastically. "And you've called me glum before."

"And so you are," Aljeron replied, smiling.

"Well, maybe one day I'll be as happy and upbeat as you are, just all smiles and sunshine, eh?" Saegan replied with a smirk.

"That's me," Aljeron nodded. "Now come on, before we're swallowed up in an unnatural darkness and destroyed by some new beast unleashed by Malek to kill us all."

They set out, and it felt good to ride faster and know that they were making better time. Their horses seemed to embrace the chance to run on solid ground, for the frozen sand beneath the snow was as hard as could be.

About the start of Eighth Hour, the relatively flat terrain was interrupted by a long ridge running parallel to the beach, not far back from the water's edge. A little past it, farther back from the water, was a small grove of trees, the only trees they'd seen for a few days. As they drew nearer, Cinjan and Synoki stopped, examining the strange formation. When Aljeron and the others came up alongside them, Cinjan turned to Aljeron. "Should we check it out?"

"Sure, why not," Aljeron answered. "The horses could use a rest."

Cinjan and Synoki pushed up the beach toward the ridge, but Aljeron stayed put. Evrim leaned over. "Are you going to look too?"

"No," Aljeron replied. "Unless they find something worth seeing, I'm happy just to have a rest here."

Aljeron dropped down from his horse and stretched, watching Synoki and Cinjan ride along the ridge toward the eastern end. When they reached that end, they stopped, calling back to the others. "We've found something you all might want to see."

"What?" Aljeron called.

"It looks like the entrance to a cave."

"A cave?" Aljeron said, looking at Saegan, Evrim, and Erigan. "Here?"

"Let's take a look," Evrim said. "Who knows what we might find?"

"Yes," Saegan said, "that's what worries me."

"You think we shouldn't?" Aljeron asked.

"I don't know," Saegan replied. "What if it's a den rather than a cave? Like you said, we aren't well equipped for the dark."

"Well," Aljeron said, looking back to Cinjan and Synoki, "it probably won't hurt to examine the entrance. Still, we should be cautious."

They joined Cinjan and Synoki at the eastern end of the ridge and examined the mouth of the cave. It was small, just a little taller than Aljeron, and only wide enough for maybe two men to walk abroad.

"It doesn't look like much," Aljeron said.

"Are we going in?" Cinjan asked.

"I don't know," Aljeron answered, turning to the others. "Any ideas here?"

"The entrance looks manmade," Erigan said. "Look, the opening is smooth and rounded, almost symmetrical."

"You think men made this cave?" Aljeron asked, surprised. "In the First Age?"

"I don't know. Perhaps it was only widened by men."

Aljeron turned back to the cave. "All right," he said. "I'm curious now. I say we go in."

"The cave is too small for our horses," Saegan said.

"And probably too small for me," Erigan said, "even if I could squeeze through the entrance."

"Well, if you don't mind waiting up here at the entrance, Erigan, we'll tie our horses to those trees over there and go see what we can see."

Two torches were produced from their dwindling stores, and everything but their swords was left behind. Again, Cinjan and Synoki took the lead. As Erigan had suspected, the cave narrowed, so that they eventually had to proceed single file. Koshti walked before Aljeron, between him and Synoki.

Not far from the entrance, Aljeron stopped, noticing a stone in the base of the cave wall. It was oval and seemed to be glowing a faint, iridescent blue. "Am I seeing things?" Aljeron said to Evrim and Saegan. "Or is this stone emitting a pale blue light?"

"It is," they answered.

"Ever seen anything like this?"

"No."

They pressed ahead, and a few spans farther on they saw another one, and a few spans beyond that, another. In fact, they began to appear at regular intervals, augmenting the light of their torches and keeping the downward sloping corridor reasonably well lit.

The corridor started to drop more steeply, and eventually, it became challenging to keep their footing. Twice, Evrim slipped and fell, apologizing profusely both times. "I'm like a baby learning to walk," he said the second time, sounding disgusted with himself.

"Give yourself some time," Aljeron replied. "You're doing pretty well, all things considered. Now take my arm. It's hard going here."

Together they continued their descent, and when it grew so steep that they could hardly keep their feet, they sat down and slid down the remainder of the way, until the corridor opened into an wide room.

"What's this, I wonder?" Aljeron said, lifting his torch high.

"Let's check it out," Cinjan said. He held the second torch.

They examined the walls and found the room wasn't all that big, but there was an opening leading to another room beyond. "Should we go through?" Cinjan asked, standing at the entrance.

"Might as well," Aljeron replied. One by one, they passed into the interior room, which was larger. An echo reverberated around them, and no roof was visible above them.

"It's a cavern," Aljeron said, with memories of the enormous caverns below Nal Gildoroth coming back to him. "I'm not sure I like this."

"Do we go on?" Saegan asked.

"Why not?" Cinjan answered. "We've come all the way down; let's see what there is to see."

"Aljeron?" Saegan stubbornly persisted.

"We'll go, but stay together."

They walked away from the door, out into the room. Koshti padded along silently beside Aljeron, while the footsteps of the others slapped on the stone floor. It was large and spacious, as Aljeron had suspected. They walked for several moments, without any change in their surroundings, then a wide stone structure appeared out of the dark, rising up almost a span above the worn floor.

"What is that?" Evrim asked.

"A forge," Aljeron answered. "Just like the forge below Nal Gildoroth."

They drew closer and stopped beside it. Aljeron couldn't believe what he was seeing. Scattered thoughts whirled in his mind. Memories from seventeen years ago mixed with stories and legends from the First Age. "It can't be, but here it is in front of us."

"Aljeron," Evrim said, "you're saying this is a copy of the forge you saw below Nal Gildoroth?"

"Or that was a copy of this," Aljeron replied. "All I know is that they are exactly alike. Wouldn't you say so, Synoki?"

"They are very similar," Synoki replied. "I couldn't say if they were exactly alike. It's been a long time."

"Aljeron, do you think this is the place?" Saegan asked.

"The place?"

"You know, where Malek made the first weapons for Andunin. The stories all say Malek made them here, in Nolthanin, not on the Mountain where the rest of the Twelve could have found them."

"More nonsense from a distant past," Synoki sneered.

"It's not nonsense. It's history," Saegan replied.

"If it's history," Synoki said, "then so is the fact that the Nolthanim must have made thousands of weapons for themselves. Why couldn't this be their secret workshop? Why must you see Malek and mythical moments in everything?"

"If Malek did make the first weapons for the Nolthanim at a forge in Nolthanin, and if the Nolthanim made more weapons thereafter, it would make perfect sense that they would use the same place," Aljeron said, stepping up to the forge and running his fingers along the smooth stone. "And where would be better than here? As far from the Mountain as you can get while still being central to Nolthanin. What's more, the Water Stone we found on the plateau suggested that the Nolthanim met not far from here at Andunin's bidding. If that was their meeting place, it would be easy enough to carry the weapons from here to there."

"This is the place," Saegan agreed. "It all began here."

Aljeron drew Daaltaran and gently laid it on the forge. His weapon was one of the Azmavarim, a Firstblade, and it may have been made on this very spot, perhaps by Malek himself. He ran his fingers lovingly along the finely wrought handle and along the side of the long, strong blade.

Synoki stepped up to the forge and leaned in close. "Is it strange to think you treasure so highly something so often associated with the ruin of our world?"

Aljeron looked at Synoki, who met the intensity of his gaze, but he said nothing. He sheathed Daaltaran and stepped away from the forge. "There's nothing more to see here," he said. "Let's go back."

"What about the rest of the cavern?" Cinjan asked.

"What about it?" Aljeron replied, starting back across the large open room. "Surely there's nothing here of more interest than this. We've uncovered the secret of this place."

Back in the rounded room at the foot of the long, sloping corridor, a debate broke out among them. Cinjan continued to press his point. "Here, we are out of the wind, the snow, and to a large extent, the cold. Why not spend the night?"

"I don't want to stay down here," Aljeron protested, looking at the dark opening that led to the cavern that housed the forge. "Not now that we know what this place was."

"Whatever it was thousands of years ago, it isn't that now," Synoki said. "It is shelter for a night, nothing more and nothing less."

"It would be nice to be out of the snow and on a dry surface for a night, Aljeron," Evrim said, almost timidly.

Aljeron looked at his friend, and after a moment, nodded. "All right," he said. "We'll stay here tonight, but we're staying in this room, not the next."

"Fine," Cinjan said, "if that's what you'd like."

"It is, and we'll need to let Erigan know."

"I'll go up," Saegan volunteered. "Be back in a little bit."

"Bring what wood we have left," Aljeron said as Saegan started to scramble up the steep corridor. "We might as well enjoy a fire here where there's nothing to blunt it. As long as we're staying, we might as well live it up."

Saegan was back before long, and soon a small fire was stoked and burning. For a while they sat up beside it, but the utter dark of their surroundings put a damper on their conversation, despite their relative comfort. Before long, each of the others lay down to sleep, and Aljeron lingered up, having told Saegan he'd take the first watch.

The fire crackled pleasantly, and Aljeron's face grew warm. The end of his cloak-sleeves were dry, a strange feeling to his thawed out fingertips. Beside him, Koshti slept peacefully, his warm soft side rising and falling rhythmically.

It felt strange to be inside. It felt stranger to be in a cave. It was hard to shake the feeling that this was a place very much like the large cavern below Nal Gildoroth, even without the piles of bones and the extensive pool of black water. He thought of that day, of finding the forge and the creature lurking in that deep, dark place. It was a place he often revisited in his dreams, which, when he had them, were more like nightmares.

He could see the still, dark water now, and Koshti running back and forth along the edge. The burst of light from

Valzaan's staff. The image of the creature falling back into the water. The splash. His eyes flickered shut.

A growl and a bump in the dark awoke him. Koshti was on his feet beside Aljeron, crouching to spring, and a dark figure was moving stealthily beside the fire. Suddenly, Koshti leapt over him, an orange and black blur to Aljeron's sleepy eyes. He scrambled to his feet, drawing Daaltaran. His eyes focused, and he saw Cinjan, long, cruel dagger in hand, struggling toward him with Koshti's powerful jaw locked on his lower arm. With his free hand he struck the side of the tiger's head a vicious blow, but Koshti maintained his grip. If anything, his jaws tightened, because Aljeron could hear the cracking of Cinjan's bone. Blood ran freely down the side of Koshti's mouth.

In an instant, Aljeron seized Cinjan's free hand. Cinjan looked in rage from the tiger to Aljeron, the same hatred from the day before burning in his eyes.

Cinjan screamed. Koshti had bitten all the way through. Even so, Cinjan's first move when the stump of his arm came loose was to strike Aljeron in a violent attempt to wrench his good hand free.

"I said you'd die if you drew your weapon against me again," Aljeron said, driving Daaltaran deep into Cinjan's chest. "I meant it."

He slid Cinjan's dead body to the floor and turned toward the fire. Saegan and Evrim were on their feet, watching, and Synoki was sitting on the other side of the fire. Seeing Synoki sitting there, calm and quiet, watching impassively, enraged Aljeron. He strode around the fire, reached down, grabbed Synoki's cloak, and hauled him roughly to his feet. "You too, Synoki. Time to join your friend."

"But Aljeron—" Synoki started.

"Saegan," Aljeron said, directing his attention to his friend. "Bring a torch."

Saegan quickly lit a torch in the fire and followed hard after Aljeron as he half carried, half dragged Synoki into the neighboring cavernous room. Synoki did not struggle hard against him, and it likely wouldn't have done much good. In fact, Aljeron was perfectly ready to kill him where they were, so it was wise on Synoki's part not to resist.

When they reached the forge, Aljeron pinned Synoki against it, raising the blood-stained blade to his throat. "This forge was made by your master, and I'm going to kill you right here beside it, so your blood spatters on it. Your death will serve both as justice for your treachery and as an act of defiance against the one who sent you."

"If you kill me, you will only stain your hands with innocent blood," Synoki said, his eyes focused on Aljeron in the dark.

"Innocent? After helping to rescue you from the Forbidden Isle seventeen years ago, you bring that viper along on our journey so he can kill me? Innocent? When the giant that killed Arintol and Karras probably tracked us or found us because of you? How dare you call yourself innocent? You may not have held the dagger, but you are no more innocent than your friend."

"He wasn't my friend."

"What?" Aljeron looked closely at Synoki for signs of desperation, but the man was completely calm and apparently serious. "What do you mean? You two are thick as thieves."

"I know it must appear that way to you," Synoki replied, "but if you would just let me explain—"

"Why should I?"

"Why not? There are three of you and a tiger. I'm under no illusion that I'll be able to break free and escape. If you don't believe my story and choose to kill me anyway, what have you lost? But, if upon hearing you understand my innocence, then I get to live and you don't make a mistake that would make you just as much a murderer as your old friend Rulalin."

Aljeron's grip tightened on Synoki's cloak. "You would compare me to my enemy?"

"I would compare one murderous act to another."

Aljeron let go and stepped back. Synoki breathed deeply and leaned wearily against the forge. "All right," Aljeron said. "Tell us your story."

"I have deceived you."

"So you admit it?"

"Not in all things. I am, as I have told you, a merchant of Col Marena. Almost all the background I gave you when we met in Col Marena is true."

"Almost?"

"Almost, but not all. I was returning to Col Marena when the city went up in flames, and though everyone bid me go with them, I was determined to see what had become of my home and my warehouse and my ships. It was foolish, I know, but I did.

"I managed to slip into the city unnoticed, but while I was walking from my burned-out warehouse to my home, I was caught by a patrol of Nolthanim. They bound and blindfolded me and brought me to a tent outside the city, where they left me in the wet grass. When they removed my blindfold, I saw that I was one of about twenty or thirty captives who had been bound and deposited there. Most were men I knew, merchants like me who had all but run the city only a few days before.

"Inside the tent, I heard voices. They were arguing, but I didn't know was about what. Shortly thereafter, a small group of men emerged, and as they walked past, I heard one of them say, 'I haven't been outside the Mountain in years. How am I to know what this Aljeron Balinor looks like?'

"I called out to them, and they stopped. 'Were you talking about Aljeron Balinor? I know him. He was my friend.'

"They came back. At first they didn't believe me. They thought I was attempting to escape, but I was able to convince them that I did know you. They untied me and took me inside the tent. The man inside, I didn't know, but I would come to know him as Cinjan, the man you killed tonight.

"He questioned me at length, and when he also was satisfied that I knew you, he told me I would live only as long as I helped him. On the day I ceased to be useful, I would die.

"He explained that they had a small boat and were hoping to get men onto the ships out in the harbor by dressing them in rags as though refugees from the city. The point of the expedition was to get a couple of men close to you so that you could be watched. I never found out the intent of the surveillance. Cinjan, who had been charged with finding and observing you, knew you were scarred but not much more than that. When he realized I could identify you without question, he told me I was going to help him do so.

"I told him I couldn't, that you had saved my life. He threatened to kill me, and though I wavered, I refused. Then, he took me by the arm and led me out into the night and down a little way from his tent to another surrounded by women and children from the city. 'If you do not do as I say,' he said, 'I will kill each of these one by one, right in front of you. Do you understand?'

"I agreed, and we set off from Col Marena, but the plan failed. The boat that they had pulled from dry-dock was more damaged than anyone could see. When we set out in it, Cinjan, myself, and two others, it sank. Cinjan was furious and commanded the withdrawal of the Nolthanim in the hopes that if he could not get out to you, maybe you would come ashore to him.

"I thought it a vain hope and believed that soon he would be through with me, and I would be dead. But then you came ashore. When we met that night in Col Marena, a small patrol of Nolthanim were observing from a distance. I was sent to confirm that it was really you. This I did, and Cinjan wanted to bring a handful of men with us, but I persuaded him that you would suspect something was amiss. I thought that with just Cinjan among us, not only your life but mine might be saved. The giant was as much a surprise to me as it was to you. After that, Cinjan didn't let me leave his side. He kept me close, which is why we were always together, but—and I swear by the Mountain—I was not part of his plan to kill you."

"That day I drew my sword on you, why would he come at me with daggers drawn? Why would he care what happened to you? You had served your purpose."

"I don't think he was coming at you."

"What do you mean?"

"I think he meant to kill me. Your questions and accusations were not so far from the truth, only directed at the wrong person. I don't think Cinjan wanted to be exposed."

Aljeron stared at Synoki. There was much about his story that could be true, but so deeply ingrained now was his mistrust of the man that he just didn't know what to think. "Saegan, examine him and remove any weapons he may be carrying or concealing."

"Aljeron," Evrim said as Saegan obeyed. "You don't believe this, do you?"

Aljeron shrugged. "I don't know what the whole truth may be. I doubt we've heard all of it, but the cost of being wrong is too high. He will go with us unarmed, as our captive and prisoner. If we perish on the way, he will perish with us. If we ever return, his story will be investigated. If he tries to escape or harm any of us, he will die."

Aljeron turned to Synoki. "Is all this clear?"

"It is."

"Time will tell, I suppose," Aljeron answered, wiping the blood from Daaltaran on the dark forge as best he could. "This blood I do leave here, a symbol of Malek's handiwork turned against Malek's own servant."

Aljeron watched the dark blood ooze down the stone, then turned and followed Saegan and the others out of the cavern.

Synoki lay in the darkness. He knew he was being watched as closely now as before, but he was just glad things had turned out as well as they did. Cinjan acted without permission and almost ruined everything. *The fool, had he just waited a little longer, Aljeron would have been his.*

9
THE CLAN OF ELNIN

BENJIAH SAT ON HIS HORSE, looking up at Dravendir, whose great golden wings were outstretched as he landed on the dragon tower in the distance. He had left the tower almost two weeks before, riding hard with his uncles to reach Caan, and now he had returned with the army they had sought. On top of the tower, the powerful wings contracted, and Dravendir overlooked the great open plain, his chest and head still visible above the rim of the tower. Though the sight of dragons had become something of a regularity, Benjiah still marveled at the power and majesty of the dragon's form.

All along the road ahead of him, the soldiers and Great Bear were spread out, winding like an enormous snake across the saturated fields. The road, though muddy and slow going, was decidedly firmer and more stable than the ground around it, more than half of which was under several hands of water. Benjiah could see the marked difference that thousands of men and horses had made since he passed south along it.

Deep ruts creased the road and shoulders, and these ruts were becoming small reservoirs of water, even though the deluge was now a drizzle. His horse strained with every step to pull his hooves out of the mud that sucked them in and latched on as though the earth itself was trying to prevent them from getting away. His only consolation was that their enemy would get the worst of the road as well.

Of course, this hadn't proved to be much of a barrier in the past week. Though Allfather's armies took more than a day's head start, the dragons informed them that the enemy had closed the gap. Reports came up all morning that Bryar and the scouts anchoring the rear guard had been engaged multiple times by packs of Black Wolves. What's more, if Dravendir had just landed on the dragon tower, then he was no longer engaged with the enemy, as he had been. Benjiah wondered about Eliandir and Gralendir, the third dragon that had survived the battle five days ago beside the Barunaan. He was also a blue dragon like Dravendir. Both seemed to defer to Eliandir when the dragons had contact with Benjiah or any of the others, but Benjiah wasn't sure that deference was exactly the right word. It was strange to think of any dragon deferring to anyone, even to a brother. He didn't know how to describe it, but the three dragons seemed simultaneously united in agreement and fiercely independent.

Eliandir's graceful, golden form glided overhead. Benjiah looked up to watch him fly, his wings moving almost imperceptibly, but he covered the distance between Benjiah and the distant dragon tower in a matter of moments. Benjiah turned to look for Gralendir, but there was no sign of him. There could be many reasons for this, but he feared the worst.

Eliandir did not remain at the dragon tower for long. After a moment he was back in the air and flying their way. Circling overhead for a few moments, he alighted on the ground not far from Benjiah and the captains of the army, who were a few horse lengths behind. Benjiah rode back along the line until he reached Caan, who was turning off the road to meet Eliandir.

"Eliandir," Caan said, "what news?"

"The rear guard has broken and is fleeing north as quickly as they can. The enemy's progress is unimpeded."

"How close are they?"

"Not far, and closing fast. The children of Vulsutyr have sent about a third of their force ahead of the main body of our enemy. They are following this group."

"So only a third of the enemy is coming?" Caan answered.

"Yes, but I reckon their number is equal to our own, and with the Vulsutyrim following them, the engagement could be devastating."

"What do you recommend?"

Eliandir raised his head to its full height and surveyed the line of weary men and Great Bear winding northward toward a distant hill that led up to the southern border of Elnin Wood. "All possibilities look bleak without more aid."

Silence descended on the small gathering once more. "Eliandir," Benjiah said, "where is Gralendir? He did not return with you?"

"Gralendir was wounded. A spear of the Vulsutyrim pierced his left wing. He was able to get off the battlefield, and we protected his retreat, but he has left for the Arimaar Mountains. He can be of no further aid to us here."

"Will he live?"

"He will live."

"Good," Benjiah replied.

"Is there any chance of more help?" Gilion asked.

"Not before this battle comes," Eliandir answered.

There was nothing further to ask, so Caan thanked Eliandir for all his aid, adding at the end, "Eliandir, I'm sorry for the injury to Gralendir. I hope that he heals fully and quickly."

Eliandir bobbed his head slightly as a nod, then leapt from the ground. They watched him fly off over the field, returning to the dragon tower.

"So what do we do?" Caan asked.

This time the normally quiet Great Bear spoke up first. "We must head as quickly as possible to Elnin," Sarneth said.

Both Elmaaneth and Kerentol agreed.

"You think we'll find help there?" Talis Fein asked.

"Regardless," Elmaaneth answered, "the Great Bear from Taralin could form a new rear guard in Elnin that could give you time to get your people through to the other side. The forest is our home, and even if we're outnumbered, we could put up more resistance than our enemy expects. He may pass through after us, but his price for passage will be high."

"There is neither time nor need to debate it," Caan said, forestalling further discussion. "The people of Cimaris Rul have already passed into the wood by now, and the front of our own column will reach it soon. We need to move that way as quickly as possible. If we are caught before we can get in, we'll form defensive positions and do our best to slow down our pursuers so that at least some of us can get in and get through."

The gathering of captains broke up and spread out along the line to encourage the retreating men to move faster if they could. Everything about the situation, the overwhelming fatigue, the intractable mud, the news of another dragon's aid lost to their cause, all combined to demoralize Benjiah. He had not been this discouraged in a long time. Allfather's victory through him over the Grendolai and the coming of the dragons had given him real hope. Watching the dragons swoop over the battlefield beside the Barunaan was like seeing the sunrise after a long and dark night. Even the appearance of the great beast in the flooded waters of the river was not enough to dampen his good spirits. They survived the day and left the battlefield reasonably intact.

What hope he felt that day, though, disappeared as their movement north bogged down. The captains hadn't discussed it, but everyone knew it. And now the gap was closed once more, except this time aid from more dragons was unlikely.

Pedraal and Pedraan dropped back beside him. "One day and one task at a time," Pedraal said, looking at him closely.

"I know," Benjiah answered.

"Just make the woods," Pedraan added.

"Just the woods," Pedraal echoed.

Benjiah shut his eyes and saw, instantly, the rushing, howling forms of hundreds and even thousands of Black Wolves. They were running along the road and beside it, two and three deep, a black, rolling wave overtaking the mud and water. He saw not far in front of them the galloping forms of riders, trying desperately to outrun them. In the midst of the riders he saw Bryar, head lowered over her horse's neck, pushing it ahead, faster and faster.

He opened his eyes and saw again the great column, slowly winding up the long road. The heads of the soldiers were barely lifted high enough to see the man in front. He looked back at his uncles. "Just the woods," he said.

"Just the woods," they answered.

He spurred his horse on, looking nervously over his shoulder.

Benjiah sat midway up the last steep hill before the road disappeared into Elnin Wood. Dusk was deepening. Still, a few thousand men and Great Bear had not yet entered the protective cover of the wood. Most of them were clustered on the hill, but the narrowing of the road as it entered the wood had slowed their progress.

"Look!" a voice cried out above him, and he saw a soldier pointing back over the plain they had spent the day crossing.

He turned. Horses with riders were approaching in the distance, riding hard. Behind them, a great host of the enemy came, moving just as fast.

Then everything started to happen at once. Caan called for the men and Great Bear still outside the wood to form a line. "Along the ridge! Form the line!" he called as the horsemen and their pursuers drew nearer.

He summoned a messenger to his side. "Ride into the wood and summon all who will come to return here. We'll need help to slow them down. We must buy the others time to get farther in."

Benjiah and the twins positioned themselves in the newly formed battle line, and Benjiah nocked an arrow in preparation for the moment when their enemy would come within range. After hurrying to prepare the line, they were all forced to wait now. The riders in front, which were of course the scouts serving as their rear guard, started up the gentler slope that led to the hill.

They were all still too far for Benjiah to take a shot. He turned to look at Pedraal and Pedraan beside him, their war hammer and battle-axe ready. As he did, he saw dark shapes moving forward out of the trees.

"Pedraal! Pedraan! Look!"

His uncles turned, and so did many of those around him. Emerging from Elnin Wood as far as he could see, were Great Bear. He turned and looked the other direction, and sure enough, they were coming out from there as well. A cheer went up from the soldiers in the line, and without being told, men moved to allow the Great Bear passage through their midst. One, whose fur was almost completely grey but was a head taller than all the others, moved along the line toward Sarneth, who was standing with Elmaaneth not far from Benjiah.

"Turgan, you are a welcome sight," Sarneth greeted the enormous Great Bear.

"You've brought a host of troubles to our doorstep, Sarneth," Turgan answered. "I guess you thought that if you couldn't talk us out of the draal, you'd force us out."

The nature of Turgan's answer worried Benjiah until he saw Sarneth's response, which was almost a grin. "Trouble was coming to your doorstep whether you wanted it to or not, Turgan. I've just brought you some aid."

"For that we thank you," Turgan replied. "And to return the favor, I've brought some help to you. It looks like you need it."

Both Great Bear turned to the pursuit. Black Wolves almost without number were leading the chase, as Benjiah had seen. Not far behind, Malekim and men on horseback came after. Of the Vulsutyrim that Eliandir had mentioned, there was no sign.

The enemy's front lines were within Benjiah's range now, but the riders coming up the hill obscured his view. He relaxed his hand. He'd get his chance, but not as quickly as he thought.

The riders were upon them, and all along the line, gaps opened to receive the scouts and their horses. Relieved, Benjiah saw Bryar come up and through down the line.

"Now," Caan shouted, "with the aid of the Clan of Elnin, let's take advantage of the slope and bring the battle to them!"

Horses, men, and Great Bear plunged down the hill. Benjiah held back, because he knew he would be more effective with Suruna up here. Pedraal and Pedraan though, didn't hesitate, and he could see them as they rushed down, their massive frames charging eagerly.

Soon the two lines met, and Benjiah saw little more than confusion. The staffs of the Great Bear were whirling all along the battlefront, knocking wolves out of the air and riders out of their saddles. He saw the large, greying Great Bear personally drive the end of his staff through the skull of a Black Wolf that made the mistake of trying to leap over another of his kind.

Benjiah found his uncles again, and sure enough, both war hammer and battle-axe were flying with speed and skill, crushing and chopping as both men dropped from their horses to better utilize their weapons. He could see, even from where he was, the muscles in their shoulders straining and tensing with every blow. They were incredible to behold, and he knew he was quite possibly watching the two strongest men alive.

Nearby, Caan, still in the saddle, was using his sword both as a weapon and as a tool to direct the battle. His loud voice rose above the din, shouting directions and instructions to all who would listen. His horse reared, but Caan held the reins firmly and kept his seat.

Not all that Benjiah could see was encouraging. A rider separated from the rest of the line was taken out of his saddle by a couple of wolves. Several others descended upon his body as soon as it struck the soggy ground, and he was completely covered by wolves, ripping furiously into him.

A little farther down, a wedge of Malekim cut their way through the Great Bear and caused lots of trouble for the men on horseback. One of the Malekim drove his cruel, curved sword through one of the riders, and the man, grasping at his side, toppled off the horse.

Benjiah focused on the Malekim who had killed the rider. He was a long way down the hill, but he had made shots this hard before. He took a breath and released his arrow. It flew wide, striking the horse of the fallen rider. The horse staggered and fell. He quickly nocked another one, and taking aim again, fired. This one hit its mark, and the Malekim struggled for a moment to pull the arrow from his side, but the cyranis did its work, and the Silent One soon keeled over.

Great Bear rallied toward that place, and the fighting intensified. Swords and staffs clashed, and many Great Bear and Malekim were pulled under in the surging ebb and flow of the battle. Suddenly, from the other direction, a sound Benjiah didn't recognize echoed above the battle, and the enemy began to fall back. Slowly, the enemy disengaged, and Caan held his line from advancing.

Benjiah began to relax and laid Suruna across his horse's back.

"I wouldn't put the bow away just yet," Bryar said from beside him. Dirty and bedraggled, she was looking beyond him at the battlefield. "Look."

The enemy was coming again. This time, with no slope to give the men and Great Bear momentum, the enemy drove their line back, so that they had to fight as they backpedaled uphill. Benjiah, using regular arrows, started to target Nolthanim on horseback, and he dropped several. Eventually, the forward progress of the enemy front was halted, and with renewed vigor, especially among the Great Bear, the enemy was driven back down the small slope.

After a while, the sound echoed across the field again, and the enemy began to disengage again. This time Benjiah did not relax. He kept an arrow ready and Suruna in position. Likewise, the men and Great Bear pulled the line together, preparing for a third charge.

But the charge didn't come, and momentarily, Benjiah understood why. Looking up, he saw the golden forms of Eliandir and Dravendir approaching from the dragon tower. They came up behind the enemy, which was scrambling to avoid the streaks of flame that were falling upon the battlefield.

Caan did not waste any time ordering the men back up the hill and into the wood. The Great Bear followed, and soon the procession into Elnin resumed. The dragons, who had not come to fight so much as to stop the fight, continued to circle, keeping the enemy at bay as the retreat continued. They were still circling when Benjiah, near the end of the long line of men and Great Bear, turned his back on the open plain and rode into the shelter of the trees.

Their passage through the wood was a long blur of marching in darkness and near-darkness. Caan did not call a halt to their movement at all the first night, and the second night only for a few hours. He knew, and they all knew, that they had been fortunate to get inside Elnin, and that they needed to make the most of its relative security.

The Great Bear of Elnin stood aside as the men passed, then formed a new rear guard. Benjiah felt enormously relieved to be inside Elnin with a host of Great Bear between him and the enemy. In some ways, he felt even safer than he had when the dragons appeared overhead the first time. He didn't know if he was as safe, but he felt safe, and even that was a relief.

Their progress at night was made possible by great lamps lit at even intervals and manned by pairs of Great Bear, presumably to make sure that the fire inside them didn't spread, though Benjiah could hardly imagine a fire starting accidentally in a world so wet that even deliberate fires were all but impossible. Still, as they past each successive lamp, he nodded to the silent attendants, grateful for the selfless provision of the Elnin clan in their time of need.

When on the second night they did stop, at last, Benjiah dropped wearily from his horse. He made little fuss over choosing a spot to sleep and didn't even think about eating. The hunger pangs had, for the moment anyway, dissipated.

Benjiah looked up at the branches of the enormous trees that rose from the forest floor. He wished he could see this place in summer. He yawned, closing his eyes. He could imagine a great canopy of green leaves, thick in every direction. He could see the sunlight, in some places penetrating just far enough to illuminate the occasional patch of upper tree trunk, but never reaching all the way down to the forest floor. The air, though hot, kept in by the cover, wouldn't be overwhelmingly stifling because of all the space above. Some of the wind that blew through upper branches would offer some circulation.

He tried to imagine this place before Corindel's betrayal of the Great Bear. Did men travel freely along this road? Were human visitors common here? Were these lamps relics of an older time, perhaps brought out of some distant storehouse to accommodate those who, for almost a thousand years, were exiled from this place?

He didn't know, and as he felt his mind drifting, he didn't try to force it to focus. They wouldn't have long before the march recommenced, so he welcomed sleep as it stole over him.

"Hey," Pedraal said, shaking him. "Wake up."

Benjiah stirred but struggled to open his eyes. "I just got to sleep," he complained as he managed to sit up.

"Yes," Pedraal replied, "if by 'just' you mean four or five hours ago. It's almost First Hour. You can't tell in here, but dawn is almost upon us."

Benjiah could see that it was a little lighter than when they'd stopped. "Dawn?" he said, yawning. "It can't be."

"It is."

Pedraal and Pedraan were on their feet, readying their horses. "I let you sleep as long as I could, but it is time to go."

Benjiah stood, wobbling, his uncooperative legs tingling with sleep. "Have you two been here before?"

"No."

"Not even when you went to Sulare?"

"No, we went east of Elnin, through the gap. It's longer, but in those days, we thought it safer; Elnin was mysterious to us and we were only three in number. Your dad and the others came through here, though."

"I know."

"Bryar was with them; she'd know. So would Mindarin."

"Where is Mindarin?" Benjiah asked, realizing that he hadn't seen Aelwyn or Mindarin since the early hours of morning, before the big battle beside the Barunaan.

"The women were sent ahead with the citizens from Cimaris Rul. They had a long discussion with Caan. I think they were trying to argue that they should be left with the army, but Caan was pretty insistent that it had become too dangerous. The dead and fatally wounded had to be left behind anyway, so they might as well go up front where it was safer. I don't know that Mindarin liked it, but in the end, I think they acknowledged that they could be of more use among the people of Cimaris Rul."

"I bet that even if she went willingly," Benjiah said, "Mindarin did not go happily."

Pedraal smiled. "I'd say that's a safe bet."

They mounted their horses. "Only sixteen and yet so wise in the ways of women," Pedraan quipped.

"I'm almost seventeen," Benjiah corrected him, "and figuring out Mindarin doesn't take any special insights."

"No," Pedraan conceded, "I guess it doesn't."

Early the following morning, after another nearly all-night march, they reached the northern edge of Elnin Wood. The great trees started to thin out, and then suddenly, the processional was in the open.

The long line of men kept steadily onward, but off to the side, Benjiah saw a strange sight. Most of the captains of the army were huddled together near a large group of men on horseback, dressed in gold and green, the colors of Amaan Sul.

"What do you think they're doing here?" Pedraan answered.

"I don't know, but let's go ask."

They rode quickly, and the assembled men turned to greet them. The officer talking to Caan saw Pedraal and Pedraan coming, and his face broke out into a smile. "Captain Someris," he exclaimed as Pedraan rode up, then repeating the greeting as Pedraal pulled up beside him.

As Benjiah came up after, the young officer slowly realized who it was. "It is good to see the heir," he said. "Your mother will be relieved to know you are well."

Benjiah nodded but said only, "Greetings, officer of Amaan Sul."

The twins hastened to inquire as to the presence of soldiers of Amaan Sul so far south.

"Captain Merias sent us," the young officer said. "The great majority of our army is deployed south of the Kalamin River, and—"

"South of the Kalamin?" Pedraal asked. "What are they doing there?"

"Refugees from the west brought word of the war and news of Malek's march through the Erefen Marshes. We were sent south to take up defensive positions and to aid in your retreat. We're here to escort you to the main body of our army."

"How far from here are they?"

"A couple of days, though at the pace this column is moving, maybe more."

"And what strength has Merias brought south of the Kalamin?"

"We have almost twenty thousand men."

All the captains reacted to this, and Pedraal and Pedraan were almost beside themselves with delight. "Almost twenty thousand!" Pedraal said, slapping Caan on the back. "Good, hardy Enthanim, not wearied by war or the march. Give me another crack at the enemy now. We'll show them what men can do."

"You'll get your chance," Gilion said grimly, "no doubt sooner than we'd like. Don't be too eager."

"I'm just happy about the help, that's all," Pedraan said.

"Indeed, but we must rejoice as we ride," Caan said. "We have thousands of civilians ahead, including women and children, and we need to get them over the Kalamin."

The mention of the river brought the image of the great beast in the Barunaan to Benjiah's mind. "How flooded is the Kalamin?"

"It is more flooded than anyone has ever seen it. The waters are very broad."

"How are we to cross?" Gilion asked.

"Merias ordered the assembly of all the fishing boats and other vessels along the river and on the Kellisor Sea," the young officer replied. "They are ready, but even so, it will probably take a few trips to get everyone across."

"Then we should not delay."

Benjiah looked back at Elnin Wood. A small gathering of Great Bear, including Sarneth, the elders of Taralin, and the greying Great Bear from Elnin consulted with each other.

"I wonder what they're discussing?" Benjiah asked.

Pedraal shrugged. "Their next move? The movements of the enemy? The results of any engagements in the wood, perhaps?"

"The clan of Elnin protected us when we approached their border and while we were within their world, but will they come out and come with us?" Benjiah asked.

"I don't know," Caan answered.

As they watched the cluster of Great Bear, the rear of the column passed. "There is no need for all of us to remain here," Caan said. "The rest of you should ride on. I will wait for word from the elders of the clan of Elnin."

"I will wait with you," Benjiah said.

Pedraal reached out to him. "Ride with us. We're going to greet the combined armies of Enthanin."

"I know," Benjiah said to his uncles. "But my role as Allfather's prophet, which took me to the draal of the Taralin clan, is more important now than my role as heir to the throne of Enthanin."

Benjiah saw the eyes of the young officer of Amaan Sul grow wide at the mention of being a prophet of Allfather, but he continued anyway. "I'll catch up to you as I may. For now, I will stay with Caan."

Pedraal and Pedraan didn't argue, and soon they were riding north with the men from Amaan Sul, and Benjiah was left behind with Caan.

"It doesn't seem to be easy," Caan said after a moment.

"What doesn't?"

"Being a prophet of Allfather."

"No." Benjiah laughed, though not because he thought it was funny. "It isn't."

"Especially when you have to remind those who used to be your authority."

"Then, and all the rest of the time too," Benjiah answered.

Sarneth began to walk their way. Caan greeted him. "Sarneth, what news?"

"Malek's hosts have been slowed in the southern reaches of Elnin by the efforts of the clan. Elnindraal has been evacuated, and the matriarchs and those too old or too young to fight have headed east toward Lindan."

"And the warriors of Elnin? Are they still engaged?"

"Most are not, and they have assembled just a few hours south, in the wood." Sarneth looked from Caan to Benjiah. "They have not decided whether to abandon Elnin, and some of the elders have asked to meet you, Benjiah."

"Me?"

"You. Will you come?"

"Of course."

"Caan, if you'd wait here."

"I will."

Sarneth turned and started back toward Elnin. Benjiah turned to Caan, who didn't let him say a word. "Go, it's why you stayed behind, is it not?"

Benjiah nodded. "Yes, it is."

He turned and set out after Sarneth, taking a deep breath.

Of the cluster of Great Bear waiting for him by the edge of Elnin Wood, he recognized only four: Sarneth, Elmaaneth, Kerentol, and the tall, grey one that was called Turgan. As they approached, he stayed close to Sarneth's side and waited silently to see why he'd been summoned.

"This is the boy?" Turgan asked, looking at Sarneth and the elders from Taralindraal.

"This is he."

Turgan looked down at him, his deep dark eyes as hard for Benjiah to read as any other Great Bear's. Turgan appeared neither suspicious nor dubious, simply serious. He was being examined.

"You went with Sarneth to Taralindraal?"

"I did."

"You appeared before the elders of the draal?"

"I did."

"You gave the prophecy of the four peoples?"

"I did," Benjiah answered again, looking at the three Great Bear he'd been traveling with. How much did Turgan know of him already?

"You believe that part of the fulfillment of this prophecy is the union of the Great Bear and men?"

"I do."

"And the third and fourth peoples?"

"The dragons, perhaps, are the third. They've already joined us, or at least some of them have."

"That's three."

"I know, the fourth people—well, I don't understand that part yet."

"I understand. We will confer," Turgan said, and he and the rest of the Great Bear, which Benjiah took to be elders of Elnindraal, moved back toward the trees.

Sarneth turned to Benjiah. "This may take a little while. Return to Caan and await word from us on the decision of the draal."

"Will they come, Sarneth?"

"I don't know."

"Surely they must. They've engaged the enemy in Elnin Wood. They can see the danger to us all. They have to come."

"No clan has to do anything because you or I say so. Your prophecy was not a direct command from Allfather for the clan of Elnin to march to war. Nevertheless, Turgan is a warrior, and if he has his way, I suspect they will come. For now, though, go back to Caan and wait."

Benjiah did, but any hope Benjiah had for a quick decision slipped away as the moments became an hour, and then two. Then he saw Turgan come out of the wood and speak for a moment with Sarneth and the others. He tensed as the small group separated, and his spirits fell as Turgan turned away and disappeared back inside the wood.

"It can't be," Benjiah whispered softly as Sarneth and the others started back toward them. "They have to come."

"Things are not always what we'd hope, Benjiah," Caan answered. "But in the end, we do not look to the Great Bear for our deliverance, nor even to the dragons. It is Allfather who will save us from Malek. He will deliver us, or we will not survive."

Sarneth and the others approached. Caan and Benjiah waited for Sarneth to break the news.

"It has been decided," Sarneth said. "The clan of Elnin will join us."

"They will?" Benjiah answered, puzzled.

"Yes, Turgan and the others have gone to muster the clan. They will come along behind us. They should catch up to us by tomorrow night. Even with their casualties, Turgan thinks they'll be able to bring twenty-five hundred Great Bear with them."

"Twenty-five hundred!"

"Yes," Sarneth replied.

"With twenty-five hundred more Great Bear and twenty thousand Enthanim," Caan said, "we're becoming an army."

Rulalin squatted by the tower, looking west over the wide, flooded waters of the Barunaan. The other captains of the Nolthanim were gathered near the tower door behind him. He was not exactly comfortable to be here, however, and he hoped that by standing aside he might hide his uneasiness. The last thing he wanted them to see in him was fear.

Nothing had gone as planned. Progress to the tower was slow, in part because a messenger from Cheimontyr brought word of a potential engagement south of Elnin, and Farimaal had to dispatch orders. More troublesome was the scene that had greeted them when the tower first came into view of a dragon standing on the gyre.

Rulalin knew that no one, not even Farimaal, expected this. The dragon towers were abandoned by the dragons at the end of the Second Age. The Grendolai had been created precisely to render them unusable for the dragons. To see the great golden form sitting there was more than a little bit disconcerting.

His presence delayed their approach to the tower. They didn't wish to ride up with a dragon sitting on top of it. Only when the dragon went out one morning and did not return did they dare come near. Farimaal, who wore his armor and helmet, approached the great iron door at the bottom of the tower and entered, though Rulalin couldn't imagine ascending those stairs now. It was one thing to go up and possibly face a Grendolai. Now, who knew what might be there? A Grendolai or a sleeping dragon or anything else, for all Rulalin could guess.

Rulalin and the others didn't have to wait long. The sound of footsteps on the stone stairs echoed inside the tower, and Rulalin returned to the group as Farimaal emerged from the dark interior into the daylight. He reached up and pulled off his helmet, and Rulalin could see something like anger in his normally impassive face.

"The Grendolai is dead."

10

THIS FAR AND NO FARTHER

BENJIAH LOOKED OUT OVER the Kalamin River. It was as flooded as the Barunaan. There were hundreds and hundreds of boats moored along the banks as far as the eye could see. Some were almost too small to be considered boats, small skiffs that might hold two or three slight people, but most were larger, vessels for anywhere from five to twenty-five people. A very few were larger still, small commercial ships no doubt used primarily on the Kellisor before being brought here.

He turned and looked back across the open plains of Suthanin. It was the twenty-eighth day of Winter Wane. It had taken three weeks to reach this place from the northern border of Elnin, a seemingly endless succession of almost identical days, and though they had managed to move a little faster above the Barunaan than they had below, it was still no less than a miracle that they were here at all.

Three times they skirmished with the enemy, but every instance had seemed but a test, for the enemy would approach in varying formations, never with as large a number as they'd brought forward beside the Barunaan. And, each time, after the two armies clashed, the enemy would quickly disengage and withdraw.

A few days ago, after the third of these small battles, the captains had met to discuss what was happening.

"I don't understand what the enemy is doing," Gilion said, expressing the frustration growing in many of them. "It is as though he intends to annoy us more than to fight us."

"Perhaps he does," Brenim replied.

"But why does he toy with battle?" Talis Fein asked. "Why do they not come upon us in all their strength?"

"It would be hard for them to get their whole host in place for battle, if their column is even remotely spread out as ours is," Caan said. "By the time the rear had come forward, we would be out of reach, unless they intended to charge across open leagues of ground to catch us. Perhaps the difficulty of engaging a moving target, even one as slow as we are, holds back his hand."

"I have wondered," Sarneth said, "if these small skirmishes have been but a formality."

"Yes," Turgan added. "It seems as if he isn't fighting us so much as herding us, prodding us to keep us moving."

"But why?" Corlas Valon asked. "We're headed this way anyway."

"He didn't know we'd keep going north after Elnin," Benjiah said.

"Where else would we go?"

"We could have turned east, toward Kel Imlaris. We considered it at one point, didn't we?"

"Sure, we could have gone east," Corlas said, "but why would they care?"

"Perhaps because there is a swollen river between us and Amaan Sul, and nothing like it between us and Kel Imlaris," Sarneth said.

"So?" Mindarin said as silence fell on most of the others. "There are boats waiting for us. We won't be trapped."

"No," Caan said, "but they don't know that. They don't know that Captain Merias has already assembled a fleet for evacuation."

"Sounds like it will be needed," Merias said.

"You may have saved all our lives," Caan added.

"Let's not rejoice too quickly," Benjiah said. "Remember the creature in the Barunaan? If the plan is not to cut us off, but to pin us down against him, getting across the Kalamin may be a difficult challenge, if not impossible. We should make all haste to get across."

That was three days ago, and now they were here. They arrived in late morning, and preparations were underway to cross. Much to Benjiah's relief and to everyone else's, there had as yet been no sign of the creature from the Barunaan.

Pedraal walked up beside him. When Pedraan did not also come up after a few moments, Benjiah looked around in surprise, wondering why his uncles, so rarely apart, were not together. "Where's Pedraan?"

"He's talking to Caan."

"Oh," Benjiah said, understanding that the subject of that discussion was not something Pedraal was going to divulge.

"I haven't had any luck locating the beast from the Barunaan," Benjiah said, changing the subject. "I've tried the last two days at dusk, but I've not found him."

"Maybe that's good news."

"I doubt it."

"So tell me," Pedraal said, looking bashful as he formulated what he'd say next. "How does it work?"

"How does what work?"

"Seeing through the eyes of the windhovers."

"I don't know that I could explain it."

"Well, not actually how it's possible, but what happens. Like, are you along for the ride, wherever they're already going? Can you give them directions, like turn left or turn right, or go higher, or whatever? Do they talk back?"

"Well, they don't talk, at least not in any language I understand. Somehow, they understand what I'm thinking, and they will change their direction when I ask, though I can only see what is visible to them. What I see, when I'm able to connect with them, all depends on where they are and which windhovers I contact."

Pedraal nodded. "It must be strange."

"Very." Benjiah laughed.

They stood quietly together for a few moments. "What we need," Benjiah said, "is the dragons to return. It's been a couple days since I've seen them, and they might know where the beast from the river is. Maybe now that we're all here, they'll show up again."

"Maybe they will. They seem to see a lot more than you'd think they could."

"Yes," Benjiah said, looking up at the dark clouds, "that's what I'm counting on."

Before long, Benjiah turned from the river. "Well, I don't know why we're waiting. We should be loading these boats and getting underway."

"Do you want to go look for the others?"

"Yes, I don't understand the delay."

As they started back across the field, Benjiah looked up and grabbed Pedraal's sleeve. "Yes," he said, excited. "They're here. Let's go find out what they've seen."

Benjiah and Pedraal were not the only ones headed over to see Eliandir and Dravendir. The other captains abandoned their various activities to greet the dragons. Soon they set down, and Benjiah ran right up to them. Though he was the youngest, he had realized some time ago that he was far and away the most comfortable of them all before the dragons. What's more, whether because he had summoned them to the dragon tower or because he bore Valzaan's staff, the dragons seemed to look to him more than even to Caan or Sarneth as their liaison with the army.

"Welcome, Eliandir and Dravendir," Benjiah said. "What news do you bring?"

"Only this advice: If you are hoping to cross the Kalamin, you must do so at once. Danger approaches from the west as well as from the south."

Benjiah's heart sank. "It is as I have feared. Where is the creature?"

"He has spent the last two days in the Kellisor Sea, destroying homes near its flooded shores and causing a lot of damage to the town near the mouth of Barunaan."

"Is it in the Kalamin now?"

"That was the direction he was headed in."

"How long do you think we have?"

"We don't know."

Benjiah turned to Caan and the others. "We can't delay. The crossing must begin now. They mean to trap us here between the river and Malek's hosts, and we must get across while we still can."

"Everything's ready," Merias said. "We can start right away, though it will take two or three trips at least to get us all over."

"Then by all means, let's get going," Benjiah said. He turned to Eliandir. "Eliandir, what I must ask of you is very dangerous. I know that you have already lost one of your brothers to the creature from the sea, but we need you and Dravendir to do what you can to slow that beast down. Will the two of you fly back along the Kalamin and try to buy us enough time to get across?"

"Hold on," Corlas interjected. "What if Malek's army reaches us while they're away? They did say danger was approaching from two directions. We don't even know for sure that this thing is on his way here. We can't afford to leave ourselves unprotected."

"The dragons are not our only protection," Benjiah said tersely, "but the river is our only escape. If Malek's army comes, some of us can fight while the others flee. If the creature comes, what will we do then?"

He turned back to Eliandir. "Will you go?"

The red dragon rose to his full height. "We will do what we can. Cross the river now, or you will not cross it at all."

Mindarin and Aelwyn were standing inside one of the midsized boats with about ten more women from Shalin Bel. "I'm not happy about this," Mindarin was saying to Benjiah's uncles.

"We realize that," Pedraal said dryly, "but just so long as you do what Caan has ordered, that's all right."

"It isn't all right, it's degrading."

"How is it degrading?" Pedraan asked, incredulous.

"Shipping us all off first, as though we were children in need of protection," Mindarin continued. "We came along to aid the army, and half the time we get sent on ahead to be kept safe, like we're no different from the elderly and infirm of Cimaris Rul. It isn't fair."

"It's practical," Pedraal said calmly. "There are soldiers headed over in this wave of ships too, Mindarin, not just women. The point is that if we are attacked, we're all going to need to fight. It doesn't make sense to send soldiers over first and leave you to face the action should trouble come.

"In fact," he continued, "when you realize that all the Great Bear are staying behind until the last wave of ships, then you'll see that all of us, men and women, are being sent over first. I'm not insulted. It makes sense."

"Some of these boats look a little small for the Great Bear," Aelwyn said. "Will they be all right?"

"They're not going in the boats," Benjiah replied.

"They're not?"

"No, they're waiting until the last wave of ships is ready, and they're going to swim across with them."

Aelwyn looked over her shoulder at the distance from this shore to that one, which was almost out of sight.

Mindarin stood in the boat with her arms crossed, pouting. Pedraal and Pedraan didn't say any more, as the boat was ready to launch. "We'll see you on the other side," Aelwyn called as it was pushed off from shore.

"We'll see you there."

All the boats and ships were soon loaded to capacity and launched. Some moved relatively quickly, others very slowly, but it was still an impressive sight to see the broad surface of the Kalamin covered with them in both directions. Benjiah had seen some of them returning earlier, having taken the citizens of Cimaris Rul over, but that was nothing compared to what he saw now.

After all the hurry up to load and launch the boats, watching them make their slow progress across the river was almost excruciating. Time seemed to slow, as there was nothing to do but watch the river and wait.

Before long, Benjiah could see returning ships passing those that had yet to reach the far shore. It must have been confusing, or at least frustrating, to make their way back through that great fleet of moving vessels, but he was glad they weren't waiting for the slower craft to arrive before starting back.

Hundreds of boats returned and were reloaded. The gathering on the near shore began to dwindle, and as more and more boats staggered in and headed back, hope began to rise in Benjiah. He looked west along the river and saw only the waters of the Kalamin extending out of sight. He looked south across the fields and saw only the dark clouds and soaked plains. *They don't know we have the boats. They think we're trapped. They think they have time.*

As the last of the second wave of ships was being loaded, Benjiah didn't look at his uncles. He knew without needing to be told that they wanted him on one of these. He also knew that they knew he wasn't getting on one of these boats, not until everyone else was safely aboard. He looked at the men who remained. There were perhaps three or four thousand, and they would be accommodated easily by the next wave. In fact, with the Great Bear swimming and only the men to be ferried over, the fastest of the ships could retrieve the few who remained.

When the last of the second wave was safely away, he turned to his uncles. "It looks like we might make it across after all."

"Yes," Pedraal said, surveying the scant assembly of soldiers and Great Bear on this side of the river. "Now would be a most inopportune time to be attacked."

"Brother," Pedraan said. Hearing the tone in his voice, both Pedraal and Benjiah turned to him. "Is it me, or is it getting darker?"

All three looked upward, and though Benjiah didn't notice anything at first, it became increasingly clear that Pedraan was right. The dark clouds were darkening. It was only midafternoon, but shadows crept over the plains and river, covering the waiting ranks and fleeing boats.

"Do you see anything to the south?" Pedraal said after a moment.

"No," Benjiah answered. "Not yet, anyway."

"And west?"

Benjiah looked toward the Kellisor Sea. At first he thought that these skies, too, were as they had been just moments ago, but then he saw two flashes in the clouds, and a sparkle caught his eye. He continued to watch, and the flashes appeared again. "Did you two see that?"

"Yes."

"It's Eliandir and Dravendir. The beast from the sea is coming."

"Should we get Caan?"

Benjiah sighed. "We can tell him, but there's nothing we can do until the ships return. Just pray the dragons can slow him down."

The growing dark had not gone unobserved by the rest of the men. Benjiah scanned the assembly, and he could see the signs of panic. He looked back over the river, and to his relief, he saw the fastest of the ships beginning the return trek.

Just then, a soldier spotted the dragons. A shout and a hand pointing west spread the alarm, and soon all eyes turned. Two easily distinguishable golden forms could be seen racing back and forth and swooping down over the river, emitting bursts of flame as they dove before rising quickly into the sky.

Benjiah turned back to the river, just in time to see a handful of boats reaching the shore about twenty or thirty spans from where he was standing. He raised his arms with Valzaan's staff in his right hand and cried out above the crowd, his voice calm and loud over the din. "We must load and go, now! While the dragons slow the beast, we must go!"

"We can't," Caan called out. "Look!"

The men turned southward. While they had been looking to the river, where the dragons were occupied with the creature and where the boats that were their hope approached, the battle line of a vast army had appeared in the distance. When Benjiah saw it, he shuddered. Even from so far away, he could see that it seemed to have no beginning or end. He had never seen the enemy arrayed in such numbers as this. With but a few thousand men and the Great Bear, the hosts of Malek would swallow them up.

"We cannot wait here," Benjiah called out to Caan, walking toward him. "We must flee now."

"If we don't fight, we will be cut down as we board. At least if we face them we can diminish their number before we die."

"It is futile. We can't allow our men and the Great Bear to be slaughtered like this."

"What choice do we have?"

"Go!" Benjiah said adamantly. "Send the Great Bear immediately. Tell them to start swimming. Load the boats as they come; get everyone across that you can. Every man lost diminishes us far more than we will diminish them."

"Benjiah," Caan said, resignation in his eyes, "a good soldier knows when he's beaten."

"You're not beaten. I'll hold them back."

"You'll what?" Pedraan exclaimed.

"You're coming with us, right now!" Pedraal said, gripping Benjiah's arm.

"I'm not."

"Get in the boat," Pedraal said, almost angrily, starting to pull Benjiah against his will toward the nearest boat.

With all his might, Benjiah ripped free of Pedraal's hand and faced his uncle. "I'm not going. You're going. Allfather's strength is the only thing that can save us now. His power alone can win this day. Don't you see that?"

Pedraal didn't answer, and Benjiah swung around to face the others. "You all need to go, now. The enemy has already cut the distance between us in half. I don't know how long I'll be able to delay them, or how long Eliandir and Dravendir will slow the creature in the river. You must go *now.*"

After a short silence, Caan began barking orders. "To the boats. Fill no boat more than it can handle. It will do us no good if you escape the enemy but are swamped on the way over. Great Bear, help us launch as many as you can, if you will, then set out for the other shore."

The men scrambled to get into the boats that continued to arrive. Already, a pair of Great Bear were pushing back out onto the water a small boat bearing five men, who looked both frightened and relieved at the same time. Benjiah turned to go, and Pedraal took his arm again. As Benjiah turned, Pedraal preempted him.

"What will you do?"

"I don't know."

"What will we tell your mother?"

"Tell her I was faithful to my calling."

"Benjiah?..."

"I have to go. If I survive, I will swim the river."

"It's too wide."

"I'm young." Benjiah smiled. "Don't worry about the river, that's not the dangerous thing." Benjiah slipped Suruna and his quiver off his shoulder and held them out. "Take these. They can't help me today."

Pedraal took them in his hand.

"Look after them?"

"I will." Pedraal released him. "Allfather go with you."

Benjiah walked toward the approaching army.

Benjiah was vaguely aware that boats continued to land and were boarded. He was more intensely aware of the vast army and, more specifically, of two leading figures now distinguishable from the rest. He had seen them both before, but the one he had not seen since Zul Arnoth.

The first was Cheimontyr. His giant frame, even at a distance, was unmistakable, as was the hammer he carried. As Benjiah watched his enormous strides, he shuddered as he recalled seeing this terrible face beyond the broken walls of Zul Arnoth.

He could also see, above the giant, a swirling vortex of dark clouds. Whether it was descending from the sky toward Cheimontyr or emanating from the giant, he couldn't tell. Lightning rippled back and forth through the dark clouds and vortex with remarkable brilliance. It was almost as if Cheimontyr himself was charging the sky.

Several spans away from Cheimontyr rode a figure on horseback. It was the man he'd seen inside the walls of Zul Arnoth, unmoved and apparently unafraid even when Valzaan threw the rest of the enemy into a panic. He was wearing the same bizarre suit of hide or armor that made him look like some strange breed of man and beast. Cheimontyr dwarfed him, but Benjiah found him just as chilling. The rage of the Vulsutyrim was something Benjiah understood, though he feared it, but the calm, emotionless presence of this man was to some extent more unsettling. How could any man have sat so unaffected in the middle of that chaos, with power beyond all human imagining wielded on every side? What must this man be that such a thing would not move him?

Beyond these two, the enemy came more clearly into view. To Benjiah's right, great hosts of Black Wolves trotted in front of men on horseback, ostensibly following the command of the man beside Cheimontyr. To the left were rank upon rank of Malekim, marching steadily onward. Between the men and Voiceless strode the giants, the center of the enemy line, some thirty or forty across, though how deep they went, Benjiah could not see.

He stole a glance at the men on the shore. Most of them were scrambling into boats as Great Bear lined up behind them, shoving the boats back out into the river. Some of the Great Bear were already in the water, helping to drag the slower vessels out from the shore. He felt suddenly alone.

But you are not alone. He heard the voice of his dreams and visions. A calm fell upon him as he turned back to face his enemy. Cheimontyr came to a stop, and so did the man on horseback, and a moment later, all that great number behind them halted as well.

Cheimontyr, who was perhaps thirty spans away, stepped forward, moving as one with the swirling clouds above him. "So, you have managed to slip away over the river," he said, and Benjiah heard anger and scorn ringing in his booming voice.

Benjiah said nothing. For a moment, neither did the giant, for just then his attention shifted west. Benjiah looked west too, and he could see the dragons were much closer, half as far as they had been when he last saw them. They still engaged the creature, who had risen out of the water, his great hands outstretched.

Good. If he's trying to attack the dragons, he isn't swimming.

"And you, boy," Cheimontyr said, and Benjiah turned back around. "Why have you not fled with them? Why do you stand before us? Have you come to die?"

"No, I have come with a message," Benjiah answered, and his voice was clear and calm. "This far you may come, and no farther, so says Allfather."

For an instant, Cheimontyr stared at him with both fury and amazement. Benjiah was aware that at some level he was himself amazed by the boldness of the words, but the rush of light and heat he'd felt when facing the Grendolai was returning. He felt composed, ready for whatever might come next from these dread captains of this mighty host.

Cheimontyr, if he thought about a verbal reply, decided against it. Rather, he took the great, shiny hammer and raised it high above his head, then slammed it down on the earth. Immediately, lightning gathered in balls above him in the clouds and began to drop like hailstones to the earth, scarring the sky with long angry slashes of light. They fell over the field, scorching the wet earth and sending up hissing bursts of steam.

Benjiah raised his arms, Valzaan's staff in his right hand. The lightning continued to fall, an intense display of light and heat, but none of it struck Benjiah, and even the bolts that landed disturbingly close did not harm him in any way.

After a few moments, the lightning stopped falling, and again he saw the giant's fury and amazement. There was such hatred in the Vulsutyrim's eyes that Benjiah believed it was directed as much at what Benjiah represented as at him. Benjiah defied Cheimontyr and his master by standing alone against them, and he had verbally challenged them in the name of Allfather. The latter as much as the former struck the chord of malice that now resonated in his enemy's heart.

There wasn't time to think upon it, though, for as soon as the explosion of lightning strikes ended, the armor-clad man turned to the forces behind them and cried out a command. Benjiah wasn't sure what he said, but the men on horseback charged forward as one, surging across the wet and smoldering turf. The Black Wolves ran too, howling their battle cry.

Benjiah felt the surge of light and heat intensify. Pointing with his open hand at the earth on one side of him and with the staff at the earth on the other side, he saw the impossible happen. Two huge balls of earth were ripped from the ground and, with a single motion of his hands, hurtled at great speed across the intervening distance. Both struck the charging lines and toppled wolves and men. Benjiah repeated the motion faster and faster, and more of the earth was churned free and thrown.

This dazed and slowed the charge. Benjiah, grasping the staff with both hands, turned sideways and lowered the staff over the earth, swinging it forward like an oar in the sea, displacing the water. The ground began to surge forward like a great wave of mud and grass, rising as it went, until it was as tall as a man. The horse of the man in the strange armor managed somehow to keep its feet, rushing up and then down the wave, but Cheimontyr, caught off balance, lost his footing and fell. He landed with a thud. All along the charging line, riders were unhorsed and wolves were flung backward through the air.

For a single instant, Benjiah observed the havoc Allfather had created through him. He looked down at his hand and gasped, seeing that it was semitransparent and shining. The light was not just a feeling, he realized; it was flowing through him.

He looked back up at his enemy, which was reforming, and then focused on the ground between them. The closest of his foes was only perhaps twenty spans away and starting to come forward again. He took the staff in both hands again and in a swift motion raised it over his head.

The results were immediate and dramatic. A long ridge of earth, as far as he could see in either direction, shot up out of the ground and rose until it was three or four spans high. It formed a wall of solid ground, maybe ten spans thick, blocking off his enemy from the river entirely. All of them—the giant, the man in his strange hides, the charging men and wolves—disappeared from view.

He held his hands high, and he could feel his body shuddering. He shut his eyes and saw immediately in his head an image from beyond the newly formed ridge. Cheimontyr was running at the ridge, raging, striking it again and again with the hammer, but to no effect. All of the enemy came forth, wielding angry fists and swords against the wall, all to no avail. Howls and snarls joined the curses as the din floated out over the battlefield.

The scene shifted. He saw the creature in the Kalamin River, still hounded by the dragons but no longer upright. Instead of trying to snare one of the dragons, he was now trying only to fend them off as he moved eastward down the river. Eliandir and Dravendir did their best to slow him down, but they had to stay at a considerable distance to avoid the great black hands that flashed through the air and could not do much more to halt his progress.

The scene shifted again. He saw the boats, all loaded with men, headed across the river. Great Bear dotted the water, swimming faster than Benjiah would have imagined. The southern shore was vacant now, and any ships moving that direction were being waved down and turned around.

He opened his eyes and looked again at the great wall he had raised from the ground. He was trembling, and sweat was pouring out of his body. He was incredibly aware of what was happening and could feel every shudder and every drop. *Hold on. Hold on. Hold on.* He whispered over and over inside his head.

The moments passed, and he lost track of time. The dark sky remained the same, obscuring any sense of the hour. How long had it been? Half an hour? An hour? More?

His eyes flickered shut and he directed his mind to the river. No more boats crossed the water. All had reached the far shore. Even the last of the Great Bear arrived and were walking, weary and soggy, out onto semidry land.

He opened his eyes again, groaning. *They've made it. They're safe.*

His arms began to buckle, and the staff suddenly dropped a few hands, until it was about even with his head. The wall of earth shuddered and dropped too, until it was only a couple of spans above the ground.

In this way, the Vulsutyrim were revealed again, their upper torsos, shoulders, and heads now visible above the wall. They cried out in surprise and excitement as Benjiah was exposed.

He groaned again, feeling the staff shaking in his exhausted hands. A crack like the sound of a mighty tree and all of its roots being ripped out of the earth echoed across the field. The giants covered their ears, and howls of pain rose to the sky as the wall of earth exploded in every direction before falling to the ground. Benjiah looked in shock and disbelief at Valzaan's staff, which had splintered into mere shards. Two small pieces remained in his hands.

He felt his legs buckle, knew that he was collapsing, and remembered no more.

11 HARAK ANDUNIN

A MAN ON HORSEBACK swept through the main gate that opened out onto the city from the palace grounds, thundering up the stone avenue that led to the courtyard beside the fountain. Wylla, who had been walking there with Kyril, watched the rider rein in his horse and wearily slide down out of the saddle. He wore the green and gold livery of Amaan Sul and looked vaguely familiar, but she did not know his name.

"Your Majesty?" the man said tentatively. "Captain Merias sends me with news from the south."

She looked closely at the man. His clothes were ragged and his hair unkempt. His face was worn and exhaustion shone in his eyes. All in all he was as bedraggled as any man she'd seen in recent memory. "How far have you come?"

"From five days south of the Kalamin."

Wylla nodded. "And when did you last sleep?"

"Two nights ago."

"And eat?"

The man looked bashful. "A little longer ago than that."

Wylla nodded again. "Kyril will take you inside to the kitchen. When you've eaten your fill and had a moment to gather yourself, one of the stewards will show you to my parlor. All right?"

The man stared, almost blankly. "You don't mind?"

Wylla smiled. "Whatever news you bring, the half hour it takes you to eat will not change it. I'll be waiting for you when you're ready."

The man nodded gratefully and turned to follow Kyril. They started away and Wylla watched them go. The news must be urgent, and she didn't want to wait. She sighed. Waiting seemed to be her lot in life these days. When the man and Kyril disappeared inside, she started toward the palace herself. At least she would have time to find Yorek.

She did find Yorek, napping peacefully in a highbacked chair in the Great Hall. The chair was turned toward the fireplace. He looked so contented that Wylla hated to wake him, but wake him she did. He stirred for a moment, but when he saw Wylla standing over him he smiled, stretched, and stood.

"Your Majesty," he said through a yawn.

"Sorry to disturb you, Yorek."

"Never mind that, I had a lovely nap. What can I do for you?"

"A messenger from the south has come."

"From Merias?"

"Yes."

"With what news?"

"I don't know," Wylla said, brushing a loose lock of hair out of her eyes. "I've sent him to get something to eat. He looked famished. He'll join us in my parlor when he's done."

Yorek nodded. "It seemed urgent?"

"Yes."

Yorek placed his hand gently on Wylla's shoulder. "Let me come. Whatever the news is, we'll receive it together."

"Thank you, Yorek," Wylla answered. "I'm so glad you're here."

"There isn't any other place I'd rather be."

Though they did not wait in the parlor long, the delay was agonizing to Wylla. A myriad of scenarios, none of them pleasant, passed through her head. None of them were new, either. She'd imagined them a thousand times since Merias took the army across the Kalamin. She knew it was silly to worry about what might have happened when any moment she would know for sure, but it was hard not to. She had a city to govern, a people to protect, and a son somewhere out there in this world of rain and storm that Kirthanin had become.

At last a knock on the door drove the doubts and fears aside, and she stopped pacing the rug and sat down. "Ready?" Yorek asked.

She nodded.

"Come in," Yorek called.

The messenger, with his hair combed and a new cloak over his shoulders, walked hesitantly into the parlor. He looked around at the furniture and wall hangings and polished wooden table, and then at the queen. His eyes were round with wonder.

"You have something to tell me?" Wylla gently prompted him.

"Ah, yes, Your Majesty," he said, regaining his composure. "I do."

Wylla waited a moment, fearing she'd have to urge him to go on.

"Well," the man began, "our scouts north of Elnin Wood made contact several weeks ago with a large group of people who claimed to have come from Cimaris Rul, all the way north through Elnin. In fact, they claimed to be the entire city!"

Wylla looked at the man in disbelief. Of all the farfetched scenarios she imagined, this had never crossed her mind. "The whole city of Cimaris Rul?"

"Yes, Your Majesty. They said they'd fled their city because the sea was attacking it from the south and Malek was riding upon them from the north."

"The sea was attacking them?"

"Yes. They explained that the Southern Ocean had risen so high that it assaulted their walls. They fled the city before they could be trapped within by the enemy or flooded by the sea."

The man paused as though waiting for questions. "Go on," Wylla said.

"Well, shortly after the people from Cimaris Rul emerged from the wood, soldiers began to emerge too, except these soldiers were from all over Kirthanin. There were soldiers from Cimaris Rul, Shalin Bel, and even Fel Edorath."

Wylla's pulse quickened. This meant that at least some of those who had fled Werthanin were still alive. The man continued.

"In addition to the men, thousands of Great Bear came out of the wood too, and we all started the march toward the Kalamin River."

"Thousands of Great Bear?" Yorek asked, incredulous. It was his turn to look startled, and even Wylla turned to look at him. She'd rarely seen him show surprise before.

"Yes, and from what I've been told, they are Great Bear from two different places, from Elnin, of course, but also from Taralin Forest."

"And they're marching with the armies of Kirthanin?"

"Yes," the messenger said.

"Thanks be to Allfather," Yorek said, clasping his hands together. "That is good news indeed, messenger."

The man suddenly beamed. His smile broke across his face like the rising sun. He nodded.

"Tell me," Wylla said, "was there word of my brothers or son from any in the army that emerged from Elnin Wood?"

The smile slipped off his face, and the man struck himself in the forehead with his fist. "I'm sorry, Your Majesty, it completely slipped my mind when we started talking about the Great Bear, but I meant to tell you that your brothers and your son were all with the army that came out of the woods."

"And they are well?"

"Yes, Your Majesty. They were when I left them."

An enormous relief washed over Wylla. "I had hoped that this was part of your message," she said at last, looking at Yorek, "but I almost couldn't bring myself to ask for fear that it was not. Where is the army now?" Wylla asked, turning back to the messenger.

"By now, Your Majesty, they may have reached the Kalamin. They may have even crossed it. I was sent ahead to prepare you for the fact that they are coming."

"For this I thank you," Wylla replied, standing. "The steward who showed you in will take you to a room. Rest well, knowing your task is complete."

"Thank you, Your Majesty," the man said, and he turned to go.

"Messenger?" Wylla called out after him. The man stopped and turned around. "What is your name?"

"My name is Corbin, Your Majesty."

"Thank you, Corbin."

"You're welcome, Your Majesty."

The man slipped out, and Wylla turned to Yorek. "Refugees from Cimaris Rul and a portion of four armies. Where are we going to put them?"

"We will put them where we can," Yorek replied. "At least we know that Benjiah is safe."

"Yes," Wylla smiled. "At least Benjiah is safe."

Aljeron looked up again at Harak Andunin rising in the distance. They were at least a day away, but having first seen the peak and realized what it was almost two weeks ago, he now felt very close indeed.

It was the twenty-ninth day of Winter Wane, and though spring was by the reckoning of the calendar but two days away, the mounds of snow that continued to hamper them said otherwise. For four days now they had been moving south from the Great Northern Sea, and most of the way he grumbled internally over the return to what was more like plowing than riding.

They had kept to the shore of the Great Northern Sea as long as they could. For almost two weeks they rode in sight of the Tajira Mountains, and for more than half that time they kept to the shore. They delayed their turn south as long as they could, but the day came when it could be delayed no longer, and with reluctance they followed Koshti as he leapt up onto the deep snowdrifts.

Harak Andunin was aptly named, for the mountain was indeed spearlike, at least as far as mountains go. The base was unremarkable, no thicker than others in the range and less thick than some, but the peak was tall and narrow, so much so that the pinnacle was obscured from view, wrapped in the dark clouds that had been their constant companions these many months.

The ease with which Harak Andunin was distinguishable from the rest was a relief. Even after successfully crossing the high plateau and the Simmok River, even as the prospect of reaching the Tajira Mountains became less fantastical, at times Aljeron had feared that it would all be to no avail. He dreamed of arriving at the mountains and examining peak after peak, trying in vain to identify Harak Andunin. In the dream, he could not discover the mountain he sought until he climbed every one.

Now he knew this would not be necessary. They could see well enough from the ground which mountain had been named after Ruun Harak, Andunin's legendary spear. That mountain was the only one they were going to have to climb.

Suddenly, Koshti bolted out of sight past an evergreen tree with low-lying branches. They had been riding for a few days now in a lightly wooded area of unfamiliar fir trees. Koshti ran into the midst of these, and Aljeron could hear a growl, a tousle of some sort, and then a hobbled deer broke out of the thicket with blood on his leg. How he'd gotten free, Aljeron could not guess, for Koshti rarely let go of his prey once he had it in his jaws.

Koshti also emerged from the thicket, and this time the deer did not get away. The tiger leapt upon the deer, toppling him sideways into the snow, and swiftly broke the animal's neck in his powerful jaws. Just like that the fight was over, and Koshti sat down beside the dead deer, blood draining into the white snow out of the wounds.

"Well done," Aljeron said to Koshti as he dropped from his saddle and waded over to his battle brother. "Saegan, do you want to get to work skinning this deer?"

"Gladly," Saegan replied, and in a matter of moments, he was underway.

"I guess we're staying here tonight?" Evrim asked.

"It's as good a spot as any and better than most, now that dinner's been delivered," Aljeron answered, smiling.

He looked down at Koshti, who lay awkwardly on his side. "What's the matter, Koshti?" Aljeron asked, suddenly worried.

He started to examine the tiger, and after a few moments found a small puncture wound on his haunch. It was bleeding steadily, soaking the fur with blood. "He's hurt," Aljeron said, almost in disbelief. He couldn't remember the last time Koshti had been injured.

"It happened in the initial encounter," Evrim said, pointing to a spoor of blood that followed the pawprints of the tiger out of the trees.

"I wonder what happened," Aljeron said, looking at the trees with suspicion. "The deer didn't do it. It's a doe without antlers."

"Maybe a branch?" Evrim suggested, wading through the snow toward the place where Koshti had disappeared. "I'll check it out."

"I'm not sure you should go there alone," Aljeron began, but Evrim passed through the dense branches out of view.

A moment later Evrim called out, "It was a broken branch. There's a mean-looking one jutting up just a little bit through the surface of the snow. It was probably hidden from view when Koshti pounced on the deer, but it must have jabbed him when he landed."

"That's why you let go," Aljeron whispered as he took a strip of cloth out of his pack and began to bind the tiger's wound.

Evrim reappeared. "Will he be all right?"

"I think so," Aljeron replied. "He's a tough old tiger."

"A little deer meat should cheer him up," Saegan said, tossing a hunk of raw deer over to the tiger. Koshti batted the meat closer to his head with his paw and took the whole thing into his mouth.

"A little deer meat will cheer me up," Evrim said as he watched the tiger devour his supper. "A lot of deer meat will cheer me up even more."

"Well," Saegan said as he kept working. "How about starting on a fire then? It will take you as long to clear a space and gather some dry wood as it'll take me to get this deer ready. Go on and get started."

It did in fact take Evrim and Aljeron longer to get a reasonable fire going than it took Saegan to prepare the deer, so they were all good and ready for dinner by the time it was finally done and the last light of evening slipped from the western sky. They nestled in under one of the fir trees with higher branches, and all four of the men, Koshti, and Erigan ate every last bite of fresh meat. It was the best meal they had shared together in ages.

Afterward, they sat around the fire and chatted freely, though Synoki was quiet and withdrawn, as was his way since Cinjan's death. Evrim had said to Aljeron that their lame companion's sulkiness was evidence of his guilt, for if he really was the innocent merchant and friend he claimed to be, wouldn't he work harder to get into their good graces?

Aljeron and Saegan shared Evrim's suspicions but did not judge his silence so severely. They remembered Synoki as a quiet and withdrawn man seventeen years ago, and in those days he aided them and fought for them. Aljeron believed that Synoki's sullen demeanor might well be the consequence of simply having been so close to death and knowing that he was still on thin ice with his companions. Whatever the reason, the three had grown used to Synoki's general silence.

As they were chatting, a large cascade of snow came tumbling down out of the fir tree and landed squarely on Aljeron's head. It covered him with snow and left both Saegan and Evrim laughing hysterically as Aljeron, startled and sputtering, tried to stand and brush the snow off.

"You two think this is pretty funny," Aljeron said as he shook snow from his hair. "I should dump a load of snow on you and see how you like it."

"I wouldn't like it one bit," Evrim said, regaining his composure. "It looks really cold and uncomfortable."

"It is," Aljeron grumbled, taking his seat again. "It's hard to believe spring is only two days away when a great big avalanche falls on your head."

"Well, there should be some comfort in that," Evrim said. "Before you know it, it'll be raining all the time again instead of snowing all the time."

"That's not really very funny," Aljeron said, thinking about all the days they'd spent in the rain.

"I'm not really laughing," Evrim replied.

"Well," Saegan said, "if it does start to rain again, maybe the water will wash this snow away. I don't want to be drenched all the time again, but I wouldn't mind not having to forge my way forward through half a span of snow everywhere I go."

"I suppose that is some consolation," Aljeron begrudgingly conceded.

"Do you think we'll reach Harak Andunin tomorrow?" Saegan asked.

"Maybe."

"We've spent so much time just trying to get here," Saegan continued, "that we haven't discussed what we'll do next."

Aljeron shrugged. "I guess that depends on what we find."

"If we find nothing?" Saegan asked.

"Let's wait and see."

"I'm not saying we'll find nothing, but what would we do then?"

"We'd head south again, to Enthanin I guess." This was Aljeron's assumption, though they'd never contemplated the possibility of failure so explicitly. As they had struggled through the various obstacles in Nolthanin, they came to an unspoken agreement not to talk about anything beyond reaching Harak Andunin. Now that the mountain was all but reached, they could give voice to fears previously only imagined.

"We will have to cross the Zaros Mountains if we go to Enthanin," Erigan said.

"That's better than going all the way west to the Kiruan River, which might be almost as hard to cross with all the precipitation we've had," Saegan replied.

"I don't think we should worry about that now. We still have to get to the mountain and then scale it. For now, let's just hope somebody's home when we get there."

The first thing Aljeron saw when his eyes adjusted to the early morning light was a dark bird soaring high above. Aljeron sat up quickly, alarmed. He didn't know if red ravens lived in this part of Nolthanin, but he wanted to be prepared just in case.

As he looked closer, he realized it was some sort of falcon, not a Red Raven. In fact, though it flew too high for Aljeron to be sure, he thought it might be a King Falcon. He was surprised to see one in Nolthanin, though he didn't know why. He'd never heard anyone say King Falcons didn't fly in Nolthanin, but he always pictured the animal life of Nolthanin as fierce and predatory, like the Red Ravens and the Snow Serpent.

Whatever kind of falcon it was, it quickly passed out of sight. Aljeron rubbed his eyes and then started to wake the others. Before long, the camp was packed up and his companions were ready to head out. As Aljeron prepared to mount his horse, Saegan tapped him on the shoulder and whispered, "Look."

Aljeron looked in the direction he was pointing and didn't see anything but a cluster of fir trees about twenty spans away. Then he realized that he should be seeing something, because that was where Saegan had dumped the deer carcass the day before. He looked closer. A small white heap, slightly different from the white around it, lay just to the side of the trees.

"My," Aljeron said when he realized what he was seeing. "I guess your idea about not leaving the deer carcass in the camp was a good one."

"Yes, I'd say that the bones have been picked just about as clean as they could be picked."

"All this way with rarely a sight of any living thing, but something got to that deer."

"Or a whole host of somethings," Saegan said. "Under cover of darkness, maybe things came scurrying from all over to get a bite."

Aljeron nodded. He thought of the bird. He hadn't awakened to the sight of a soaring bird in months, and rarely had he seen birds at all since setting foot in Nolthanin. He doubted that the presence of the bird and the freshly devoured remains of the deer were a coincidence. Word must have gotten out that there was dinner to be had. He wondered if the falcon had come too late to have any, or if he was just setting out for home after eating his fill. Either way, he decided to take the appearance of the falcon on this, the last day of winter, as a good sign. Maybe spring really was coming after all.

They made good time except for a small delay caused by a narrow ravine. In ordinary weather their horses could have jumped it, but given the current icy conditions, that was quite impossible. The snow on the far side was just as high as the snow on this side, and the prospect of one of the horses failing to land a sure footing and slipping backward into the chasm was most unappealing. They followed it southward for about half an hour before they found a place where they could just step across and be on their way.

Despite the lost time, spirits rose as the mountain loomed before them. This was especially evident in Saegan, who must have thought all night about crossing the Zaros Mountains, because three and four times he mentioned plans and routes that would be most likely to get them safely through a pass, and so on. Then, about midday, he said to Aljeron, "If it's not too far out of the way, we could go to Tol Emuna, maybe. I'd like to see home again."

Aljeron nodded, knowing that Tol Emuna, in the far northeastern corner of Enthanin, was out of the way to everywhere but Tol Emuna. He said, "If it isn't too far out of the way, I'd like to go there. I've never seen Tol Emuna. Is it as strong as they say it is?"

"Stronger," Saegan smiled. "I don't know what 'they' say about it, but it is hard to comprehend the strength of the city without seeing it. The land surrounding Tol Emuna is arid and dry, almost a desert. The vegetation is tough and scraggly, like the land. Out of this hard, rough earth, a massive stone formation towers above the barren plain. It isn't formed perfectly like a quarter moon, but it curves inward like one, and Tol Emuna is built into the side of that formation, facing south. The northern side is protected by that great rock, and the city extends south from it. The place is surrounded by the strongest rock wall I've ever seen, except for maybe the wall of Nal Gildoroth. There is but one gate, and behind that gate on either side are great stones that can form a layer of solid stone across the gate as well. Since rainfall is so scarce, the city depends entirely upon an underground water supply, which is replenished annually by the spring rains. These are channeled by a myriad of secret ways into the great cistern under the city. In short, it would be a hard place to overcome by siege, because the water supply cannot be cut off, and it would be a hard place to take by force, because the walls are so strong and the land around it is so barren. Anyone who attacks the gates of Tol Emuna will pay a high price to get in."

Aljeron had heard descriptions of Tol Emuna and long ago fashioned an image of a wild and lonely city in an almost uninhabitable corner of Kirthanin. That image came to mind as Saegan talked, but to it was added the image of people walking about the city. The warmth and affection in Saegan's voice reminded Aljeron that certain men, women, and children called Tol Emuna home. "I would very much like to see it one day."

The reminiscent smile and tone disappeared from Saegan's voice. "Thinking of home makes me wonder what's going on, with the others and all."

Aljeron looked up into the dark sky. "Well, we don't know for sure, but I'd say the continued presence of these clouds is probably evidence that the Bringer of Storms is still alive and well. Whether his strength is weakening or the storm has served its purpose, I can't say. Like you, I worry for our army and friends. Did they make it to Cimaris Rul? Did they clash with Malek there? Did they have to flee by sea again? If so, where would they go? To try to sail northeast to Kel Imlaris at this time of year would be crazy. I can't imagine what plan they would have adopted if they had to leave Cimaris Rul, but if the Bringer of Storms still wields his power, it is hard to imagine that Cimaris Rul could hold out. "

"True," Saegan answered. "If any did survive and flee together, may they find a place as strong as Tol Emuna for their refuge."

As dusk set in, Aljeron called to the others. "I wanted to spend the night at the foot of the mountain, but I think we should look for a place to camp now. We'll be at the base by midmorning tomorrow at the latest."

The men agreed and quickly found shelter. They dismounted to prepare a fire for more of their fresh deer meat, then spread out to gather wood. A moment later, Evrim called the others to join him. "Look," he said. "Can you see anything out there, above those trees?" He was pointing at several trees, perhaps fifty spans away, closer to Harak Andunin.

Aljeron peered into the gloomy sky. He saw the slightest wisp of low-lying grey cloud above the trees, but nothing else. He shook his head. "I don't see anything."

"It's smoke," Erigan said, looking at Evrim.

"I think so too," Evrim answered.

"It can't be smoke, not here," Aljeron said, dismissing the possibility entirely.

"Look again."

Aljeron squinted, and it seemed there was indeed a tail from the thin wisp of grey cloud winding its way down into the trees. If there was a tail winding its way down, it could in reality be smoke winding its way up. "But how could it be smoke?" he finally asked.

"I don't know," Evrim replied. "There were no lightning strikes today, not that we saw. Not yesterday either. And even if there had been, a fire is almost inconceivable with all this snow and wet."

"It could be another ravine or chasm," Saegan suggested.

"What do you mean?"

"I've heard of cracks in the earth in Nolthanin where gas and smoke rise from deep underground," Saegan explained. "Maybe the ravine we skirted today was one of these, or a chasm that used to be one of these. Maybe that's all this is."

"We could go see," Evrim suggested.

As reluctant as Aljeron was to get back on his horse, he agreed, unwilling to stop for the night without solving this mystery. Slowly, cautiously, they made their way closer to the smoke. And it was indeed smoke. Not long after confirming this, Aljeron motioned to the others not to speak, and they silently dismounted.

Evrim led the way silently through the fir trees toward the source of the smoke, of the snow muffling the sound of their movements. In the middle of a dense grove, Evrim signaled for them to stop. He crouched in the snow, a strange look on his face. After a moment, he turned to the others and whispered just barely loud enough to be heard. "I think I can smell meat roasting."

"Impossible," Aljeron said.

"No," Erigan said. "I can smell it too."

Aljeron looked down at Koshti. The tiger stared alertly at the ring of trees, his nose in the air. Koshti could smell something too. "But how?"

"I don't know," Evrim answered. "But if there's smoke and roasting meat beyond these trees, you know what else must be there."

"Men," Aljeron whispered.

Evrim nodded. "So what do we do?"

Aljeron drew Daaltaran. "We go and check it out."

Saegan drew his sword as well, then Aljeron took the lead with Koshti, and Evrim dropped back. Erigan took up the rear with Synoki and Evrim, his staff ready for trouble.

They crept through the trees, winding their way in. Eventually, even Aljeron could smell the meat, and it smelled good. He followed the smell and the occasional glimpse of smoke above the trees. Then, suddenly, Aljeron rounded a tree and saw a clearing ahead. He motioned to the others to stop.

He crouched and tried to see the clearing through the dense branches of a fir tree. There was little snow there; he could actually see ground where the snow had been cleared away. A fire was burning, and meat on a stick was held aloft over the far side. He couldn't see who was holding the stick, but he could see one pair of feet beside the fire.

Aljeron turned to the others and held up one finger. "I think there is only one man," he whispered.

"It could be a trap," Saegan suggested.

"Maybe," Aljeron answered. "I'm going around to see. Watch from here. If it's a trap, help me if you think you can, or get away if you know you can't."

"But Aljeron—" Evrim started.

"I'm going," Aljeron said, and standing, he forced his way through the branches.

Flames rose between him and the solitary figure on the other side, but as Aljeron continued walking, the man became discernible. He was wearing a deep yellow, almost golden cloak that reminded Aljeron of the rising sun. He was looking down at his stick, and his face was obscured in shadow.

"Greetings, traveler," Aljeron called out.

"Greetings," the man said, looking up.

Aljeron stepped back. "It can't be."

"Not so. It can be, and it is."

EPILOGUE

FOR A LONG TIME, all was darkness. For Benjiah, it was as if he were floating in a great black sea with nothing above him or below. There was no sound, only silence, and if time existed here, he was not aware of a before or after, only now.

Gradually, though, he became aware of something beyond the void. Voices spoke to one another as though at a great distance, and he was moving. In fact, he was being dragged none too gently over rough ground. He tried to open his eyes, but even the failing light of evening blinded him, and he shut them again immediately.

The voices were nearer now, and he realized they were coming from the men who were dragging him. He was lying on a cloak or blanket, and they pulled him by his ankles.

"I still don't understand it."

"It doesn't matter if we understand it. We just have to do it."

"He should be dead. They should have killed him when they found him."

"Apparently not everyone thinks so."

"That's what I don't understand. I was up front. I saw what he did. We should have killed him."

"It wasn't him," the other man replied. Benjiah was alert enough to trace this voice to the person holding his left ankle. "It was that staff, and now it's broken. I heard that Farimaal gathered up all the pieces, and that he or Cheimontyr was going to personally see them burned. There will be nothing left of it but ash by now."

"Still, I don't see why we should risk it. He should be dead."

"Look, let's just do what we're told to do."

Benjiah's head began to swirl, the voices faded, and soon he was floating in darkness once more.

When he came to, he was lying motionless on something hard and smooth. He ran his hand along it and felt that it was wood, like a large board or maybe even a tabletop. He wanted to open his eyes to see where he was, but the memory of the blinding light the last time he'd tried made him hesitate, in part because he didn't want the pain, but also because he wasn't sure he wanted to see what his eyes would show him.

After lying there motionless for a while, he tried at last to open his eyes. The light was painful, but not overwhelmingly so. He was in a dim place. As his eyes adjusted, the first thing he noticed were dark, vertical lines. As his vision grew clearer, he sat up suddenly, despite the pain in his head. He reached out and felt the wooden slats. They ran from the edge of the wooden floor he was lying on all the way up to a matching piece that formed a wooden ceiling above. They were in front of him and beside him and—he turned around—behind him too. He was lying in an oversized crate or something like it that was serving now as a cage.

He closed his eyes, and the succession of images that had paraded through his head for years passed before him again. He saw the grey skies and the endless rain. He saw the flash of brilliant light. He saw the slats of this very cage. He had seen this very image a hundred times, looking through the bars at a dimly lit room, which now he realized was really a large tent.

Although the realization he was in a cage was not a happy one, there was some comfort in knowing this was the cage he had foreseen. He had lived to see his visions of the storm, the light, and the cage become reality; maybe he would live to see the fourth image as well—the great white city square, open and empty, beautiful and mysterious. If he would live to see that place, then today was not the day he would die.

The flap of the tent opened, and he sat back against the wooden slats. The cage blocked his view of the man's head, but he walked over to the cage and squatted to look in. Seeing Benjiah conscious and wary, he smiled a cruel smile.

"How do you like your accommodations?"

Benjiah didn't answer. The man was dressed nicely; his cloak was finely woven and his boots showed little mud or wear. He didn't look like a soldier.

"This cage was not originally meant for you," the man said, sliding his hand along one of the slats. "Farimaal had it made originally for your captain, Aljeron. He thought the captain in a cage would make a nice display after your army was subdued. Of course, there are some doubts now as to who is really leading the hodge-podge of rabble that passes for your army, if it is being led at all."

Again Benjiah did not answer the man, who was peering intently at him, perhaps waiting for a response.

"That was an impressive display you put on today. Too bad you needed that old blind fool's staff to pull it off. The staff has been destroyed, just like its previous owner. It would seem that your days as a wizard and conjurer are over. Too bad for you."

The tent flap opened again, and a second man entered. The man who was stooped by the cage suddenly stood, and the two men faced each other. Benjiah couldn't see their faces.

""What are you doing here?" the new arrival asked.

"I've just come to see how our prisoner is faring."

"Do you have permission to be here?"

"I don't need your permission to be here," the first man said, aggravation clear in his voice.

"That's a matter for another day. For now, all you need to remember is that this prisoner is off-limits. You heard what Farimaal said. I found him. I recognized him. He has been given into my safekeeping."

"Yes, he has, so you'd better keep him safe."

"I will, don't worry about that."

"Oh, I'm not worried. I'm actually eager to see what happens. If you mess this one up, you'll have to answer to Farimaal, and I'd like to see that."

"I bet you would. Now get out of my tent."

The man exited, and the new arrival remained where he was, his back to the cage. Part of Benjiah wanted to crawl forward to see the man more fully, but his body was weak and weary and unwilling to move, so he remained where he was.

"Are you all right?" the man said.

"I'm in a cage," Benjiah answered.

"True," the man said, and he stepped forward and squatted down much like the first man had done. As soon as he did, Benjiah gasped. He knew this face. It was the face of the rider he had seen with his father and Aljeron in his vision in Amaan Sul, the face of the man he had dreamed of standing at the gate of Fel Edorath. It was Rulalin.

"You are the spitting image of your father," Rulalin said.

"Are you going to kill me like you killed him?"

"No."

"Why not?"

"Because your coming into my hands at this particular moment in time is a most fortuitous turn of events." The barest hint of a smile touched Rulalin's face. "I have big plans for you."

The snow fell long
The drifts piled high
The wind blew cold
The end drew nigh.

The end of warmth
The end of light
Forevermore
Eternal Night.

The storm held sway
Engulfed the land
The end of time
The end of man.

But buried deep
A seed survived
That spring would come
And hope revive.

—excerpt from "The Last Winter"

The End
of the Third Book of
The Binding of the Blade

GLOSSARY

Aelwyn Elathien (ALE-win el-ATH-ee-un): Novaana of Werthanin, Mindarin's younger sister.

Agia Muldonai (ah-GEE-uh MUL-doe-nye): The Holy Mountain. Agia Muldonai was the ancient home of the Titans, who lived in Avalione, the city nestled high upon the mountain between its twin peaks. Agia Muldonai has been under Malek's control since the end of the Second Age, when he invaded Kirthanin from his home in exile on the Forbidden Isle.

Alazare (AL-uh-zair): The Titan who cast Malek from Agia Muldonai at the end of the First Age when Malek's Rebellion failed. Severely injured in his battle with Malek, Alazare passed from the stage of Kirthanin history and was never seen again.

Aljeron Balinor (AL-jer-on BALL-ih-nore): Novaana of Werthanin (Shalin Bel), travels with his battle brother Koshti.

Allfather: Creator of Kirthanin, who gave control of Kirthanin's day-to-day affairs to the Council of Twelve. To accomplish this task, He gave great power to each of these

Titans. Since the time of Malek's Rebellion, Allfather has continued to speak to His creation through prophets who remind Kirthanin of Allfather's sovereign rule.

Amaan Sul (AH-mahn SUL): Royal seat of Enthanin.

Anakor (AN-uh-core): Titan, ally to Malek, killed by Volrain in the Rebellion.

Andunin (an-DOO-nin): The Nolthanim man chosen by Malek at the Rebellion to be king over mankind.

Andunin Plateau: Wasteland of northwestern Nolthanin.

Arimaar Mountains (AIR-ih-mar): Suthanin's longest range, which runs between Lindan Wood and the eastern coast of Suthanin.

Assembly: The official gathering of all Kirthanin Novaana who are appointed to represent their family and region.

Autumn Rise: See seasons.

Autumn Wane: See seasons.

Avalione (av-uh-lee-OWN): Blessed city and home of the Crystal Fountain. It rests between the peaks of Agia Muldonai and was once the home of the Titans. Like the rest of Agia Muldonai, the city was declared off limits by Allfather at the beginning of the Second Age.

Avram Gol (AV-ram GALL): Ancient ruined port city of western Nolthanim known in the First Age as the City of the Setting Sun.

Azaruul butterflies (AZ-uh-rule): Green luminescent butterflies.

Azmavarim (az-MAV-uh-rim): Also known as Firstblades, these swords were forged during the First Age by Andunin and his followers.

Balimere (BALL-ih-mere): Also called Balimere the Beautiful. The most beloved of all the Titans to the lesser creatures of Kirthanin. It is said that when Allfather restores Kirthanin, Balimere will be the first of the faithful Titans to be resurrected.

Barunaan River (buh-RUE-nun): Major north-south river between Kellisor Sea and the Southern Ocean.

Bay of Thalasee (THAL-uh-see): Bay off Werthanin's west coast.

Benjiah Andira (ben-JY-uh an-DEER-uh): Joraiem and Wylla's son.

Master Berin (BARE-in): Master of Sulare.

Black Wolves: Creatures created by Malek during his exile on the Forbidden Isle.

Mistress Brahan (BRA-HAN): Rulalin's housekeeper and chief steward.

Brenim Andira (BREN-im an-DEER-uh): Novaana of Suthanin (Dal Harat), Joraiem's younger brother.

Bringer of Storms, the: See Cheimontyr.

Bryar (BRY-er): Novaana of Werthanin, Elyas's older sister, who fights for Fel Edorath under Aljeron's command.

Caan (KAHN): Combat instructor for the Novaana in Sulare.

Calendar: There are ninety-one days in every season, making the year 364 days. The midseason feast days are not numbered and instead are known only by their name (Midsummer, Midautumn, etc.). They fall between the fifteenth and sixteenth day of each season. These days are "outside of time" in part as a tribute to the timelessness of Allfather; they also look forward to the time when all things will be made new.

Calissa (kuh-LISS-uh): Novaana of Suthanin (Kel Imlarin), Darias's sister.

Captain Merias (mer-EYE-us): High-ranking officer in the army of Amaan Sul.

Charnosh (CHAR nosh): Titan, ally to Malek, killed by Rolandes during the Rebellion.

Cheimontyr (SHY-MON-teer): The Bringer of Storms, most fearful of the Vulsutyrim who can control the weather.

Cimaris Rul (sim-AHR-iss RULE): Town at the mouth of the Barunaan River where it pours into the Southern Ocean.

Cinjan (SIN-jun): Mysterious cohort of Synoki.

Col Marena (KOLE muh-REEN-uh): Port near Shalin Bel.

Corindel (KORE-in-del): Enthanim royal who attempted to drive Malek from Agia Muldonai and betrayed the Great Bear at the beginning of the Third Age.

Corlas Valon (KORE-las vah-LAHN): Fel Edorath captain whose troops join Aljeron's to face Malek.

Council of Twelve: The twelve Titans to whom Allfather entrusted the care of Kirthanin. The Council dwelt in Avalione on Agia Muldonai, but frequently they would transform themselves into human form and travel throughout the land. The greatest of these was Malek, whose Rebellion ultimately brought about the destruction of the Twelve.

Crystal Fountain: Believed to be the fountainhead of all Kirthanin waters, this fountain once flowed in the center of Avalione.

cyranis (sir-AN-iss): A poison of remarkable potency that can kill most living things almost instantly if it gets into the bloodstream. Consequently, the cyranic arrow—the head of which is coated in cyranis—is one of few weapons that the people of Kirthanin trust against the Malekim.

Daaltaran (doll-TARE-an): Aljeron's sword, a Firstblade whose name means "death comes to all."

Daegon (DAY-gone): Titan, ally to Malek, killed by Alazare during the Rebellion.

Dal Harat (DOLL HARE-at): Village in western Suthanin, Joraiem Andira's home.

Darias (DAHR-ee-us): Novaana of Suthanin (Kel Imlarin), Calissa's brother.

Derrion Wel (DARE-ee-un WELL): Town in southeastern Suthanin.

draal (DRAWL): A tight-knit community of Great Bear.

dragon tower: These ancient structures were built in the First Age as homes away from home for dragons who naturally live in the high places of Kirthanin's mountains and prefer to sleep high above the ground.

dragons: One of the three great races of Kirthanin. All dragons are descended from the golden dragon, Sulmandir, the first creation of Allfather after the Titans. All dragons appear at first glance to be golden, but none except Sulmandir are entirely golden. Three dragon lines exist, marked by their distinct coloring: red, blue, and green.

Dravendir (DRAV-en-deer): A blue dragon.

Eliandir (el-ee-AN-deer): A red dragon.

Elnin Wood (EL-nin): Forest of central Suthanin that straddles the Barunaan River, home to the Elnindraal clan of Great Bear.

Elyas (eh-LIE-us): Novaana of Werthanin, Bryar's younger brother, who died fighting for Amaan Sul in one of the first campaigns against Fel Edorath.

Enthanin (EN-than-in): Kirthanin's eastern country. Residents are Enthanim.

Eralon (AIR-uh-lahn): Faithful Titan killed by Malek and his allies during the Rebellion.

Erefen Marshes (AIR-i-fen): Swampland boundary between Werthanin and Suthanin.

Erevir (AIR-uh-veer): Major prophet of Allfather in the Second Age.

Erigan (AIR-ih-gan): Great Bear, Sarneth's son.

Evrim Minluan (EV-rim MIN-loo-in): Joraiem's best friend and close friend to Aljeron.

Fall Rise: See Seasons.

Farimaal (FARE-ih-mal): Leading general of Malek's, who brought the Grendolai into submission.

Fel Edorath (FELL ED-ore-ath): Easternmost city in Werthanin; the first line of defense against attacks from Agia Muldonai.

Fire Giant: See Vulsutyr.

First Age: The age of peace and harmony that preceded Malek's rebellion. Not only did peace govern the affairs of men in the First Age, but the three great races of men, dragons, and Great Bear coexisted then in harmony.

Firstblade: See Azmavarim.

Forbidden Isle: After Malek's failed Rebellion at the end of the First Age, he was driven from Kirthanin and took refuge on the Forbidden Isle, home of Vulsutyr, the Fire Giant.

Forest of Gyrin (GEAR-in): Forest south of Agia Muldonai, home to the Gyrindraal clan of Great Bear.

Forgotten Waters: Passage across the Southern Ocean from Suthanin to the Forbidden Isle.

Full Autumn: See seasons.

Full Spring: See seasons.

Full Summer: See seasons.

Full Winter: See seasons.

Garek Elathien (GAIR-ick el-ATH-ee-un): Novaana of Werthanin, Mindarin's father.

Garring Pul (GAR-ing PULL): Southernmost city of Enthanin, where the Kalamin River meets the Kellisor Sea.

garrion (GARE-ee-un): Mode of transport common in the First Age used by the Titans and some Novaana. Garrions came in many shapes and sizes, but they all functioned similarly: A dragon would pick up the garrion with his talons as he flew.

giants: See Vulsutyrim.

Gilion Numiah (GIL-ee-un new-MY-uh): Captain of Shalin Bel's army.

Gralindir (GRAY-lin-deer): A blue dragon.

Great Bear: One of the three great races of Kirthanin. These magnificent creatures commonly stand two spans high and are ferocious fighters when need calls. Nevertheless, they are known for their great wisdom and gentleness.

Grendolai (GREN-doe-lie): The joint creation of Malek and Vulsutyr, these terrifying creatures were used to attack the Dragon Towers when Malek invaded Kirthanin from the Forbidden Isle. The dragons call them Dark Thieves.

gyre: A manmade dragon den built on top of a dragon tower.

Haalsun (HAL-sun): Faithful Titan killed by Charnosh during the Rebellion.

Halina Minluan (huh-LEE-nuh MIN-loo-in): Evrim and Kyril's older daughter.

Harak Andunin (HARE-ack an-DOO-nin): Mountain in Nolthanin whose name means "Andunin's Spear."

Hour: See time.

Invasion, the: Malek's second attempt to conquer Kirthanin.

Joraiem Andira (jore-EYE-em an-DEER-uh): Novaana of Suthanin (Dal Harat) and a prophet, murdered by Rulalin.

Jul Avedra (JULE uh-VADE-rah): Coastal town of Enthanin about midway between Tol Emuna and the Kalamin River delta.

Kalamin River (KAL-uh-min): River separating Enthanin from Suthanin.

Karalin (CARE-uh-lin): Novaana from Enthanin (near Amaan Sul), crippled left ankle.

Kellisor Sea (KELL-ih-sore): The great internal sea of Kirthanin that lies directly south of Agia Muldonai.

Kelvan (KEL-vin): Novaana from Werthanin who died on the Forbidden Isle while battling Malekim and Black Wolves.

Kerentol (CARE-en-tall): Great Bear, elder of Taralindraal.

King Falcon: See windhover.

Kiraseth (KEER-uh-seth): Father of the Great Bear.

Kirthanin (KEER-than-in): The world in which the story takes place. Kirthanin comprises four countries on a single continent. Each country is defined by its geographic relationship to Agia Muldonai.

Kiruan River (KEER-oo-an): Marks the boundary of Werthanin and Nolthanin.

Koshti (KOSH-tee): Aljeron's tiger, battle brother.

Kumatin (KOO-mah-tin): Sea serpent created by Malek under the Forbidden Isle.

Kurveen (kur-VEEN): Caan's sword, a Firstblade whose name means "quick kill."

Kyril Minluan (KEER-il MIN-loo-in): Novaana of Suthanin (Dal Harat), Joraiem's younger sister and Evrim's wife, mother of Halina and Roslin.

Lindan Wood (LIN-duhn): Forest in eastern Suthanin, just west of the Arimaar Mountains, home to the Lindandraal clan of Great Bear.

Malek (MAH-leck): The greatest of Titans whose betrayal brought death to his Titan brothers and ruin to Kirthanin. Since the end of the Second Age and his second failed attempt to conquer all Kirthanin, he has ruled over Agia Muldonai and the surrounding area.

Malekim (MALL-uh-keem): Also known as Malek's Children, the Silent Ones, and the Voiceless. These creatures were first seen when Malek invaded Kirthanin at the end of the Second Age from the Forbidden Isle. A typical Malekim stands from a span and a third to a span and a half high and has a smooth thick grey hide. "Malekim" is both a singular and a plural term.

Marella Someris (muh-REL-uh so-MAIR-iss): Wylla's deceased mother, former Novaana and Queen of Enthanin.

Merrion (MAIR-ee-un): White sea birds with blue stripes on their wings that can swim short distances underwater in pursuit of fish.

Mindarin Orlene (MIN-duh-rin ore-LEAN): Novaana of Werthanin, Aelwyn's older sister.

Monias Andira (moe-NYE-us an-DEER-uh): Novaana of Suthanin (Dal Harat), Joraiem's father.

Mound: Central feature in the midseason rituals that focus on Agia Muldonai's need for cleansing.

Nal Gildoroth (NAL GIL-dore-oth): Solitary city on the Forbidden Isle.

Nol Rumar (KNOLL RUE-mar): Small village in the north central plains of Werthanin.

Nolthanin (KNOLL-than-in): Kirthanin's northern country, largely in ruin during the Third Age.

Novaana (no-VAHN-uh): The nobility of human society in Kirthanin who at first governed human affairs under the direction of the Titans but have since adapted to autonomous control. Every seven years the Novaana between the ages of eighteen and twenty-five as of the first day of Spring Rise were to assemble from the first day of Spring Wane until the first day of Fall Wane. Sulare is commonly referred to as the Summerland. "Novaana" is both a singular and a plural term.

Nyan Fein (NYE-un FEEN): Novaana of Suthanin (Cimaris Rul), married to commander Talis Fein.

Parigan (PARE-ih-gan): Great Bear, lead elder of the Taralindraal.

Pedraal Someris (PAY-drawl so-MAIR-iss): Novaana of Enthanin (Amaan Sul), Wylla's younger brother, Pedraan's older twin.

Pedraan Someris (PAY-drahn so-MAIR-iss): Novaana of Enthanin (Amaan Sul), Wylla's younger brother, Pedraal's younger twin.

Pedrone Someris (PAY-drone so-MAIR-iss): Last king of Enthanin, deceased.

Peris Mil (PARE-iss MILL): Town south of Kellisor Sea on the Barunaan River.

Ralon Orlene (RAY-lon OR-lean): Mindarin's late husband.

Rebellion, the: Malek's first attempt to conquer and rule Kirthanin by overthrowing the Twelve from Avalione.

Rolandes (roll-AN-deez): Faithful Titan killed by Daegon during the Rebellion.

Roslin Minluan (ROZ-lin MIN-loo-in): Evrim and Kyril's younger daughter.

Rucaran the Great (RUE-car-en): Father of the Black Wolves.

Rulalin Tarasir (rue-LAH-lin TARE-us-ear): Novaana of Werthanin (Fel Edorath), who murdered Joraiem in jealousy over Wylla.

Ruun Harak (RUNE HARE-ack): A spear given to Andunin by Malek.

Saegan (SIGH-gan): Novaana of Enthanin (Tol Emuna) who fights alongside Aljeron.

Sarneth (SAHR-neth): A lord among Great Bear, one of the few to still hold commerce with men, of Lindandraal.

seasons: As a largely agrarian world, Kirthanin follows a calendar that revolves around the four seasons. Each season is subdivided into three distinct periods, each of which contains thirty days. For example, the first thirty days of Summer are known as Summer Rise, the middle thirty days as Full Summer, and the last thirty as Summer Wane.

Second Age: The period that followed Malek's rebellion and preceded his return to Kirthanin. The Second Age was largely a time of peace until a massive civil war devastated Kirthanin's defenses and opened the door for Malek's second attempt at total conquest. Any date given which refers to the Second Age will be followed by the letters SA.

Shalin Bel (SHALL-in BELL): Large city of Werthanin.

Silent One: See Malekim.

Simmok River (SIM-mock): Nolthanin north-south river that pours into the Great Northern Sea.

slow time: See torrim redara.

Soran Nuvaar (SORE-an NEW-var): Friend and officer of Rulalin.

span: The most common form of measurement in Kirthanin. Its origin is forgotten but it could refer to the length of a man. A span is approximately 10 hands or what we would call 6 feet.

Spring Rise: See seasons.

Spring Wane: See seasons.

Stratarus (STRAT-ar-us): Faithful Titan killed by Anakor during the Rebellion.

Sulare (sue-LAHR-ee): Also known as the Summerland. At the beginning of the Third Age the Assembly decreed that Sulare, a retreat at the southern tip of Kirthanin, would be the place where every seven years all Novaana between the ages of eighteen and twenty-five were to assemble from the first day of Spring Wane until the first day of Fall Wane.

Sulmandir (sul-man-DEER): Also known as Father of the Dragons and the Golden Dragon. He is the most magnificent of all Allfather's creations besides the Titans. After many of his children died during Malek's invasion of Kirthanin at the end of the Second Age, Sulmandir disappeared.

Summer Rise: See seasons.

Summer Wane: See seasons.

Summerland: See Sulare.

Suruna (suh-RUE-nuh): Joraiem Andira's bow, previously his father's, whose name means "sure one."

Suthanin (SUE-than-in): The largest of Kirthanin's four countries, occupying the southern third of the continent. Ruled by a loose council of Navaana. Residents are Suthanim.

Synoki (sin-OH-kee): A castaway on the Forbidden Isle.

Tajira Mountains (tuh-HERE-uh): Nolthanin range in which Harak Andunin is located.

Taralin Forest (TARE-uh-lin): Western forest of Suthanin and home to the Taralindraal clan of Great Bear.

Talis Fein (TAL-is FEEN): Commander of the armies of Cimaris Rul.

Tarin (TARE-in): Novaana of Enthanin, Valia's cousin.

Tashmiren (tash-MERE-in): Servant of Malek, originally from Nolthanin.

Therin (THERE-in): Faithful Titan killed by Malek and his allies during the Rebellion.

Third Age: The present age, which began with the fall and occupation of Agia Muldonai by Malek.

time: Time in Kirthanin is reckoned differently during the day and the night. Daytime is divided into twelve Hours. First Hour begins at what we would call 7 AM and Twelfth Hour ends at what we would call 7 PM. Nighttime is divided into four watches, each three hours long. So First Watch runs from 7 PM to 10 PM and so on through the night until First Hour.

Titans: Those first created by Allfather who were given the authority to rule Kirthanin on Allfather's behalf. Their great power was used to do many remarkable things before Malek's rebellion ruined them.

Tol Emuna (TOLL eh-MUNE-uh): Heavily fortressed city of northeastern Enthanin's wastelands.

torrim redara (TORE-um ruh-DAR-uh): Prophetic state of being temporarily outside of time.

Turgan (TER-gun): Great Bear, elder of Elnindraal.

Ulmindos (ul-MIN-doss): High captain of the ships of Sulare.

Ulutyr (OO-loo-teer): Vulsutyrim captor of the women on the Forbidden Isle.

Valia (vuh-LEE-uh): Novaana of Enthanin, Tarin's cousin.

Valzaan (val-ZAHN): The blind prophet of Allfather.

Voiceless: See Malekim.

Volrain (vahl-RAIN): Faithful Titan killed by Malek during the Rebellion.

Vol Tumian (VAHL TOO-my-an): Village along the Barunaan River between Peris Mil and Cimaris Rul.

Vulsutyr (VUL-sue-teer): Also known as Father of the Giants and the Fire Giant. Vulsutyr ruled the Forbidden Isle and gave shelter to Malek when he fled Kirthanin. At first little more than a distant host, Malek eventually seduced Vulsutyr to help him plan and prepare for his invasion of Kirthanin. This giant was killed by Sulmandir at the end of the Second Age.

Vulsutyrim (vul-sue-TER-eem): Name for all descendants of Vulsutyr; both a singular and a plural.

War of Division: Civil war that weakened Kirthanin's defenses against Malek at the end of the Second Age.

Water Stones: Stone formations created by the upward thrust of water released from the great deep at the creation of the world.

Werthanin (WARE-than-in): Kirthanin's western country. Residents are Werthanim.

windhover: Small brown falcons that are seen as "holy" birds in some areas of Kirthanin because of some stories that associate them with Agia Muldonai.

Winter Rise: See seasons.

Winter Wane: See seasons.

Wylla Someris (WILL-uh so-MAIR-iss): Queen of Enthanin and widow of Joraiem.

Yorek (YORE-ek): Royal advisor.

Zaros Mountains (ZAHR-ohss): Mountain range bordering Nolthanin on the south.

Zul Arnoth (ZOOL ARE-noth): Ruined city between Shalin Bel and Fel Edorath; sight of many battles during Werthanin's civil war.

ABOUT THE AUTHOR

L. B. Graham was born in Baltimore, Maryland, in 1971. He loved school so much that he never left, transitioning seamlessly between life as a student and life as a teacher. He and his wife Jo now live in St. Louis. They would like one day to have a house by the sea, which he wants to call "The Grey Havens." His wife is Australian, which he thinks is appropriate since his grandfather was Australian and his father was born in Melbourne. The fact that he has these Australian connections and that his father grew up in Ethiopia all make him think he is more international than he really is. He went to Wheaton College outside of Chicago, where Billy Graham went, but they aren't related. He likes sports of all varieties, especially basketball and lacrosse. His biggest sports achievement was scoring 7 goals in a lacrosse game when he was a junior in college (a 10–6 win against Illinois State). He and his wife have two beautiful chidren, Tom and Ella, who love books, which pleases him immensely.